TURN THAT RIVER RED

A SLASHER ROMANCE

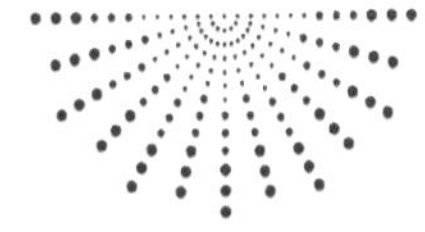

ROSE BITTERLY

A NOTE FROM THE AUTHOR

Thanks so much for picking up *Turn That River Red!* This is a dark horror romance featuring a murderous, morally black MMC. It also deals with themes of religious trauma and abuse.

As you might expect, it contains some potentially upsetting material

Because a certain online bookseller has a history of removing books with comprehensive content warnings, I have opted to put the full, detailed list of content notes on my website, which you can access at rosebitterly.com/content-notes or via the QR code below.

Once you're on the site, just click or tap on the book's title to expand the full list of warnings.

However, there are a few triggers that I did want to list here:

- Graphic depictions of sex, violence, and blasphemy (aimed at fundamentalist Christianity)
- The FMC's backstory involves religiously motivated abuse, including forced marriage, grooming, and domestic violence. I want to stress that these triggers DO NOT involve the MMC.
- SA (NOT between MCs, not graphically depicted)

If you have any questions or would like further clarification, don't hesitate to contact me through the email on my website.

-Rose Bitterly

PROLOGUE

AMBROSE

I crouch in the thick, muggy shade of an old metal shed, listening to the road two hundred feet in front of me. Rust has eaten holes into the metal so the baking Texas sun comes streaming in, filling the shed with stars even though it's two in the afternoon and I think I might sweat away into oblivion.

Who knows how long this thing has been sitting out here, or why it was built in the first place; I've claimed it for my purposes now.

I take a long drink of water and swish it around in my mouth. Silence. No one comes out this way unless they're headed to the Church of the Well compound, and that works in my favor. Because that compound is exactly where I need to be.

Something stirs in the distance, the faint hum of tires on asphalt. I spring into action, launching myself over to the little slat I peeled away when I set up my trap this morning. When I look out, I see the road, mirage heat shimmering like an oil slick. Everything around us is flat and dead and dusty. Not a lot of places to hide, but tacks on the road are an old trick, and they'll get the job done.

The van comes into view. White-paneled and plain. Nondescript. The sort of van you're meant to not look at twice. When the Church of the Well sends one of their members out into the secular world, they don't want to draw attention to themselves.

I peer out through the slat, holding my breath like I'm watching deer in the woods. When the van hits the tacks, it's like a gun going off. The tires explode, the rubber shreds to ribbons, and the metal frames rattle and scrape along the asphalt. Sparks fly up, pale in the sunlight, as the driver slams on the brakes, the van screeching and spinning. For a minute, I think it's going to tip over. It doesn't.

I pat the knives hanging on the side of my belt: a carving knife on my right, a gutting knife on my left. Just reminding myself they're there.

The van idles. I steady my breathing, waiting to see if this van really does belong to one of Sterling Gunner's flock.

A dark-haired man gets out, wearing the loose, old-fashioned shirts the men all wear. I grin, excitement bubbling up even though this is a killing of necessity, not pleasure.

He mills around the van, cursing to himself in Spanish. I slick back my hair and plaster on an affable grin and shove out through the shed's rickety door.

"Hola!" I call out. "Tienes problemas con tu camioneta?"

The man looks up at me, confusion and suspicion warring across his features. If his clothes didn't give him away as being from the Church of the Well, his distrust certainly does. "Who are you?"

"Name's Gabe," I say. "I was doing some deer hunting and I heard your tire blow out." It's a dumb story, but he's not going to be alive long enough to really think about it.

"This close to the highway?" He frowns and looks around, as if a deer might come trotting out of the endless flatlands.

"Well, hey, it ain't exactly hunting season, you know?" I

amble up to him with a touch of cowboy swagger, and he keeps watching me with narrow, guarded eyes. Fair enough. He should be suspicious of me.

I notice his gaze dropping down to my knives.

"What happened?" I ask.

"Something on the road." He kicks at the asphalt. "Shredded my tires. Nails or something."

I peer through the front windshield of the van. The passenger side is empty. I walk closer, aware of the man watching me with suspicion, as I crouch down beside the tires and let out a low whistle.

"Damn," I tell him. "These things are shredded to hell."

"Hijo de puta," he mutters softly. He pushes his hands through his hair and drags open the passenger side of the van. "Let me get my phone."

"Where you headed?" I rise to standing. "You from that church down the road?"

He glances over my shoulder at me. "Yes," he says stiffly.

Perfect. I just needed the confirmation.

"You want me to give you a ride? Hot as balls out here. No sense in you waiting for the tow truck."

"I can't leave the van alone," he says, burrowing around in the front seat.

"It'll be fine. Ain't nobody comes out this way. Why do you think I was doing my hunting out here?"

As I talk, I walk toward him, my steps soft and light. Too light for a human like him to hear.

The man slides out of the van, holding his phone, and that's when I attack with my carving knife, slamming it straight into the base of his spine. He goes rigid; the phone drops out of his hand and cracks on the asphalt.

"Lo siento." I breathe it into his ear. He's not dead yet, just paralyzed, and I can smell the fear wafting off him, thick in the heat. "Nothing personal. Wrong place, wrong time."

I ease my gutting knife out of its holster, running my thumb along the glossy wooden handle. The entire set is over a hundred years old, crafted by a knifemaker down in my hometown of San Angelo when I was still a young man. Or youngish man.

"Esto terminará rápido," I tell him, which is the truth. I didn't trap him here, on the road to the Church of the Well, to feed my bloodlust, strong as it is. No, I need a body. One of the faithful, so I can display him by the river, throw them into disarray, and worm my way into their trust.

I need to get through those compound gates. And this is the easiest way I know how.

Plus, I could do with some more meat.

So I gut this poor Christian like he's the deer I said I was hunting. He doesn't feel it when his belly splits open and his intestines spill out. That's why I stabbed him in the spine. A killing of necessity like this doesn't require suffering.

But I *feel* it. The heat, the coppery stench, the slippery delicious wetness of all his insides. When he tilts forward, I catch him and lick the blood off my fingers. The van's keys are in his pocket, and I pull those out before I toss him over my shoulder and take him to the back of the van, which isn't even locked. It's full of groceries from the store in Cocana, nearly forty minutes in the opposite direction. Bread and milk, big chunks of cheese.

He was alone. Good.

I take the keys and the body and hike back across the flatlands, moving quickly in the hot sun. My Oldsmobile is parked about a quarter mile away, on an old dirt road that'll lead me back to my ranch house, where I can get to work on the next part of my plan.

If I'm going to earn a spot on that compound, I need them afraid.

Good thing I've been sowing fear for two hundred years.

CHAPTER ONE

MERCY

The golf cart whines as I steer it across the thin, scrubby grass. The sun hasn't even risen yet, but the air is already warm, and I know today is going to be another miserable triple-digit day. At least Reverend Gunner doesn't forbid air conditioning.

The headlights on the golf cart flash over the landscape, revealing the pair of spindly mesquite trees that mark the embankment down to the Concho River. I'm technically stealing right now; the river isn't part of the church's property, and women aren't supposed to drive the golf carts. We certainly aren't supposed to take them off the premises. But if I leave early enough, I'll be back behind the gates before anyone notices. I can slip into the kitchen and start preparing breakfast early, a dutiful helpmeet to the entire congregation.

I stop the golf cart, turn off the engine, and, just for a moment, sit there, staring out into the eerie pre-dawn darkness at the river rushing below. It's my favorite place in the whole world, small as my world is. This was where I was baptized when I was eight years old. Reverend Gunner did the honors himself, squeezing my nose and tipping me backward into the shockingly cold water. I felt such an enormous peace in that moment, suspended beneath the surface, Reverend Gunner's face blurry and smiling.

He hadn't decided I would be his helpmeet yet.

I step out of the golf course and shine my flashlight, stolen from the supply closet last year, across the embankment so I don't trip as I make my way down to the river. We've been having afternoon thunderstorms, short-lived and wild, and the river is swollen. The water babbles like the wives when we're doing chores—hanging laundry, scrubbing the communal bathrooms, tidying up the chapel.

It also glimmers softly, a hint that the sunrise has started even though I can't quite see any light on the horizon.

I slip my shoes off and walk out onto the cool, slippery rocks until the water laps around my ankles, still as shockingly cold as it was the day I was baptized. It's a relief, though. The heat is unrelenting this time of year, even at night.

I wade through the rocky shallows, the beam from my flashlight reflecting off the water's surface, until I find my favorite sitting rock, a big stone that juts out over the bank. I heave myself up, arranging my skirts around my knees, lean back on my forearms, and breathe deep.

The wind stirs, hot and dry. Somewhere, a bird twitters, the first sign that morning's on its way. I check the time on my wristwatch, a one-year anniversary gift from Reverend Gunner: a little past 5 AM. I still have plenty of time. We don't start cooking breakfast until 6.

Nearly forty-five minutes to myself. It's an unimaginable luxury, and a rare one now that I've come of age and been bound to Reverend Gunner as his helpmeet. Most nights, he calls me to the little mother-in-law suite attached to his house —Madelyn, his first wife, prefers I don't perform my wifely duties in their shared home. And although the mornings after those nights are the times I need the river the most, it's too hard to pull myself out of bed when I've been up until two in the morning.

Last night, though, Reverend Gunner never summoned me, and I finished my chores early and went to bed early so I could wake up before sunrise and come here to have this time to myself.

Something splashes in the water. A fish or an owl, maybe. I think it's still dark enough for them. I sit up, my flashlight trained on the water. I like the way it looks, like a ribbon of the starry night sky has fallen from the Heavens and landed in the middle of West Texas.

Something floats past. I think it's log at first, even though there aren't a lot of trees out here. But it's strangely shaped. Ragged. I sweep my light over the water, trying to chase it, but it's gone.

Another splash. A little louder, this time. It's coming from my right, from upriver, and for the first time, a little quiver of fear works down my spine.

Is someone else out here?

I stand up slowly, my heart thudding. If there *is* someone out here, they probably aren't from the church. Maybe it's someone doing some early morning fishing. I've never known people to fish in this part of the Concho River, but it's certainly possible.

Another splash.

I scurry down the rock, fumbling around in my dress pocket for the key to the golf cart. It's not there. I left it in the cart, the way I always do when I come out to the river. Because I assumed I would be alone out here.

In a sudden surge of panic, I switch my flashlight off. But just as I'm plunged into darkness, one of the rocks beneath my feet dislodges, and I fall sideways, splashing into the river.

Thanks to the afternoon thunderstorms, the current is strong. Before I can find my footing, it sweeps me out into the center of the river. I cry out, water sputtering into my mouth, and try to stand. But my feet don't quite touch the bottom.

I know how to swim, but I'm out of practice—swimming is for children, and I'm an adult now. I'm also wearing a calf-length cotton dress, another mark of womanhood in the Church of the Well, and the fabric tangles around my legs as I kick them out, trying to get my body upright. Water keeps splashing over me, and my dress drags me down below the surface, and I wonder if it's finally my time to walk into the dazzling light of Heaven and fall into the arms of Jesus Christ.

And, just for a moment, I stop struggling. I let myself sink.

But I can't do it. Not when my lungs start burning for air. A sinner's instinct for survival kicks in, and I push myself up, gasping when I break the surface. I gulp down air, furiously treading water. The river pours around me, but I realize with some relief that I'm out of the eddy that dragged me away from the shore.

But it's still dark, and the water is black and unfathomable. However, I'm not as worried about cottonmouths as I am the rage of Reverend Gunner if he finds out I left the compound without permission.

I take a deep breath and dive under the water, swimming with the graceful butterfly stroke I learned a lifetime ago, before my parents died and I lived in a leafy Dallas suburb and wore whatever I wanted. It's hard, with the way my dress keeps wanting to drag me down, the fabric heavy and waterlogged. But I use every ounce of my strength and push forward, moving toward the bank.

But something's in the water.

It's too dark for me to see what it is. Certainly not a snake, but not a log, either. It's round and shaggy, and I think it's a soccer ball at first. Someone kicked it into the river and didn't bother to retrieve it.

But then the river surges it toward me, and I see the gleam of—

Eyes?

And suddenly, I'm staring at a man's face, his gaze blank and unseeing, his mouth twisted in terror.

I scream and water floods into my mouth, and then I realize it's the same water that a dead body has been floating in and that just makes me retch and choke and try to splash away, but somehow splashing away brings the body—no, the *head*, it's just a head—closer to me. It kisses against my shoulder and I shriek and push it away, which means I touch it, the skin clammy and cold.

The head rolls up, eyes staring at the heavens, and it looks—

It looks familiar?

"Raul?" I whisper, my voice cracking.

No, it can't be. It's dark and I'm panicking and what I need to do is get out of this river and not convince myself I'm seeing a friend in the water.

I kick away, but my eyes don't leave the head. Because even in the dark, it does look like Raul. His dark hair. His high cheekbones. I know what Raul Alvarez looks like because I used to bring him cold water every day when he was training with the rest of the Soldiers of God. Or at least I did until Reverend Gunner told me it was untoward for a helpmeet to spend time with single men.

But I still talk to him, when the reverend or one of his spies aren't around.

"Raul?" I keep swimming backwards, staring at the head bobbing in the water. My voice cracks. "Raul?"

My feet touch the surface, and I turn around and splash up the embankment—thank the Father I'm actually on the right side of the river. My golf cart sits where I left it, and I half-run, half-stumble up to it, flinging myself into the seat. The key sits in the ignition, right where I left it, too. I let out a sob of relief when the engine comes on, that I'm not a girl in a horror movie who's been stranded with—

With a killer?

I throw the cart into reverse and peel away from the river, tears streaking over my cheeks, mixing with the river water streaming out of my hair. I turn the cart around so quickly that it tilts up on its left wheels and then lands with a terrible crunch. But it's still working, and I drive away, pushing it as fast as it can go.

Which is not that fast. It's a golf cart, not a car.

I glance in the rearview mirror but all I see is the faint grey line of the sky. The sun is starting to rise.

My panic doesn't subside, though. I'm not being followed. But I found a dead body. And that means I'll have to tell the reverend, a thought that gives me a sick feeling in the pit of my stomach. But I can't leave the body there to rot.

Especially if it is Raul, who's always so kind and respectful, who teaches me how to say things in Spanish. Raul's the sort of man I always imagined myself marrying, before Reverend Gunner told me my calling was elsewhere.

I squeeze the steering wheel tightly, my tears hot and desperate. *It can't be Raul. It can't be.*

But it was someone.

Someone who had been decapitated and tossed into the only place in this world I've ever known peace.

CHAPTER TWO

AMBROSE

Well. *That* didn't go how I expected, although I can't say I'm disappointed by the result.

I had intended to take some inspiration from my friend Jaxon and set up a vaguely blasphemous sculpture with the inedible body parts on the bank of the Concho. Considering I'm doing this entire thing as a favor for his girlfriend Charlotte, it felt fitting, even though I normally prefer not to leave evidence of my crimes lying around.

Especially since, in the last fifty years or so, I've developed a taste for the meat.

At this point, I'm nearly two hundred years old, counting any time spent in the dirt recovering after a death, and I've had a baker's dozen of those in my lifetime. You get tired of things, living this long. You get tired of sex and sleep. You get tired of food. But back in the '70s I befriended another one of my kind who argued we ought to treat humans the way the better humans treat deer and wild boar. Got to use them up completely.

She was an unusual one, and older too, about a hundred years older than me. She had fallen into the hippie shit that had been popular a few years earlier. Back to the land. Long hair and bare feet. Kill for food, not pleasure.

Still, eating her big succulent roasts gave me a taste for human meat, and so I started to collect the best cuts from my victims: the rump, the thigh, the belly—which makes a fine, salty bacon. The man from the church was no exception. Waste not, want not, my old hippie friend would always say. Sometimes, I wonder what she's up to, if she's still using every part of the human. She's not in Texas anymore.

Anyway, my point is that most of my victim is currently sitting in my freezer. What I'd brought with me for my bait was just the unusable parts, since using every part of the human really isn't feasible. The head, sans its teeth, being the main one. I also had both forearms and his hands, fingertips still intact since I want him identified. The feet. Big, awkward pieces that are so obviously what they are. Soft meats, like the innards and the lungs and such, I feed to my dogs. I was ready to get to work.

But when I arrived at the river, someone was there.

I smelled her before I saw her *or* heard her, a soft lilac scent that drifted on the balmy early morning air. I stood beside my Oldsmobile, dragging that sack of hands and arms and a single severed head, and breathed it in, trying to place where it was coming from.

Then I heard her over the rushing babble of the river—her soft, rhythmic heartbeat and the gentle whisper of her breath. I dropped the sack and crept forward along the riverbank until I saw her: Young, pretty, her long pale hair up in a braid and silvery in the starlight. As I watched from the brush, she waded into the ankle-high water, a flashlight dancing over the surface.

I knew immediately she was from the church because of how she was dressed, in one of those shapeless calico dresses. But what the hell was she doing out there at five in the morning?

I had to consider my options then. Clearly, I couldn't set up any displays. But I had my witness here already. A pretty little thing who could run screaming to the church and set off the turmoil I needed to worm my way inside.

Fortunately, we've had all those thunderstorms, which do little to break the heat but do put on a great light show and, more importantly, flood the rivers. This morning the Concho was churning its way through the West Texas desert, right past my witness. My job just got a lot more easy.

So I went back upriver and tossed in the body parts, one after another, throwing them toward the center of the river where she was shining her flashlight. I knew there was a chance she wouldn't realize what she was looking at, but I figured if it didn't work, I could just drive downriver, recollect them, and try again tomorrow night.

But then the poor thing slipped and fell into the water. And then I heard her start to scream.

In my many years walking this earth, I've become a connoisseur of screams. Humans can't tell the difference between them, but I can. Screams of pleasure have a throaty undercurrent like good whiskey. Screams of pain have a desperation to them, a pleading, that always goes straight to my cock. And screams of fear—well, those are the classic, aren't they? Pure adrenaline converted to audio. It's like hearing the creation of the universe.

That girl screamed with fear, mingled with a touch of disgust and—most deliciously—sorrow. As soon as I heard it, that braided, multilayered scream, I knew she had found the head.

Even better, though, I suspect she recognized its former owner. That's what the sorrow was.

At that point, I was about a half-mile upriver from her, but I'm not a human. I'm the boogeyman, and it only took me about a minute and a half to clear the difference. I got there just as she was dragging herself out of the other side of the river, the head still in the water.

She didn't see me.

Of course not; it was still dark and she was panicked and I wasn't about to follow her up to the church compound. But I saw her. She practically dove into her golf course and peeled out across the dirt, heading straight to the church in a cloud of panic.

Like I said, it all worked out better than I had expected.

I'M HOME NOW, home being an old ranch house set off the highway. I've got a half dozen houses scattered across the western half of the state, having collected them over the years. It's easier to hunt if you have a wide area, a bigger pool of victims, and traveling's a lot easier when you've got a semi-permanent home to go to.

This is always the hard part. Biding my time. Letting them steep before I sweep in and destroy their lives.

I pace around my hot, sunny living room while one of my dogs, an old mutt I call Max, follows around at my heels, hoping I've got more wet meat for him. I keep thinking about the girl I saw—my second victim, technically, even though right now I've got no intention of killing her. Sometimes, humans are better use to you alive.

I sink down on my couch and flip open my laptop and type in *Cocana County murder,* even though I suspect the church will try to keep this out of the press for as long as they can. I'm right. Nothing. I slam the laptop shut and toss it aside and Max hops up on the couch beside me, his big curling tail wagging. I pet his head distractedly, rubbing him on the spot between his ears that he likes, and just kind of stare at the wall.

I haven't hunted like this in years, although there was a

period of time when it was my preferred method. What got me on this kick was Charlotte. She's another of my kind, but unlike most of us, she didn't know what she was for the first thirty years of her life thanks to her upbringing in the California branch of the Church of the Well. Her adoptive parents—not Hunters themselves, of course—did some kind of charm meant to stave off the devil, but instead, it bound her nature. Kept her from killing. It wasn't until Jaxon broke her open that she found herself.

I have a habit of collecting young Hunters—like Jaxon, when he first came up in the world, and now Charlotte, and our mutual friend Sawyer, currently stalking the balmy streets of Pensacola, Florida. Last year, I told Charlotte I wanted to find the names of her parents. Her *birth* parents. Because at least one of them has to be a Hunter like her and me and the rest of us. I'm finally getting around to it.

As it turns out, she was adopted through the Church of the Well. And, lucky for me, their main cell is up here in West Texas, so close to my own personal hunting grounds. Another convenient fact? I used to be a preacher myself, and I know exactly what to do and what to say to endear myself to someone like the Reverand Sterling Gunner, former televangelist and current High and Holy Prophet of the Church of the Well, whose gated compound is just a forty-five-minute drive north of the ranch house where I currently sit.

All I need to do is talk my way into the compound, find Charlotte's adoption records, and get out. Once I have the names, Charlotte can find out where she came from, and I can get back to hunting the way I prefer.

I stand up and pace around, rolling my plan through my head. The girl at the river has almost certainly planted those first few seeds of fear and panic. I'll let them marinate for a day, even though I'm itching to get this over with. I'm not terribly keen on the idea of going back to my old preacher persona, truth be told. All this nonsense with Charlotte has me thinking about my own youth, when I was a completely different person.

I grew up the illegitimate son of a Catholic priest in Mexican Texas with a murderess for a mother—a murderess who strangled me at twelve years old so she could put me in the ground and make sure I came back out like her. The boogeyman. El Coco.

A Hunter.

My father being a human priest always made me interested in human religions, which was why, when I was older, I went traveling across northern Mexico and the newly-formed Republic of Texas as an itinerant preacher, spreading the word of a god that hates me so I had a way to do the things my body needs to do. I'd go into frontier settlements and spread the Good Word for a few days. Earn their trust.

Then I'd slaughter them and slip off into the darkness like the wind.

I stop by my window and push the curtain aside. There's not much of a view: just the flatlands around the house, my dusty old car, the dirt road winding up to my property.

A tail thumps my leg; I look down to see Max staring up at me, his long pink tongue lolling out of his grinning mouth. I've always kept a dog, ever since I left my mother's side and struck out on my own. What's a hunter without a hound dog, after all? His sister Roxi is around here somewhere, too. She's the really vicious one.

I reach down and scratch his head. "I think you'll be good at doing it this way," I tell him. "You always liked being friendly, huh? I'll need that."

Max barks, his ears perked up.

"I just hope your sister can behave herself." I turn my gaze back to the window, thinking through my plans. Give them a day for the initial shock. Keep an eye on the news, not that I expect to see much. The Church of the Well keeps to themselves, from what I've seen. Living off the grid and all that. But if someone does report something, I need to know.

Then I'll drive up to the gate with my two dogs and ask them for a bit of Christ's grace. An itinerant preacher, in this day and age? They'll eat it up, I think. I hope so. Otherwise, I might have to kill my way in, which I'm not too keen to do.

I want to do this cleanly. Invisibly. And then I want to move on with my life.

Something snags in my thoughts, though. The blonde at the river. Her lilac scent and her lovely, symphonic scream.

I'll get to see her again, won't I?

The thought sets a fire in me—one I haven't felt for a long, long time.

CHAPTER THREE

MERCY

I knock lightly on the door to Reverend Gunner's office. Male voices drift out, low and serious, but I don't hear permission to come inside.

"He's meeting with someone."

Mrs. Harrison startles me, and I jolt a little, the tray with Reverend Gunner's coffee jostling. She's his receptionist, an older woman who's followed him since his days as a televangelist, before God the Father appeared to him for the first time. She wasn't at her desk when I came up to the office to bring him his coffee like I always do, at 10:30 AM on the dot.

"Oh," I say. "He didn't mention—"

"The guest just arrived." She settles down behind her desk, smoothing her dark skirt. We're all wearing dark colors today, of course. For Raul.

Images from yesterday morning flash through my thoughts. The cold river. Raul's frozen, mist-covered eyes. The coffee tray wobbles again, and I take a deep breath to steady myself.

"—traveling preacher," she says. "Like Jesus himself."

"What?" I'm not sure what to do. Reverend Gunner gets upset when his coffee is late. He also gets upset if I interrupt his meetings. And he's already furious with me for going down to the river without permission.

"That's who's in there," Mrs. Harrison says. "A traveling preacher named Ambrose Echeverría."

The voices in the Reverend Gunner's office go quiet. Chairs scrape against the linoleum.

"We weren't expecting anyone like that," I say.

"I know. That's what I was saying." Mrs. Harrison drops her voice a little. "He showed up at the gate early this morning. Said he goes where God directs him, then insisted on seeing the Reverend."

I turn back to the shut door, and something tightens in my chest right it swings open.

Reverend Gunner stands in the doorway, bearing down on me. "Mercy," he says. "I see you've pulled yourself together."

I don't say anything, just tighten my fingers around the coffee tray.

"That's good. It's unbecoming for a helpmeet to be hysterical. Come, I want you to meet someone."

I found Raul's corpse in a river! I scream inside my head. Of course I was hysterical. All day yesterday, I couldn't stop crying. I want to cry now, but I'm holding back my tears because I don't want Reverend Gunner to discipline me.

I'm a helpmeet. It's important that I be helpful.

Reverend Gunner guides me inside his office, shuts the door, and takes his coffee. "Pastor," he says. "This is the woman I was telling you about. The one who—found the body."

A tall, rangy man rises up and turns toward me, the sun from the window behind him casting him in a golden halo. He's older—not as old as Reverend Gunner, but in his early forties at least—and roughly handsome, with dark hair slicked back from his face and salt and pepper stubble across his jaw. His intense brown eyes burn straight through me.

A fire-and-brimstone preacher if I ever saw one.

"This must be Mercy," he says, never taking his eyes off of me. "I heard you've experienced some suffering these last twenty-four hours."

I nod cautiously and set the empty coffee tray down on the little table in the corner. I'm wary of handsome men. Handsome men make Reverend Gunner jealous, and when he gets jealous, my life gets significantly harder. It doesn't even matter if I'm attracted to them or not. It doesn't matter if they're kind, like Raul, or a fellow preacher, like this man, who looks at me like he's rooting around in my soul to dig out my sins.

I'm Reverend Gunner's helpmeet, and if another man looks at me, I'm the one who suffers.

"Answer him, Mercy," Reverend Gunner says sharply.

I swallow back my worry and my grief. "Yes, sir. I—something terrible happened yesterday morning—"

"I know." Pastor Echeverría gives me a gentle smile. "I felt it. An immense darkness coming from this place."

I stiffen and slip a glance over to Reverend Gunner. But he's watching us approvingly.

"God led Pastor Echeverría here," Reverend Gunner says. "Right when we needed him most."

I turn back to Pastor Echeverría, who nods, his eyes never leaving mine. "That's what I do," he says. "That's my calling. I go where I'm needed." He moves closer to me, his movements easy and graceful, and then stops beside the table, placing one hand beside the tray. My eyes drop down to it, to his strong, graceful fingers. Organist's fingers, as Mrs. Harrison would say. "Reverend Gunner tells me you knew the deceased."

My whole body goes stiff, and for a moment all I see is Raul. Raul grinning at me as I hand him a bottle of cold water, Raul walking across the campus with the other soldiers, Raul surrounded by cold black water.

"Y-yes," I spit out, because I can feel Reverend Gunner

staring at me. "Yes, of course. I know everyone in the congregation. I—"

My words lodge in my throat, and my eyes prickle with tears. I clutch at my dress and try desperately to blink them back, because if Reverend Gunner sees me crying in front of one of his guests, his punishment will be quick and furious. "You're a reflection of me, Mercy," he said to me last night, curled up beside me in bed. "We have to show the congregation that we're stronger than the devil."

I fumble in my skirt pocket for the rag of Kleenex I shoved in there this morning. But Pastor Echeverría offers me a handkerchief instead. A *cloth* one, bleached clean, with a delicate *AE* embroidered in the corner.

"Take it," he says softly.

I glance at Reverend Gunner for permission, anxiety knotting my stomach. He gives me a sharp nod even though his frown cuts deep lines into his face. I snatch the handkerchief away from Pastor Echeverría and press it against my eyes, catching the tears just before they fall

"It's all right to cry," Pastor Echeverría says gently. "It's a terrible crime, what happened, and it's terrible that you had to be one to discover it."

I dab at my eyes again, sniffling. My heart feels like it's twisting in my chest, and I suddenly taste the cold, steely water in the back of my throat, and I see Raul's empty eyes, his mouth twisted in fear. And although Reverend Gunner is still sitting behind his desk, watching me, Pastor Echeverría makes me feel safe. Reverend Gunner might punish me later, when we're alone, but he won't do it here.

"Raul was my friend," I say primly, staring down at the handkerchief crumpled in my fist.

Reverend Gunner makes a hoarse noise in the back of his throat, and I immediately regret saying anything. But Pastor

Echeverría only smiles gently and says, "Then this must be exceptionally difficult for you. Would you like to pray about it?"

I wipe the last of my tears away and fold up the handkerchief, aware of Reverend Gunner watching us. "Pastor Echeverría, I appreciate—"

"Call me Ambrose."

I immediately look over at Reverend Gunner again, heart pounding. I know he won't approve of such a thing, but there's something about the way Pastor Echeverría—Ambrose—is staring at me, eyes dark and burning, that makes me want to disobey Reverend Gunner's wishes.

Ambrose notices my hesitation and glances back at Reverend Gunner. "I know it's informal," he says. "But I prefer to eschew formality in my ministry. Only the Lord Jesus Christ requires a title."

Reverend Gunner quirks his mouth into a smile. "I appreciate that," he says. "One outsider to another."

Ambrose turns back to me, smiling again. There's something sharkish about his smile, like his mouth is almost too big for his face. Like he might devour me whole. "What do you say, Mercy? Allow me to pray with you?"

"I think you'd benefit," Reverend Gunner says. "This is a holy man, Mercy. I can see God's fire in him."

I swallow, my throat dry. Ambrose waits, his face impossible to read. But I don't think he looks at me the way a pastor is meant to look at their flock.

It's not exactly how Reverend Gunner looks at me in our marriage bed, but it's close.

"Of course, it's your choice," Ambrose says. "But it seems you are in need of a little prayer—"

"I am." I flick my gaze over to Reverend Gunner one last time, who gives me another encouraging nod. If he approves of this man, this traveling preacher, there must be something holy about him. Some strength that can help defeat the evil trying to creep its way into our congregation.

Then I focus on Ambrose again. His face is sharp and angular, his nose slightly hooked, his lips full. There's something wild about him.

Fire and brimstone.

"Then it would be my honor." His eyes glitter. "Even if I can't help the entire congregation, at least I know I helped you, Mercy Gunner."

Hearing my full name in the dark rasp of his voice makes the hairs on my skin stand up.

"Thank you." It barely comes out a whisper.

He nods toward a nearby chair.

"Sit," he says, a touch of a command to it. My skin prickles again.

I sit, and he walks over to me.

"Bow your head."

I do. Ambrose spreads his palms against the top of my hair, his touch warm. I breathe in shakily, trying to fix my gaze away from where it wants to go—which is his groin. It's nearly eye level, and my thoughts curdle at what might be tucked behind those dark pants.

"Lord Father," Ambrose intones, his fingers sinking into my hair. "Please help ease this woman's suffering in this time of darkness. Help guide her journey on the path through her grief, and help her find solace in your vast and holy light."

I flutter my eyes closed, giving myself over to the prayer. When Reverend Gunner prays with me, he doesn't touch me. Touching is for something else.

"Heavenly Father," Ambrose continues, his voice intensifying. "Lord of All. Show this woman that death is only the beginning. That there is nothing to fear from the end, for all those who reject the devil will resurrect in the coming End of Days."

Ambrose's hands seem to tighten against my head, and something shifts as he slips into the Aaronic blessing:

"'The Lord bless thee and keep thee; the Lord make his face to shine upon thee and be gracious to thee; the Lord lift up his countenance upon thee and give thee peace.'"

Warmth washes through me, starting in my core and spreading out through my limbs. Slowly, Ambrose draws his hands away, and I lift my head to meet his gaze.

It's so black, so intense, I nearly have to turn away.

"Amen," I say shakily.

Ambrose drops his hands to his sides and gives me a faint smile. "Amen," he repeats.

Then he crouches down beside my chair so he's looking at me, almost, I think, in supplication. The warmth from his prayer is still there, lingering in places it probably shouldn't.

"Did it help?" he asks.

I nod wordlessly. I'm not sure what I'll say if I try to speak, and the last thing I want is for Reverend Gunner to suspect I'm feeling any of the things I'm currently feeling.

"Good. I'm glad." Then he turns away from me, back to Reverend Gunner, who's leaning back in his chair, watching us with his hands steepled. The spell snaps, and I'm a helpmeet again. I stand up and smooth my skirt, hands shaking.

"That's what I do, Reverend Gunner. That's the gift God gave me, and I think it can be an immense help to the people here."

Reverend Gunner tilts his head. I know he's considering Ambrose's words, and I'm afraid he's going to say no and send him away.

Ambrose grins. "I have two dogs, by the way, if that sways your decision at all."

I bite back a laugh. My grief isn't gone, but in those moments that Ambrose was touching me, it receded a little. And I think I believe him, about possessing God's gift.

After all, isn't Reverend Gunner always saying that those backwoods preachers are the closest to God, the ones who best know how to defeat the devil? I know he sees all that in Ambrose, just as I felt it while Ambrose was praying over me.

I felt it as much as I've ever felt God's presence.

"Where are you staying?" Reverend Gunner asks Ambrose.

"Nowhere. It's just me, my car, and my dogs," Ambrose says easily. "But I do have a cell phone. I'll give you the number."

"You're not at a motel?" I ask, genuinely surprised. Reverend Gunner gives me a dark look, reminding me to be silent. But Ambrose smiles gently.

"No," he says. "Motels aren't necessary for me. I travel as our Savior did." He winks. "Well, as he would have if he'd lived in the twenty-first century."

"You'll fit in well around here," Reverend Gunner says. "And I can't deny we need all the strength we can. The devil wants to destroy us. I think that's something we can all agree on." He stands up. "Mercy, show Pastor Echeverría—"

"Ambrose." Another sharkish grin.

"Yes, of course. Ambrose." He gives a thin-lipped smile, barely hiding his discomfort. "Show Ambrose to one of the empty cabins. Then come right back here." His eyes glitter darkly. "We need to make arrangements for tonight."

My whole body suddenly feels like it's been dropped in ice. I discovered Raul yesterday and already Reverend Gunner is asking me to perform my wifely duties? But I only nod and mutter, "Yes, sir," knowing full well that I can't give anything else away in front of Ambrose—in front of a stranger, even one Reverend Gunner approves of. The outside world doesn't understand why Reverend Gunner requires a helpmeet. They don't understand the stress he's under.

Especially now, I suppose.

Reverend Gunner gives us both a dismissive wave, and I lead Ambrose out of the office and past Mrs. Harrison's empty desk.

Once we're outside of the building, I spot two dogs tied up to one of the fenceposts, tails wagging as we approach.

"Max and Roxi," Ambrose says, rubbing one of them between their ears. "My constant companions."

We aren't allowed pets on the campus, not permanently. Reverend Gunner says they distract from our work and that animals don't have souls anyway. But I like these dogs, with their big friendly eyes and curled tails. When Ambrose unties them, one of them runs up to me and sniffs my hand.

"That's Max," Ambrose says with a smile.

"Hi, Max," I whisper, my fingers sinking into his soft fur. It feels like a sin, petting him.

Just like it felt like a sin when Ambrose was praying over me.

I stand up, forcing myself to focus. I belong to Reverend Gunner. "It'll be about a five-minute walk to get to the cabins," I say, keeping my gaze lowered.

"That's quite all right, Ms. Gunner."

Ms. Gunner. The name slams straight through my chest. I curl my hands into fists.

"Please," I say, even though I know I shouldn't. "Call me Mercy."

CHAPTER FOUR

AMBROSE

I was not expecting my most recent victim to stroll into Gunner's office like that. I was certainly not expecting her to be the wife Gunner was going on about, especially since he already has one—Madelyn Gunner, who used to show up on his old television programs back in the '90s, her honey-blonde hair teased halfway to Heaven.

But no, the woman who came into that office, my victim, is definitely not Madelyn Gunner. But the door swung open and there she was, as blonde as the first wife but younger and sadder and clutching a tray with a single cup of coffee.

When she looked at me, I felt a sudden bolt of electricity go through my body. For a few exhilarating seconds, I was certain she was going to recognize me. My muscles corded up beneath my skin, preparing for me to lunge forward and intercept her before she could start screaming that the itinerant preacher Ambrose Echeverría was really a murderer.

But she didn't. Her big brown eyes just blinked at me, red-rimmed from crying.

Mercy Gunner. Sterling Gunner's backup wife. His *helpmeet*.

Seeing her in his sunny office was unnerving. It still

unnerves me, even though I'm currently tucked safely away in a prefab cabin on the edge of the compound—excuse me, *the campus*, as if this place is a regular church and not a fucked-up fundamentalist cult run by a money-hungry grifter who claims he has a direct line to the Christian god.

Claws click on the laminate flooring; Max and Roxi have completed their initial survey of the little cabin and are now sitting at my feet, blinking up at me, waiting for instructions.

"Welcome home," I tell them. "At least for the next few days. Behave yourselves."

They both thump their tails against the floor in excitement.

I do a quick round of investigation myself. The cabin is small, just three rooms: a common area with a little kitchenette, a cramped bathroom, and a bedroom with a twin-sized bed and a simple writing desk stocked with a notepad, a pen, and a pristine Bible.

I take off my cowboy boots and sit down on the edge of the bed. The dogs curl up on the floor beside me, patient and obedient. I've left my supplies out in my Oldsmobile, which I packed to look like the itinerant preacher I said I am. No suitcase, just clothes folded up in the backseat. A battered old Bible, of course. A big bag of cheap dog food, some plastic bowls. Roxi and Max are gonna be whining for real meat soon enough, but they'll survive.

At least the hard part is over; Reverend Gunner isn't exactly some frontier town leader desperate for spiritual counseling. But I could tell, talking to him in his office, that he was shaken up by my handiwork. He's convinced these people he's the key to Heaven, after all—it looks bad if one of them kicks it, especially when they're chopped up and thrown in the river. They don't know I severed Raul's spine first so he didn't feel any pain. *Raul*—I finally learned his name from the good reverend.

It wasn't as hard as I expected, though, getting in Gunner's graces. I've dealt with enough religious con men to know how to present myself so I don't look like a threat to their empire. Make myself seem small and poor and humble so they think they can control me—that'll do it, every time.

I will say I wasn't expecting him to make me pray over his pretty little wife, though. I had a quiet moment of panic where I forgot all my old tricks—it didn't help that *she* was the one in need of prayers, the woman with the gorgeous scream. Or the gorgeous speaking voice, lower than you'd expect from her appearance. Throatier, with a slight roughness that suggests she knows the taste of whiskey and cigarettes.

I very much doubt that woman has ever had a drop of alcohol in her life.

I keep hearing her say, *Something terrible happened to me yesterday morning*, and I love knowing I'm the terrible thing that happened to her. Love that I was able to put my hands on her and pretend to pray her sorrow away. I haven't prayed in decades. Longer, even, and while I found the words easily enough, the sight of Mercy bowing her head in front of me didn't exactly put godly thoughts in my mind.

She had her hair up in braids, giving me a glimpse of the back of her neck, and—more deliciously—the faint ridges of her spine. I'll admit a part of me wanted to slide my hands down and twist her neck with one sharp thrust. A clean, quick death so I could take her back home and slice the meat away, big thick woman steaks I'd fry with butter.

Another part of me, though, didn't want to kill her at all. The truth is, I wasn't thinking about killing her *or* eating her while I fumbled through my prayer. I was imagining her in that exact position, her plump pink lips wrapped around my cock while I skull-fucked her.

I fall back on the bed, the image running through my head again. I haven't fucked a woman in a while. Men are easier when all you want is to come in some nice, warm hole, and I've made it a point in the last century to avoid getting romantically entangled with humans of any gender. Granted, Sawyer's little escapade with Edie Hensner certainly worked out—not just for Sawyer, but for Charlotte and Jaxon, too. Charlotte, especially. If Sawyer hadn't let himself get infatuated with a human, I'm not sure Charlotte would have ever discovered what she is.

And *that*, I remind myself even as I rub my quickly-hardening cock through my pants, is the real reason I'm here. I need to find those adoption files. Find the names of Charlotte's parents.

I do *not* need to fuck Gunner's backup wife, even if she did help get me inside the compound with her panic and her screams. Even if she did stare up at me with a kind of blinding adoration because she thought I had filled her with the Light of God, not knowing that I was really just thinking about filling her with my cum.

But fuck if it's not fun to fantasize about. Fun enough that I put aside any thoughts about why I'm here at the Church of the Well and pull my cock out to pump it into my fist, imagining she's bowing before me and not her god, her tongue tracing the vein that wraps the full length of my dick. I imagine clutching onto the back of her head to show her how to suck cock properly—a good Christian girl like her wouldn't know.

I grunt, squeezing tighter around my cock. My orgasm's coming fast, a hot tightness coiling in my balls. In my head, Mercy Gunner weeps for me, tear tracks running down her soft cheeks. I thrust into her mouth. She makes small, frightened whimpers.

When I come, I groan, lifting my hips as my cum oozes up between my fingers. Then I slump back against the bed and catch my breath. There. Now that I've got that out of my system, I can focus.

But even as I go to clean up, Mercy's pretty brown eyes and golden hair linger in my thoughts.

CHAPTER FIVE

MERCY

Even after three years, I hate when Reverend Gunner forces me to visit him at midnight. I hate even more that he's making me do it *tonight*, a day after what happened at the Concho River.

I know I should be grateful. I know that I'm lucky Reverend Gunner and his first wife Madelyn adopted me after my parents died when I was eight, that they brought me into the Church of the Well and raised me out of the secular world, in the shining umbrella of God's light. For ten years, Madelyn taught me how to be a good wife, how to cook and clean and be obedient. I thought I would be partnered with one of the soldiers, maybe even Raul. I fantasized about us leaving the compound and starting another ministry in some far-off place, like the ministries in California and Tennessee.

Instead, when I turned eighteen, Reverend Gunner told me I was to be *his* wife, that God told him he needed two help-meets if he was to do all that he had been set on this Earth to do.

Three days later, I married him in the chapel, wearing my

favorite blue dress. Favorite then, anyway. Not favorite anymore.

Madelyn sat in the front row and watched me with daggers in her eyes.

I think that's why Reverend Gunner gave me a cabin of my own, a copy of the guest cabins, small and cramped. He doesn't like visiting me there, though. So when he asks me to tend to his needs, I have to meet him in the suite attached to his and Madelyn's home, the home where I grew up, the largest and grandest of all the houses on the compound.

He calls it our marriage suite. I walk there now.

The night is hot and sticky, even this close to midnight, and my dress sticks to my legs as I trudge across the campus. My cabin is only a few minutes away, and I know exactly when to leave so that I arrive at our marriage suite at midnight on the dot.

The door is unlocked, as always, and I push it open to find Reverend Gunner stretched out on the big, lavish bed in his boxers and a white undershirt, tapping away on his laptop. He glances at me as I step into the suite, eyes passing briefly over my body, my hair, my face. "Perfect timing," he says, the way he always does. "Don't forget to lock the door."

As if I would.

I step out of my shoes and then turn the lock, sealing us into the marriage suite.

"So what do you think of that preacher?" Reverend Gunner says without looking away from his laptop. "A bit earthy, isn't he?"

I reach back and unzip my dress, then pull it over my head and fold it up and drape it on top of the chest of drawers. I know I need to choose my words carefully.

"He's intense," I say. "But I felt God's strength in him." I don't say what I actually felt—that it was as if God's love flooded my entire body, and that I want to pray with him again, to feel that warmth radiating out from my center over and over.

"Mmm, yes, I sensed that, too." Reverend Gunner shuts the laptop and sets it on the bedside table, then peers at me over the top of his reading glasses. "We'll need that, you know. The devil is here, Mercy. Trying to destroy all that I've built."

I think of the cold water of the river, of Raul staring at me from the darkness, his soul already gone to Heaven, and swallow the lump in my throat. "I know," I whisper.

Reverend Gunner keeps studying me over his glasses. "The Deceiver was trying to get to me through you," he says sternly. "That's why he compelled you to disobey. Why he drew you out to the Concho."

I don't say anything, just stand there in my underwear, my body still warm from the heat of the night.

"This is why you're not allowed to leave the compound," Reverend Gunner says. "Why none of the women are. Women are too susceptible to the devil's trickery."

"I know." I don't meet his gaze, just stare at the quilt on top of the bed. Madelyn made it when I first came to live with them.

"You have to be careful. More careful than most." Reverend Gunner shifts forward, forcing himself into my line of sight. "The Deceiver wants to see me destroyed, and you're his way into me."

I nod. This is not a new conversation.

"I told this Pastor Echeverría he can stay," Reverend Gunner continues, "because we need all the help we can get. He might be unorthodox, but he'll fight the devil. I can sense that in him." He smiles. "Now, you'll help set him up in the meeting hall tomorrow morning, won't you? He's going to lead a prayer session."

"Of course, Rev—Sterling."

It still feels strange, even three years later, to use his first name

"Good. Now." Reverend Gunner licks his lips. "Why don't you come over here and help me destress?"

Dread shoots through me, but it's not like I can refuse. I unhook my bra, letting my breasts fall free. My panties are last. Reverend Gunner watches me the whole time, his erection already tenting his boxers.

"Have you lost weight?" he says lightly, eyeing me up and down.

"I don't know." I haven't, but I know better than to contradict him.

"You look good."

My skin crawls beneath Reverend Gunner's gaze. He watches me as I walk across the room, past the window that looks out into the Gunners' grand backyard, full of flowers that Madelyn planted and tends to every day. She told me once, before I became Reverend Gunner's helpmeet, that she wanted something lovely for the Soldiers of God to witness when they walked past their house on their way to training.

Raul. My throat constricts. I can not think about him. Not here. If I cry while I'm underneath Reverend Gunner, he'll hit me.

"I've needed this," Reverend Gunner says as I crawl into the bed beside him. He rubs himself over his boxers, and I already know what he wants me to do. It's the same thing every time.

I pull the waistband down and guide his penis out. Even after three years, I think it looks strange, like some alien from a secular horror movie. I take it into my mouth anyway, and at least Reverend Gunner is always clean, so all I taste is his skin and the occasional burst of saltiness.

He groans as I tend to him, settling back into the pillows. Usually, when I do this, I let my mind go blank. In the first few months after our wedding, as he showed me what he needed in the marriage suite, I would try to pray. But that felt wrong. So now I just let my mind go empty.

But something's different tonight. My thoughts won't *stay* empty.

I keep thinking about Ambrose.

I think about him standing over me, his hands pressed against my head. I think about how my eyes were in line with this part of him, and I wonder, even though I know I shouldn't, what he looks like behind his pants.

If he looks like an alien from a horror movie, or—

A strange, unfamiliar heat throbs between my legs. I pull Reverend Gunner deeper down my throat, and for a split second, it's Ambrose laying on that bed, and it's Ambrose's manhood between my lips.

The heat brightens. I squeeze my thighs together as if that might bring some relief.

"That's enough." Reverend Gunner's voice breaks the spell. The image of Ambrose dissipates in my head, and I'm left with an uneasy wash of guilt.

He's a good man, a true soldier of God, and I should not have thoughts like that about him.

"I want you on your back tonight," Reverend Gunner says.

We change positions. I settle into the warmth he left behind on the blankets and spread my legs, knees pointed at the ceiling. If I drop my head to the side, I can look through the window and out at the garden. It's brazen, how Reverend Gunner left the curtains open, baring our marriage to the world.

Reverend Gunner slides into me without any warning, grunting a little in surprise. "You feel good, Mercy." He says it the same way he's always complimented me, like he's a teacher awarding me with a gold star.

"So do you," I say by rote, even though he doesn't, not really. He doesn't feel bad, like he did those first few months, when every time he entered me it was like he was ripping me in two. Now it just feels odd, the way his hardness moves inside my body.

Reverend Gunner grunts, his thrusts quick and arrhythmic. I close my eyes and wrap my legs around his hips the way he likes, lifting my behind to meet him so he doesn't complain that I'm not putting in any effort. *If I wanted a wet fish, I'd fuck Madelyn*, he told me once, then flipped me over and spanked me like a child, hard enough that it hurt to sit the next day.

That was still better than the first time I cried.

I pull my thoughts away from the past. I need Reverend Gunner to think I'm enjoying myself, and I rock my hips a little, making him groan in appreciation. With my eyes closed, it's easier to think of pleasant things.

Like Ambrose.

The heat comes back, a molten gold between my legs. It's wrong to think of Ambrose on top of me, thrusting himself up into my body, so I think about how he laid his hands on me instead. His hot touch. His dark, velvety voice.

The Lord bless thee and keep thee.

Ambrose drawing me against him and kissing me the way no one has ever kissed me before, so slow and deep that he has to hold me up or else I'll collapse across the ground.

The Lord make his face to shine upon thee and be gracious to thee.

Ambrose unzipping my dress with a careful, tender precision, then kissing my bare shoulders after he slips the fabric away.

The Lord lift up his countenance upon thee and give thee peace.

Ambrose rising above me as I kneel in front of him, lips parted and eyes lifted as he presses his hands against my head, as he unzips his pants, as he—

I gasp, eyes fluttering open. The hot, rising tide inside my core recedes, and Reverend Gunner keeps grunting on top of me. He's nearly done; I can tell by the way his thrusts get harder and the way he squeezes the pillow beside my head. Sweat gleams on his brow, and his eyes are wrenched shut in concentration.

I turn to look out the window again. Madelyn has small garden lights installed in the flowerbeds, so they shine on the hibiscus and calla lilies, lush from the rains we've been having. Everything else is just shadows.

And then one of the shadows moves.

I tense beneath Reverend Gunner, instinctively lifting my chest. He pushes me back down.

"Almost—done—" he pants.

Someone's out there. The thought stirs, but I don't say it. There can't be someone out there. Not at midnight. Not in Reverend Gunner's backyard.

Someone killed Raul.

My heart pounds wildly. Not on the campus, I remind myself. Out in the secular world. The campus is locked at night. Guarded during the day by the Soldiers of God, all the young men of our congregation.

Young men like Raul...

The shadow moves again, fluttery as a ghost. There *is* someone out there.

"Reverend," I whisper, fear tight in my chest.

"Say my name, Mercy," he moans softly. "You're gonna say my name as you come."

I want to shove his sweating, thrusting body off me. I want to jerk the curtains shut and run into the little bathroom and stand under the hot water to rinse all this sin away.

But I can't. Reverend Gunner has me pinned down against the mattress, and the shadow moving outside comes closer. Steps up to the window.

I cry out, my voice strangled and terrified. Reverend Gunner chuckles.

"That's it, baby," he grunts. "Come for Daddy."

A pale face peers into the glass, and with a shuddery, horrible jolt, I realize who it is.

Pastor Ambrose.

It's undeniably him. I memorized his face this morning. He peers into the glass, sweeping his gaze around--

And then his eyes meet mine.

I want to scream. I want to weep.

Ambrose tilts his head, eyebrow arched. Reverend Gunner keeps thrusting into me, oblivious that we have an audience. And I'm too terrified to tell him.

And then Ambrose lifts his hand like he's waving to me.

He smiles.

His lips move. I have no idea what he's saying, but his eyes never leave mine. They bore into me with that same intensity as earlier, like he's flaying my soul apart.

"There it is!" Reverend Gunner shouts, slamming himself completely into me, groaning as his hot, sticky wetness floods into me. Every muscle in my body goes rigid.

"You liked that," Reverend Gunner says. It's not a question.

"Y-yes," I stammer, forcing myself to look up at him.

"Felt you come."

I have no idea what he's talking about. I've never had an orgasm. I don't think I can. But still, I nod, too scared to speak.

When Reverend Gunner rolls off me, I flick my gaze back over to the window.

It's empty.

CHAPTER SIX

AMBROSE

I jump the fence surrounding Gunner's well-manicured backyard and crouch down behind a trash can, breathing heavily and waiting—for screams, shouts, a slamming door. Anything. Some hint as to what's going to happen next.

There's only silence.

I sit back on my haunches and let my senses go wide. Those senses are what got me into this stupid fucking mess in the first place; I was headed to the administrative office with every intention of breaking in to see if I could find the church's adoption records. But then the wind stirred up and I caught Mercy's scent, as sweet as night-blooming jasmine. I should have ignored it, but the memory of her pretty, wide eyes gazing up at me while I pretended to pray over her was too much.

I wanted to see her again.

So I did what I'm designed to do, and stalked her from the shadows. I watched her go through the fence gate, then did the same thing I'm doing now, which is listening and smelling and *sensing* to get a feel for my surroundings. But what I mostly felt was Mercy: her trepidation, her disgust.

And that intrigued a monster like me.

Should I have hopped the fence into what I realized quickly enough was Gunner's backyard? No.

Should I have crept up to the window when I realized what was happening in the little suite growing off the side of his oversized house like a barnacle? When I felt Mercy's quickened heartbeat and smelled the faint pungent undertones of sex? Absolutely not.

But I did it anyway. I told myself I could use it, somehow—blackmail Gunner or something—and that might have been true until I let myself get caught like a goddamn fool. But I'll admit I was intrigued by the thought of the lush, curvaceous body hiding beneath that baggy cotton dress.

Of course, what I wound up seeing—

Mercy didn't want to be there, poor thing. She clearly wasn't enjoying herself at all. Any arousal I sensed was a bodily response, protecting her from Gunner's fumbling incursions. I haven't fucked a woman in a while, but I know what it looks like when you're fucking them properly.

And Gunner certainly wasn't.

That's what got me caught, ultimately. My desire, however stupid, to kick the door down, slash Gunner's throat, and show Mercy what a good fucking is supposed to look like. What's it's supposed to *feel* like.

In fact, I was fantasizing about it in rather embarrassing detail when Mercy turned her head and spotted me, and for a few bizarre seconds, it was like I was a deer caught in head-lights, blinded by the unknowable.

The way she looked at me—with confusion, desperation, sadness—I felt something I hadn't felt in a long, long time, which is pity. Genuine pity. I couldn't help but tell her I was sorry.

Now, crouched behind this filthy trash can, I try to find her again. She's still inside, along with Gunner, and I don't think she's told him anything. Because I can sense both of their heartbeats: hers is still quick and frantic, but his is calm. Steady. I keep waiting for the spike of his rage or fear or both, but it doesn't come.

She's kept her mouth shut.

That intrigues me even more, which I dislike. I'm at the Church of the Well for a reason, and it's not to pursue this bizarre fascination for a human woman.

I slip out from behind the trash can, keeping my senses alert. It's easy out here in the west Texas flatlands, which is why I've always hunted in the western half of the state. The emptiness. The enormity. It's not just sound that carries for miles, but everything, all the traces humans make without realizing it.

And although the compound is full of people, most of them are asleep right now, their bodies a quiet susurration in the background, not quite as loud as the electricity humming through the wires stretching between buildings.

I move along the fence, away from Gunner's house. The administration building is to my left, and I know that's where I should go. I need to find a way in, then figure out where they're keeping the adoption records. They have to be here somewhere.

But then a click ricochets through the night. I freeze, melting into the shadows. It's the gate on Gunner's fence latching shut, and in the middle of the night, it's as loud as a gunshot.

So are the footsteps. Light. Quick. Feminine.

Mercy.

I turn around, away from the administrative building and toward her. My thoughts hum. Intellectually, I know I should just leave her alone. But I'm curious—curious as to why Gunner's backup wife is walking through the compound at one in the morning instead of curling up beside him in that big bed where he fucked her so poorly.

Mercy helped me get into the compound, even if she didn't

realize it. Maybe she can help me get to the adoption records, too.

It's a lie I tell myself. Really I want to follow her fear like rabbit tracks. I want to feel her terror spike when I let her hear my footsteps in the dark, a sweet memory I can take home with me when I'm done with this ridiculous place.

So I go back the way I came, following her scent until I can see her, walking at the brisk pace of someone desperate to be where they're going. She has her arms wrapped around her chest, her head dropped low.

Pity flares through me again.

I'm getting soft. Sawyer and Jaxon are rubbing off on me.

Mercy's footsteps thud against the dusty foot trail. I slip behind her, as silent as a mountain lion. She senses me; I can tell by the way her shoulders stiffen, by the intoxicating eruption of fear that floods into her sweetness.

Her head swings, hair gleaming in the moonlight. I slip sideways and out of her line of sight.

She keeps walking, quickening her pace. I follow, slow and steady and silent. It's not enough, following her. I want to touch her. Taste her.

Maybe she *can* help me find the adoption records. It would certainly be so much easier if I have her telling me where they are.

Maybe I'm deluding myself. But still, before I can convince myself otherwise, I glide up behind her, sliding between the shadows. She hears me just as I wrap my hand around her mouth, and she unleashes a small, startled gasp right before I silence her. I drag her off the walking path and into the gap between two of the industrial-looking houses that wrap around Sterling Gunner's mansion like guards.

"Mmph!" Mercy cries, her breath warming my palm. Her plush body squirms against mine, and I wrap my free arm around her waist to still her.

"I'm not going to hurt you," I rasp into her ear.

She freezes. I actually feel her muscles snap into place.

She tries to twist her head toward me, but I hold her firm.

"I'm taking you back to my cabin," I whisper, nudging her along, keeping my senses open for anyone moving through the compound. There's nothing. Just insects. A few flapping bats. Night birds. "I want to talk."

Mercy whimpers and her tears bead along the top of my hand. It's been so long since I've licked tears off someone's skin, and the urge to do so now soars inside me. I promised I wouldn't hurt her, but fuck, I want to. Not in a way that would kill her. Just in a way that would make her scream—that gorgeous, melodic scream I heard nearly two nights ago on the river.

"Plhmph," she says into my hand. I've done this enough times in my two hundred years to know she's saying *Please*.

"I said I'm not going to hurt you." I drag her along with me, keeping to the narrow paths formed between the compound's prefab houses. My temporary cabin is maybe a two-minute walk from here, and I move quickly. I make Mercy move quickly.

Her tears flow faster, but she doesn't fight back. I suppose even she knows how dangerous men can be.

I'm not exactly a man, though. Not in the way she's thinking.

My cabin appears up ahead, and relief surges through me even though I take pains not to let Mercy know. I left the porch light on, the only light in the ring of cabins. Mercy sniffles.

"Almost there," I tell her, and now she does try to fight back, although she does so half-heartedly, squirming against my grasp. It does little but send blood shooting down to my cock, another fact I try to conceal from her.

"Mmmphhnn!" she shrieks, and I tighten my hand around her mouth, squeezing her face perhaps a little too hard. As I drag her up to the door, Max lets out an excited bark from inside. Mercy keens.

"Don't be scared of him." I shove the key into the lock and turn it and push the door open at the same time, then heave Mercy into the cabin, tossing her onto the couch while I lock the door. She scrambles to her feet as both dogs run up to investigate—although she takes their appearance as a threat and screams and tries to bolt forward. I catch her around the waist, slap my hand over her mouth.

"Don't do that again." I put my lips on her ear, and she shivers against me. "Do not scream. Do you understand?"

"Nmn!" Her tongue licks my palm.

"No, you don't understand?" I drag her back over to the couch, pressing her body up against mine. I need to play this carefully. I don't want her thinking I'm anything but a preacher.

Her only answer is a kind of choking sob. Her face is drenched in tears, and so is my hand, and I'm enjoying this far more than I should.

"I don't want to hurt you," I tell her. It's good to tell them that, even when it's a lie—which, here, it isn't. Not really. I certainly don't *intend* to hurt her, anyway. "I just want to talk about what I saw." I pause, then add, "And come clean about something."

Mercy jerks her head in something close to a nod, and I slowly move my hand away from her mouth. She doesn't move, doesn't scream. She blinks at me with tear-damp eyes.

"Who are you?" she asks, voice trembling. "Why are you doing this?"

For a fraction of a second, I consider telling her the truth, that the devil really has come to the Church of the Well. That I am, in fact, the closest thing to Satan she'll ever meet. It would be worth it to drown in the miasma of her terror.

But I refrain. I'm not Sawyer, making decisions with my dick.

"I'm Ambrose Echeverría," I say smoothly. "And I am a traveling preacher, and God did call me here. He works in mysterious ways, as the saying goes."

Mercy twists her head toward me, her brown eyes big and glossy and bloodshot from crying. Her cheeks are ruddy. I will not be forgetting this pretty picture anytime soon.

"Why are you here?" she snarls, with more vehemence than I'd expect.

I give a hapless sort of sigh and rearrange my features into an expression of sheepishness, as if I'm not used to doing this sort of thing. "I originally thought God brought me here for one reason—"

"You're taking advantage of us," she snarls. "Our grief—"

"No," I interrupt. "I came here for one thing, yes. But when I arrived, I knew my presence was needed for other reasons as well. My desire to see the church through their grief is genuine."

All lies, of course. But ones she wants to believe, given the way her eyes soften.

"I'm not supposed to be alone in a man's home," she snaps. "And you dragged me here against your will."

"I apologize for that." I hold my hands up, trying to look as hapless as possible. "Truly. But I wanted to speak to you privately. About what I—" I swallow as if this topic upsets me. "Saw."

Mercy's eyes darken. "You were spying on me and my husband."

There's the slightest pause before she says *husband*, a small quiver of hesitation. I make myself look hapless again.

"We all have our vices," I say, channeling every disgraced preacher I've ever seen—and I've seen a lot of them. "I'll admit the sins of the flesh are something I struggle with."

Mercy's fear flickers like a candle. Just for a moment, it turns to lust.

Interesting.

"There's something I need," I continue. "And with what I saw—well, Sterling Gunner is still married to his first wife, isn't he? It would do some damage to his reputation if his arrangement with you were to become public knowledge."

Blackmail, the last refuge of a coward. But if it'll get me those adoption records so I can move on with my life—

Mercy lets out a sharp, bitter laugh. "I should have known." Her fear has subsided somehow, giving way to a kind of darkness I don't know how to read. "You want to fuck me, don't you?"

It is utterly bizarre hearing this woman of God say the word *fuck*. So bizarre, in fact, that I don't even register what she's getting at until she says, "You don't need to threaten me. Just ask Reverend Gunner. He's willing to share if you give him something."

"What?" I didn't expect to be surprised tonight, but Mercy just pulled it off. "You think I brought you here to *rape* you?"

I'm almost offended. I'm a murderer and a cannibal. I hunt humans the way humans hunt deer.

I'm not a fucking *rapist*.

Mercy's brows draw together. "What do you want, then?"

I tilt my head toward the couch. "Sit."

Mercy stares at me in defiance.

"Do it," I say, and I let just enough of my true self through that this time, she listens.

CHAPTER SEVEN

MERCY

I sink into the cheap, flimsy sofa, my entire body trembling. Ambrose ambles toward me with a slow, lazy swagger, and I peer up at him, my tongue dry and thick in my mouth.

"What do you want?" I manage to whisper.

Ambrose stops a few feet from me, his eyes pinned to mine. "The Church of the Well organizes adoptions."

Of all the things he could have said in this moment, this sentence is the absolute last thing I expected.

"What?" I squawk out. I can't help myself.

"Adoptions," he repeats. "I'm helping someone find her birth parents. She was adopted through the Church of the Well in the '90s."

I stare at him in confusion. "So she's a member of the church?" That's what the church does—rescue lost souls to bring them into the fold. It's how I came here, although I don't say that to Ambrose.

"She was," he says. "Although now she's—she's part of my flock. And I agreed to help her."

I knot my skirt up in my fists as warring emotions clash in

my chest. One of them is a strange desire to know more about this woman he's helping. If she's a wife. A girlfriend.

Why do you care?

"So that's why you brought me here," I say numbly. "To blackmail me." I look at him—dangerous and handsome, his lean, rangy frame towering over me. For a moment, I'm reminded of him praying over me this morning. All that warmth I felt was the opposite of the emptiness I feel right now.

I thought he was different. I thought he was like Raul.

"I want to blackmail Reverend Gunner," he says, somewhat stiffly. "If anyone on this compound has access to those files, it's him. But you'll need to deliver the message. Tell him if he doesn't help, I'll go straight to every news outlet and—"

"He won't care."

Ambrose stops and frowns at me. I stare down at my lap. "He doesn't care what the secular world thinks of him."

"I'm not talking about the secular world," Ambrose says sharply. "I'm talking about his followers. He was a powerful man in the old televangelist days."

I laugh. "He's not a televangelist anymore. Not since God revealed the First Prophecy to him." I narrow my eyes, regarding Ambrose with a new suspicion. "Do you know anything about the Church of the Well? Anything at all?"

Ambrose's face is impossible to read. "I know enough," he says darkly.

"Clearly, you don't." I straighten my shoulders and look him in the eye as I speak. "God Himself told Reverend Gunner that he was allowed to take a second wife because he's a prophet, and his work is important enough that he needs extra support."

Ambrose studies me for a second—

And then he laughs.

"Is that what he said?" Ambrose sits on the couch beside me, leaving just enough space between us to count as decent.

Not that Reverend Gunner will care if he finds out that I'm in this cabin unchaperoned. "What about him being willing to *share*? Did God reveal that to him, too?"

I freeze, my skirt balled up tightly in my fists. "Yes," I say, and Ambrose laughs again, shaking his head. "He wouldn't actually share me with you," I add. "I only said that so you wouldn't—"

"I won't do anything to you that you haven't agreed to."

Ambrose's words shoot straight through me, and I jerk my gaze up to him.

He's not laughing.

"He only shared me with Pastor Sullivan," I say, not totally sure why I'm telling him this. "He's another prophet. My job here, in this life, is to serve as a helpmeet to the prophets. To help them—" The word curdles on my tongue. "Relax."

Ambrose studies me for a long time. "I see," he finally says. "And the congregation knows."

"Of course they do. It's a great honor."

"Do you really believe that?"

I take a deep breath and look away from him, staring across the living room and into the open bathroom door. His cabin has the same layout as mine. Because that's what being bestowed a great honor means—having the woman who raised you kick you out of her home because her husband wants to fuck you.

"Well?" Ambrose prompts.

I squeeze my eyes shut. I know I should say yes. But Ambrose would know I'm lying.

"No," I whisper.

Ambrose shifts on the couch, and I glance over at him. He reminds me of Raul. They're handsome in the same way, with their dark eyes and high cheekbones. But Ambrose looks at me in a way Raul never did.

Because Raul knew better.

"Forgive me for saying this." Ambrose leans closer, his hair falling a little into his eyes. "But what I saw earlier—you didn't seem to be enjoying yourself."

Heat rushes to my cheeks. "You shouldn't have seen that."

"You're right." Ambrose straightens up. "I shouldn't have watched. But—" His eyes are black holes. "I stand by what I said. Reverend Gunner doesn't seem to care about your needs."

I swallow, my throat suddenly very dry. "Reverend Gunner is the prophet," I say, reciting what I've heard a thousand times. "I'm there to help him carry this burden."

"But you don't enjoy it." Ambrose shifts closer, close enough that the space between us isn't decent anymore

And yet I don't move away.

"Of course I do." I say it too quickly. Too defensively. A smile curves up on Ambrose's lips.

"Like I said," he murmurs. "My one weakness is the pleasures of the flesh."

The couch's armrest digs into the top part of my back, and Ambrose's thigh nudges up to the seam of my legs. I bite back a gasp of surprise, but he notices. I can tell because his smile turns to that sharkish grin that splits his face in two.

I still don't move away.

"What if I make you another offer?" he asks, looking me dead in the eye. "For the adoption records."

He's hunched over me, his mouth inches from mine. Three years as Reverend Gunner's helpmeet means I know what this position is. I ought to push Ambrose away, get out of here, and run to tell Reverend Gunner that the itinerant preacher needs to be expelled from the church immediately.

And yet I don't want to push him away. His thigh between my legs feels good, not odd and certainly not painful. Heat blooms in my belly.

"What kind of offer?" I whisper.

Ambrose tucks a lock of my hair behind my ear, his touch so gentle I can almost forget that this is a sin.

"You agree to help me get the files," he says. "And I'll reward you."

"Reward me how?"

Ambrose grins again. Then, as gently as he tucked my hair, he starts to saw his thigh back and forth between my legs.

"How about I show you what it's supposed to feel like?" he murmurs.

"I knew it!" I cry, and then I try to roll out from under him. But he catches me and pushes me back against the couch.

"I'm not going to fuck you," he says. "I'm just going to touch you."

He grinds his thigh up against me, and even with the layers of fabric between his skin and the most private part of my body, I'm struck dumb. It's not that I *can't* protest. It's that I don't want to.

"Like that," he purrs, quickening his pace. "You like that, don't you? Reverend Gunner never does this for you, does he?"

"Why would he?" I whisper.

"Because he doesn't give a shit about you."

I jerk my gaze up to meet Ambrose's. He stares down at me like he's daring me to contradict him. And all the while, he keeps sawing his leg up against my body.

"You don't know that," I finally say. Even though it's a thought I've had myself, more than once, in the empty darkness of my bedroom.

"I know what I saw." Ambrose snakes his arm down between us and grabs my dress's skirt and peels it upward, removing one of the layers of fabric between us. He never breaks eye contact with me.

I won't do anything to you that you haven't agreed to.

I haven't technically agreed to this. Not out loud.

But I do want it, don't I? Because, God forgive me, I don't want him to stop.

"What do you say, Mercy?" Ambrose pulls his knee away

from me, and its absence makes me gasp. "I make you feel good, and then you help me get access to the files?"

"I don't have access to the files," I whimper.

"But you know where they are. So what's it going to be? Yes or no?"

My breath shudders in my throat. I can't say yes. I *can't*.

No is on the tip of my tongue. But it never escapes—

Because I nod my head in agreement instead.

Ambrose smiles at me, dazzling and toothy. "Wonderful," he says, and I expect him to press his knee back against me—I *want* him to—but he doesn't. Instead, he slides his hand back down and gently trails his fingers over my underwear. Not *there*, not where I expect him to touch. He's a little higher, and he works his fingers in a slow, gentle circle.

I gasp, my body shuddering. It's never felt like this, not with Reverend Gunner or Pastor Sullivan.

"That's it," Ambrose slips his fingers sideways and curls them into the leg band of my underwear. They feel impossibly hot against my skin. "Once you come, you can tell me where the files are."

Before I can say anything, he pushes my panties aside, and then his fingers are *on me* on me, rippling over my most private area.

"But I can't—" The words slip out before I can stop them. Ambrose looks down at me, his pupils flooding out his dark irises, turning his eyes solid black.

"Can't what?" He doesn't put his fingers inside me like I expect him to. Instead, he touches that spot that makes my whole lower half feel hot and shaky.

"Can't come." I sigh the words out, shame burning in my face.

Ambrose keeps rubbing me in slow, lazy circles. "Yes, you can." He leans closer, and for a moment I think he's going to kiss me. "It might take some time, but I can be patient when there's something I want."

"I've never—"

"Stop talking." He says it like an order. A command.

And one I want to follow.

So I do stop talking, sealing my mouth shut.

"Relax."

That's harder to do. Every muscle in my body feels like it's contracting toward the place he's touching.

"Good girl," Ambrose says. "Now stop arguing with me and just focus on my fingers. Do you understand?"

Stop talking, he said, and so I nod wordlessly, gazing up at him. He smiles a little. His touch quickens.

"Then let's begin."

CHAPTER EIGHT

MERCY

I thought we had already begun, considering Ambrose is currently swirling the pads of his fingers over some impossibly sensitive patch of skin. He's not even inside me, and I already feel a quaking, unfamiliar heat between my thighs.

"Why don't we get you more comfortable?" He smooths his free hand over my hair. "That armrest looks like it's digging into your back."

As soon as he says it, I feel it, the firm wedge of foam and particle board jutting between my shoulder blades. "O-okay."

Ambrose takes his hand away, and I squirm, shocked by how much I miss his touch. "Stretch out," he says, standing up. "And spread your legs."

That last sentence, it's a *command*, dark and throaty. All I want is to do as he asks, and I don't know why. Because all my life, all I've ever done is what men tell me.

But this—feels different somehow.

"Go on," he urges.

I shimmy my hips down, not caring that my skirt rides up

around my waist, not caring that my underwear is twisted to the side, exposing me to the cool air of the AC. Ambrose watches me the entire time, his hands at his side, his eyes fixed on me—

His *excitement* is more than evident.

I try not to look at it, the tent in his trousers. But as I settle back on the stiff cushion, my eyes keep flicking that way.

If Ambrose notices, he doesn't say anything.

"That's an improvement." He kneels on the floor beside the couch. "But let's really give me access."

He flashes me that sharkish grin. I feel like he's about to devour me whole.

But he doesn't. Instead, he gently pushes my thighs apart, draping one leg against the back of the couch and arranging the other so my toes graze the linoleum floor. Then he reaches between my legs again, sliding his fingers up between my folds.

I cry out and smother my voice with my hand.

"Make all the noise you want," he says. "It's one in the morning. Everyone's asleep. The other cabins are empty."

"You told me not to talk." I look up at him, and he's looking at my face, not—down there. It's like he knows my body by touch.

Ambrose raises an eyebrow.

"So I did." He slides a finger inside me and does something, makes some kind of movement, that draws another gasp out of my lips. "But I like hearing your desperate little pants." He leans close, and when I breathe in, I smell him—cedar and cold wind and something that might be leather. "I'm definitely going to want to hear you moan when you come."

Heat surges through me. He's touching the outside of me again, although one finger still works inside me. There's none of the painful stretch of intercourse. Ambrose is barely inside me at all. But it feels—

It feels like the light of God.

"You're wet," he says softly. "That's the first stage of arousal."

I just look at him, silent the way he asked me to be. With his free hand, he runs his thumb over my mouth. "So are these red lips," he mutters. "You're on your way, sweetheart."

Sweetheart. It's so innocent-sounding, but it shoots right through my core. My muscles jump and tremble, and Ambrose grins and touches me a little faster.

"See what I mean?"

"What are you—" I stop, remembering I'm not supposed to speak. But Ambrose tilts his head at an inquisitive angle. Keeps touching me. It's like he's stoking a fire between my thighs.

"Go on," he says.

"What are you doing?" The question comes out in a rush.

"Touching you."

Heat floods into my cheeks, and then he does something down there that makes my hips jolt into his hand. "How are you touching me?" I ask, my voice ragged. "It feels—it feels better than when Reverend—"

"Don't say his name." He massages me, inside and out. My body shakes, and that heat has started to become a kind of pleasurable irritation. I have the sudden, worrying thought that I need to use the bathroom, but I'm too embarrassed to say anything.

Ambrose changes something in the way he touches me, increasing the pressure on the outside. I cry out, my voice strangled.

"That's your clit," he says. "And something tells me the good Reverend Gunner has never found it once in his miserable life. He can't be bothered."

Some part of me—the part of me not currently quivering with pleasure—knows I should be offended on Reverend Gunner's behalf. But the rest of me kind of curls inward that this man, this liar who nonetheless still knows how to lay on hands, can see straight into my marriage after a single day.

"Now this," Ambrose says, and he hooks his finger up inside me, pressing against something that makes me keen and arch my back. "They call that the G-spot. But from what I understand, that's just your clit, too."

He evens out the pressure of his touch, and I can barely stand it, all this heat inside me. I don't understand how he knows my body so well, or why he wants to do this to me just so I can show him where to access the adoption records. In truth, I keep waiting for him to give up and take out his penis and put it inside me the way Reverend Gunner does. The way Pastor Sullivan does too, whenever I'm asked to serve him.

"You touch these things together," Ambrose says. "And you'll come."

He's going faster now, and I can feel an embarrassing flood of wetness between my legs. I know I'm probably staining the couch. Dirtying his fingers. But Ambrose doesn't seem to care. He just leans over me, his face close to mine. For a moment, I wonder if he's going to kiss me.

"How does that feel?" he whispers.

I don't have the words to describe how it feels. I feel vulnerable and exposed. I feel like I'm burning alive. I feel like something's trying to split me apart and I want it to happen but I'm also afraid it's going to happen.

All that, and what comes out of my mouth is—

"I think I need to use the bathroom."

Immediately, humiliation floods through my cheeks, and I grab Ambrose's wrist and shove it away and move to get up. I shouldn't be here. I belong to Reverend Gunner. And yet—

The absence of Ambrose's touch is almost painful.

Ambrose pushes me back down on the couch. "You don't need to use the bathroom."

"Yes, I do." I try to push my skirt down, but he stops me.

An agitation works up between my legs. A faint, treasonous tugging. I want him to touch me again.

But he *can't*.

"How about this?" He slides his palm against my nether lips, making me gasp and buck up into touch. He laughs. "I know you're enjoying yourself."

"It feels like—"

"Like you're going to piss yourself?"

He arches an eyebrow mischievously, and I jerk my gaze away from him, my face flaming with heat.

"I told you. I think I need to use the bathroom."

"And I'm telling you that you don't." He grabs my chin with his free hand and tilts my face toward him as the heel of his other palm grinds against my clit.

His fingers move through my slipperiness, my humiliating wetness, and find their way back to their previous positions: one inside me, one outside, both moving in tandem. I keen and squirm beneath Ambrose's weight, that pressure building up again in my belly.

Ambrose presses his lips to my ear. It almost feels like a kiss.

"If you need to piss," he rasps. "I want you to piss on my fingers."

"*What?*" I try to sit up again, but Ambrose pins me down and rubs me faster, his finger sliding in and out of me with a steady rhythm that feels dangerous and sinful and fiery and impossibly good. Like Heaven and Hell got all entwined together.

Just like Ambrose, I think distantly.

"I mean it." He works me with his entire arm, his breath hot against the sensitive skin of my neck. "I want you to let go, Mercy. If that means pissing on my hand, then fucking piss on me."

His words shoot straight through me—their vulgarity. Their harshness. They aren't the words of a preacher.

And yet Ambrose prayed over me like a preacher. He talks like a preacher, when he wants to.

But he clearly doesn't want to right now. He keeps rubbing me with that same frantic rhythm, and even though it feels slatternly, I can't help but match that rhythm with my hips, until the two of us are locked together, moving as one.

I groan and drop my head back, and Ambrose brushes his lips over my neck, then does the same with his tongue. More noises come out of my mouth, and it feels like someone else is making them, all those rough little grunting pants.

"That's it," Ambrose murmurs, moving his mouth to the other side of my neck. "That's it, Mercy. Just let it go."

I feel like I should tell him to stop. But I also think that if he stops touching me, I'll die.

"That's it," he whispers, over and over like a chant. "That's it. That's it. Come on, darling. That's it."

I moan, and the pressure is going to erupt, and I *am* going to pee on his hand, I'm certain of it, but I don't care because all I want is to keep feeling his fingers sliding through me, back and forth, fast and unceasing, and then—

All that pressure explodes. Every nerve in my body flares like I'm doused in Holy fire. I can't catch my breath. I can't stop myself from jerking and flopping around, and it almost feels like I'm lifting up in the air, like it's the End of Days and my body is ascending into Paradise.

Ambrose groans softly, a sound that draws me out of the Heavens and back to Earth—back down to this stiff, uncomfortable couch, where my legs are splayed, my dress hiked up. It's the most unladylike I've ever been in my life.

I take a deep, shuddery breath, trying to slow my racing heart. I blink up at Ambrose, who grins down at me.

"Told you didn't need to piss," he says.

And that's when I realize what happened.

"That's—that's what it feels like?" I push myself up to

sitting, all my movements shaking and trembling as I smooth my skirt down, wriggling my hips to adjust my panties back into place.

Ambrose doesn't try to push me down this time, only sits back and then, to my horror, holds up the hand he used to pleasure me. His fingers are shiny and wet.

"Yeah," he says. "Like Heaven itself, right?"

I can't dwell on his blasphemy, though, because he slides his fingers into his mouth, sucking them clean like chicken bones. I can't tear myself away from the sight. From the way his eyes flutter closed and his cheeks hollow out. When he drags his fingers out of his mouth, he looks right at me.

"You taste fucking delicious, Mercy."

The way he says my name sends little quakes shooting through me, like a miniature version of my first orgasm.

"Thank you?" I whisper, squeezing my dress up in my fists.

Ambrose chuckles and stands up. The tent of his erection seems even larger than before, and I tense myself, waiting for the inevitable.

It doesn't come. Instead, he holds out one hand. He doesn't have preacher's hands, a detail I hadn't noticed in all the times he's touched me. They're rough. Calloused. Strong.

A carpenter's hands.

More blasphemy. But I take his hand anyway, and he pulls me up to standing.

"Did you enjoy that?" he asks.

I hesitate, not sure how to answer, and I'm grateful when I hear the click of a dog's nails on the tile because it means I can look away from his black, piercing gaze to the big, black dog that comes trotting into the room.

"Hello, Roxi," he says.

She sits on her haunches and stares at me. I keep studying her—she's big and vicious-looking, although she doesn't seem interested in hurting me. Ambrose brushes his knuckles against my cheek.

"You didn't answer my question."

I force myself to look over at him. There really is something in his features that reminds me, distantly, of Raul, and my chest clenches up. Now, grief intermingles with my guilt. Still, I answer honestly.

"Yes." I take a step back from him, trying to get out of his reach. "But you can't—I'm Reverend Gunner's helpmeet. His wife."

Ambrose shakes his head, his expression unreadable. "No. He's forcing you to be his mistress."

The truth of his words slices straight through my heart.

"God sent me to him," I say quietly. "That's why my parents died. So I could come here to him and support his work here on Earth."

I've said these words, or had them said to me, hundreds of times. They've always felt hollow.

At this moment, they feel like a lie.

"Your parents died," Ambrose says, interest curling in his voice. "So you were adopted, too?"

"I should go." I turn to leave, and I'm not completely surprised when Ambrose catches my arm and pulls me, somewhat roughly, up toward him.

"We had a deal." He speaks into my ear, and little shivers work through my body. "Tell me where the adoption files are."

This really doesn't feel like a fair trade, that he gave me all that physical pleasure and asked for none in return. I swallow nervously. "Remember, I don't have access to them."

"That's fine. Just show me where they are."

"They're in the emergency bunker," I say softly, his rough fingers burning a bracelet around my wrist. "On the western side of the campus, past the training fields. I can show you tomorrow morning before I get you set up for the prayer sessions."

Ambrose immediately releases me and gives me a dazzling smile. "Excellent. Thank you, Mercy."

We stare at each other for a few moments. My whole body still feels shaky. Weak.

I'm weak, for letting him do that.

And yet I desperately want him to do it again.

"I'll see you tomorrow," I say, and then I flee.

CHAPTER NINE

AMBROSE

I wake up the next morning to harsh sunlight falling across my eyes and Max's big sloppy tongue slurping against my cheek. "Yeah, I know, I know," I mutter, tackling him into a hug. Roxi sits patiently by the door, thumping her tail against the tile. "Well, I'm up now. Give me a second and I'll feed you."

As soon as Max hears the word *feed*, he's off like a shot, skittering into the kitchen. He's gonna be disappointed, though, since they're getting dry grocery store kibble and not their usual chopped-up organ meats.

I drag myself out of bed, splash some water on my face, and try to ignore Mercy's lingering scent on my fingers. I showered last night, but I've got a Hunter's heightened senses, and I can still smell her all over my hand—sweet and musky, like dried roses. I had to jerk myself off as soon as she left, the memory of her moans and thrusts and the horny, horrified expression she gave me when I told her to just piss on my hand seeing me through to completion.

The dogs follow me around as I pour the kibble into the bowls—Roxi gives me a baleful look when she sees it, although Max dives right in. I put on a pot of coffee and lean against the counter, trying to get myself back into preacher mode. I let it slip last night when I dragged Mercy back here, and although she clearly doesn't suspect I'm the one who killed Raul Alvarez —she would have been much more afraid—it was still stupid. *I'm* being stupid, honestly. I'm not here to get laid. I'm here to get those fucking adoption records for Charlotte and then get out.

But fuck, Mercy squirmed so deliciously while I stroked her to orgasm. And I can't get over the shock on her face after she came for the first time. And before that, too, while she was in the middle of it. Her eyes rolled back and she arched her back and her cunt fluttered furiously around my finger, like a butterfly desperate to get free. The crimson flush above her breasts. Her bright eyes staring at me like she had just seen God.

And I did that to her. Gunner has been using her for his own pleasure for fuck knows how long, but *I'm* the one that made her come. Helpmeet, my ass.

An orphan, too. *God sent me to him*, she said, and I wonder how old she was when that happened. She changed the subject real quick when I brought up her being adopted.

And then there was shit about how he "shared" her with his right-hand man, Sullivan. Gunner is lending her around like a library book, a thought that makes my stomach clench up and the void surge up in my throat—

I'd love to dismember the fucker limb by limb and smoke his thighs like a brisket.

The coffee machine gurgles, and a soft wet nose nudges against my calf—Max, drawing me out of his bloodlust. I take a deep breath and reach down to rub between his silky ears. It's a good thing I kill regularly. Otherwise, I don't think I'd be able to stop myself from going after Gunner. I'm fighting the urge enough as it is. Wanting to fuck and wanting to kill have always felt the same to me, so Mercy's presence, however intoxicating it may be, is complicating my little mission.

"Thanks, buddy," I tell Max, who barks and wags his tail and nudges against me again before trotting into the living room and settling down next to the door like a good guard dog. Roxi just watches me. She's more ruthless, and I bet she felt the spike in my blood. I bet she's waiting for instructions to attack.

"Not today, girl," I tell her as I fix my coffee. "Today, you're a pastor's dog."

She has nothing to say about that. I take my coffee over to the front window and peer out through the curtains. The little courtyard in front of the houses is empty and quiet, the grass yellowing from the heat despite the rain we've had. There's a spray of wild sunflowers bursting along the walkway, heads tilted toward the east.

I need to get ready. Mercy will be here soon enough, and I've got to keep this preacher ruse up for a little while longer.

Assuming I haven't blown my cover enough already.

Rap rap rap.

Max immediately starts barking, claws scrabbling over the tiles. I slick my hair back with some water and go to pull the door open.

There she is.

She's wearing another one of those shapeless cotton dresses, the skirt voluminous enough that it hides her big hips and soft thighs and the entrance to Heaven nestled between them, and her hair's up in braids again, a style that makes her eyes seem even more soft and doe-like. She gives me a shy little smile and says, "Sorry. I know I'm early."

"That's just fine. You want to come in?"

She gives me a strange look. "I really shouldn't. I'm not supposed to be alone in a man's home."

That makes me want to drag her into the cabin, throw her on that pitiful excuse for a bed, and fuck her until she's screaming her savior's name. Because how the hell can she follow a rule like that when Sterling Gunner's treating her like his own private sex toy?

I keep my mouth shut, though. Preacher. I'm supposed to be a goddamned preacher, and Mercy is clearly trying to pretend last night didn't happen. And honestly, I probably should, too. I've got no business getting mixed up with a human woman, much less a Christian.

"Right," I say. "Of course." I flash her a grin, trying to disarm her. "What about dogs, though? Can you be alone with them?"

Mercy smiles. A genuine smile, one that reaches all the way up into her eyes. "Of course."

"Good. You can keep these two out of my hair while I finish getting ready." I whistle, and Roxi and Max come bounding out, tails wagging and tongues lolling. We've got a whole language of whistles worked out between us. That one means, *Play nice*.

And they do, running around Mercy and nosing at her hands until she pets them. I leave the door open when I go back inside, and I can hear laughter drifting in from the courtyard.

I finish getting ready—throw on a tie for good measure, work some gel through my hair so it'll stay put, slap on some cologne. Mercy's giggles trail in through the open door as I take one last look at myself in the tiny bathroom mirror. It's been a hundred years at least since I last played preacher, but I think I look convincing. A little rough around the edges, maybe, but that just makes it easier to lean into the aw-shucks backwoods shit that always puts my prey at ease.

"Having fun?" I ask as I step out onto the little cement patio. Mercy has plopped down in the yellowing grass, her skirt flared out around her, as Max—always the charmer—keeps trying to lick her cheek. Roxi watches the whole thing with her usual bored detachment. She doesn't like the *play nice* command as much as Max does.

"Your dogs are so adorable." Mercy fights past Max to stand up, and he keeps nipping around her ankles, his tail a blur. I think he actually likes her, which warms my heart a bit, even though it shouldn't.

"Yeah, I know. That one can be a pain in the butt, though." I nod at Max, then whistle to him: *Come here.* Both of them trot over to me.

"They're well-trained," she says.

"Gotta be," I answer smoothly. "They're around strangers all the time. They're a key part of my ministry."

That, of course, is not the *real* reason they're well-trained, but it sounds good.

Mercy flashes me a sweet little smile, kind of shy and soft. I latch both dogs up on their leashes, then squint up at Mercy through the sun. It's already hot as hell, and it's not even 9 AM yet. And unfortunately, I have to wear long sleeves to cover up my tattoos.

"So are you going to show me what we talked about?"

A shadow passes over Mercy's face. I know damn well she didn't forget about it; I'm not scheduled to show up at the meeting hall until 10. She's actually *very* early. If I didn't know better, I'd think she might want to see me.

"Well, yes," she says, her shoulders stiffening. "It's on the other side of the campus, though. I can get a golf cart if you want."

"Don't be ridiculous." I pat Max's head again. "These two need a walk anyway."

"It's just so hot," she says. "And you've got a tie and everything—"

"I'm happy to walk." I move up beside her, and we set off

down the sandy pathway. "Assuming you won't get in trouble for being alone with me."

She blushes bright red, and my cock stirs because it's the same shade she turned last night before I made her come.

"Not out in public like this," she says softly. "And I already told Reverend Gunner that I was going to give you a tour of the grounds before your prayer session."

"Clever." And I mean it. Gunner might have her under some fucked up kind of control, but she's working with what she's got. I admire that in a human.

We fall into step together, the dogs sniffing the path as we walk. It *is* hot as hell, but there's a bit of a morning breeze. I wouldn't call it cool, exactly, but it stirs everything around.

"This is the residential area," Mercy says, gesturing toward the houses rising up on either side of us, all bigger and somewhat more elaborate versions of the prefab cabin they put me up in. "About 200 people live on the campus. Of course, Reverend Gunner's followers are much more numerous than that. We have nearly 7,000 members across the United States, with satellite campuses in Florida, California, and Tenn—"

"I don't need the official tour," I turn toward her, and she's blushing again. It's dangerous, that blush. Reminds me of the blood pumping through her body and how much I might like to see it outside of her. "I knew all that before I came here, anyway."

Mercy's blush deepens. "Of course, I'm sorry," she says. "I'm just used to—"

"No need to apologize." I put my hand on her arm without thinking about it, and I immediately feel her muscles tense. But she doesn't try to shrug me away. "Tell me what you think people are looking for from the prayer sessions today."

I know I'm laying it on a little thick, but I need to make up for my serious lapse in judgment last night. Make sure she doesn't suspect I'm anything but a horny preacher.

"Oh, any guidance you can provide would be wonderful." She sighs and gazes blankly up ahead. The houses have given way to the administrative buildings I was trying to investigate last night before I got distracted by her scent. "And your prayers—you do have God's touch."

I sense the shift in her heartbeat as she realizes what she's said. God's touch, indeed. I certainly helped her see God last night.

"Grief is hard," I tell her, "but it also can't be rushed. God might work through me to help, but it is God in the end."

She looks sideways. I wonder if she thinks my bullshit is as gibberish nonsense as I do. "Of course. I felt God working through you. I felt—" Her voice fades, and all her systems quicken. Her heart, her breath. She's nervous. Not *afraid*—that has a much different rhythm to it, and one I'd like to experience from her again. But I do find her nervousness endearing.

"It felt good," she says in a very, very low voice. "What you did to me. I felt—" She takes a deep breath. "Thank you."

Roxi tugs on her leash, moving to investigate something in a flowerbed beside a bland brick building. I use that as an excuse to stop, letting her leash out as I turn to Mercy. She looks up at me, her lips parted and her eyes bright.

She's *definitely* not talking about my prayers.

I can smell her arousal, sweet and dark and musky. The scent goes straight to my cock, which is probably why I say what I say next, even though it's foolish as hell, given she's a human and I'm a Hunter and it's really not my place to fuck her kind, but to kill them.

Still, the words slip out anyway.

"If you never need release like that again—" I stop closer to her, and her eyes follow me, dark with lust. "You know where to find me."

CHAPTER TEN

MERCY

For a long moment, all I can do is stare at him, handsome in the harsh morning sunlight. *Too* handsome. *Dangerously* handsome. When he answered his door this morning, he looked like the preacher who had been sitting in Reverend Gunner's office yesterday. But right now, he looks like the man who set me on fire last night. Like someone I absolutely shouldn't be alone with, even if we are out in public.

Then, quick as lightning, that shadow disappears.

"So, this bunker," he says. "It's nearby?"

"About five more minutes."

The big black German shepherd mix lunges forward, her ears flattened against the back of her thread, a hint of teeth peeking from her jaws.

"Roxi," Ambrose says sharply, and when she ignores him, he whistles three short notes. Immediately, she turns back toward us, tongue wagging.

It seems Ambrose isn't the only one who can change personalities on a dime.

"She saw a squirrel," he says apologetically. "Shall we?"

As if he hadn't just said what he said. As if my body doesn't feel like a live wire.

"R-right," I say quickly. "This way."

I lead him down the walking path, away from the administration center. We're on the western side of campus now, and being here sends a sharp burst of grief twisting through my belly. It's where the men do their training when the weather isn't so hot, and where I used to hand out bottles of cold water. It's where I became friends with Raul.

Of course, no one is out this morning. Reverend Gunner says that what killed Raul can't be defeated by guns and weapons but by prayer and faith. Guns can't kill the devil.

So for now, it's just an empty shooting range, a dried-up obstacle course. I see Ambrose looking at it, but he doesn't say anything.

We cut across the grass, walking in silence. The dogs snuffle around, curious and alert. I smooth my palms against my dress; nine in the morning and I'm already sweating.

"Almost there," I say with an apologetic little laugh. Ambrose glances at me sideways.

"This place is bigger than I thought it'd be."

"Nearly a thousand acres." I bite back the urge to give him the rest of the tour, which I've done dozens of times for Reverend Gunner's guests. How he purchased the first five acres in the 1980s shortly after he married Madelyn, thinking he would build a house for his family. How, a year later, God came to him while he was on the property, near an old dried-up well, and told him to build a church instead, and that was the beginning of the Church of the Well. Now that well is the altar of the chapel where Reverend Gunner preaches and where, thirty-five years later, he took me as his wife.

But I don't say any of it, because I don't want to talk about Reverend Gunner with Ambrose. And because, before I know it, the bunker entrance appears up ahead, a grey block jutting out of the middle of the western field.

"There it is," I say.

Ambrose frowns. "Damn. When you said bunker, you meant it. It's underground?"

"Well, yes." Why do I feel like he's judging me? Judging the Church of the Well? "It's an emergency bunker. In case of government interference."

"Hmmn." The dogs stop to investigate something in the grass, and Ambrose stops with them, studying the bunker entrance. "And the files are in there?"

"We use parts of it for storage."

"Until the government comes rolling in, anyway."

I glare at him, irritation fluttering in my chest. "Reverend Gunner is a *prophet*. Of course the government wants to see him destroyed."

Ambrose tilts his head, his eyes glittering. "Do you really believe that?"

His question brings me up short because although I know I'm supposed to say yes, my immediate response is *no*—not only to the threat of the government, which I've always been doubtful of, but to the idea of Reverend Gunner as a prophet. It's something I've been told since I came here at eight years old, but no one has ever asked me if I believe it until now. It was always just taken for granted that I did.

Ambrose arches an eyebrow, waiting for my response.

"You can't deny the devil is out there," I say, knowing I'm evading the question. "In the secular world. And he wants us dead. He killed—" The sentence lodges in my throat.

"Yes," Ambrose says softly, his eyes dark as pitch. "Yes, he killed poor Raul."

Then he strides forward, pulling the dogs with him. As he walks, his voice rings out, and there's the hellfire and brimstone preacher I saw in him yesterday morning: "'Be sober! Be watchful! Your adversary the devil, as a roaring lion, walketh about, seeking whom he may devour.'"

I recognize the words from the Book of Peter, and goosebumps prickle along my arms. Something about the way he says the verse—it's like he's faced the Deceiver himself head-on.

I scurry after Ambrose as he makes his way up to the bunker entrance. It really isn't much to look at. A door leading to nowhere.

"Have you ever been inside?" he asks over his shoulder.

I stop at his side. He's studying the lock—a digital keypad. Only Reverend Gunner has the code. Memorized, supposedly.

"Yes, a couple of times." I run my finger over the keypad. "But like I told you, I don't know the code."

"I suppose it's safe to assume Reverend Gunner does." Ambrose crouches down so he's eye-level with the lock, and the dogs sniff around him. He bats them away distractedly, his attention focused on the door.

"Yes." Then, for some reason I can't fathom, I add, "He's the only one who does."

Ambrose makes a soft *mmm* sound in the back of his throat.

The wind picks up, hot and dry and blustery enough to tug strands of hair out of my braids, and I hold my breath, waiting for Ambrose to demand I use my sinful feminine body to wring the code out of Reverend Gunner.

But he doesn't. He only stands back up and turns toward me, dogs still snuffling around in the grass.

"Thank you," he says. "I appreciate your help."

"I didn't do much." I cross my arms over my chest even though it's blazingly hot and my skin is coated in sweat. There's something about the way Ambrose looks at me, like I'm split open just for him.

I don't dislike it. But it feels wrong. Just like last night felt wrong.

Just like it feels wrong to be standing here, alone together, away from the eyes of the congregation.

Away from Reverend Gunner.

"You did quite a bit." Ambrose steps closer to me, and his gaze is so intense I can't help but turn my eyes toward him, my heart pounding.

With a start, I realize where I've seen his expression before. It was on Raul—not when he was looking at me, though. When was practicing his rifle aim. When he had his eyes set on a target.

"Can I thank you?" Ambrose says. And just like that, the expression is gone, replaced with a soft, seductive smile. My heart beats so fast that I feel like I might faint in the heat.

"Thank me how?"

His smile just deepens, and he presses his hand around the back of my head and pulls me into him. I realize what's going to happen a split second before it does, and my body reacts on its own. I tilt my head, part my lips, and welcome Ambrose's mouth on mine.

The only man who has ever kissed me is Reverend Gunner. On the occasions when I served Pastor Sullivan, he didn't bother. But even with the reverend, I never truly participate. I've never kissed anyone back.

This morning, I do.

Ambrose's kiss is slow and measured. He slides his tongue through my parted lips and laps gently at my mouth like he's tasting me—like he's savoring my taste. The sensation is as warming as his fingers were last night, and I open my mouth a little wider, letting more of him in. He brings up his other hand and presses it gently against my cheek, his palm warm and slightly rough.

I moan softly, pressing myself into him. A gentle, pulsing heat floods between my legs. The world falls away. The church campus, the bunker entrance, the hot bracing wind, the hellish sin of what we're doing—it's all gone. There's nothing but me and Ambrose and our bodies melting together.

Then he pulls away, as slow and measured as he started. He smooths his hand over my braided hair, catching some of the glinting strands that had come loose in the wind.

"That's how I wanted to thank you," he says.

I swoon a little, stumbling away from him. Max follows me, tail wagging, and I reach down to scratch behind his ears. His stiff fur grounds me.

"We shouldn't have done that," I murmur, even though my body is aching for us to do it again.

Ambrose steps closer to me, the hot wind ruffling his brown hair. "And why not?" Another step. "Because you're Sterling's *helpmeet?*"

He spits out the last word so that it's dripping in sarcasm. I take a deep shuddery breath and allow myself to acknowledge a single truth: that I don't care about Reverend Gunner. I care about his rage, of course, if he ever found what we've done. But Ambrose and I are alone out here, and that's not why I said why I did.

It was guilt. Because Raul is dead, and the devil is trying to destroy the church, and I have no right to experience such pleasure.

"You don't owe Sterling Gunner anything," Ambrose says, taking another step toward me. "You don't, Mercy. He didn't fucking marry you."

"It's because of Raul!" I spit out, my words ringing on the wind.

Ambrose stops at that. For a moment, I think he looks genuinely surprised. "Oh."

"Raul was my friend," I say stiffly. "His funeral will be this week sometime. And I can't—I shouldn't—"

Ambrose clears the rest of the space between us with two

steps and pulls me into his arms. It's not suggestive. It's the embrace of a preacher.

"Raul is with his Creator," Ambrose says into my hair. "He's surrounded by glory. You're the one that needs comfort. Not him."

"That wasn't comfort," I tell him, my chin resting on his surprisingly muscular shoulder.

"Of course it was." Ambrose releases me enough that he can gaze down at me, his hands still on my upper arms. "I'm here to comfort you, Mercy. Whether with prayers or with—"

"Maybe we should stick with prayers." I step away from him, smoothing my hands down on my skirts.

Ambrose's eyes glitter. "Then let's pray."

It feels like a trap, with the way he's looking at me like he wants to devour me. But Lord forgive me—despite my protests, I want to be devoured.

"I can show you to the meeting hall."

"It's still early." Ambrose never takes his eyes off me. "And maybe I want to pray over you without anyone watching."

This is wrong. I know it's wrong. Getting on my knees before God is not supposed to feel like getting on my knees for a man.

And yet that's *exactly* what's happening, fire coursing through my body. I remember last night's orgasm. Last night's pleasure.

"Kneel."

He says it softly, but it still feels like a command. A command I yearn to follow.

Still, I sweep my gaze around, looking out at the empty field. The church's buildings seem far away, and the training grounds are empty.

"Kneel, Mercy."

I snap my gaze back to him, my breath tight and my body

crying out for his touch. He stares at me, his eyes black. His dogs flank him, making him look—

Well, not exactly like a preacher.

"I'm not asking," he says.

This isn't holy, what we're doing. And yet I sink down to my knees anyway, my body trembling. Ambrose steps up to me. There's a lump in his pants, and it's so close I could tilt forward and kiss it.

"Bow your head," he says in that same commanding tone.

This time, I obey immediately.

He puts his hands on my crown, just like yesterday morning. I suck in shallow breaths like my body's not getting enough air.

I force myself to look down at his black cowboy boots. For half a second, I imagine kissing those, too. I imagine falling prostrate before him, kissing his feet like Mary Magdalene before Jesus. Because that's who I am, isn't it? Mary Magdalene.

And last night Ambrose was the closest to Jesus Christ I've ever been.

"Lord God in Heaven," he intones, and I force myself to tame my thoughts. This is just a prayer. Just a blessing. Nothing more. "Show this woman that her grief need not consume her. I remind her of your words—'Blessed are they that mourn, for they shall be comforted.' And as your servant, I comfort her now."

His fingers tighten ever so slightly against my skull.

"Help her to put her hope in you, Lord God, that she will find the comfort she seeks." He pauses, and the wind blows around us, and warmth floods through my body. "And help her to see that comfort which has already been shown to her. In your name, we pray. Amen."

"Amen," I whisper, my tongue dry.

Ambrose lifts his hands from my head, and I let my gaze slide up him—over those boots I still yearn to kiss, then the physical evidence of his lust I feel mirrored in my own body, and then finally his black gaze, staring down at me.

"You look beautiful on your knees," he says.

My lust swells. I squeeze my thighs together so flesh presses against the place where Ambrose unbound me. But it's nothing compared to the dexterity of his fingers.

Ambrose offers me his hand and helps me stand up. I'm grateful for it, too, because I feel lightheaded. Dizzy. His rough palm is a reassurance.

"Feel better?" he asks.

I don't. I'm burning alive. And when I look up at him, he squeezes my hand tighter, a gesture of possessiveness that makes my heart flutter.

He leans close. I think he might kiss me again, but instead he just presses his mouth to my ear. "Thank you for helping me."

He braids his fingers through mine.

"And for letting me help you."

CHAPTER ELEVEN

AMBROSE

I spend the rest of the day lost in thought, alternating between the absolute fucking vision of Mercy kneeling in front of me, her cheeks flushed and her delicate arousal perfuming the air around us, and working through the puzzle of how to break into that goddamn bunker.

Oh, and playacting as a preacher. But slipping into that role is easier than I remember.

The meeting hall they set me up in is small and dim—yet another prefab building with thin walls and an echoing linoleum floor. Ancient metal folding chairs lined up in neat rows, a particle board folding table set up at the front as some kind of makeshift pulpit. When Mercy sees the setup, she sighs, shoulders hitching a little.

"I wish we could have put you in the chapel," she says softly. "But Reverend Gunner said he wanted to keep it open."

"This is fine." I flash her a grin. "I'm preached in worst places."

That's true, actually, although Mercy wouldn't believe me if I told her—a weary wagon train in Utah before it was Utah, a snowed-in settlement up in the New Mexico mountains, a village along the Rio Grande that had been decimated by cholera. To be fair, I always chose places that had been tainted by death. Made my true work easier.

The only thing that's unusual about this place is the little twists of twine and sticks pinned to the walls. They're magic—a soft sort of Christian magic that buzzes in the back of my head. I figure that these are the charms Charlotte told me about, the ones that poisoned her as a child so she wouldn't know what she was.

Charms to keep away the devil.

They don't keep me away, fortunately, although I do have a faint, dull headache throughout the prayer sessions—which go smoothly otherwise. Congregants file in, and I put on my brightest smile and quote the Bible at them and then lay hands like I did for Mercy, although it doesn't have quite the same effect on them as it does on her. I speak platitudes I first developed 150 years ago: "Death is not an ending, but an exaltation," and "Don't allow grief to control you," and other pithy sayings that apparently offer the comfort humans seek when they're faced with death head-on.

I'll admit I'm tempted, on a couple of occasions, to slip into my old routine—offering prayers and guidance that worm little seeds of doubt and fear into their minds. That's what the boogeyman does, isn't it? Sow fear? But I'm at the Church of the Well for a specific reason, and that reason isn't killing. It's getting the names of Charlotte's birth parents.

I don't see Mercy for the rest of the day; whether she's avoiding me or got swept up in Gunner's demands, I don't know.

Around lunchtime, a familiar-looking woman shows up with a sandwich and some kind of dubious macaroni salad, which she sets in front of me when the other congregants have cleared out.

"Pastor Echeverría," she says. "I've heard a lot about you. I'm Madelyn Gunner, Reverend Gunner's wife."

So that's why she looks familiar. As soon as she says her name, I see the younger version of her, with the teased blonde hair and glittery blouses. She's dressed much more demurely now.

I also notice the way she stresses the word *wife*.

"It's a pleasure," I say, slapping on a smile. "I take it this is my lunch?"

"Yes. We thought you might be hungry."

I wonder, briefly, who *we* is, but don't comment on it. "Well, you were right. I'm starving." I give her an affable grin, which she returns—years of being Gunner's wife must have taught her that much. She's a bit guarded.

"Was Mercy helpful this morning?" she asks.

Is that suspicion in her voice? I wonder how much she and Mercy talk. Surely Mercy didn't tell her what happened. She's guarded, but she's not distrustful.

"Wonderfully helpful," I say. "Got me set up in here and everything."

Madelyn nods, face set in a firm expression. "Very good. She can be a... helpful girl when she needs to be."

I don't say anything. Madelyn straightens her spine, clears her throat.

"Sterling and I were hoping you could stay here for another few hours," she says. "The congregants have found your prayers reassuring."

"That'll be just fine."

Madelyn nods and stands up. "Pastor Sullivan wants to meet you," she says. "He works closely with my husband. He'll be along in a few hours."

Then she's gone, leaving me alone with the sandwich, which turns out to be ham and cheese. It's not bad.

The afternoon is more of the same, with me pushing

through the dull throb of my headache and trying to ignore the constant flurry of blood and breath roiling off the Church of the Well congregation. This was always the hard part—keeping up my ruse when what I really want is to kill.

Pastor Sullivan comes in around mid-afternoon, right after I finish praying over a mom and her baby, the baby with one of those wretched charms tucked into its swaddling clothes. The mom weeps while I pray—tears of fear, mostly. I can taste it in the back of my throat.

Pastor Sullivan, though, is not a man who's afraid. I sense that immediately. Like Mrs. Gunner—the real one—he's cautious. Distrustful. He hides it in front of the mom, flashing her a smile and pressing his hand on the baby's forehead, but when the two of us are alone he fixes me with a cold, icy gaze.

"So you're the traveling preacher," he says.

"Ambrose Echeverría." I hold out my hand for him, and when he grabs it, I'm struck with a sudden, nearly overpowering urge to hurl him to the ground and slam my cowboy boot into his jaw.

He fucked Mercy.

The thought comes to me out of nowhere, as hot and furious as summer lightning.

"Henry Sullivan," he says, giving me a fake smile.

This scrawny, thin-necked man used Mercy to fulfill his own needs. I drop my hand to my side and study him with a Hunter's eye: picking out strengths and weaknesses, measuring the steady beat of his body.

He'd be easy to kill.

We make small talk for a few minutes, a dull back-and-forth in which he tries to assert some kind of dominance over me and I pretend that I'm too friendly and oblivious to notice. The whole time, all I can think of is killing him. Him and Gunner both.

And it's all because of a human woman and her big brown eyes.

CHAPTER TWELVE

AMBROSE

By the time night falls and the campus tucks itself in for the night, I've managed to turn my attention back where it needs to be—getting into that bunker.

I still don't know how I'm going to do it. In some ways, seducing Mercy again seems my best bet. I can draw her into me, get her addicted to the pleasure she's been denied, and convince her to extract the code out of Gunner.

There are a couple of problems with that, though. It'll take too long, for one. The longer I'm here, the more likely it is that people will start looking me up and get suspicious—the Internet and social media have made my old schemes impossible in the long term. Worse, getting Gunner to give up the code would probably involve her having to fuck him, a thought that sends rage boiling through me, not dissimilar to the rage I felt when I spoke with Sullivan this afternoon. And thirdly—

Well, I run the risk of getting addicted myself. I've already jerked myself off twice since I got back, my head filled with an escalating kaleidoscope of depravities: Mercy on her knees so she can worship my cock instead of God. Mercy bent over a pulpit while I ram into her tight asshole. Mercy naked while I open up the throats of any man who's ever touched her against her will, their blood streaming over her lush body as she touches herself like I showed her last night.

But she's a fucking human, and my obligation is to other Hunters. It's bad enough that I kissed her this morning when I said I was going to leave her alone. But I gave myself a taste of something sweet and it was too hard to resist the temptation.

So no, I won't use Mercy. Instead, I put on some dark clothes and head out to the bunker on my own. I'm strong. Maybe I can pry that door open.

I leave Roxi and Max at the cabin—if there's trouble, I'd rather they not be involved—but I do take my hunting knife with me, a big mean blade that fits neatly in the holster on my hip. Then I slip out onto the compound, moving quietly through the shadows. It's like last night, except when I take a quick detour by Gunner's house, the room where he was fucking her is dark and empty.

Thank fuck for that. Maybe now I can focus on the actual task at hand.

I make it out to the bunker easily enough. The night is cloudy, with a new moon and hardly any starlight, but I've got a predator's night vision so I don't have to announce my entire presence to the Church of the Well with a flashlight. I go up to the door and crouch down so I can study the keypad. It's mechanical, not digital, which means I might be able to break it. I've got the strength and I've got a knife. It's worth a try.

Like most Hunters, I've picked up some basic lock-picking skills over the years—enough to know that this isn't a standard lock that can be cajoled open with a few strategically placed hairpins. However, I also have a general idea of how to crack open a standard keypad lock, and I suspect the general prin-ciple applies here. I start by trying to wedge my knife behind the keypad, hoping to pull it away from the door so I can get to the innards inside.

It doesn't budge.

"Fuck," I mutter, standing up straight so I can get leverage on my knife handle. I wrap both hands around it and brace one foot against the big steel door and pull with every ounce of my strength.

The knife whips upward. The lock remains unbroken.

"Dammit." I try again, gritting my teeth at the metal-on-metal screech. I'm fucking up my knife blade, doing this.

I step back, studying the lock. There's got to be something else I can do. Maybe if I can find a sledgehammer or something over in that training area on the other side of the field—

Something stirs in the grass behind me.

Something *human*.

I whip around, putting my senses out. The intruder is behind the big metal gym in the training area. I can hear the steady pace of their heart, and I catch a whiff of male pheromones.

"Who's there?"

A flashlight shines around the corner, bright as the sun. I only have a few seconds to consider my options, which boil down to two choices: hide or kill.

And then the flashlight sweeps across my face, and a man shouts, "You're not supposed to be out here!"

Kill it is, then.

My blood immediately surges at the thought. All that sexual tension with Mercy has left me hungry for destruction. Seeing Sullivan this afternoon didn't help, either.

"Sorry!" I call back, pulling the knife behind my back. The flashlight bobs toward me, its owner barely visible behind the glare, even to me. But I know other things about him. He's not particularly scared. His heartbeat is slow and steady, so he'll probably put up a decent fight. There's a faint whiff of metallic smoke from a gun that is, presumably, resting on his hip. "Sorry, I was going for a walk."

"All the way out here?" He comes closer, close enough that I can see his face above the sphere of light. He's older, a little grizzled. "You're that traveling preacher, aren't you?"

"I am. I like my night walks." I amble toward him, fingers tightening around the knife handle. I can leave it alone if I spin a pretty enough lie. But he'll probably report to Gunner that I was sniffing around the bunker, and that'll make getting access harder than it already is. Assuming Gunner doesn't run me off the campus.

"It's not safe out here." We meet in the middle of the grass, and the guard lowers his flashlight out of my eyes. "Not with what happened to Raul."

"He was killed on the campus?" I inject a touch of fear into my voice, hoping I can get this man to talk while I work up my plan of attack. I'll need to do it fast. This isn't exactly a pleasure killing, even if my cock hasn't gotten the memo. Right now, it's as hard as it was for Mercy when she was in the throes of the first orgasm of her life.

"We don't know where he was killed." The guard frowns, and his emotions shift; suspicion wafts off him. "All we know is the devil has come for us. It's better not to come to the outskirts. The protections are thinner here."

Devil this, devil that. It's not the devil these people need to worry about. It's me.

"Of course." I take a step toward the guard, and his suspicion curdles into a little burst of fear, delicious in the balmy night air. "I'll make sure to stay closer to the center."

And then I dive toward him, swinging my knife out so it's the first thing that makes contact. I sink the blade into his upper back and press my hand up against his mouth, muffling his shout of surprise. It takes him a second longer to realize what's happened, and by then I've yanked the knife out and sank it into his flesh again, a little lower down, right at the base of his rib cage. His blood gushes over my hand, and I groan at the release of it.

He struggles against my grip, trying to pry my hand away from his mouth. I shove him, hard, and he flies across the field and lands with a hard thud on the dried grass. Then I leap on him before he has the chance to sit up, pressing the blade up against the bottom of his chin to force him to look into my eyes.

"Deceiver!" he rasps, blood bubbling up between his lips. "Satan! You will be struck down! You will be—"

I slap my hand over his mouth.

"Wrong on both counts." I leer down at him, dancing my blade through the dark night. "No one's coming for me. And I'm not the devil." I lean close, like I might draw his soul into my body. "I'm the boogeyman."

The guard whimpers, bucking beneath me, his fear pungent and thick. I breathe it in deep, then run my tongue along my blade to taste the fear in his blood. It's fucking delicious. Pity I can't carve him up and take him back to my freezer.

His eyes go wide, and he bucks against me. But I'm stronger than any of the men in this place.

"What should I do to you?" I ask in a soft sing-song, pressing the blade against his cheek. He trembles beneath me, his lips desperately trying to move against my hand—to pray or protest, I'm not sure which. Honestly, I know exactly what I should do—kill him fast and hide the body.

But the idea just feels so damn unsatisfying. And I keep thinking of Mercy's beautiful scream when I first saw her by the river. I want to hear that scream again. I want to lick the terror from her skin.

The man bucks beneath me, his blood pulsing out of him in spurts. "You're just making it worse," I tell him.

He lets out a wet, choking sob. I lean over him and breathe

in his last, panicked breaths. A scene, I realize, just like I'd been planning to do with Raul. I'll use him to set a scene in the residential area, where she'll be sure to see it.

No, not just the residential area. Reverend Gunner's house.

"You're going to frighten her so beautifully," I murmur.

And then I plunge my knife straight into his heart.

CHAPTER THIRTEEN

MERCY

The sun is just starting to rise when I leave my cabin to help prepare breakfast for the congregation. This is one benefit of summer, even with the heat—I won't have to walk across the still, quiet campus alone in the dark. If I were unmarried, and living in the single women's dormitory, I would never have to be alone. But as Gunner's helpmeet, I'm always isolated.

But even with the dawn's pale, sherberty light, even with the Texas morning heat, I still feel a chill as I pad down the dirty walkway. Something feels—off.

The devil, I think, drawing my arms around my chest. *The devil is close*.

The others have noticed it, too, I think. I see more houses marked by charms than usual. Some of them are painted on, the lines neat and even, and others are made out of twine and ribbon. Women's nonsense, Reverend Gunner always calls them, although he says it with an indulgent smile. Madelyn is more forthright—she calls them witchcraft. When I still lived with them, she would always complain about them. "I don't see how you can allow them," she would say to

Reverend Gunner, and he would respond with, "If it makes the women feel better, leave them. They aren't an affront to God."

I've never cared about the charms myself. Maybe it was because Madelyn was the closest thing I had to a mother after my own mother died, and so I tend to see them as needless superstition. "Your prayers are what really matter," Madelyn told me when I was young, although, in the last three years, it feels like that's not true, either.

All these thoughts swirl around in my head as I make my way toward the kitchen. Which is good, because they keep me from thinking about Ambrose and his slow, soft kisses and the fantasy I nurtured as I tried to fall asleep last night, the two of us standing side by side in front of the well in the chapel, me in a bridal veil.

The idea makes me feel warm and sick with guilt at the same time. Easier to put it out of my head.

I keep walking, my footsteps echoing softly. I'm nearly to Reverend Gunner's house, rising taller than all the others. I miss living there. Miss being Reverend Gunner's ward instead of his helpmeet.

But then I turn down the side street, and the wind gusts, bringing a thick, coppery sweetness that lodges in the back of my throat. My empty stomach turns. It smells like someone threw out old meat and let it rot in the sun

And then I see Reverend Gunner's fence.

I see that there's something *on* it.

I stop on the walkway, not comprehending what I'm looking at. At first, I think Madelyn draped some of Reverend Gunner's clothes over the fence to air dry. But she never does that.

And then I realize it's not just clothes. There's a face. There are hands.

There's blood.

I stumble backward, and the world draws away from me. I

hear the ocean in my head. I recognize the face, hanging slack and twisted in fear. It's Burl Marsh, one of the gruff old soldiers.

He's stretched out like a Catholic crucifix on Reverend Gunner's fence, his throat split open, his chest covered in blood. His eyes stare blankly ahead, right at me.

Just like Raul's did.

That's when I scream, all my terror exploding out of me in one terrible sound that shatters the silence of the campus into a million pieces.

Then I turn and run. I'm not even thinking clearly; all I know is I can't do this again. I can't stare at another dead body. I can't answer the torrent of questions from Reverend Gunner and Pastor Sullivan and Deacon Price, the head of the Soldier of God. I can't sit shaking in a room, sobbing and confused.

I run harder than I have in my life, my skirt streaming out behind me, and I don't even realize where I'm going until I wind up in front of the guest cabins.

Ambrose's cabin is shut up as tight as all the others, and I wonder, idly, if God sent him to us because He knew the night-mare that was about to unfold.

I wonder if God sent him to me.

Shouts ring out behind me, coming from Reverend Gunner's house. A woman screams. I know I should go back. Instead, I jog up to Ambrose's door, still panting and trying to catch my breath. Before I can even press the doorbell, his dogs start barking, my presence announced whether I want it or not.

I shouldn't be here. The devil has come for us again, for another of my brothers, and here I am standing on the porch of the place where I sinned, and all I want, with a sudden and painful clarity, is to sin again.

I stumble backward, telling myself I have to go back. But then the door pulls open, and when I see Ambrose filling up the frame, dressed in dark slacks and a dark long-sleeved shirt like a priest, I burst into tears. I know I shouldn't be here. But this is the only place I want to be.

"Mercy?" His brow furrows. "What's wrong?"

I wipe at my eyes like I can press the tears back into their ducts. "I'm s-sorry," I stammer out. "I know it's early. But there was—there was—"

Grief and terror overtake me again. I cover my face with my hands and weep. I'm not even crying over Burl Marsh. I'm crying over Raul, and the fact that not even our gated campus is safe from evil, and that the only thing that comes close to bringing me comfort is a sin.

"Come inside," Ambrose says softly. "Tell me what's wrong."

A scream rings out suddenly, and Ambrose jerks his gaze past me. "What happened?" he says, mare sharply now.

I sob. "I'm not supposed to be alone—"

"Mercy," Ambrose says. "Are you in danger?"

More shouts. Someone wails, long and dark like a siren. I wonder if it's Burl Marsh's wife.

"No," I whisper. "But—"

"Get inside," Ambrose says. "Tell me what's going on."

I look over my shoulder, although all I can see are cabins. And then I step over the threshold. When Ambrose closes the door, the shouts go quiet, and I feel a rush of relief, like he's locking all the evil out in the sun.

"Tell me what happened," he says, his hands on my shoulders, his eyes boring into mine.

"There was another murder," I whisper.

Before I can say anything more, he pulls me into him, his arms wrapped around my shoulders. My cheek presses into the bare skin above the collar of his shirt. This is wrong. This is the only thing keeping me from flying apart.

"At the river?" he says.

"No." I burrow my face into his shoulder, my whole body

shaking uncontrollably. "Here. At Reverend Gunner's house. *Inside*. The devil—"

Ambrose squeezes me tighter and presses his mouth against the top of my head. "You're safe," he says softly. "No one can hurt you here. Not even Satan."

"Why is this happening?" I pull away from him. "Who's doing this? They—they *crucified* him, like our Savior—"

I dissolve into tears again, ugly and choking. I wait for Ambrose to tell me to calm myself, the way Reverend Gunner did after I found Raul, but he doesn't. Instead, he takes my hand and leads me to the sofa, where Max is sitting, watching us. I sink down next to him and then run my fingers over his head, hardly feeling his stiff fur. His tail thumps against the cushions.

Ambrose sits beside me. Not close enough to be inappropriate, but close enough that I could, if I wanted to, sink into him until I forgot all my terror.

"Who was it?" Ambrose asks gently. "Was it someone you know, like—like before?"

I stare down at my hands. "I know everyone who lives here. But he wasn't my friend, like Raul."

Ambrose considers this. "You still feel grief, though."

Grief isn't the right word, not for Burl. I'm not sure what the right word is, though. "I feel afraid," I finally say. "The campus is supposed to be safe. It's supposed to protect us from the secular world. And then this—"

I see Burl's body, his arms stretched wide, the blood garish in the dawn light, and sob again

Ambrose puts his hand over mine, his touch warm. "They'll find who did it."

"Who will?" I blink back tears. "Reverend Gunner refuses to call the police! And we still don't know what happened to Raul. Now this? It hasn't even been a week!'

Ambrose tightens his fingers around mine. "Nothing's going to happen to you."

"You don't know that." I jerk my gaze over to him. "Why would someone kill Raul? He was kind. Burl—Burl wasn't the world's nicest man, but he didn't *deserve* to—" I can't get the rest of the words out. "They left his body like a warning. Like they're going to pick us off one by one until there's no one left—"

"Mercy. Stop." Ambrose's voice is firm and commanding, and he's still squeezing my hand. I don't want him to let go. "You'll drive yourself crazy trying to make sense of it."

I look up at him. His living room window faces the east, and sunlight pours in, hot and lemony. My tears turn the light to glass.

Ambrose reaches over and smooths away a few strands of hair that worked themselves loose from my braid. Then he leaves his hand against my cheek, not even caring that my skin is sticky with tears.

I realize what I want, even though I shouldn't. But the devil's cruelty has weakened my will.

"Kiss me again," I whisper.

Ambrose's face is unreadable. He brushes his knuckles against my cheekbone. "Are you sure?"

"Yes." And it's true. I want the oblivion of sin. I want the oblivion of desire. I don't dare ask him to touch me again, but a kiss—a kiss is innocent. "Please. I know we shouldn't, but I just want to forget—"

His mouth catches mine. His tongue parts my lips. And I kiss him back, unsure where to put my hands—on his arms, on his face. But he decides for me. He presses me back against the couch, our mouths never disconnecting, and he pins my hands over my head. His body covers mine, and I feel the evidence of his arousal as much as I feel my own—an unfamiliar rigidity digging into my thigh.

"Are you needed somewhere?" he asks the questions against my lips.

"They probably want to ask me questions about the—about the—"

"No," Ambrose's voice is firm. "You don't need to do that."

Relief surges through me. "What if Reverend Gunner goes to my cabin?" I whisper. "What if he's looking for me?" The last thing I want right now is to talk about Reverend Gunner. I want Ambrose's mouth on my lips. I want to never stop kissing him.

Ambrose kisses along my neck, all the way to the edge of my neckline. "I'll call him and tell him the truth," he mutters. "That you saw the body and need grief counseling. I'll let him know he can speak to you once you've calmed down."

Then he nips at my skin with his teeth, making me cry out. "This isn't right," I gasp out, but Ambrose interrupts me.

"Yes, it is." He kisses my mouth again, deeper than before. "I'm going to make you forget all your fear, Mercy Gunner. Just trust me."

And I do.

CHAPTER FOURTEEN

AMBROSE

Mercy moans beneath me as I kiss along her throat and scrape my teeth against her skin, something I've been dying to do since I heard her beautiful, melodious scream this morning. I've been awake all night, the windows cracked open, waiting for it.

I know this is stupid. But she tastes like the jugo de cana that I used to drink when I was a young man and knowing that she actually *saw* my work has me delirious. Her loud, sobbing tears alone were enough to send all the blood straight to my cock.

I kiss up along her jaw so I can taste the salt residue left by those tears, and she whimpers again. I half-expect her to push me away, but she doesn't. One of her hands drapes around my shoulder. The other runs up and down my spine. Her body rocks against me, her legs spread, opening up for me despite the thick layers of her dress.

"Wait here," I mutter into her ear before dragging myself away. Mercy blinks up at me, dazed, her lips plump and swollen. Fuck, I want them around my cock. But I also need to show *some* restraint.

"What are doing?" Mercy asks breathlessly.

"Told you. Calling Gunner." *Reverend* Gunner, I remind myself. I'm still playing a role here, even if seeing Mercy like that, red-eyed from weeping and spread out for me on the sofa, is enough to make me forget. "Reverend Gunner. I'll tell him you're safe, I'm calming you down, and he can speak to you when you're ready."

Mercy sits up, her skirt rustling, and her fear takes on a unique undertone: she's afraid of *Gunner*. "Don't let him get jealous. I'm not supposed to be alone in your cabin."

I jerk my gaze over to her, more sharply than I intend. That motherfucker gets *jealous*? He uses her, passes her around, and he has the nerve to get *jealous*?

"You saw something unimaginably awful for the second time in a week," I tell her, trying to keep my voice even. "And came to me for guidance."

I resist the urge to ask what would happen if Gunner did get jealous. What he would do to her. I can tell that her fear is a fear of experience.

I pull out the cheap burner phone I bought for this mission, then look at Mercy expectantly. She hesitates, but only for a second. Then she rattles off a phone number.

Gunner doesn't answer, thank fuck. I don't actually want to talk to him. "Reverend," I say when the voice message beeps. I never take my eyes off Mercy—I want to drink in every aspect of her fear and her lust and her despair. "This is Ambrose Echeverría. I have Mercy Gunner here with me. She told me what happened. She, ah, unfortunately saw the body—"

Mercy blinks, big fat tears shimmering on her eyelashes. I've never wanted to taste salt so badly.

"She's very upset. She did tell me she's not supposed to be alone in my cabin, but I think we can make an exception here, yes? She'll need some time before she can come in to speak with you about it. Please, call me if you have any questions."

Then I hang up and switch my phone over to silent.

"There." I go back over to Mercy and kneel down in front of her. A tear streaks over her cheek, and this time, I really can't help myself. I nestle between her legs and rise up to catch the tear with my mouth.

"Ambrose," she murmurs.

"Shhh." I guide her back to where I want her—on her back, with her legs spread wide.

"This isn't right," she whispers. "We should—we should *pray*, or—"

"You want to pray?" I push her skirt up enough that I see the simple cotton panties underneath. They already have a damp spot, and I desperately want to taste it.

I look up at her, waiting for her to answer. The sharp, piquant fear she experienced when I mentioned Reverend Gunner is gone, although a richer fear remains—a fear of me. Not Ambrose the preacher, not the Ambrose she thinks she knows, but Ambrose the boogeyman. Ambrose the killer.

But it's intertwined with the scent of her desire, and I think I might lose my mind from the combination. Probably I already have.

"We *should* pray," she whispers weakly.

I notice that she has not pushed her skirts down.

"I have an idea." For the second time this morning, I drag myself away from her trembling, willing body. But if she wants to bring God into this—well, I'll invite him in. "Wait here."

I go into my bedroom and dig out the old pocket Bible I brought with me. I've had it for years, since the 1970s, at least —if you're going to hunt in Texas, having a Bible in your pocket doesn't hurt.

I flip through it as I walk back into the living room. When I step through the doorway, Mercy yelps a little and jerks her hand away from between her legs.

She'd been touching herself.

"Practicing what I showed you?" I grin as her face turns red with embarrassment. She doesn't even bother to deny it.

"Is that a Bible?" she asks instead.

"Yes." I amble across the room, each step slow and careful. Making her wait. Making her tremble. "You said you wanted to pray." I hand her the Bible and flip it open to Song of Songs. "So you'll pray."

Mercy looks down at the open pages. "You want me to—" Confusion mars her pretty features as she glances up at me. "To read this?"

"Out loud." I settle down in front of her and curl my fingers around the band of her panties. Her muscles contract; I feel the sudden siege of tension on the air.

"While you're—" She blushes again.

"While I'm eating your cunt, yes."

The reaction I get from her is like a shockwave. Lust and arousal flood the air. Should I have said it like that, when I'm supposed to be a preacher? Probably not.

Do I regret it? Not in the slightest.

I yank her panties down and, for the first time, get a real look at the cunt in question. It's gorgeous—wet and swollen with need, covered with a fine pelt of light brown hair. I arrange myself between her legs and breathe in deep that scent of human prey in heat.

"Read," I order, and Mercy gasps softly. I know she's going to obey, and it's not because she's a good Christian girl trained to be subservient. This goes deeper than that. She witnessed death, and when humans witness death and want to survive, they need to fuck. If there's anything I've learned in my two hundred years, it's that.

Mercy takes a deep breath and looks down at the Bible. "'L-let him kiss me with the—'"

And I do. I press my mouth against her wet labia and lick them with my tongue, savoring the first musky taste of her. Mercy cries out, hips jolting against me. I pull away.

"Read," I command, and I realize a second too late that I've just spoken to her the way I speak to someone I plan to kill.

But she doesn't know that. And, with the pulse of her blood, I feel how much she likes it.

"Do not stop until you come." I keep using my Hunter voice on her, because fuck, I love how her body reacts. Her eyes turn all to pupil. Her breath quickens. Her thighs push further apart.

For a moment, she stares at me over the pages of the Bible. I don't move. I won't touch her until I hear her read.

Then she drops her gaze down and starts again.

"'Let him kiss me with the k-kisses of his mouth—for thy love is—is—is—'"

I lick along her slit and push my tongue up into her pussy, relishing the way she momentarily stutters and loses her words. But she's a good girl, and she finds them again, even as I flick my tongue against her swollen clit.

"'—Better than wine,'" she gasps out, thick thighs trembling beside my head. "'Th-thine oils have a go'—oooooh." That last word dissolves into a moan as I kiss her deeper and nudge my nose up against her clit.

"Keep reading," I say into her drenched pussy, right before I attack her again, devouring her essence. I've eaten so many humans in my long life, but nothing compares to this.

"'Thy name is as oil poured forth. Therefore do the—ah! Therefore do the virgins—*love thee*!'"

I smile at that, the way she shouts out *love thee*, and then fixate on her clit again, strumming it hard with my tongue as she stutters out the rest of the verses. It's getting harder for her to read; her voice is jagged and shuddery, and she stumbles over her words as much as she pronounces them.

But it just makes me harder, knowing that I'm unraveling her completely.

"'F-for why sh-should I b-be as one that-that is v-veiled—'" Mercy pants and shakes, legs quaking on either side of my head. I tongue-fuck her in response, lapping up against her inner walls, giving her clit a rest so she can catch her breath. I know Song of Songs by heart, and I'm going to make sure she comes with the final verse.

"'—be-beside the fl-flocks of thy c-companions? If th-thou know not—oh thou f-fairest'—Ambrose, oh my god, oh my—"

"Keep going," I growl after withdrawing my tongue and licking her soft, silky cleft. I bite gently against her inner thigh, making her screech and jolt. "'Oh, thou fairest among women,'" I recite, peppering her thighs with kisses. "'Go thy way forth by the footsteps of the flock, and feed thy kids beside the shepherds' tents.'"

I punctuate the verse by attacking her clit again, flicking my tongue fast against its pulsing heat. Mercy shrieks and thrusts against my face, and I love that wantonness. I bring one hand up and slide a finger into her pussy, gently massaging the pad of flesh that drove her wild the other night. "I don't hear you fucking reading, Mercy."

"'Go thy way forth!'" she shouts, still jerking up against my face. I lick her clit and finger her pussy as she struggles through the rest of the verse. "'By the footsteps! Of the flock! And feed!' Feed thyyyy oh my god!"

She's getting too close to coming, and we're still only halfway through Song of Songs. I force myself to draw back, denying her the release I know she wants. Her gasps, her moans, her arousal soaking my chin and lips—it tells me everything I need to know.

"Keep going," I purr, licking her labia—licking everywhere but her clit, the way I know she wants. And my good little Christian girl obeys me again, panting out the next verse:

"'—feed thy kids beside the shepherds' tents. I have ccompared thee, oh m-my love, to a-a steed in Pharaoh's ch-chariots. Thy cheeks—'"

I settle into my slow, lazy teasing, relishing both the salty-hot taste of her cunt and her ragged reading of the Bible's version of erotic poetry. I've always liked Song of Songs, with its litany of strange compliments— Pharaoh's horses and bags of myrrh and eyes like doves. But I've never listened to it while buried in a beautiful woman's pussy, and I have to say, I think this should be the preferred reading.

"'My beloved,'" Mercy whispers, her voice ragged, "is unto me—unto me a c-cluster of henna-flowers—'"

We're almost to the end. Time to reward Mercy for her obedience. As she whimpers out *henna-flowers*, I thrum my tongue against her clit, faster and harder than I have before. She bucks in response, her hips slamming up against my face. But God help me, she doesn't stop her recitation.

"'Behold, thou art fair!'" she screams. I don't actually know if she's reading. I think she might be screaming the verses from memory. "'My love! Behold—thou art!' Oh—right there—that feels—"

I slap the side of her thigh, hard enough to remind her what she's meant to be doing. And maybe it's my imagination, but I swear her clit jolts when I smack her. Is it possible my sweet human Mercy is a bit of a pain slut?

I can't imagine the Reverend Sterling Gunner, prophet of God or not, has any idea what to do with such a treasure.

"'Thine eyes are as dooooooves,'" Mercy moans, thrusting against my mouth. Fucking my face. I barely have to do any of the work at this point—just keep my tongue out so she grinds against it. "Be-behold! Thou art! Fair! My beloved!'"

I think she's going to spill over before she finishes the passage, but even I'm not cruel enough to pull away. In fact, I shove her thighs open and match my hungry licks with her thrusts, a rocking, perfect rhythm that rolls underneath her recitation of the verses.

"'The beams! Of our! House are! Cedars!'"

The couch scrapes against the tile. I bury myself deeper in her, dig my nails into her soft creamy flesh. She's screaming words—are they from Song of Songs? Are they prayers to her god? Blasphemies for her devil? I don't know—I'm so focused on bringing her over the edge that I can't register them.

Finally, I swipe one long lick up her her slit, landing hard on her clit, and it happens. Mercy arches her back like she's possessed. Every muscle in her body vibrates. I keep my tongue pressed against her clit as it flutters furiously, matching the frantic racing of her heart.

And fuck, the sound that comes out of her mouth—a deep, throaty moan, at least two octaves lower than her speaking voice. Her fists beat against the cushions. Her pussy quivers. My face is a glorious fucking mess, and when I'm certain she's finished coming, I pull away and draw the back of my hand against my mouth, wiping it away—only to lick the flavor off my skin.

Mercy stares at me, a vision of destruction. Her cheeks and lips and chest are all ruddy from excitement, and I can smell the coppery tang of her blood from underneath her skin. Her eyes are as bright as glass. Her hair's a nest of golden tangles.

Seeing her like that, I know I have to keep desecrating her. I have to mark her. *Baptize* her. I am playing the preacher, after all.

"Don't fucking move," I say, and then I pull out my cock.

CHAPTER FIFTEEN

MERCY

My body is boneless. Liquid. So when Ambrose unbuckles his fly with one deft hand, I can only stare up at him—my legs still spread, the Bible a weight on my chest.

"Don't fucking move," he purrs, an order I wouldn't disobey even if I could.

Then he pulls out his manhood. I have, at this point, seen exactly two penises in my life, but Ambrose's is the first that I actually want to look at. It's thick and hard, the skin shiny from being stretched and the tip already beading with his arousal.

"Are you going to—" I lick my lips, watching as he strokes himself, his fingers tightening rhythmically around his length. "Do you want to—"

"Fuck you?" Ambrose drops his penis and leans over me until I feel his hardness digging into the soft flesh of my belly. When he speaks, his breath blows softly across my skin. "Do you want that?"

I do want it. My entire body is burning for it. But instead of telling him that, instead of reaching down and sliding him inside me the way I do for Reverend Gunner, I whisper, "I can't."

Ambrose runs his thumb over my lips. "That's not what I asked."

Then he pulls back, situating himself so he's kneeling over me, and begins to stroke himself. Even though I'm still reeling from his mouth, heat coils inside me again as I watch him pleasure himself, his hand moving slow and languorous up and down his length.

"I want you too," I whisper, my voice trembling with fear. "But I can't. I have to tell them what I saw—"

Something flashes in Ambrose's eyes. An unreadable bolt of lightning "Didn't I make you forget about that?"

He had, actually. And he's making me forget it again, the way he's quickening his strokes, smearing around the liquid beading out from the thick mushroom of his head. There's a word for what's between his legs, and it's not penis or manhood. It's *cock*, a word that makes my cheeks flush. His *cock*—thick and veiny, straining for release—is pointed right at me.

And I don't want to it be anywhere else.

"Well?" he prompts. "Didn't I?"

"Y-yes," I stammer out. "But I can't—"

"We won't." He's still stroking. "Don't get me wrong, Mercy. I'm going to fuck you." He grins, teeth sharp and predatory, and thrusts into his fist. "But not now. Not when we're rushed."

My breath catches. I'm not sure what to say to that. That I want it, desperately? That we shouldn't be doing any of this?

"Right now," Ambrose says. "I want to baptize you."

And just like that, I'm not thinking about the nightmare I found this morning. The blasphemy of his words sends lust coursing through my core—an angry, terrifying lust. I'm afraid of it, but I also want more of it.

"W-what?" I stammer out stupidly.

"You heard me." His breath has quickened. His voice has

gone ragged. "You're mine, Mercy. Not Reverend Gunner's. Do you understand that?"

I don't look at his face when I answer him. I look at his cock.

"Yes."

"Good. I know he's going to want to touch you again, and I know you can't say no." Ambrose's eyes flutter shut. A vein bulges on the side of his neck. I can almost feel his tension as my own—that agonizing, pressurized heat. "If he makes you go to him, go to him. But you'll still be baptized in my name."

He throws his head back and groans and I whimper and have a sudden, delirious thought that I need to throw the Bible off to the side, but it's too late. Ambrose's groan turns to a roar and he thrusts his hips toward me and ribbons of warm, thick cum splatter across my cheek and my neck and the Bible, still open to Song of Songs.

I stare at him, stunned and far more aroused than I am disgusted. He squeezes his cock twice more, then drops his hand and lowers his head to meet my gaze.

"Look how fucking beautiful you are," he mutters. "Marked by my cum like that."

I should hate this. I should feel used and degraded. But Ambrose looks at me with the kind of worshipful expression I've only seen when men pray, and so instead I feel more beautiful than I ever have in my entire life.

"Do you want to taste me?" he murmurs, already dipping his fingers in the cum dripping down my chin. "Eat of my body?"

I can't answer that, not with words. But I want it. I've never wanted anything more. And so I drop my mouth open like I'm about to receive communion.

Ambrose grins and slides his cum-sticky fingers across my tongue. I wrap my lips around them and suck, moaning softly at the saltiness of him. He tastes like Reverend Gunner. But he also tastes divine.

"That's it." He pulls his fingers out and scoops up more cum from my cheek. "Do you want more, my greedy little princess?"

He doesn't wait for a response this time, just sides his fingers into my mouth again, and I lick it off his fingers, my hips writhing against the sofa.

"You can have that any time you want." Ambrose pushes off the couch and takes the Bible out of my hands and slams it closed.

That feels like too much. "You need to clean it!" I cry out, sitting up.

"I need to clean you," he says. "The book can wait."

He tosses it on the end table, as if the matter's closed, and then disappears into his hallway. I stare at the Bible. It's old. Obviously well-used. I don't understand how he can just let it be *desecrated* like that.

He doesn't see it as a desecration, whispers some voice deep in my head. A voice that feels dangerous.

Ambrose steps back into the living room holding a damp bath towel. I can't speak as he helps me up to sitting, then settles down beside me and gently, carefully, wipes his seed away from my skin.

"As much as I want to leave it," he says softly. "I can't have Reverend Gunner seeing you like this."

"Don't talk about him." I'm surprised by the vehemence in my words. So is Ambrose, it seems, because he jerks his dark eyes up to meet mine.

"Feeling guilty?" He arches an eyebrow.

"No." I force myself to meet Ambrose's gaze. "But I don't want to think about him. Not right now."

"Fair enough." Ambrose smiles softly—sadly, I think, and I wonder if he doesn't want to think about Reverend Gunner, either. I can't say I blame him.

He finishes cleaning me up, then tosses the towel on the ground and kisses me softly. I don't want to get up from the couch, even though I know I need to. I have obligations outside of this cabin. What's happened here—it leaves me dizzy and hot. But it won't last. It can't last.

It was just a temporary oblivion to help me forget the horrors of last night.

"I should go," I mutter, pulling away from Ambrose, straightening up my dress. He doesn't protest. Doesn't try to stop me. I run my hands over my hair, trying to smooth it down, and in the flurry, I catch Ambrose's dark, heavy gaze.

"Do you want me to set up the prayer circles again?" he asks. It takes me a moment to register to his question.

"Y-yes. That would be—that would be good, I think." I stare at him, lounging on the couch, his arm stretched over the back cushions. I don't want to leave. I have to leave. "I can't believe this happened again."

Images flash through my head. Burl's gaping neck. His bright red blood. His outstretched arms. I try to force them out.

"There are a lot of monsters in this world," Ambrose says.

"Do you think they'll catch this one?" *Assuming it's not the devil.* But I don't say that out loud.

Ambrose studies me for a long time, like he doesn't know how to answer.

"I'm sure they will," he finally says.

REVEREND GUNNER'S office is thick with panic. When I come in through the front door, Mrs. Harrison is talking with Mrs. Sullivan, their heads tilted together, their voices low and urgent. They both look up at me, but it's only Mrs. Harrison who rushes over, her arms outstretched.

"Are you all right, Mercy? I heard you *saw* the body."

I let her pull me into an embrace, even though I'm afraid

she'll smell Ambrose on me. But of course her hug is as quick as it always is. Mrs. Sullivan watches me coolly from afar. She knows what her husband did to me.

"Yes, it was—I didn't mean to, but—" I try to offer a brave smile. "I don't want to talk about it."

"I know. It's awful," she says. "Just awful. We're having a prayer meeting tonight. We have to drive the devil out."

"Yes, we do." Mrs. Sullivan's heels click against the linoleum as she comes to join us. "We need to drive the *sin* out."

She looks at me when she says that, and I swallow back my sudden bolt of fear. Even though I know she's not talking about Ambrose.

Mrs. Harrison clears her throat. "Mercy, you should join us, of course. And mark your door. I'll make a charm for you."

I glance sideways at Mrs. Sullivan, but she doesn't say anything.

"I know Reverend Gunner wants to speak with you," Mrs. Harrison says quickly. "He's meeting with Deacon Price right now to set up twenty-four-hour patrols around the compound."

"They should have done that after Raul," Mrs. Sullivan says. "That's why we have the Soldiers of God in the first place. To protect us from our enemies."

"These aren't human enemies," Mrs. Harrison says, shaking her head. "It's the devil. I can feel it."

I think of Burl stretched across the fence just like the Savior, his head dropped against his chest. Whatever sinful magic Ambrose worked to help me forget has faded.

Before I can say anything, however, Reverend Gunner's door bangs open. He comes out with Pastor Sullivan and Deacon Price, along with a couple of Deacon Price's favorite soldiers. It all feels so awful and so familiar. There's that same sick coil around my stomach, the constant, shivering reminder that the church campus isn't safe the way it's supposed to be.

"There you are," Reverend Gunner says. "I was concerned when Pastor Echeverría called me."

Hearing him say Ambrose's name makes my skin crawl. I straighten up my shoulders. "I'm sorry," I say. "But I panicked. I know I should have gone to you—"

It's the right thing to say, of course. Reverend Gunner's expression softens a little. The other two hang back, watching us. Especially Deacon Price. I know he wants to question me. He questioned me after Raul.

"Of course you did," Reverend Gunner says softly. "This is a lot for a woman like you to have to deal with."

Then he does something he never does, which is walk right up to me and hook his fingers under my chin to tilt my gaze up to meet his. My heart is frantic, remembering how Ambrose did the same thing. Even though the position couldn't, at this moment, feel more different.

"I know this is upsetting," he says softly. "I know you're frightened. And Deacon Price does want to speak to you."

I wait for the *but*. Because I know, with a sick, sinking dread, that it's coming.

"But I still expect you to perform your duties," he says, eyes hard. "Now more than ever. You can not imagine the stress I'm under."

Two of your congregants are dead! I want to scream at him. *And I found both of their bodies!*

And yet I did the same thing he's proposing, didn't I? I went to Ambrose.

No, that was different. I wanted *prayer*. And he offered something—

He offered something better.

I think about it now, staring up at Reverend Gunner. My body goes hot.

"Do you understand?" Reverend Gunner asks. "I'll need to see you soon. Tonight, after the woman's prayer session?"

There's only one answer to that question. It doesn't matter if my heart is broken, if I'm grieving, if the entire campus is burning down around us. But this time, when I answer it, I have a secret of my own.

"I'll be there," I say, voice ringing out clearly.

But my thoughts are focused on Ambrose's dark, hot eyes.

CHAPTER SIXTEEN

MERCY

"I'm here to accompany you to Reverend Gunner's house."

Deacon Price stands on my porch, his arms crossed over his chest, his gaze dark and glowering. He wears a pistol on his hip and one of Mrs. Price's charms around his neck.

"Oh." I wasn't expecting him, and I'm not scheduled to arrive at the marriage suite for another fifteen minutes. For the last hour, I've curled up on my couch, the Bible open on my lap —not to the Book of Solomon, but to the Sermon on the Mount. I wasn't reading, though. I was just staring at the words until they became illegible, my thoughts trailing between the horrors I saw today and the pleasures that unraveled me.

Deacon Price's knock on the door nearly scared me out of my skin.

"He didn't tell you I was coming?" Deacon Price's frown deepens. "It's late, Mercy. He doesn't want you wandering around by yourself."

Then he shouldn't ask me to perform my duties. The thought slams into my head, but I hold my tongue. "Of course."

"And I'm leading the patrol tonight. I swore to him I'd get you there safe."

He stares at me, his gaze hard.

"He also said to tell you to pack a change of clothes. You'll be sleeping in the suite tonight."

My chest tightens—he never asks that. Madelyn doesn't allow it.

"It's dangerous, Mrs. Gunner," Deacon Price says. "You can't be wandering off by yourself. Go on and pack. I'll wait here."

I nod and slip back into my cabin, my thoughts numb. I don't want to spend the night in the marriage suite. I don't want to go to the suite at all. I want to stay here, with the doors locked tight, and curl into my bed and daydream about riding into the sunset with Ambrose, my hair loose from its braids, Max's head in my lap. All of us going somewhere far, far away.

But that's not a life I'm allowed to have.

I pack quickly, folding up my nightgown and fresh clothes and sliding them into a little knapsack. Deacon Price is still waiting for me when I step out of the cabin, and he stares at me as I lock my door. I can feel his eyes burning through my skin.

"It's good you're here for him," Deacon Price says as we step onto the walkway. "Sterling. He needs someone vivacious to keep up his spirits."

My cheeks burn. I stare at the dark street.

"For the devil to get so close to his home—" Deacon Price tsks. "Our enemies are closing in. And you help keep him clearheaded."

"Thank you," I murmur, because there's nothing else I can say.

When we round the corner to Reverend Gunner's house, my chest squeezes so tight I think I'm going to stop breathing. But of course the body is gone. All the blood has been washed away. A large slice of the fence has been taken down, leaving an entranceway into the backyard.

"Did you call the police?" I ask.

"Of course not," Deacon Price says. "This is spiritual warfare. The police can't help us."

I knew he was going to say that; he said the same thing after Raul's death, although I hadn't asked that time. Madelyn had, her voice hard and glinty and frightened. And she disapproved of the answer, I could tell. Not that she said anything.

"Don't worry," he continues, briefly putting his hand on my shoulder. I tense up, and he snatches it away—he's not supposed to touch me if we're alone like this. No man is.

I think of Ambrose and shiver.

We go into the backyard through the gate, and Deacon Price doesn't follow me into the yard, only gives me a little salute, his eyes still boring through me as I walk up to the door of the suite. All the lights are on, but the curtains are closed tonight.

Lord Jesus, I hope Ambrose doesn't try to sneak around the bunker entrance tonight.

The door's unlocked, and when I go in, Reverend Gunner is waiting for me like always. He's upset. About the murders? About me going to Ambrose this morning instead of him? Probably both. I can feel the anger in his silence as he watches me go through the usual motions: locking the door, peeling out of my clothes.

"On your back." The first words he says to me.

I do as he asks. It's not like doing what Ambrose asks, which is like sliding into a warm bath. This makes me feel cold and empty.

Maybe that's why I let myself think about Ambrose as Reverend Gunner pants on top of me. I think about his long fingers sliding up inside my body, his wet tongue probing against my clit, his fist clenched tight around his cock as his cum spurts out, marking me as his.

If he makes you go to him, go to him. But you'll still be baptized in my name.

Thinking about the way he said those words, his voice soft and dark and his eyes boring into me, changes something. It makes Reverend Gunner's arrhythmic thrusts feel—good, sort of. Not as good as Ambrose's hands or tongue, not good enough to undo me, but good enough that my breath quickens and Reverend Gunner mutters that I must have needed this as much as him, didn't I?

When he finishes, I look at the curtain pulled tight across the window and imagine, with a tight hot pulse, that Ambrose is watching me like before, stroking himself to completion.

Reverend Gunner rolls off me with a sigh, and I don't move, just stare up at the ceiling as he heaves himself off the bed and fumbles around for his clothes. "Stay here until sun up," he tells me. "This is where you're safest. Not with—"

He cuts himself off. *Not with Ambrose Echeverría*, I finish in my head.

I drop my head to look at him, skin crawling. "I will."

Reverend Gunner pulls his shirt over his head and slips his shoes on. "I mean it," he says. "Deacon Price has set up multiple guards. But this killer—" Reverend Gunner's eyes flash. "He wants to see me destroyed. He wants to see the whole church destroyed."

"I understand."

Reverend Gunner studies me like he's trying to decide what to say next.

"We could use some prayers," he says. "The whole congregation."

And then he's gone, the door slamming shut behind him.

I count to ten, then slide out of bed, pad over to the door, and turn the deadbolt. The suite is completely silent, the window unit AC having kicked off at some point while Reverend Gunner was on top of me. I slide back into bed, still naked, and stare up at the ceiling, my thoughts swirling around. I feel hot and distracted. Unfinished. I wish Ambrose were here.

There's a devil hunting our church, and all I can think about is Ambrose. And I keep thinking about him—because I'd much rather think about him than the killer, actually. I know I'm safe in the marriage suite, the door dead-bolted from the inside and the windows locked. Not even Reverend Gunner can get in here, and he has a key.

So I close my eyes and once again let my thoughts go where they want—to Ambrose. I imagine us in the chapel, sunlight pouring in through the tall thin windows to shine on the altar. He's standing. I'm kneeling in front of him, my bridal veil streaming out behind me. Praying to him. *Worshipping* him.

Worshipping his cock.

That's it, he purrs, and I can hear his voice in my head, dark like cigarettes and twinged with a faint whiskey drawl. *You suck my dick so well, Mercy.*

Here in my bed, my body heats again. I run my hands over my breasts and squeeze them in tight handfuls, my nipples hard against my palm. I squirm against the mattress, pressing my legs together, trying to relieve the pressure from my fantasies.

Don't get me wrong, Mercy. I'm going to fuck you.

I imagine it, Ambrose fucking me. I imagine he's here in the marriage suite, that it's *our* marriage suite and he's thrusting his thick, veiny cock inside my body, and I spread my legs across the bed, moaning softly. I drop my hand down over my stomach, slow and trembling, and try to touch myself the way Ambrose does.

It doesn't feel quite right. But it doesn't feel bad, either.

You're mine, Mercy. Not Reverend Gunner's. Do you understand that?

"Yes," I whisper, just as I did this morning. "Yes, Ambrose. I belong to you."

I run my fingers in clumsy circles, dragging them through my moisture until it almost feels like Ambrose is touching me. There's a hard, throbbing nub—my clitoris. It's the first time I've ever touched it.

"I belong to you," I whisper, squeezing my eyes shut. Pornographic images flash through my head. My mouth around Ambrose's large penis. Me on my hands and knees as Ambrose thrusts inside me, his hands squeezing my fleshy hips. Me kneeling in front of him as he prays over me—except he's naked, his body lean and muscular as he strokes himself with one hand and presses the other against my head.

Behold, thou art fair, my love. Thine eyes are as doves.

I groan in the bed, lifting my hips as if Ambrose were here and I could pull him inside me. Instead, I make do with my fingers, rubbing and rubbing in this one particular spot that makes my legs shake and my heart pound.

Worship me, darling, the Ambrose in my head mutters, and I do worship him, there in the middle of the chapel of my mind, sunlight shining over both our bodies. In the real world, in the bed, my pleasure builds into an uncomfortable tension. I would give anything to be kneeling in front of Ambrose for real. I would give anything to pull his cock into my mouth and taste his seed again. I would give anything to be *his* helpmeet, to come willingly to his bed every time he asked it of me.

Worship me, he growls in my head, and I whimper, "I do! I worship you! Ambrose, I—"

And then the pleasure splits me open. It tears through my body and makes me jolt against the bed. I slap my free hand against my mouth to keep from crying out, and I pant against my palm, touching myself until it hurts too much to continue. Ambrose would have kept going, and I would have worshipped him for that, too.

I pull my hand away and sink into the mattress, shivering with the aftershocks of my orgasm and the chilly air of the AC, which kicked on while I was touching myself. My thoughts feel tattered, like old clouds. I wish Ambrose were here, wish he would gather me up in his arms and tell me I needn't fear the demon stalking our church. And not because God would protect me.

But because Ambrose would.

CHAPTER SEVENTEEN

MERCY

Islam awake in the middle of the night, gasping for breath. For a moment, I don't know where I am. My room feels too dark. The bed feels too hard. And then I remember.

I reach over and switch on the bedside lamp, which illuminates a patch of the bed and floods the rest of the suite with shadows. Then I sit and listen, my heart pounding fast. Did something wake me up? Some killers' knife scraping on my window?

The suite is silent, though, and I think what actually woke me was a dream. It's fading, the sense memories lingering longer than anything else. A blinding, paralyzing terror. Rough hands on my skin. A blade flashing like lightning.

"Jesus, you are good and wise," I mutter, one of the first prayers I ever learned. "You will be there when I rise." Madelyn taught it to me when I first came to live at the church. I got nightmares then, too.

And despite everything, whispering that prayer does help calm me down, just like Ambrose's prayers do—his *actual* prayers. Ever since I became Reverend Gunner's helpmeet, God has felt farther and farther away, but I still like to pray some-times. Even if I'm not sure it does anything.

I curl back up in the bed, listening to the AC unit rattling in the window. I'm wide awake, though. My nightmare, whatever it was about, spiked my adrenaline, and now every noise in the suite makes my heart jump and my skin crawl.

I throw the blankets aside, roll on my back, and stare at the ceiling. Would I sleep better if I was in my cabin? Probably, but as much as I don't want to be in the suite, I don't actually want to go walking through the compound alone at night, either.

Maybe that's what my dream was about. Seeing Burl strung across the fence, his face slack and his body drenched in blood.

"No," I whisper, sitting up. No, I won't think about that. No, I won't let myself sit here in trembling terror. The door is deadbolted. And neither Raul nor Burl were killed in their homes.

Still, sleep feels a million miles away, so I crawl out of bed and pace around, trying to calm my body down. It helps a little. It would help more if Ambrose were here.

No, I can't think about him, either. It's not like that can—go anywhere.

Although I wish it could. And as I pace around the small room, I let myself think about him anyway, because it's better than thinking about the murders. What if he *did* ask me to leave with him? Would I go? He's not married—there's no ring on his finger. And legally, I'm not either. But I do know how to perform wifely duties. Not just the sexual ones, either. I can cook and clean and organize a household. I can take care of finances. I like kids...

My thoughts unwind from there, vivid and bright in my imagination. Ambrose down on one knee, proposing. I imagine it by the Concho River, the sun sinking into the horizon and turning everything pink and golden. A beautiful memory to wash away the terrible one.

I imagine a wedding, something I haven't let myself fantasize about since I became Reverend Gunner's helpmeet. Me in a lacy white gown, Ambrose taking my hand above the well in the chapel, the sunlight streaming around us.

I know Reverend Gunner would never let us marry there—he and I exchanged vows in front of God, even if we didn't do it in front of a judge. But it's *my* fantasy, and I let it unspool. It's so different from what I imagined when I was touching myself. It's sweet. Me and Ambrose riding in his car with his dogs, going from church to church, spreading the word of God. My hair loose and long, streaming in the wind blowing through the open windows. The two of us laughing. Country music on the radio.

I stop in front of the suite's door. It's a stupid dream, I know. I can't leave the Church of the Well. I made a promise to God and to Reverend Gunner. I'm his wife, his helpmeet.

So why does the thought of my actual future make me sick to my stomach when the thought of a future with Ambrose doesn't?

My chest feels tight, but it's not with fear, not anymore. I'm not worried about the killer. I'm worried about my *life*. What if I could show Ambrose that I might be worth fighting for?

The bunker codes.

The thought comes to me like a lightning bolt. I told him I had no way of getting them, which is mostly true. They certainly aren't stored anywhere in the administration building.

But I know Reverend Gunner. He's a prophet of God, but he's also forgetful and absent-minded. When I was eighteen and he explained what I was to become, he said that was why God granted him permission to take two wives. It's not that he's greedy. He just needs more *help* than other men.

He's supposed to have memorized the bunker code. But I have no doubt they're written down somewhere in his home office.

I press against the door, the wood cool against my face. Because I lived here for ten years, I know where the Gunners hide their spare key, in a little lock box hidden behind some shrubs. I know the code—0928, Madelyn's birthday. I could slip in easily. If I get caught—

If I get caught, I can tell them I thought I heard someone prowling in the yard. That I was afraid for my life.

It's shocking, how quickly I settle on my decision. I don't even give myself time to talk myself out of it. I just throw on one of the silky robes in the suite's closet and slip on my shoes and step outside.

The night is hot and damp and very, very dark. It only takes a minute for me to dart across the backyard, but it feels like hours, knowing that there could be a killer out there, watching me. But there's not. I make it to the back patio safely. Find the lockbox, open it, pull out the key. My heart's beating quick, but my hands are surprisingly stable. It doesn't feel like I'm doing something wrong, not even when I step in through the back door.

Since Reverend Gunner took me as a helpmeet, I haven't spent much time in their home. But it's still the home where I grew up, and I remember its layout well. The master bedroom is downstairs and the office is upstairs. I don't want to linger down here in case one of them wakes up.

I slip through the dining room and into the living room, keeping my eye on the hallway leading to the master bedroom. Everything is still and quiet, and I let out a long breath when I make it to the steps. Those I climb quickly, my feet light. I don't feel completely relieved until I'm in the office, though.

It's neat and tidy, decorated with the same expensive, masculine wood furniture Mrs. Gunner picked out for the reverend's main office. I gently shut the door behind me and tug open the curtains to let in the porch light, which gives me just enough light to see by.

Reverend Gunner, as a rule, doesn't trust computers. He writes notes to himself down by hand, on whatever paper he has handy. I remember Madelyn would always gather them up and organize them every Saturday evening after prayer circle. "This man would lose his head if it weren't attached to his body," she always said, smiling down at me. She was kind before I turned eighteen.

I scan the bookshelves first but don't see anything. The desk is tidy, more evidence of Madelyn's presence here. I slide the drawers open one by one. They're full of pens and paperclips and sticky notes and loose notecards, like Madelyn shoved his mess into the drawers and forgot about it. But there's one drawer that's essentially a filing cabinet, deep and heavy. The files are all personal, I realize, as I thumb through the tabs. One for IDs. One for property deeds. One for fertility documents.

I stop at that one, my chest heavy. The Gunners were never able to have children, something Reverend Gunner always blamed Madelyn for. But it's been three years and I'm not pregnant yet, either.

I shove the thought aside. Maybe I can escape the threat entirely, if Ambrose takes me away.

I keep looking. I'm about to give up when I find a slim file shoved in the very back of the cabinet—one without a label. I ease it out and carefully fold it open on the desk. It's full of Reverend Gunner's notes. They're loose and disorganized, but I recognize them immediately for what they are. I paw through them—phone numbers and addresses and computer passwords. Notes he didn't want Madelyn to have access to, I think.

And then I find one, a folded-up piece of yellow legal paper, that simply says:

REVELATION

I know this is it. God told Reverend Gunner to build a bunker, and so he did.

I unfold the paper and there's nothing on it except for six

numbers. Not a birthday—not even Reverend Gunner is that careless.

I scribble the code down on a blank sticky note, fold it up tight, and slide it into the waistband of my panties—I could still get caught, and if I get caught with *that*, there'll be no talking my way out of it. But my waistband feels like a safe option.

I replace everything so that the office looks exactly as I found it.

Then I creep down the stairs and out into the backyard, replacing the key and the lockbox. Frogs and insects fill the night with their chirping, croaking songs. Somewhere in the distance, coyotes yelp at each other.

Those sounds were always my soundtrack whenever I would go down to the Concho River in the early mornings. The thought sends a sadness stabbing through my chest because I don't know when I'll be able to do it again without remembering the last time. Without remembering Raul.

But at least I have this gift for Ambrose.

CHAPTER EIGHTEEN

AMBROSE

My kind don't really have to sleep. It's a good idea if you've been really busted up, or if you *really* need your wits about you for a kill, but for the most part, sleeping is more of a want than a need. Unfortunately, with this whole damn compound on lockdown thanks to my handiwork, that leaves me restless and bored in my cabin.

I can only jerk off to the thought of Mercy's gasping face and trembling tits so many times. And I shouldn't even be doing that, truth be told. She's a fucking human woman, and she about had a breakdown when she saw my work.

Two hundred years old and I've managed to catch feelings like a goddamn teenager.

I've got to figure something out, though. I need to get those birth records and get the hell out of here before I mire myself deeper in with her. There's a reason I haven't fucked her properly yet, and it's not just because I want to take my time.

I mean, that's *part* of it. But I also know better than to fuck human women. I'm not Sawyer.

My point is that by the time the sun rises, two days after I killed Burl, I'm going a little stir-crazy. Back in my traveling preacher days I never stayed in one place too long. I said my spell, left them wanting more, and then slashed them down while they were too God-struck to notice.

Wish I could do that here. But I promised Charlotte I'd get her the names of her birth parents and going on a killing spree won't make that any easier.

And, yeah, maybe I want another go with Mercy, too.

I'm actually thinking about that, about what I'd like to do to her next, when someone raps on my door. My nerves are a little on edge, but then I smell her through the walls. Sweet and musky. A little afraid.

What has my human seen this time? Certainly nothing I've done. I was a good boy last night.

Max is waiting at the door by the time I get over there, tail wagging and thumping, his ears perked up. "Don't get too attached, boy," I mutter to him right before I pull the door open.

I know it's Mercy, but my body still reacts at the sight of her standing there, looking rumpled and not quite put-together. Her long hair's loose again, not in those fussy braids.

"Can I come in?" she says urgently. "Before someone sees me?"

I just step aside in response, then shut the door once she's safely inside. Part of me wants to tell her there's no one around, but then she'll want to know how I know, and I can't have her suspect that I'm anything other than a lascivious human preacher.

"Is everything all right?" When I turn around, I find her smiling and petting Max, who's lapping it all up. Damn dog. At least Roxi has the good sense to keep her distance and not fall in love. "There hasn't been another—attack, has there?"

Of course I already know the answer is no, but I'm playing a role here.

"No, nothing like that." Mercy gives Max one last scritch

between his ears and straightens up. She's nervous, though, another thing I can't tell her I sense it. She tries to cover it up with a shy smile. "I, um, I brought you something."

I blink, surprised—I'm used to people being afraid around me. That goes with the territory. This is different, though. She's acting more like a schoolgirl who got caught breaking the rules.

"Brought me what?" I step closer to her, relishing the way her biorhythms change, her heart and breath speeding up. She lifts her eyes to meet mine, her lips parted. I'm not a mind reader, but I know what she's thinking. My heightened senses tell me exactly how my closeness affects her.

And since I'm a fool who loves having this power over her, I step closer. She doesn't step back.

"What'd you bring me, Mercy?"

She slips her hand into the big pocket of her dress and pulls out a square of yellow paper. "I had to go to Reverend Gunner last night."

Jealousy flares in my chest, hot and burning. I'm surprised by how intense it is.

God, I want to cut that man's dick off.

"I um..." Her cheeks turn bright red, and she looks down at the paper, squeezing it in her hands. "I thought about you while he was..."

Oh, that goes straight to my head. And my cock.

"Did you now?" I grab her chin and guide her gaze up to meet mine. The way she yields to me, the wide, submissive gaze in her eyes—it drives me wild. Even though it's so, so dangerous. "Did you come, thinking about me?"

Her blush deepens. "After he left. I—I touched myself the way you—the way you showed me."

I slide my fingers around her throat, smiling at the spike of her fear and her lust. Then I pull her up to me and kiss her, slow and deep. She relents for a few seconds, then jerks away, her gorgeous tits heaving beneath that baggy dress. "And then I got you this," she mutters, not looking at me as she shoves the yellow paper to my chest.

I catch her wrist, then fold her hand in mine. She lifts her gaze, and I want her on her knees for me. I want her eating my body. Not just my cum. I want to feed her my literal flesh, thin delicate strips of it. And then I want to consume her in kind, bite by fucking bite.

"It's the code to the bunker," she says breathlessly.

That jerks me out of my fantasies. "What? How?" I unfold the paper and stare at the six numbers written out in Mercy's neat, feminine hand. "I thought you said you don't have access to it."

"I don't." She sounds sheepish. "I just didn't tell you that Reverend Gunner writes all his passwords down. I figured this one would be, too, but..." Her cheeks turn bright red. "But I didn't really have a way to get it. I knew it would be in his home office—"

"And you had a sleepover last night?" I hear the sharpness in my words. The idea of that piece of shit touching her, touching what's mine, is too damn much, even if I did baptize her. Even if she was thinking about me the whole time.

"He made me stay in the suite afterwards," she says. "Because of the killer."

Damn. Well, I've got no one to blame but myself for that one, I suppose.

"I couldn't sleep," she continues. "And I was thinking about you, and—"

She blushes again, and I wonder what exactly she was thinking about. I wonder how filthy my little human can get.

"I thought it was worth a try." She shrugs, then peers up at me. Her hair glints around her like a halo, and somehow it just makes her eyes darker, two deep pools I'd be willing to drown in a thousand times over.

You really are being a fool, Ambrose.

"And it paid off." I fold the paper back into a square and then slide it into my wallet for safekeeping. "Thanks."

"I know it's not safe," she says, worrying her hands. "But if you're going to go, it should be at night. I just don't—" The earnestness in her expression nearly undoes me. "I just don't want you to be the next—"

"Nothing's going to happen to me." Part of me wishes I could tell her why, if only to hear her melodious scream again. But if I do that, I can forget fucking her. Me and the dogs'll be on the lam. Or I'd have to kill her, which is not something I'm terribly interested in doing. She's more fun to me alive.

"You don't know that," she says.

"I do, actually." I smile at her, wondering if she'll put the connection together. I doubt it; even if some part of her subconscious has figured it out, she doesn't want it to be true, so she won't see it. Not until there's hard evidence.

And, if all things go right, I can protect her from that. I can get my files, fuck her proper the one time, and be on my way. Down south to Big Bend, a handful of delicious new memories to use whenever I want to fuck my hand. And I'll leave her with a handful of memories, too.

"Why?" she asks. "Because of God?"

For a moment, I have no idea what she's talking about. But then my false identity kicks into place. "Exactly," I say, then pull out a Bible quote: "'Fear thou not, for I am with thee.'"

Mercy smiles a little, although I don't think she believes me.

"I'll go tonight," I say. "Midnight."

Then I step close to her and wind my arm around her waist. She doesn't try to push me away, and when I nuzzle her neck, she sighs softly and puts her hands delicately on my chest. I speak into her skin.

"And you're going to come with me."

Mercy jerks away with a jolt of fear. It's not true terror,

although it's close enough that my cock strains against my pants and I breathe the scent in deep. Mercy stares at me.

"Why do you want me to go with you?"

I look at her, considering all the ways I can answer that question. I go with the most practical. "So you can help me find the right files."

But also because I want to make sure I see her one last time before I sneak out of this fucked-up church and back to my normal life. Because even though I shouldn't, I really, really want to fuck her. It surprises me, honestly, how badly I want it. How much I've needed to get her sweet fear out of my system since I heard her scream down at the Concho River.

"Oh. Right. Of course."

"Don't worry." I can't stop myself from coiling my fingers around her throat—gently, of course. Not that it bothers her. I can sense everything about her body's reaction. The way her fear melts away and is replaced with a warm, pulsing lust. I run my thumb along her trachea, into the hollow at the base of her throat, and when she swallows, I feel the movement. "I won't let anything happen to you."

That, at least, is a promise I can keep.

Mercy lays her head against my chest like she wants to listen to my heartbeat the way I like to listen to hers. "The woman you're doing this for," she says softly. "Who is she to you? Really?"

Is that a twinge of jealousy I hear from her? I squeeze her shoulders a little, pressing her into me.

"She's the girlfriend of a long-time friend of mine," I say honestly, and immediately, the tension slips out of Mercy's shoulders. "She needs to know the identity of her birth parents for a—a medical reason."

"Oh. That makes sense." Mercy pulls away from me. "What's her name?"

"Charlotte Careta." I smooth Mercy's hair back, smiling down at her. "I think you two would get along."

It's the right thing to say, and it's not even a lie. Mercy smiles, although there's a sadness to it. "I feel like all the women here hate me," she says. "Because I'm—" She stops and bites her lower lip, but she doesn't need to say anything more. Because I get it. Sterling Gunner pitted her against the wives. Mercy represents their biggest fear, doesn't she?

"That's not your fault," I say softly. "Because there's nothing hateable about you, Mercy."

She smiles and falls back into my arms. I pull her close, and I'll admit this position is strange to me. Holding her without intending to fuck her. Just comforting her. Making her feel safe. That's not what the boogeyman is supposed to do.

"When do you want to go to the bunker?" she asks.

I press my nose into her hair to breathe in her scent. I can't put this off. I'm digging myself into a hole with her, and if I don't get out soon, I don't think I ever will.

"Tonight," I tell her. "We'll go tonight."

"You're a terrible influence for a preacher."

Oh, if you only knew, darling. But the only response I give her is another kiss, a promise of what I'm going to do to her.

CHAPTER NINETEEN

AMBROSE

I blur into the shadows outside Mercy's little cabin, watching the dark windows and listening to the sounds of humanity inside. One of the benefits of being a Hunter is that my senses come alive at night; the deeper the ichor, the more the world lights up for me. Not in sight, of course, but in sound and scent and taste. And I can tell that Mercy is awake inside that cabin.

It's about ten minutes until midnight. Mercy told me that the church's paramilitary is patrolling the campus, so I went sniffing around earlier today to find out more from Deacon Price, the one who's supposed to be in charge. He let slip that they're keeping to the periphery of the compound since they assume it's an outsider coming in. Still, I keep some feelers out for the guards, but they aren't nearby.

Movement from Mercy's cabin. A shadow passes by the window, dark on dark, and I drift forward, moving with my light predator's steps. I have my switchblade tucked into my pocket, just in case, but I doubt I'll need it. This isn't a killing night, assuming I keep my wits about me.

I move up to the little plastic picket fence that wraps

around Mercy's postage stamp yard, still keeping to the darkness. Her heartbeat thuds through the walls. She's nervous. Excited. Frightened, too. My cock twitches, eager to be inside her.

A whisper of footsteps; Mercy steps out of the house through the front door, dressed in a black dress like I told her to wear, her hair up in those braids. For a moment, she stands on the porch, sweeping her gaze around like a frightened rabbit. She doesn't see me even though I'm right in front of her, watching her, but I bet her skin prickles and the soft downy hair on her arms stands on ends. That's the effect I have.

I move forward, letting myself be known. When she sees me, she jumps and slaps her hand over her mouth, smothering a yelp of surprise. Then she scurries across the yard, her footsteps thunderous.

"You frightened me," she whispers.

Oh, she only knows the half of it.

"There's nothing to be frightened of," I tell her instead. "But we don't want to dally. Come along."

I grab her hand, her skin cold and clammy with anxiety, and pull her forward, leading her on a path only I can see—one that's marked by shadows and darkness. While my heart is as calm as ever, hers is as loud as a thunderstorm, and I find myself squeezing her hand, trying to soothe her.

What is it about this woman, that I want to *soothe* her as much as I want to terrify her?

We make it to the bunker without incident. I keep my senses on the guards pacing around the fence, which allows us to cut across the center of the compound without being noticed. Although I'll admit, when I finally see the bunker's big metal door, I do feel something like relief. I really want to protect my last few hours with Mercy.

Mercy's relieved, too. She sighs next to me when we get to

the door. "I can't believe that worked," she whispers. "I was *sure* we were going to get caught."

The danger's exciting her. I can feel it. I can see it in the glassy shine of her eyes.

"Told you," I murmur back. "I'm not going to let anything happen to you."

I punch in the code to the bunker. A split second later, the keypad turns green and there's a quiet, hydraulic hiss as the door cracks open. I glance over at Mercy.

"Good girl," I tell her, grinning.

The way she flushes with pleasure absolutely perfumes the air.

I push the door open and let her go inside first, glancing over my shoulder to confirm, one last time, that there aren't any humans around to see what we're doing.

"You can close the door," she says. "It doesn't lock automatically. And besides, the code will work to get us out."

I peer through the doorway to find her standing in a narrow, dimly-lit hallway. "You sure about that?"

She smiles a little. "Yeah. I've been down here before, remember? There's also a phone. We'd be able to call for help. Not that—" She tucks her hair behind her ear, looking away from me. "Not that I'd really want to do that."

I pull the door shut, the clang echoing around us. She's right; the door doesn't lock, which is a relief. I don't really like the idea of leaving it shut, but leaving it open is inviting trouble, too.

"See?" she says.

"We should probably work fast," I tell her. "Do you know where the files are?"

"Not *exactly?*" Mercy gives me a shy, sheepish look, which just makes me want to bend her over and smack her on the ass, punishment for not being prepared.

"Not exactly?" I stroll up to her and curl my hand around

her throat like I did this morning. She stares at me expectantly, her lips parted and her eyes bright. "So we're going to have to go looking?"

"I have a vague *idea*." Her eyes glitter mischievously, and my cock jumps.

I had planned to wait until we were back at my cabin, the file secured, before I fucked her. Now I'm not sure I can hold out that long.

"Well, let's see it, then. Your vague *idea*." I slide my hand away from her throat. "Lead the way."

She does, taking me down the narrow metal hallway, the automatic lights casting everything in an eerie, yellowish glow. It tilts down, taking us deeper underground, and I wonder what the hell Gunner thinks is going to happen, building a structure like this.

I wonder what he's planning to *do*.

And I wonder, distantly, what that might mean for Mercy.

Not your concern, I tell myself as we wind deeper into the bunker. *She's human. Your obligations are to your own kind.*

"If I had to guess, they'd be in here." Mercy's echoing voice jars me out of my thoughts. She stops in front of a doorway and pushes it open, releasing a rush of stale, cool air. "The last time I was down here, Mrs. Harrison had me drop off a box of old files in this room."

She reaches inside and hits a light switch, flooding the room with more sallow lighting. The room is bigger than I was expecting, a cavernous labyrinth of cardboard boxes. Mercy spins around, her skirt flaring up so I catch, ever-so-briefly, a flash of her calf.

It really is like I'm a fucking teenager again.

"This is going to take all night," I tell her.

"So we'll just have to come back." She arches an eyebrow, and I get a strange, tight knot in my chest—because she wants to be here. Even if it means sneaking out and breaking the rules.

She has no idea what I am. If she did, she would not be this excited to be trapped in an underground bunker with me.

But her big, bright grin sloughs away any doubts I have. She doesn't have to know what I am or what I've done. We'll have our fun together, I'll leave her with some good memories, and that'll be the end of it.

"That's risky, you know." I stride up to her, loving the way she gazes up at me with that worshipful expression. I cup her face, rubbing my thumb over her lips—

Which she parts, drawing my thumb into her mouth. Her eyes never leave mine.

Fuck, I really do need to get her out of my system.

"Are those files even down here?" I ask her, using my killing voice so I can feel her squirm against me. It works. "Or was this just a ploy to get me alone?"

Mercy releases my thumb, giving me a glimpse of her pink tongue in the process. I want it on my cock, want it plunging up into my asshole. I want to make her do things the good Reverend Gunner wouldn't *dream* of.

"They're down here," she says primly. "And I think I know where."

"You said you weren't even sure they were in this room."

Mercy grins and pulls away from me, disappearing down one of the aisles of boxes. I take the opportunity to adjust my cock, which has grown uncomfortably hard. I'm already thinking about the things I want to do down here—a reward if she gets the file, a punishment if she doesn't. I don't even know which I'd prefer.

"Are you coming?" she calls out.

I'm about to, I think, but I don't say anything, just follow her scent through the dim light. I find her on the far side of the room, kneeling next to a stack of boxes. She looks over her shoulder at me. "Help me with these."

"You think the files are over here?" I hoist up the top box, an easy weight given my Hunter's strength. Mercy's eyes go wide, though she doesn't say anything.

"Um, yeah, I think so. It looks like they're connected to the adoption program, anyway. And you said she was adopted in the '90s, right?"

"Yeah. Early '90s."

She shoves a box aside and drags another one out. The way she's positioned highlights the thick curve of her ass, like she's situating herself just for me. Like she's putting herself in a position to be fucked.

"Oh my god, I think—" Her voice is muffled as she burrows deeper into the boxes, lifting her ass even higher. I have to bite back the urge to tell her to freeze. "I think I found it!"

She falls back on her heels, breaking the pretty picture of her submission. But she also drags out another tattered old banker's box, scraping it across the floor to bounce against my feet.

"There you go," she says, a little breathless. "Adoption files from 1990 to 1995."

Well, well, well. It seems my little human might get rewarded tonight, after all.

"Not as many as I thought there'd be." I'm surprised at how well I keep myself composed, especially when Mercy sits down on the floor, her skirt hiking up around her thighs. I lower down into a crouch and pull the lid off.

"We don't do that many," she says. "At least from what I understand." She hesitates, chewing on her bottom lip. "I heard it isn't—well, it isn't exactly *legal*."

I snort. Big surprise there. "Yeah, well, I'm not worried about it. Like I said, Charlotte just needs her parents' names so she can track them down."

The tabs flash by. *Bronson. Buford. Callen.*

"I wish I could meet her," Mercy says softly.

I pause, just for a second. Part of me wishes that, too, but I keep pushing through the tabs. Because *that's* an impossibility.

Careta, Franklin. There it is.

I yank the file out of the box, flip it open.

"Did you find what you were looking for?" Mercy asks.

"Yeah," I say. "I think I did." I glance down at the papers in the file—an intake form for *Baby Medina.* Medina. I don't know any Hunters with that name, but that doesn't mean much.

I scan over the intake form, looking for anything that could point to the full name of Charlotte's birth parents. Mercy leans close to me, her breath warm on my shoulder.

"You know," I say, still skimming the form as I talk. "I decided when we came in here I was either going to punish you or reward you."

Mercy's heart rate picks up, and I glance at her over the top of the file, give her a slow, easy grin. Her eyes widen.

"I-I don't understand," she says shyly.

I think she does, though. She squeezes her dress up in her fists, and the blood is rushing to her face.

"If we didn't find the file, I was going to punish you." I flip the intake form over, and there, finally, I see it:

Mother: *Julia Medina.* Father: *Johnny Dobsals.*

There's an address next to the mother's name, some small town in Oklahoma. Next to the father's, it just says, *Location unknown.*

Well, damn. It looks like Charlotte's mom was the one who put her up for adoption, which means she's almost certainly not a Hunter—no Hunter would give their child to a fucking church. But I don't recognize this Johnny Dobsals, either. Granted, most of us change names like we change clothes.

At least I've got a starting point, though.

"But you did find the file," Mercy says softly. "Didn't you? Is that it?"

I snap it shut and peer up at her.

"I did," I say. "Which means you get a reward."

I stand. Mercy doesn't move, just gazes up at me. Fuck, I love her like that. Pliant. Supplicant. Eager to please.

Sterling Gunner doesn't deserve her.

"What kind of reward?" But she knows. I can see it in the gleam of her eyes. I can smell it in the arousal perfuming the air.

"Take off your clothes," I tell her. "And you'll find out."

CHAPTER TWENTY

MERCY

I t feels like a dream, being down here. Or a fantasy, like the fantasies I conjured up when I was in the marriage suite alone, sliding my hand between my legs. But it's neither.

It's real. I broke Ambrose into the bunker; I helped him steal a file that's supposed to be sealed. And there's a killer stalking the church, one who could walk through the unlocked bunker door and attack both of us.

"Don't you *want* your reward?" Ambrose says softly, kicking the box aside to step up closer to me. He presses his fingers under my chin, tilting my head upward.

His erection is more than evident.

"Y-yes," I whisper, my thoughts hazy. "But I wish you would tell me what you're going to do."

"You'll find out," he says. "Now undress."

I know I should refuse. I'm married—before God if not legally, which is all that matters. I made a vow.

A vow you never meant.

"Mercy." Ambrose's voice lilts in a warning. Then he reaches into his pocket and pulls out something small and slim. I don't know what it is until he squeezes it and a narrow silver blade whips out. I gasp, a sharp lance of terror moving through my chest—

"Don't make me cut that dress off you."

"Why do you have that?" I whisper.

Something dark flashes through Ambrose's features. "There's a killer loose. I needed *something* to protect you."

My chest flares with heat. *He wants to protect me.*

But then he presses the flat side of the blade against my cheek, and any warmth is swallowed up by the chill of the metal.

"However," he continues. "I will use it on that dress if you don't get moving."

This time, the fear that curls through me is almost indistinguishable from lust. I twist my arm around to pull down my zipper, the sound impossibly loud in the bunker's echoing silence. Ambrose keeps his eyes fixed on me as I shrug out of the sleeves, revealing the ugly, industrial-strength beige bra I have to wear. I push the dress down and stand at the same time, letting the stiff fabric fall around me in a pile.

Ambrose's eyes gleam, taking me in. I have to resist the urge to cover my body, even if I'm still in my underwear, because the way he looks at me—

It's like he wants to eat me.

He fingers the handle of the knife, and the blade catches the dim lights and flashes like a camera.

And then he *moves*. He moves so fast I don't see him. One second, he's watching me, and the next, he has his arm around my waist, pulling me into him, and the knife has slipped between my panties and the skin of my hip.

"I was going to take them off," I gasp, stunned by his quickness.

Ambrose's eyes burn. "But this is so much more *fun*," he murmurs, pressing the knife blade against my hip as he kisses along my neck, making me tremble and gasp. I wait for the sound of shearing fabric, but it never comes. Instead, Ambrose slides out the knife and slips it under my bra band.

"Or should I start here?" he rasps into my neck.

"I-I thought you were rewarding me."

Ambrose chuckles and slides his free hand between my legs to my palm my sex, the heel of his hand grinding into my clit. Even with the layer of cotton, my body explodes with heat.

"Is that enough of a reward for you?"

Then, in another lightning-fast movement, he yanks the knife sideways. I feel my bra band snap more than I hear it, and then I feel it when he slices away the straps with two quick slices of the knife. The ruined bra falls to the ground as Ambrose steps away.

For the first time, he sees my bare breasts, his eyes dark as he drinks me in.

"God, you're fucking perfect," he says.

The compliment surprises me; Reverend Gunner has made it clear, on multiple occasions, that I should be a little thinner, with smaller breasts and smaller hips—that if I were, maybe I would be worthy of being a first wife and not a helpmeet. *You have a Jezebel's body*, he told me once, right before he took me over to tend to Pastor Sullivan's needs.

But with Ambrose, the way he compliments me—it's like he can't believe I'm here in front of him.

"Get the panties off," he orders, in that rough, dark voice he uses sometimes. "I want to see all of you."

I shove the panties down without hesitation, eager to obey him. He watches me, eyes roving over my body, as I step out of them and stand there in the damp, warm air of the bunker, utterly exposed. I'm not sure what to do with my arms—hang them at my side? Wrap them around my waist? I do the latter on instinct, but Ambrose moves fast again, grabbing my wrists and jerking my arms overhead.

"No," he says darkly. "Don't cover yourself. You're too fucking gorgeous."

He walks me backward, my bare feet skittering over the cool, dusty floor as he guides me through the maze of old boxes. His eyes never leave mine, and I have no idea how he sees anything. How he knows where to step. But he does.

Suddenly, he shoves me, and I yelp as my backside presses into the wall. Ambrose leans into me, still pinning my arms overhead, and trails his mouth along my neck. It's not a kiss, not even close. He breathes in deep, smelling me.

"Delicious," he purrs, the movements of his lips teasing my skin. He steps backward, his hand already fumbling with his fly.

"What would you like me to do?" I breathe out.

Ambrose smiles at that and jerks his pants down over his hips just enough to pull his cock out, as big and meaty as I remember. Bigger.

"You're so eager to please, aren't you?"

I stare at him, not quite sure how to answer. "For you," I finally say. "I am for you."

It's too dark to really see his face. The lights are behind him, wrapping him in shadows, and I worry I misspoke, that it was too much for him—too close to telling him that I *want* him, not just sexually, but—

But for real.

"Good," he says. "Then you'll do exactly as I say, won't you?"

Heat burns through my core. I nod.

He steps closer to me, his cock bobbing, and presses his hand on the top of my head. Then he presses down, and I fall to my knees, eyes lifting to him. I know what he wants, but I still wait for the order.

"Open."

I do, dropping my jaw, still looking at him. He keeps his hand on my head and uses the other to guide his cock over my waiting tongue.

"Worship me," he commands, his voice black as the shadows.

And I do. I draw his length into my mouth even though it's more than what I'm used to, pulling it as deep in as I can go—so deep my throat constricts and my eyes water. I keep going, though. I brace myself against his thighs and bob my head back and forth, worshipping every veiny inch of him with my mouth and tongue. He puts both his hands on my head, just as he did when he prayed over me, his fingers drawing up clumps of my hair.

I moan around him. Suck a little harder. I desperately want to taste him again. I want to swallow every drop of his release without wasting it like before. The idea spurns me on, and I roll my hips, my sex so drenched with my arousal that it almost feels cool against the air.

Ambrose grunts and pulls hard on my hair. But the pain doesn't deter me. If anything, it drives me on. I use every trick I learned to mollify Reverend Gunner, even though it's harder with Ambrose's size. I suck on his sensitive head, then lick his entire length, all the way down to his testicles, still half-buried in his underwear. I try to swallow him whole again, although I can't quite manage it.

But I know he likes it because he groans and sighs and pulls harder on my hair, digging his fingers into my scalp. I'm so sure he's going to finish. So sure I'll get to take his communion again. To eat of his body—

Would I drink of his blood? I think I would.

But then Ambrose wrenches himself out of me, so roughly that his cock slaps across my mouth like a warning.

"No," he says roughly. "Not like that."

I stare at him, my body so flushed with desire I feel like I'm going to lose my mind.

"I want to come in your cunt," he rasps, staring down at where I kneel before him. His words send heat shooting through me, even though I know I could wind up pregnant. But I don't care.

"I'd like that," I whisper, and Ambrose smiles.

"Then turn around and get on your hands and knees. Show me how wet you are for my cock."

His vulgarity just stokes lust inside me, and I immediately do as he asks, arranging myself on the floor. For all that I've been used as a helpmeet, I've never done this position before, and I feel degraded and exposed and desperate all at once—but because it's Ambrose towering over me, it all just heightens my lust.

"There it is." Ambrose runs his hands over my behind, his touch soft and reverent. "There's that pretty pussy." A single finger slides inside me, and I yelp and jerk back against him.

The movement is met immediately with a sharp slap across my bottom. It stings, but it's just like when he pulled my hair. The pain and the pleasure meld together into something new.

"Hold still," Ambrose says. "If you move, you'll get another slap."

I hold my breath, bracing myself on my forearms, my hips lifted to meet him. He works another finger inside me, his strokes firm. I whimper, using every ounce of willpower to stay still.

"That's it." He runs his other hand over my lower back like he's holding me in place. "You're going to come around my cock, do you understand?"

I bite my lip, trembling. I want to, more than anything. But orgasms are new for me, and I've still never experienced one during actual sex.

Ambrose slaps my ass, harder than before, and I cry out.

"Do. You. Understand?" He strokes my sex in time with his words, and that's harder than before, too.

"Yes!" I cry out. Then, in a rush: "I'm just afraid I can't!"

Ambrose's fingers go still inside me. "You will," he says softly. "I'll get you good and ready before you take my cock."

As he speaks, he slides his fingers out and rubs them against my clit, making me moan and buck back against him. That earns me another slap on my behind.

"What did I tell you to do?"

I shiver. "Hold still."

"Good girl. You really do like to obey me, don't you?"

"Y-yes." I squeeze my eyes shut and clench my hands into fists. He keeps rubbing my clit in quick circles, and that still-unfamiliar pressure builds up in my belly.

"Then obey. I want you still while I fuck you. I'm in control here."

"Y-yes, sir."

I don't know where the *sir* comes from, but at this moment, it feels right.

"Fuck, you're a treasure," Ambrose groans. His hand falls away from me, and I moan softly at its absence.

"Oh, you don't like that, do you?" He's touching my hips now, arranging me into position. "Don't worry, darling. You'll like this even better."

I wish I could look at him. Wish I could see his face as he stares down at me, stroking my skin while I tremble and shake beneath his touch.

"After all," he purrs, and I feel something press against my sex, something much bigger than his fingers. "This is your reward."

And then he pushes his cock inside me with one firm stroke, filling me to the brim.

CHAPTER TWENTY-ONE

AMBROSE

Mercy's pussy is drenched with need, and when I slide into her, its walls flutter around me to welcome me home.

This cunt is going to be my fucking undoing.

"Oh my god!" she gasps out, her legs trembling. "Oh, it feels —you feel—"

"Don't move," I warn her.

She drops her forehead against the floor, shoulders hitching. All I can see of her is her long, graceful back and the puddle of her blonde hair and, most deliciously, the wide curve of her ass as I pull my cock halfway out of her pussy just so I can drive it in again.

She makes a noise halfway between pleasure and pain. A noise I want to hear over and over again.

"Remember what I told you." I start my thrusts off slow and teasing. Warming her up. "You're going to come around my cock. Do you understand?"

She nods and moans wordlessly.

I tap her ass, lightly. "Use your words. Do you understand?"

"Yes, sir!"

Sir. Fuck, I didn't even ask her to say that. It didn't even occur to me. But when she let it slip earlier—

It's too damn bad she's human. It really is.

"Good girl. Now relax while I fuck you."

Mercy lets out a soft sigh and slumps lower against the floor, and I do exactly what I promised—driving my cock in and out of her soaking wet cunt, angling my hips so I'm massaging her G-spot with the underside of my dick. The animalistic yelps currently coming out of her mouth tell me I'm right on target.

"Does that feel good, Mercy?" I dig my fingers into her flesh.

"Yes!" she cries out. "Yes, oh yes oh yes oh—"

Her words dissolve completely when I hunch myself around her so I can reach down and press my thumb against her clit. She jerks at that and gives a shriek of pleasure. It's not quite as good as a shriek of fear, but I'll take it.

"You're going to come for me." I speak into her spine, her skin beading with sweat in the damp air. "You're going to come harder than you ever have before. Do you understand?"

"Yes, sir!" she shouts into the ground. I grab hold of her hair with my free hand and jerk her head up, holding her in place.

"Don't move," I growl, driving myself into her. "I'm about to show you God."

Mercy whimpers. Her whole body is shaking, her muscles quivering. She's close. I keep up my pace—my cock inside her pussy, my hand on her clit. Part of me wants to show her what I am when she comes. I want to dig my switchblade out and slam it into the thick flesh of her thighs and carve out a chunk of skin so I can taste the pleasure in her flesh. Then I'd let her taste me. Let her eat of my body for real.

The thought drags me dangerously close to orgasm, and I have to pull back, focusing on a blank spot on the wall. I wind my fingers up in Mercy's hair, binding myself to her. It's hurting her—I can hear it in the way her moans pitch a little higher.

But I can also tell she likes it because the first sparks of her orgasm fire around my cock.

"Almost there, darling." I pull harder on her hair, yanking her head back so her throat is exposed. I could split it open if I wanted. Bleed her all over these boxes and then lap the blood up like a dog.

I yank her hair a little harder, and she keens in pleasure.

"A-ambrose!" she cries out, voice cracking and shuddering. "Don't stop. I—"

She doesn't have to say what she's doing because I feel it, the fluttery, frantic contractions of her cunt around my cock. Mercy lets out a low, dark groan from deep in her throat, and it's the sexiest goddamn sound I've ever heard. Better even than the scream I got out of her when she realized she was swimming with a corpse.

She jerks against me, spearing herself on my cock as she fucks her way through her orgasm. I don't chide her for moving. I don't want to; it feels too good, the way her pussy clamps down in desperation. I spread my fingers over the back of her neck and drop my head back and match her rhythm. My balls tighten up against my dick, everything ready to spill.

"You ready for me?" I rasp. "Ready for my cum?"

Mercy moans in response, dropping her head against the floor. I smack her ass. "Answer me!"

"Yes!" she cries. "Please!" That's what pushes me over the edge—knowing she wants me to finish inside her, like my cum can wash away whatever dregs Reverend Gunner's left behind. My whole body goes rigid and I roar as my orgasm tears through me, quaking up through my belly. I told her she was going to come harder than she ever has before—I promise I know I kept—but it seems she just did the same to me.

Depleted, I slump over her, covering her body with mine. I can barely think from the head rush, and it takes me a moment to realize I'm covering her neck with eager little kisses and licking away her salty sweat. Scraping my teeth against her skin, trying to bite at her. To *eat* her.

I jerk away before I do something I regret. Mercy lifts up, looking at me over her shoulder, her face flushed and her eyes glassy and adoring.

This was so stupid. She's looking at me like she loves me.

I could end it. I could end *her*, which would be the easiest and cleanest thing to do. Cut her throat like I was imagining and carry her body back to my house in the desert and cut her body up into meat. I've got the files. Got what I came for.

The switchblade burns in my pocket.

Then she speaks, in a soft, throaty whisper—

"Thank you."

And I realize just how much I don't want to kill her. Eat her, yes. Make her bleed, absolutely. But *end* her?

I couldn't. I *can't*.

Christ, I'm getting soft in my old age.

"Thank you," she says again, and then she pulls away from me, our bodies finally separating. She crawls around and sits back on her heels, gazing at me through the mussed tangle of her hair. "I didn't—I've never—" She glances away, shy, and it feels like my heart might burst with whatever it is I'm feeling for her. Affection, lust, I don't know. "Thank you for showing me what it's supposed to feel like."

That nearly melts me on the spot. For the first time since I was a young man I almost wish I was human, not a Hunter, so I could drag her away from this shithole church. I know that's what she wants from me. I can see it in her expression.

But she doesn't want *me*. She doesn't want the boogeyman. She wants the itinerant preacher, and that man doesn't exist.

"You're welcome." I stand up and help her to her feet, too. She's shaky, and I hold her hand to steady her. But she pulls away from me to gather up her clothes and get dressed. I watch her move through the shadows, and I realize I'm trying to memorize what she looks like.

It hits me, then, that I'm never going to see her again. And she has no fucking idea. Just like she has no fucking idea what I truly am.

Mercy twists around, trying to zip up her dress, and I step over and do it for her without thinking. That just earns me another shy glance over her shoulder and a quivering sense of normalcy. "Thanks," she says in that small voice, and I can just tell that she's imagining us doing this for the rest of our lives.

You don't want me, I think, like I might be able to plant the idea in her head.

"Now what?" Mercy gathers up her mangled bra and tries to fold it down as small as possible. I pick up the file I came here for. It feels absurd, now.

"I'll walk you back to your house," I say.

She's disappointed, even though she tries to hide it.

"I can take that, too." I pluck the bra out of her hand. "Get rid of it for you."

Her cheeks pinken, but there's delight in her eyes. It's killing me, knowing I'm about to break her heart into a thousand pieces. She's gonna come by the cabin tomorrow and find me and the dogs gone. But I can't say goodbye. It'll invite too many questions, and I've fucked up enough in the last few days as it is.

So this is it. Me, Mercy, and a long walk through a quiet, terrified compound.

CHAPTER TWENTY-TWO

MERCY

True to his word, Ambrose gets me home safely, winding us through the darkness as if he's lived at the Church of the Well his entire life. It's almost like he doesn't even *need* to see the walking trails.

"Don't worry," he whispers as we pass by the administration building, closed up tight for the evening. "The closest guard is patrolling along the fence. We're in the clear."

"How could you know that?" I whisper back, glancing sideways at him. It's so dark out here that I can barely make out his features, but I know when he looks at me, because his eyes catch the light strangely, and for a moment, they gleam like a cat's.

"Just do."

I wonder if it's God speaking through him. That feels blasphemous to consider, given what we just did in the bunker. Or rather, it feels like it *should* be blasphemous—the truth is, everything that's happened tonight has felt completely right in a way I've never experienced before. I'm used to the opposite, to everyone in the Church of the Well telling me that something's right even though it feels deeply, profoundly wrong.

Like being Reverend Gunner's helpmeet. Or offering myself to Pastor Sullivan.

I know what Reverend Gunner would say, that sin always feels good and doing the right thing always feels difficult. That it's God's way of testing us and Satan's way of seducing us. I've always accepted that.

But tonight—tonight I wonder if maybe I've had it backward all this time.

We turn onto my street, which I recognize even in the dark. My heart constricts. I don't want to go home. I want to go back to Ambrose's cabin and fall asleep in his bed.

"There you are," Ambrose says as we come to my porch. I stare up at my front door, fear twitching through my body. Not fear of the killer, though. Not fear of the devil. Fear that everything I've learned has been a lie, that Ambrose gave me my first glimpse of Heaven and I'll never get to experience it again.

But I still can't bring myself to ask Ambrose to take me with him. Because why would he agree to such a thing?

"I'll see you tomorrow," he says stiffly, and he presses his lips against my cheek. It's not chaste. His kiss lingers, and then he repeats it on my mouth—quick, urgent, hungry.

Tomorrow. Maybe I'll gather up the strength to ask him tomorrow.

I nod, my mouth too dry to speak. I can feel him staring at me through the dark even though I can't really see him, his face a blur of shadows.

"Good night," I manage to whisper.

"Good night, Mercy."

I love it when he says my name. It makes my whole body light up like Christmas.

He reaches over and smoothes his hand over my hair, his touch gentle even as it reminds me of how hard he pulled on it earlier, like he was trying to drag me up to meet him. The space between my legs flares with heat.

"Good night," he says again, and then his hand falls away, and then he's gone.

For a minute, I stand there, listening to his footsteps retreat into the darkness. They're faint, and I have to strain to hear them, to let myself know this wasn't all a dream.

It wasn't a dream. But whatever it was—it's over.

At least for now, I tell myself, and then I hear Ambrose's smoky voice:

See you tomorrow.

I let myself into my tiny yard but don't go back into the house just yet. I want to stay out in the damp night air, the dew settling on my skin. Part of me wonders if I'm tempting the killer. Maybe if I can draw him out, Ambrose will appear to save me.

I pace around my tiny garden, my thoughts racing. I don't want to go back inside. I don't want to go back to my bedroom and strip out of my dress and fall asleep in my little twin bed.

What I want, truly, is to walk out of here and all the way to Ambrose's cabin. I want to kneel in front of him and beg him to take me far, far away from the Church of the Well. Away from the murders. Away from Reverend Gunner. Away from all of it.

I barely realize what I'm doing until I'm walking swiftly along the sidewalk beside my house, arms crossed over my chest, heading straight to Ambrose's cabin.

Walking alone is terrifying. I can barely see in front of me, and the darkness amplifies the night sounds, turning every insect rattle and frog croak into a killer's footsteps. I'm halfway to his cabin when my speed-walking becomes a jog, my breasts bouncing uncomfortably without their bra. I keep my gaze focused ahead, working on kid logic—if I don't see the killer, then the killer can't see me.

It doesn't work, of course.

"Who's there?"

I freeze when I hear the voice, just around the corner from

Ambrose's cabin. A flashlight sweeps across the road and shines in my eyes, blinding me like a deer. I'm too terrified to move.

"Mercy? What are you doing out here?"

And then, like that, I know who it is.

"Deacon Price?" I squint into the light and wrap my arms tighter around my chest. My voice sounds quick and panicky, and I know I need to come up with an excuse for being out at night. And fast.

"You can't be out here." Deacon Price moves the flashlight out of my eyes and steps up to me, frowning. "It's not remotely safe. There's a *killer*."

"I kn-know," I stammer out. "But I—Reverend Gunner wanted to see me, and—"

"And he sent you home alone?"

Deacon Price knows I'm lying. I can hear it in his voice, the chiding, vaguely patronizing tone.

But what other excuse do I have? I can't tell him the truth.

"Yes." I try to add an air of authority to my voice.

"So why are you here?" Deacon Price says. "You would have passed your cabin five minutes ago."

My heart pounds furiously in my ears. He's right. I messed up. "I—I must have gotten turned around—"

"You're going to see that traveling preacher," Deacon Price says lightly. "Aren't you?"

Panic surges in my chest, and I shake my head no because if I try to say it out loud, he'll immediately tell that I'm lying.

"Does Reverend Gunner know that?" Deacon Price steps closer to me. Close enough to be uncomfortable. "That you're —*visiting* someone else? In the middle of the night?"

His voice drips with contempt, and I can feel him leering at me in the dark.

"We shouldn't be out here," I say shakily.

"No." Deacon Price shakes his head slowly. "No, *you*

shouldn't be out here. *I'm* the congregation's first line of defense against the devil that's been stalking our people."

I take a shuffling step backward. "I'll go home now," I say quietly, my throat dry with fear.

Deacon Price just stares at me, the flashlight at his hip.

"Good night, Deacon." I whirl around on my heel.

But Deacon Price grabs me by the arm, his grip firm. I cry out, and he jerks me up to him and slaps his hand over my mouth. "What are you going to give me?" he says softly, his breath warm on my ear, "so that I don't tell Sterling you were going to see Ambrose Echeverría in the middle of the night?"

"I wasn't!" I cry out, although my protests are muffled by his hand.

"Here's what we're going to do," Deacon Price walks me backward, away from the sidewalk and into the yard of the closet cabin. An *empty* cabin. "The two of us are going to have some fun. And in exchange, I won't tell anyone I saw you out here. Understood?"

I close my eyes, trying to trap the tears, and tell myself this isn't as bad as it could be. Deacon Price could have marched me to Reverend Gunner's house and told him everything.

Or I could have met the killer.

Instead, I just have to do what I always do as a helpmeet: lay back and let him take what he needs.

But I don't want to. I'm sick of this life. Sick of being used. I struggle against Deacon Price's grip and try to bite at his palm, but it's no use. He's too strong for me.

"Stop that," he snarls. "Behave, or I'll tell Reverend Gunner everything."

I whimper, a few tears streaking over my cheeks. But I do relent, because what choice do I have?

Deacon Price pulls me sideways, one hand still on my mouth and the other wrapped around my arm. The empty guest cabin looms beside us.

"Good thing these places are fully furnished, huh?" he laughs. "Henry told me how familiar you are with the beds in here."

Shame and humiliation surge through me. Henry is Pastor Sullivan. He wasn't supposed to tell anyone what we did, aside from his wife—part of his arrangement with Reverend Gunner. But it did happen in one of these empty guest cabins.

Deacon Price unlocks the back door and shoves me inside. The cabin is cool and dark. He finally lets me go when he kicks the door shut, and I fold my arms over my chest, heart pounding, all my senses on high alert. He grins down at me, his teeth very white.

I wish I could punch them and watch them shatter. But I know I'm not strong enough.

"Now, I gather you know what to do from here?" He unbuckles his belt and slides it out of the loops with a snap. "Get to it. I can't be gone too long."

I feel numb. Not even thirty minutes ago I was on my hands and knees for Ambrose, moaning with an intense pleasure that felt so unbelievably right even though, technically, it was a bigger sin than what I'm about to do now.

Because I wanted it. Because I wanted *him*.

"Reverend Gunner will be upset if he finds out—" I start, but Deacon Price just cuts me off with a sharp laugh.

"When he finds out you're fucking that preacher?"

My face flares with heat. *He can't possibly know that. He's just guessing.* "I'm not!" I cry. "He's just been offering me counseling, and I was upset, and—"

"It's nearly two in the morning." Pastor Price peels his shirt off, revealing the firm muscles underneath. "No one goes to counseling at two in the morning." He grins, then, and runs his hands over his ridged stomach. "Like what you see?"

No. I don't. I jerk my gaze away, fix it on an empty spot on the floor.

"Better than Sterling, no doubt." Deacon Price grabs my chin and forces me to look at him. There's no tenderness in it, the way there is with Ambrose. "Better than that preacher, too."

I don't say anything. Deacon Price lets me go, steps back, and pulls a cell phone out of his pocket. My chest constricts, and then I can barely breathe when he swipes it open and shows me what he's pulled up:

Reverend Gunner's phone number.

"Get to work," Deacon Price says. "Or I'm telling him everything."

CHAPTER TWENTY-THREE

AMBROSE

I throw the last few days' worth of dirty clothes into my suitcase, burying Charlotte's adoption file. Once I'm back at my ranch house, I'll give her a call with the names. She's more than capable of tracking her parents down, especially if she has Jaxon helping her out. He's got a couple of decade's worth of experience stalking prey.

Over in the living room, Max whines, then scratches at the door. I frown and put out my senses. A couple of humans are nearby, moving around, but they aren't in the little cul-de-sac where my cabin is. Just the guards, no doubt.

Whatever it is that's got Max worked up, Roxi doesn't care. She's sitting at my feet, ears perked up, watching me pack.

"What's your brother doing, huh?" I ask her, slamming my suitcase closed and then zipping it up. She tilts her head, eyes curious.

"No idea, either, I take it." I heave the suitcase off the bed, and she stands up, tail wagging. Ready to go on our next mission. She's bloodthirsty enough that she probably hopes it's a killing job.

Max's whines grow louder, his scratches more urgent.

"Max, knock it off! No one's there!" I wheel the suitcase into the living room to find Max up on his hind legs, pawing furiously at the door. He's on the alert, big time. His ears are flat against his head, and his tail sticks straight out behind him.

His whine turns into a low growl, then a loud, sharp bark.

"Shh!" I drop the suitcase and rush over to him, running my hand over his raised hackles. He looks at me, his pupils black, then turns back to the door. Barks again. Scratches the wood.

"What's going on, boy?" I don't like this. My dogs work as a team; they're both trained to alert me to a threat. So I don't understand why Roxi's calm and Max is losing his mind.

He lets out a loud, thunderous chorus of barks and scrabbles so hard against the door that it's like he's trying to pull it down.

I glance over at Roxi, my breath tight. She sits on her haunches, head cocked with interest.

"What the fuck is going on—"

That's when it hits me. A sudden whiff of sweet, smoky fear. After the last few days, I'd know it anywhere.

"Mercy," I breathe.

Max barks more furiously. I press my hands against the door and close my eyes and put my senses out—only this time, I have a target. That target *should* be tucked away in her bed, sated after the good fucking I gave her. At least, that's what I've been telling myself so I don't feel guilty about ditching her without warning.

Something's wrong, though. She's definitely not in her bed, because I can sense her nearby. My first thought is that she's coming to see me again, which I'll admit gives me a warm little swell in my chest even though it shouldn't. But no. Her fear wouldn't be that strong just from walking through the night, even alone.

And Max wouldn't be acting like this, either. He senses danger. Just not danger to me.

"You motherfucker," I tell him. "You like her, don't you?"

I step away from the door, squeezing my hands into fists. I ought to just leave it. I like her well enough that I don't want to kill her, but I can't get involved with this bullshit arrangement Gunner has set up with her—even if it does send a sour twist of jealousy through my belly. I have no business getting involved with human women, even one who managed to charm my guard dog.

And yet I'm still standing here. Not grabbing my suitcase. Not loading up my car and planning how I'm going to get around the patrol.

Max slams against the door, his teeth bared and a growl emanating from deep in his throat.

Then Mercy's fear spikes.

It's not just fear, though. It's sorrow. That same sweet, overpowering sadness I felt the first time I saw her down by the river.

"Fuck." I try to shove Max back as I fling the door open, but he tears out of my grip and takes off across the courtyard. "Fuck!" I shout, louder, and I follow him. I know exactly where he's going because I'm following the same scent.

It leads me around the block to another set of empty cabins. Visually, they all look abandoned—no lights, no movement. But the one closest to the walkway is throbbing with life. Mercy is in there—frightened, angry, upset. Someone else is in there, too. A man. And he's not fucking upset at all

I know, with a sudden and blazing clarity, that I'm going to kill him.

Max bounds up to the cabin's front door, barking furiously. "Heel," I order, and to my relief, he listens, falling silent and backing off from the doorway. His hackles are still up, though. Teeth bared.

"I've got this," I tell him. "Wait."

Then I kick the door in, the flimsy wood splintering beneath my boot heel. A male voice shouts from inside the house, a mix of surprise, confusion, and guilt. I stomp inside, my bloodlust surging inside me as I follow the delicious trail of Mercy's fear.

I know what I'm going to find, but knowing it intellectually and *seeing* it are two different things.

There's Mercy, *my* Mercy, on the couch, naked, tear tracks over her cheeks.

And there's one of the goddamned church guards scrambling away from her, his pants shoved down over his hips.

"What the hell?" he shouts. "What are you doing here?"

I look over at Mercy, and she lets out a soft, hiccupy sob. She's not afraid anymore. But I can still sense her shame and her sorrow. Her self-loathing.

"I'm sorry," she whispers.

I look back at the guard. I've seen him before. He's always hanging around Gunner and Gunner's right-hand man, Sullivan. I don't remember his name, just his smarmy smile. He's not smiling now, though. He's glaring at me as he tries to tuck his cock back in his pants.

"This is none of your business," he spits out, although I hear the fear behind his words. Not real fear, not life or death fear, although that'll be here soon enough. He's just afraid of getting caught. "Go back to your cabin, preacher. This is a church matter."

I step toward him. Cold. Calm. His fear twists and darkens, and I can't help but smile a little.

Because he's slowly realizing what I am.

"Mercy," he says softly. "Mercy, you need to run."

"Mercy doesn't need to do anything she doesn't want to." The words come out slow as molasses. "Mercy's safe."

That's all I need to say before I let the bloodlust take me completely.

I launch myself at Mercy's rapist using all my speed. He shrieks and tries to duck away, but I'm much too fast for him. I grab him by the neck and slam him up against the nearby wall, hard enough that I leave a smear of blood behind. Then I fling him down to the floor, slamming his head against the cheap vinyl floorboards. He chokes and sputters, blood oozing between his lips. I pin him there one-handed, fury surging through my blood.

"You shouldn't have touched her," I snarl, tightening my fingers around his throat. He grabs at my wrist, kicking desperately up against me. But he's human, and I'm furious.

I drag his head up by his neck and then slam it back down again. Again. Blood splatters across the floor. "Don't fucking touch her," I growl, over and over. "Don't touch her. Don't *fucking touch her.*"

He's dead. I sense it when his life cuts out, when he goes from being prey to being meat. And with that death, the rage washes out of me. I drop him, staring down at his ruined head and the gore splattered across the floor, trying to catch my breath. Trying to calm myself.

Behind me comes a choking, terrified whimper.

The full realization of what I just did slams into me. I jump to my feet, whirling around to face Mercy. She's pressed up against the wall, still naked, tears streaming over her face, her mouth twisted in anguish.

"You're safe," I tell her immediately. "I'm not going to hurt you."

Even though I should. She knows what I am now. She knows, and she's horrified by it.

"It was you," she chokes out, shoulder hitching with her sobs. "All this time. You—you killed—*why?*" She screams the last word. "Why did you do that? Why did you—"

She doesn't finish her last question because she breaks down into tears instead, but I can guess what she was going to ask. Why *did* I fuck her?

Because I thought I would get out of this compound before this happened. Before she discovered what I am.

"I'm really not going to hurt you," I murmur, reaching out to her on instinct—only to realize as I do that my hand is covered in blood and specked with brain matter. Mercy screams when she sees it and darts sideways, her panic making her thoughtless. I grab her around her waist before she bursts out of the house and ruins this for both of us.

"No," I whisper into her, pulling her up to me without thinking about how painfully hard I am. When she feels my erection, she screams again. Tries to get away. "No, I can't let you do that."

"Why?" she sobs.

"I don't want to get caught."

Mercy slumps down, weeping. I whistle softly, and a few seconds later, Max shoots into the house. He goes straight to Mercy and licks her fingers, which makes her hiccup and jerk back in fear.

"He's *really* not gonna hurt you," I murmur into her hair, still holding her tight. "He's the reason I even knew you were in trouble."

Mercy wails out her terror, and I know we can't stay here. I got what I came for, which means it's time for me to vanish into the desert. As for Mercy, I've got two options:

Kill her, or take her with me.

"Why?" she whispers, over and over like she's reciting a prayer. "Why? Why me? Why did you do this to me? Why?"

Max keeps licking at her fingers, trying his damnedest to bring her a little comfort. I slide my hand up over her chest, inching closer to her throat.

Because you're beautiful, I think, even though I know better than to say it aloud. Because of the way she yields to my touch. Because of the sound of her scream shattering the early morning silence beside the Concho River.

I have one hand squeezing around her waist, pinning her up against me. The other lays over her heart because I can't bring myself to kill her.

Fuck. *Fuck.*

"They're going to arrest you," she babbles. "They're going to arrest *me*, they'll think I had something to do—"

"That's not going to happen." Her fear scent is overpowering in its sweetness, and I wish, with a sudden, violent clarify, that she was one of my kind. That I could throw her into the puddle of blood oozing across the floor and fuck her until we're both drenched in death and moaning with pleasure. It would make this so much easier, wouldn't it?

God, Jaxon really lucked out.

But I'm not Jaxon, and I'm not lucky, and right now I'm holding a panicked, terrified human woman that I don't want to kill.

"Mercy," I whisper softly. "Mercy, I'm not going to hurt you, okay? I need you to remember that."

It doesn't do any good. She screams and kicks against me, which I expect. I clamp my hand over her mouth and drag her into the kitchen, Max trotting behind us, still trying to lick at Mercy's fingers. These cabins are furnished, just like mine is. There'll be something in here I can use.

I keep my hand clamped around Mercy's mouth as I jerk the drawers open, the contents rattling. Mercy screams in terror, her breath hot and damp against my palm, but I skip right past the drawer of knives, even if my belly tightens at the sight of them.

"Fuck." I drag Mercy across the kitchen, over beside the stacked washer/dryer, and that's where I finally find what I was hoping for: a roll of black duct tape. She wails when she sees it, thrashing against me. Her panic is thick as syrup, and I'll admit I like it. A lot. But I've got to focus on getting us out of here.

I let go of Mercy's mouth just long enough to wrap the tape

around it, silencing her once again. She stares at me from over the top of the tape, her eyes wide with fear and red from weeping. It's the hottest fucking thing I've ever seen, but I snapshot the image for later and keep going. Lord knows Mercy's never gonna let me touch her again.

I really should kill her. But I just don't want to.

I wrench the tape around Mercy's wrists, binding her hands behind her back. Do the same with her ankles. It takes a few minutes, with all her squirming and all those betrayed, terrified glances from above the tape. By the time I'm done, my cock is so hard, so sensitive, that the fabric of my underwear is almost enough to set me off.

I ease her down on the kitchen floor, where she rolls back and forth in a panic. My balls tighten like I'm about to come.

"Watch her," I tell Max.

He barks once, then curls up at Mercy's side, tail thumping. Mercy's muffled screams follow me into the living room, where I grab a blanket off the sofa and gather up her clothes—the dress, the panties. No bra. Because three hours ago, I was cutting it off her, and she was willingly spreading her legs for me.

Now she's seen what I really am, and I'm afraid it might have broken her. The idea doesn't exactly diminish my erection, though.

Back in the kitchen, Mercy lays sideways, bound and weeping and naked. And for a moment, all I can do is stare at her—her anguish and suffering and terror are so beautiful. Exquisite. Perfect. And I want more than anything to mar that perfection, to pull my throbbing cock out and jerk off until she's strung with my cum.

I don't, of course. I just stomp over to her, throw the blanket around her, and heave her up over my shoulder. She screams and kicks and having her on me like that is too much.

Her fear wafts around me, as delicious as the scent of her lust, and I can't stand it—

I come with a strangled choke, a wet spot growing across my underwear.

I stare at the empty wall, sucking down breaths of air. "I'm not going to hurt you," I gasp out, for what it feels like the millionth time.

I know she doesn't believe me. I know it's pointless. But at least it's the truth.

CHAPTER TWENTY-FOUR

MERCY

I sob into the duct tape, my eyes sticky with my tears. I keep expecting to run out of them somehow, like I'll sob so much that all the moisture will leach out of my body. But of course that doesn't happen. I keep weeping.

Tires scrape against asphalt. I'm in the back seat of Ambrose's ancient sedan, still bound in duct tape and wrapped up in the blanket from the cabin. Static-laced country music plays softly in the background. Max is curled up next to me, his body warm and soft and comforting. I don't understand it.

I'm not going to hurt you, Ambrose keeps saying, but he already has.

He's the demon that tormented my home. He's the killer.

I'm so, so stupid.

I close my eyes. My weeping is mostly silent now, just an endless river of tears and an all-encompassing web of despair that wraps around me like a blanket. Ambrose hasn't said anything since he got in his car and started driving. I don't even know how he got off the compound without anyone seeing. He never stopped and talked to anyone. Just laid me in the back seat, got behind the wheel, and drove away.

This is what you wanted, some small, vicious voice whispers in the back of my head. *You wanted to abandon Reverend Gunner. Now the devil's stolen you away.*

The devil also stopped Deacon Price, another thought I can't bear to consider.

I let out a soft sob against the duct tape, my body shuddering. Max lifts his head and whines a little. Then he licks my face. I shouldn't trust Ambrose's dog, should I? But I think Max is the only thing keeping me from losing my mind.

"Is she okay back there?" It's the first thing Ambrose has said since we left the Church of the Well.

Max barks once.

"Good."

I lay still, holding my breath. I feel like a little girl hiding from a monster. If Ambrose doesn't hear me, he'll forget I'm here.

"I'm taking you west," he says, shattering the illusion. He sounds exactly as he did before I knew what he was, his voice low and rough with that reassuring Texas twang. "Got a place out in the flatlands. It's nice. You'll like it."

"Take me home!" I scream into the duct tape, although it doesn't sound anything like that. But somehow, Ambrose seems to understand.

"Yeah, I can't do that," he says. "Can't risk you telling them what I am."

I scream in frustration, kicking my legs out. Max whines and nudges at me, but I roll away from him, trying to flip onto my other side. I can't, though. The back seat is too narrow.

"We'll be there in about an hour," Ambrose says. "Just try to relax."

My vision floods with tears, and I slump against the seat, my tears wet and choking.

"You're completely safe," he says, as if he hasn't carved my heart out a million times over.

MY EYES FLUTTER open to dusty, hazy sunlight. There are a few seconds where all I feel is a vague stir of confusion—*How did I oversleep? I never oversleep*—and then the memories of last night come slamming through me.

I jerk up to sitting, shocked when I realize my hands aren't bound. Neither are my feet. I'm also in a bed, the blankets tucked around me. I'm still naked, through.

Terror courses through my chest, and I scramble up to standing, dragging the blanket up to cover my nudity. I'm in a small, tidy bedroom, the furniture dated but clean. There are thin curtains across the windows and a chest of drawers in the corner, my dress lying across the top.

I scurry over and grab the dress and slide it back on, along with my underwear. I'm not sure how to feel about it, that Ambrose—if that's even his name—left my clothes for me. I don't see my shoes, though.

I have to get out of here.

I go to the window first, shoving the curtains aside to get a look outside. All I see is pale, fluttering grass rolling out from the house and a few twists of mesquite trees. I try to open the window, but it only slides up about four inches before it jams. Hot, dry wind blows across my face.

I whirl around and eye the door. He didn't leave me bound and gagged, but he's still a psychopath. A monster.

And suddenly I'm thinking about what he did to Deacon Price, slamming his head against the floor while blood splattered up against the wall. I keep hearing the sound of it, crunching and wet, and my stomach lurches, bile rising up in my throat. I swallow it back down.

Don't fucking touch her.

Ambrose's voice swirls around in my head. More images come flooding in: The way he chanted *Don't touch her* while he brutalized Deacon Price. The way he broke down the door to get at me. Max running up to lick my hand when he was done. *He's the reason I even knew you were in trouble.*

I suck down a deep lungful of air, my whole body trembling. I stare at the doorknob. I know it's locked. Ambrose is a murderer—

But is he *the* murderer? Did he kill Raul? Burl?

I sit down on the bed, my whole body vibrating. Of course he's the murderer. Who else would it be? I saw what he was capable of. I watched those hands that brought me so much pleasure rip the life out of another human being.

My stomach lurches again, and this time I can't stop my sickness. I lean over and retch across the floor. When I'm done, I stare up at the door again, tears streaming out of my eyes, my mouth burning.

I have to try it. I know it's going to be locked, but I have to try it.

Moving in a panic, I surge forward, yanking hard on the knob.

It turns.

I'm so shocked that I release it and stumble back. The door swings open, revealing a dim hallway outside.

I jerk back, frozen with a new fear. This is a trap. A test.

But there's nothing even close to a weapon in my room. Why would there be? And it's not like I can fight against Ambrose, anyway. I know firsthand how strong he is. How easily he can pin me down and overpower me.

How easily he could kill a grown man barehanded just for touching me.

I sniffle back tears and take a hesitant step toward the doorway, straining for any sounds in the house—footsteps, breathing, anything. But nothing waits for me on the other side. Just a dim hallway, the walls covered in a faded floral wallpaper from the '70s.

I creep out, shaking so badly I can barely walk. The house is quiet save for the persistent hum of an air conditioner. My room is at one end of a hallway; at the other are two entrance-ways, both glowing with dim sunlight.

Something moves in one of the rooms.

I scream and bolt forward, my fear calcifying into a need for survival. But I don't get far, because a dark shape leaps out of one of the bedrooms and slams me up against the wall. I scream until I realize it's a dog—it's Max, actually, and he's not attacking me. He's licking my face.

"Let me go!" I sob, trying to push him away. He whines and wags his tail, wanting to play. I scramble out from under him—

And run straight into Ambrose's strong, unyielding chest.

"You don't need to do that," he says softly.

I scream again and try to jerk away from him. He's faster than me, and stronger, and he grabs both of my arms and pulls me up to him, never letting go even as I screech and thrash against his grip.

"Let me go!" I scream. "Let me go, you devil!"

"Can't do that," he says softly. "But I told you I'm not going to hurt you, and I meant it."

He drags me into a living room filled with the same old-fashioned furniture as the bedroom. A couple of ancient recliners. A velour sofa. Bookshelves covered in dust. Thick curtains that block out most of the sun.

"Sit," he tells me, forcing me down on the sofa. I do, lifting my gaze to take him in.

He towers over me, looking nothing like a preacher. He wears a tight white tank top and cut-off black sweatpants. Faded tattoos crawl over his biceps and shoulders, a melange of shapes that bleed together into smoke. I let this man inside me and I didn't know he has tattoos because he was always completely covered up. A wolf in sheep's clothing.

"You're not a preacher," I whisper, the first thing I think to say even though it's stupid.

Ambrose stares at me for a long moment, his eyes black as pitch. Why didn't I see that before?

"No," he says. Then: "Not anymore."

We stare at each other. My breaths come out shuddery and ragged and I keep waiting for him to grab me by the neck the way he did Deacon Price and slam my head against the wooden floorboards.

"Is your name really Ambrose?"

He tilts his head, frowning. I don't expect him to answer.

"Yes," he says. "Actually, it is."

Then he crouches down in front of me, putting us closer to eye level. I jerk away on instinct, twisting my hands up in my skirt. Ambrose keeps drinking me in. It reminds me too much of our first night together. I had been afraid then, too, but for different reasons. It never even occurred to me he could be what he is.

"Why?" I whisper.

"You're gonna need to be more specific."

For some reason, that sends a new wave of fear shooting through me. I press myself against the back of the couch, eyes darting around. Ambrose shakes his head.

"Don't try to escape," he says. "I'm faster than you. Stronger than you. I can sense things you can't. I have every advantage over you."

I choke back tears. Choke back at my fear. "Why?" I scream it this time, and he sighs, pushes one of his hands through his hair. His tattoos ripple across his muscles.

"I'm the fucking boogeyman," he says.

I stare at him in disbelief—because of all the ways he could answer, *that's* what he goes with?

His face is as handsome as it was the first time I saw him, but now I recognize the darkness lurking there. I see the devil in his sharp features. A devil that dragged me to hell with him.

"You killed Raul, didn't you?"

It's not until the question is out, hanging in the air between us, that I hope the answer is no. But Ambrose flicks his gaze away from me, and I know it was too much to hope for. Blood pounds through my head, and I drop my mouth open and wail, a long toneless sound I barely recognize as coming from me. Ambrose says nothing. Does nothing. Just watches me, his eyes glittering.

Max clicks into the living room, hops on the sofa beside me, puts his head on my lap. I want to push him away, but I'm too afraid. I'm too afraid to do anything but cover my face and wail out my terror.

Ambrose lets me.

I sob into my hands, trembling and shaking. When I finally lift my gaze, Ambrose is still there, watching me with a predator's gaze.

"Why me?" I whisper. "Why did you do this to me?"

Ambrose sighs a little, his shoulders hitching. "I didn't—" He drops his gaze to Max. "What I am. Why I did this. It's complicated." He lifts his gaze to meet mine. "You probably won't believe me if I told you."

"Try me," I snarl.

Ambrose rises to his feet, his eyes never leaving mine. "You wouldn't," he says, more firmly. "Which is why I'm going to show you instead."

Fear surges through me again, and Ambrose sniffs the air, his eyes burning the way they did when we were in the bunker together. I press my thighs together, hating that my body floods with a sudden flare of lust.

He's a killer. He killed Raul.

"I'm fond of you," he says roughly. "Which is as unsettling for me as it is for you."

I curl into myself, sinking my hand into Max's fur for support. Ambrose's cut-off sweatpants don't leave much to the imagination, and I can see the outline of his erection, which sends another wave of black lust surging through me.

"I'm not going to kill you," he says, walking over to the dusty bookshelf. "Don't *want* to kill you."

He picks something up. I shiver, digging my fingers into Max's fur. Max nudges at me with his wet nose, but I don't dare take my eyes off Ambrose's lean, muscular back.

When he turns around, he's holding an enormous hunting knife. I stifle a scream.

"I'm not going to kill you," he says calmly. "But I've got to show you I'm not human."

Then he shoves the knife into his belly and drags it sideways, splitting himself open.

CHAPTER TWENTY-FIVE

MERCY

I scream and jump to my feet as blood gushes out of the wound Ambrose just carved into himself. He looks at me with that black, glittering gaze and tosses the blood knife to the ground with a metallic clatter.

"Come here," he growls.

"What did you do?" I can't move. I can't even believe what I'm seeing. His blood looks too red, too bright. *Just like Burl's blood.*

I swoon in place, throwing out my hand to balance on the couch.

"Cut myself open." Ambrose pushes one blood-soaked hand through his hair, leaving streaks of crimson in its wake. Max nudges at my hand, seemingly completely unconcerned for his person.

"But why?" I whisper, my whole body trembling. "Why did you—you'll *die.*"

Ambrose grins. "No, I won't. Now come here." He uses that same rough, demanding voice from when we were intimate, and despite the horror of the situation, my body reacts as it did before, with a curl of shameful heat. However, it's just as quickly overpowered by something like worry—

Surely I *want* him to die? He kidnapped me.

But no. I don't.

"You have to stop the bleeding." I stumble over to him, acting on some deep-rooted instinct to protect a man that I had, up until twelve hours ago, wanted to love. I press my hands against the wound, and blood seeps hot and sticky through my fingers.

Ambrose grabs my wrists and yanks my hands away. "I told you," he murmurs, leaning in close to rasp into my ear. "I'm not going to die."

"You disemboweled yourself!"

He cups my jaw with his blood-streaked hands, positioning my gaze on his. "I did not," he said evenly. "I didn't cut deeply enough."

And then he kisses me.

I'm stunned by the fervor of the kiss, his hot and hungry mouth devouring my own. His other hand, equally blood-soaked, comes up and cups the side of my hair, holding me in place as he deepens the kiss, as I—

As I kiss him back.

I know I shouldn't. He's a murderer. He killed Raul and Burl and Deacon Price. And he just sliced himself open in front of me, and now his blood is soaking through the fabric of my dress until I feel it cling to my belly. But his kiss still inflames me, and as he devours me I try to devour him back, my hands on his shoulders. I'm afraid to press into him. Afraid I'll hurt him.

Ambrose breaks the kiss with a groan and clutches at my face, smearing my cheeks with more blood. His eyes blaze with —not lust. It can't be lust, even though it looks like it.

It's pain, I tell myself. "You need to go to the hospital."

"No, I don't." He pushes me backward until my legs bump against the couch. "I'm proving something to you."

"What?" I screech. "What could you possibly be proving with this?"

His only answer is a sharp, shrill whistle. There's a jangle of dog tags as Max scrambles to the floor and out of the living room. Then Ambrose pushes me down on the couch, and I stare up at him, legs akimbo beneath my blood-soaked dress. His tank top is crimson, so drenched with blood I can't even make out the wound.

"I'm proving to you what I am." He runs his blood-sticky hand up the inside of my thigh, making me shiver. "A human man couldn't survive what I'm about to do."

"What?" I scream, scrambling backward. Ambrose grins and catches my arms, pinning me down.

"I'm not human," he purrs. "I'm the boogeyman. But I'm not going to hurt you. I'm going to make you feel good."

I swoon, my eyes rolling back in my head as he presses his lips to my neck and licks the blood away. I can smell it everywhere, coppery and pungent.

"You're the devil," I gasp out, terror coiling around me.

"A devil," he says into the hollow of my throat, his breath making me shiver. "More or less." He pulls away, eyes blazing with a madness that makes lust flare deep in my belly. He never looks away from me as he reaches down and pulls out his erection, as covered in gore as the rest of him.

"You can't," I gasp.

"Why not?" He pushes his hand up along the inside of my thigh again, and despite my best intentions not to, I still moan with pleasure as his fingers find my clit. "Because you don't want me?"

"Because you're hurt," I gasp out, trying not to think about the blood on his fingers as he parts my folds to gather the wetness between my legs—a wetness I can't deny as he swipes it around my clit, making me moan.

"So you do want me?"

"You're a killer!" I scream, and Ambrose pulls his hand away from my clit and presses it against my thigh.

"That didn't answer the question," he says.

I stare at him, sucking down breaths. He looks like a nightmare towering over me, his entire midsection drenched in blood.

"Why are you doing this?" I whisper.

Something flickers across his expression. His fingers drift up into my folds again, and he slides two fingers inside me, making me gasp and squirm with pleasure. I try not to think about the blood on them. About the blood on his thumb as he circles it around my clit.

"I don't know," he says. "There's something special about you."

"You're hurt," I whimper, squirming beneath his touch. "You're a killer. You're—"

"Let me fuck you." Ambrose shifts forward, his blood-sticky erection pressing into my thigh as he continues to touch me in that way that makes me feel like I'm falling apart. "One last time. I want to remember how good this fucking pussy feels around my cock."

I moan at his filthy words, at his filthy touch. His rubs me faster, and to my horror, I buck into his hands, groaning and arching my back.

"Well?" He crawls on top of me, shoving my bloody skirt up around my waist until I'm exposed for him.

Waiting for him.

"If I say no, will you even stop?"

A dark cloud crosses Ambrose's face. "Yes. But you're not going to say no."

He's right. I hate that he's right. I hate that I like what he's doing to me, our bodies both drenched in blood. I hate that I don't understand how he's even doing all of this, that his belly is gaping open and still his eyes are bright and his touch is firm.

He really is the boogeyman. He really is the devil.

"What'll it be, Mercy?" He slides another finger inside me, and I quake with pleasure. He's the only man who knows how to touch me. The only man who knows how to make me feel pleasure.

"Yes," I scream. "Take me, you damned monster!"

Ambrose breaks into a manic, terrifying grin. He doesn't look human at all.

He's *not* human. That's what he said.

A devil. More or less.

"That's what I've been waiting to hear," he growls, and I know I'm damning myself for moaning beneath his pliable fingers, for spreading my legs for this abomination.

But I don't care.

I don't care when he grabs hold of his bloody cock and presses it against my entrance, his eyes fluttering closed and his lips parting. I hold my breath, squeezing my hands into fists, and when Ambrose slides his full length inside me, I sob with pleasure, all the nerves in my body on fire.

"I thought I'd never get to feel this again," he sighs, rolling his hips against me. His belly presses against mine, the blood hot and slippery between us. "This perfect human cunt."

"You're not human," I gasp. "You're the Deceiver."

"Well, I'm *a* deceiver, certainly." His mouth latches onto mine, pulling me into another hungry, desperate kiss as he rolls his hips against me to fill me over and over with his hardness. "And a killer. A monster. I don't deny any of those things."

"You lied to me," I moan, clutching at his hips. His wound doesn't seem to slow him down at all. He thrusts into me as hard as he did last night in the bunker, striking so deep inside my body that I see dots of light in my vision.

"I know. But I'm not lying now." He kisses down my chin to bite and suck at my neck—it hurts, a little, but it feels good, too. Just like everything about him. He plunged a knife into my heart as surely as he did his own belly, but I can't feel it anymore. All I feel is the pleasure of his cock inside me, of his bloody skin grinding against my clit, his teeth sinking into the delicate skin of my throat.

I'm going to come for him. I feel the certainty of it building into a pressure in my core, and I grind up against him, desperate for my release.

He doesn't give it to me, though. Instead, he pulls back and gives me another terrible, manic grin. And still he's thrusting into me, the muscles in his body tensing beneath his tattooed skin. He looks exactly like the devil of my nightmares, the devil that Madelyn said would devour me if I disobeyed Reverend Gunner.

And he *is* devouring me.

But it isn't the horror I thought it would be.

"I'm showing you exactly what I am," Ambrose says softly, sliding his fingers up through my hair. "And you like it, don't you? You like what you see?"

I moan because he's right and because I'm on the precipice of my orgasm.

"Answer me." He pulls hard on my hair, and I don't have to answer with words because my body does it for me. My orgasm explodes outward in a rush of feverish pleasure, and all I can do is let out a string of whimpering, desperate moans. Ambrose never stops fucking me, even when the heat of his cock almost feels too much to bear. His face twists up, and he bares his teeth and rasps, "Was that a yes? You like what you see?"

He's fucking me harder than should be possible with the wound in his belly. We're both drenched in blood. But all that seems to matter to him is drawing a single word from my lips.

I stare at him, my gaze unfocused: this monster who destroyed my life. He's the most beautiful man I've ever seen, and the most terrible.

"Yes," I whisper.

Ambrose roars and slams so deeply inside me that pain bursts in my core, just for a second, like a kind of dessert after the dinner of my orgasm. Then he draws back, pulling out of me completely. I feel his seed leaking out between my thighs, as thick and hot as his spilled blood.

For a moment he stays like that, his arms braced against the couch, his sweat- and blood-soaked hair falling into his eyes. I'm too afraid to move. But then he lifts his gaze to meet mine, his expression unreadable.

"Give me your hand."

"What? Why?" My fear brightens, and Ambrose runs his tongue over his lips, his eyes boring down into me.

"Told you I'm not going to hurt you." He grabs me by the wrist and pulls my hand up to him—

Up to the bloody patch on his belly.

"No!" I cry out instinctively, afraid he's going to make me hurt him more somehow. Ambrose laughs, hard and cruel, and presses my hand to his stomach.

At first, I don't understand what I'm feeling. His shirt is soaked with blood, and I can feel the slow rise and fall of his breath and the faint ripple of his muscles contracting beneath his belly's softness. But then I realize something's missing.

He isn't cut.

I gasp and jerk my hand away. Ambrose grins and slumps back on the sofa, his arms draped over his knees. He looks like the demon he said he was—a vile, gore-soaked monster.

"You were cut," I whisper.

"I was." He shifts around, stretching out beside me, and pushes up the ruin of his tank top. "But I healed up fast."

"That's impossible." I shake my head, my fear sparking through me. "That's—I *saw* it. I saw the knife go into—" I gag on the words, and Ambrose reaches over and tucks my hair behind my hair, leaving blood streaked across my cheek.

"It did. Hurt like shit, too." He runs his fingers down my

arm to circle them around my wrist again. I'm too confused, too frightened, to try and fight when he pulls my hand forward and presses it once again to his belly. "There'll be a scar. Feel it."

I don't feel anything but blood and firm, warm skin. But then he slides my hand a little lower, and my fingers graze across a ridge of scar tissue. Trembling, I let my hands trace along the scar as it runs from one side of his torso to the other.

"I sliced eight inches into myself to show you what I am," Ambrose says softly.

I yank my hand away. "A demon."

But he shakes his head. "No. A Hunter."

CHAPTER TWENTY-SIX

AMBROSE

Mercy's fear is like the fine, smokey tequila I used to drink in my youth. The Aguirre family in my hometown distilled it in a little wooden building outside their house, and I always carried a bottle with me whenever I went on my travels. But that branch of the Aguirre line died out sometime in the 1950s, and I haven't tasted anything like it since.

Until now.

Mercy stares at me from where she's curled up on the couch, a vision drenched in blood. She's tucked her skirts around her thighs, but I saw what her cunt looked like when I slid out of her, how my wound painted it crimson while I fucked her. There's a part of me that wishes I could skip the conversation we're about to have and dive between her legs and clean her with my tongue.

Maybe I'll do it when we're done. A reward for breaking a promise to myself and my mother to never tell a human about the nature of my people.

"What do you mean when you say you're a Hunter?" she asks, her voice trembling. "You hunt people?"

"Yes," I say. "That's exactly what I mean."

Her fear spikes, and I breathe it in, getting drunk on it like I used to the Aguirres' tequila. But not so drunk I can't stop her when she tries to scramble off the couch. I grab her by the waist and pull her onto my lap, all in the span of a few seconds. Mercy lets out a terrified gasp and goes petrified on top of me. Can't say I mind.

"Let me explain," I mutter into her ear, smoothing her hair away from her neck. The blood looks so pretty on the blond, violence mixed with sunlight. "I keep telling you I'm not going to hurt you, and I mean it."

"Why not?" she sobs. "Why do you keep—touching me and making me—" Her voice falters.

"I'm fond of you." I shift her around so she's draped across my lap sideways and I can stare down at her blood-streak face, her features even more delicate when she's terrified. "Would rather keep you in this world than take you out of it."

"But you weren't *fond* of Raul," she spits out.

I sigh. "Raul was a means to an end. If it makes you feel any better, he didn't suffer."

He's also currently tucked away in my deep freeze, or at least the meaty parts of him, but I don't mention it.

"But *why?*" she demands, fury momentarily working through her fear. I like it. A sprinkle of cayenne mixed in with the smoke.

"I needed to get on the Church of the Well compound to find Charlotte's file. That part was true." I smile at her, hoping to reassure her a bit. It doesn't work. "But Gunner keeps y'all isolated, and I needed a way to destabilize things so I could get on the campus." I brush my fingers through my hair, and it pleases me when she doesn't pull away. "Fortunately for me, there was a beautiful woman down by the Concho when I—"

"Don't do that," Mercy snarls. "Don't *compliment* me like that."

"It's true, though." I smooth her hair away from her face, and she keeps glaring at me, but she doesn't bat my hand away. Doesn't try to scramble off my lap. Maybe she's too afraid to move—but I don't think so. She did let me fuck her, after all.

"You still haven't told me what you are," she says. "Why you were able to cut yourself like that."

My chest squeezes with tension. Talking about killing is one thing. Human men kill all the time. But this, the truth of what I am—this is what I don't want to tell her.

"You called me a demon," I say carefully. "But I'm not from hell. I'm not a spirit. Not in league with Satan."

Mercy glares at me, even though the fire of her anger still hasn't overtaken her fear.

"But I am—more than human." Her body is warm against mine, her heart thudding wildly. "Better than human. Capable of hunting humans to fill an urge I don't think you could ever understand."

Mercy pales beneath the blood. "But what *are* you?"

I consider this question for far longer than I probably should. "There's no word for what I am," I finally say. "My people, people like me—we have different names for ourselves. My mother called us los cocos."

"The coconuts?" Mercy says flatly.

I bite back a smile—she's terrified, my pretty blood-soaked human, but she still has some fight in her.

"No," I say. "El Coco is an old name for the boogeyman in Spanish."

Mercy studies me. I risk snaking my arm around her waist to pull her a little closer. She frowns.

"You're the boogeyman."

"Sí." I trail my fingers along her arm so that the delicate hair there stands on end.

"Why did your cut heal so fast?"

"Why can I hear your heart beating, pretty human?"

She scowls when I say *pretty human*.

"Why can I smell your fear?" I tuck my fingers under her chin and force her to look at me. "Your arousal?"

Her eyes widen and she squeezes her legs shut. I laugh.

"I'm designed to hunt humans like you," I tell her. "I can sniff your kind out in the dark. I'm stronger and faster." I lean close, tilting my head like I'm going to kiss her. And although I had been teasing earlier, now I *do* catch a whiff of her arousal, faint beneath the coppery tang of blood and the maelstrom of her emotions. "But most importantly, I'm impossible to kill."

Mercy's eyes are enormous as she stares up at me. And I take a deep breath. Because this is it. This is the part my mother told me I should never tell another human. *Es nuestro vantaja mejor, mi cielito*, she would say, her long fingers stroking through my hair. *Nunca deberías regalarlo*.

"That cut I gave myself," I say. "If I were a human man, I would be bleeding out right now. I certainly wouldn't have been able to fuck you."

Mercy's cheeks turn crimson.

"I healed quickly because I was—" I grin devilishly. "Engaging in vigorous activity, shall we say? If you had been fighting me, you might have thought you had the upper hand. But the harder I fight, the faster I heal."

"We weren't fighting," she mutters.

"Fighting and fucking are the same as far as the boogeyman's concerned."

That scares her. I breathe the scent in deep. "Now, if I had cut deeper," I continue. "If I had sliced through my organs, I unfortunately would *not* have been able to fuck you. And you would have thought I was dead."

Mercy watches me warily. When I run my hand up her leg, she jolts a little.

"Remember," I purr. "I can smell your arousal."

"You w-wouldn't have really been dead?" she stammers out, my fingers slipping between the thick press of her thighs.

"Not in the way you'll die someday." I stop and look her straight in the eye. "Which won't be anytime soon, by the way. Not for decades."

Mercy doesn't say anything. I keep going.

"But I would have appeared dead." I gently pry her legs open. "My heart would have stopped, I wouldn't be breathing, all that shit. But I would have been able to drag myself outside and burrow in the dirt like a cicada. Then I would have revived."

I stop, my hand nearly to Mercy's softly throbbing clit—I can feel it, undeniable to my Hunter's senses. She's still draped across my lap and my head's still bowed over hers. We're like a bloody pieta. Except she's not dead, and I meant it when I said she won't be.

"Revived?" she whispers.

"Come back from the sort-of-dead," I say. 'That's what I am, humanita. A nightmare. And you can't kill nightmares."

I wait, unmoving. Whatever we do next, it'll be up to her. If she wants to try and test if I'm telling the truth—well, the knife is still lying in my blood a few feet away. I won't let her do any real damage, of course, but I also hope she at least tries it. It'll be fun to let her sink my own blade into my skin, let her know what it's like to be a killer.

But Mercy doesn't go for the knife. She shifts in my lap, rubbing her plump ass against my semi-stiff cock. When she feels it, she bites her lip and presses her thighs around my hand. But she doesn't say anything. Instead, she slides her hand over my belly, feeling once again for my wound.

"It's closed up," she whispers. "It shouldn't—that's impossible." She looks at me, her eyes wet with tears. "You're telling the truth, aren't you?"

"Yes." Something surges up in me, a kind of strange protective desire. "I know I lied to you, Mercy. I'm not a traveling preacher anymore, although I was, a long time ago—"

"How long?"

"A little under two hundred years."

She goes pale again and kind of swoons against me. I can feel her blood pressure dropping, and I scoop my hand behind her head and prop her up.

"But there's a lot I didn't lie to you about," I say fiercely. "Every time I touched you—I meant that. I did. And when I say I'm not going to kill you, that's not a lie, either."

"Why not?" she whispers. "What's so special about me?"

The question brings me up short. Because I don't actually know.

I wonder, briefly, if this is what Sawyer felt like the first time he saw Edie.

"It just feels wrong," I finally say. "To kill you."

Then, because I'm not sure what else to do, I kiss her, taking her face in both hands and pulling her up close to me. She yields to me as beautifully as she did in the Church of the Well bunker, her lips melting into mine. For a long time, all I do is kiss her mouth, slow and sweet, neither of us making a sound.

And then I start working my way down, kissing over her throat to taste the salt of my own blood. Mercy whimpers softly, her hand coming up to tangle in my hair, and I keep going, over the place where her breasts strain against the blood-soaked fabric of her dress. Then I slide her off my lap so I can go even lower, until I'm able to push up her skirt and find the treasure hidden inside.

"What are you do—"

I bite the inside of her thigh, making her yelp. "Licking you clean."

"You can't," she gasps, shifting her hips into my face.

I don't tell her how much I like the taste of blood. Baby steps. But I do drag my tongue along the blood caking her thighs until I find the soft silk of her pussy—and effectively silence any of her protestations. Mercy falls backward, hips bucking up as I dive into her blood-encrusted cunt, devouring my taste in hers with long swipes of my tongue.

"Ambrose," she whimpers, tangling her hands in my hair.

"Be quiet and come for me," I growl before attacking her pussy again, parting her lips open with my tongue so I can give her a good fucking. She groans her appreciation, thighs already starting to tremble around my ears.

And she thought she couldn't come.

I chuckle at the thought as I withdraw my tongue from her pussy so I can lick the blood away from her clit, which just makes her moan and writhe on the couch. I know she's close; all the signs are there in her body, all that fluttering and pounding and rushing. And that just makes me eat her harder, my own blood bursting on my tongue. It's almost enough for me to imagine that I'm devouring her for real, pulling her into me bite by bite.

"Ambrose!" she cries, arching her back with ecstasy. "You shouldn't be doing this—The blood—"

I tear myself away from her sweet cunt to look at her over the ruined mess of her dress. "I'm the fucking boogeyman, remember?" I grin at her, knowing my mouth is smeared with my blood and cum and her arousal, and Mercy's fear spikes, and I nearly come in my goddamn pants again.

"You like this," she whispers.

"No." I shake my head as I slide two fingers inside her to stroke along her inner wall. That undoes her, the way I knew it would. "No, I fucking love it."

Then I dive between her legs again, licking the blood away as I fingerfuck her closer and closer to release. Mercy's leg muscles quiver wildly, and her heartbeat is like a thunderstorm filling up the room.

"Come on, humanita," I murmur. "Come for me."

Then I press my lips to her swollen clit and suck.

Mercy screams, a beautiful shattering sound that goes straight to my dick. Her orgasm moves through her body in waves, and I keep licking her—licking up my blood, licking up her desire.

I keep licking until she's nothing but a quivering mess, melting at my command.

CHAPTER TWENTY-SEVEN

MERCY

I can't believe I let him do that to me—twice. I let him have me twice, even though I know what he is, a murderer and a monster and an abomination.

The boogeyman.

And yet the boogeyman lets me take a shower to wash the rest of his blood away. I stand motionless under the spray, the water steaming around me, my thoughts empty. I'm too exhausted to be confused.

He also brings a change of clothes—an oversized T-shirt, a pair of men's boxer shorts. "Don't have any ladies' clothes," he says apologetically, but that actually makes me feel better. It would be so much worse if he had women's clothes in this house. Women's clothes, but no women.

He's a murderer, I think as I slip on the T-shirt and the boxers. They feel utterly strange to me after a lifetime of dressing for modesty. Decadent, almost. They aren't even particularly revealing, and yet I *feel* exposed, with my bare thighs peaking below the boxers, my knees open to the cool air of his house. Ambrose glances at me when I walk into the living room after my shower, sweeping his gaze over my body, making me feel naked and beautiful all at once.

"Want something to eat?"

I should say no. I should fight. I should run. I'm not chained up. But Ambrose would certainly catch me. I've seen what he's capable of, even if it feels impossible.

And even if he didn't—where would I go? I've looked out the windows. We're in the middle of nowhere.

So I just nod, smoothing my shirt down distractedly. "Yes, " I tell him. "Yes, something to eat would be nice."

What he fixes for lunch isn't anything fancy: just a can of tomato soup heated up on the stove, a grilled cheese sandwich. I eat it because I'm hungry, and I feel dizzy with everything that's happened.

And because it tastes good.

When we're finished, Ambrose clears the dishes. I sit at the table in the dining room, listening to him clatter around in the kitchen, fighting the urge to get up and help him the way I was taught. Max snoozes at my feet, his body warm against my leg. He's followed me everywhere since—

Since what happened earlier.

Roxi keeps her distance, though, sitting on her haunches in the kitchen doorway, her eyes on Ambrose. He sings as he puts the dishes away, a soft, haunting melody, the lyrics in Spanish. I catch every other word—something about a witch, something about children.

When he finishes, he comes to stand in the doorway next to Roxi, wiping his hands on a towel before flinging it over his shoulder and then, to my dismay, smiling at me in a way that makes my stomach clench up.

He's so handsome. As handsome as the devil, especially with the dark, blurry tattoos crawling over his bare shoulders.

All of Reverend Gunner's sermons were right. Satan really is Heaven's most beautiful angel. And now I'm in hell with him.

Even if it doesn't feel like hell.

"You've got free run of the house," Ambrose says, leaning in the doorway. "You can go out in the yard if you want, although with this heat—"

I stare at him from across the table. "And if I run?"

His expression doesn't waver. "You're welcome to try. We're fifteen miles from the closest highway. Twenty miles from the nearest gas station. There aren't any other houses out here." He smiles a little, and fear and lust both quiver down my spine. "Plus, I told you. I'm faster and stronger than you. I'll hunt you down before you reach either one."

"And kill me?" I shoot back.

"No."

We stare at each other, neither of us speaking. The silence burns around me.

"What about clothes?" I finally say. "I can't wear T-shirts and boxers for the rest of my life."

"I told you—your life isn't going to end in the next few days."

Icy fear shoots down my spine; I hadn't even been thinking of it in that sense. I don't say anything, though, just wring my hands together under the table.

"We can order some things for you," he says. "Have them delivered in the next few days."

"Why are you being so kind to me?" I spit out the question before I can stop myself. Ambrose tilts his head.

"I thought I made it clear that I'm fond of you."

Then he disappears back into the kitchen, leaving me alone in the dining room. For a long time, I just sit there, trying to process everything that's happened. This is the murderer who terrorized the Church of the Well. This is the man who cut off Raul's head and threw it in the Concho River, the man who cut Burl's throat and then crucified him against Reverend Gunner's fence.

The man who brutalized Deacon Price because he touched me when I didn't want it.

It does not escape my attention, even though I feel strange about it, that Ambrose didn't brutalize *me* for giving in to Deacon Price. Because that's what Reverend Gunner would have done. Well, not literally. He wouldn't have killed me.

But he would have hit me. He would have called me a slut and a whore and reminded me that I belong to him. It wouldn't matter that I hadn't wanted Deacon Price, because it never mattered that I didn't want Reverend Gunner.

But I did want Ambrose.

And Ambrose protected me.

Maybe that's why I still—why I still want him.

how can you want him he killed Raul

I shove away from the table and stalk into the living room, my heart racing. I half-expect Ambrose to be in there, waiting for me, but he isn't. The couch is, though. It's still soaked with his blood.

I whirl away from it and sit down in the overstuffed recliner instead. Turn on the TV. The women aren't allowed to watch TV on the Church of the Well compound, just as we aren't allowed to have cell phones or learn how to drive.

I remember TV, though, from before my parents died. Hazy memories of cartoons and toy commercials. I flip through the channels, gazing at one image after another. Actors I don't recognize. Commercials for drugs I wasn't allowed to take. The Church of the Well compound—

I freeze, my finger hovering over the channel button as I stare at the familiar entrance. A woman's voice speaks over the image.

"—tragedy this month," she's saying. "The church's leadership is urging anyone in the local community to come forward with information."

The image cuts to Reverend Gunner, and I nearly shriek, seeing his face fill up the screen. He looks straight into the camera. His eyes are dry, but that's not a surprise. He's never wept in his life.

"Although three of our brothers have joined their creator," he says solemnly, "we may still be able to save the life of our sister in Christ, Mercy Gunner."

My whole body goes rigid, hearing my name When my photograph appears on the screen, I feel myself disassociate, like I'm rising out of my body. It's the photograph from my marriage ceremony with Reverend Gunner, me in a simple blue dress with flowers braided into my hair. I'm smiling, but only because I had to.

"You don't look happy to be there."

Ambrose's voice makes me scream. I jump up in the chair and turn to find him standing behind me, smirking at the TV.

"They're looking for me," I snap, changing the subject so I don't have to admit to him that he's right. "They actually went to the press about it. To the *police*. Reverend Gunner doesn't do that."

Ambrose frowns and walks around to stand beside me just as the screen fills with a police sketch of his face.

"Police believe this man, calling himself Ambrose Echeverría, may be responsible for all three murders and the disappearance of Mercy Gunner. They ask that if you have any information, please come forward."

I'm petrified, staring at the line drawing of the man who did, in fact, kidnap me. But it's a new fear, and a strange one.

I'm afraid that the police will find Ambrose—that they'll find *me* and take me back to the Church of the Well.

Ambrose picks up the remote and switches the TV off. The silence in the living room throbs in my ears.

"That made you afraid," he says quietly.

I pull my knees up to my chest, staring at the black TV screen. I want to deny it because I'm supposed to be afraid of him, not Reverend Gunner. I'm supposed to want to be rescued.

Ambrose kneels down beside the chair. "Do you want to go back to the Church of the Well, Mercy?"

No. I don't.

The realization hits me hard, as hard as Reverend Gunner's beatings, and leaves me just as breathless. I wanted to be free of that place, and now I am. Maybe I'm not truly free here, either, but it's—

It's different, somehow.

"They know who you are," I say quietly.

Ambrose tilts his head, studying me. "They don't, actually." He smiles thinly. "Ambrose Echeverría's my real name, but that's not the name I bought this house with. Or the car parked in the garage."

I don't say anything.

"I didn't let anyone take my picture while I was on the compound," he continues. "That's why they had to do that police sketch in the first place. And it wasn't even that good of a likeness." He leans close to me, close enough his breath warms my cheek. "I'm designed to hunt your kind, humanita. Which means I know how to blend in and how to hide."

He trails his hand up my arm, and I take a shuddery breath, not wanting him to sense the relief in my chest but knowing he probably does.

"You're a monster," I say, thinking it will hide my true feelings.

"Never denied it," he says. "Also, you didn't answer my question."

"What question?" Even though I know. It's been searing in my thoughts this whole time.

"You don't want to go back," Ambrose says. "Do you?"

My skin prickles with goosebumps. And he notices. His eyes flash, his red tongue shoots out and licks his lips. He looks at me like a meal—

And my body goes hot for it.

"Do you?" Ambrose purrs, his fingers trailing softly along my arm.

There's no point in lying. He can sense everything I feel, and if I try to fight him, his body will stitch back together. I squeeze my shirt hem up in my fist.

"No," I whisper, my voice jagged. "I don't.'"

Admitting that feels like throwing up.

"You'd rather stay here than be there?"

I look over at Ambrose. His black eyes are unreadable. His fingers are still curled protectively around my wrist.

And he's right. I would rather be here, with the devil, than back at the Church of the Well. I don't want to be Reverend Gunner's wife or helpmeet. But I also don't want to be alone in the terrible, secular world.

"Why are they looking for me?" I ask. Anything to avoid answering Ambrose's question. "Why do they care?"

Ambrose releases my wrist to brush his fingers against my cheek. "Sterling Gunner is not really a prophet of God," he says. "God never told him he could take two wives. God never told him he could abuse his adopted fucking daughter."

"I was just his ward," I mutter, shaking beneath Ambrose's touch.

"You're dangerous," Ambrose grabs my chin, his eyes flinty. I relent to his touch, letting him guide me to look up at him. "You can show the rot of that place. That's why he's looking for you."

I tremble. That can't possibly be true.

But it *feels* true.

"I won't let him find you." Ambrose ghosts his hand over my hair and stands up. "As long as you're here with me, you're safe from Sterling Gunner."

And then he stalks out of the living room, leaving me alone with my fear and my confusion.

CHAPTER TWENTY-EIGHT

AMBROSE

I don't know what the fuck I'm doing.

"She's human," I mutter to myself that night while I stroke my cock in the shower. "She's human. She's *human.*"

But all I'm thinking about is her blood-covered cunt, her wide and fearful eyes.

I groan and shudder as cum splatters across the shower tile, then step back with my eyes closed to let the water run over me. I send my senses out to pick up on her—she's still in the house, her body calm with sleep. I'm honestly surprised she hasn't tried to escape, and I'm not sure what it means, exactly. If some part of her really does want to be here with me or if I frightened her enough to stay.

The fact that I hope it's the former, even just a little, is a testament to how foolish she's made me.

I cut the water off, get out of the shower, and towel down. The whole time I can sense her in the background, a human heartbeat pounding through the walls. It's unnerving, truth be told. Being surrounded by humans at the Church of the Well was one thing—that was temporary, and I had a purpose. But this house is my *home*. I don't bring humans here except as meat. Matthew, my delivery driver, has, up until now, been the one exception, and I don't let him inside. He knows his place, knows he can live as long as he's useful to me. As long as he obeys.

I learned years ago the benefits of keeping a few humans around on a long but undeniable leash. They can connect me to the human world and ensure I don't have to worry about details. But that's not what Mercy is.

She's something dangerous.

I get dressed, pulling on the same shorts and tank tops I've been wearing. It's abominably hot, and the house's creaky old AC unit can barely keep the heat at bay. I ordered similar outfits for Mercy this afternoon—sleeveless tops, loose cottony shorts, a handful of sundresses. I didn't want to see her in any more loose-fitting bags.

If I could convince her to walk around naked for me, I would.

I check on her before going back to my bedroom—she *is* asleep, lying on top of the covers. Max is curled up on the floor beside her bed, and he lifts his head when I come in, tail wagging.

"Good boy," I whisper to him, and he settles his head back down on his paws. I like that he's keeping Mercy company. I also like knowing I'm not the only fool in this house.

Roxi, of course, is waiting by my bed, just like she does every night. "You're the smart one," I tell her. "Not a good move, fucking around with humans."

She tilts her head, ears perked up. I scratch her head and sit down at my desk, where I've got my laptop and Charlotte's adoption files. I haven't called her about them yet, mostly because I want to see if I can figure out who these people are. Give her a little something more to go on.

I flip the files open and stare down at the two names: Julia

Medina and Johnny Dobsals. I still think there's a good chance Julia's the human and Johnny's the Hunter.

Still, I type both names into Google and click around, trying to see what I can find. There's not much, not for either of them, and it's hard for me to focus anyway. I keep thinking about this afternoon, Mercy staring in horror at Sterling Gunner on the TV. It is a little concerning that he's finally got the cops involved. Maybe I should have taken a page out of Sawyer's book and tried to make it look like Mercy was dead. Because it seems obvious to me that Gunner doesn't think she is, which puts the heat on me.

On *us*.

I sigh and click through to one of those people finder websites. Julia Medina's on there—last known address in Kansas. No Johnny Dobsals, though. Or John Dobsals, for that matter.

Something shifts in the house, like lungs filling with air. Mercy's awake.

I force myself to focus on my search, even though her being awake is distracting. Her body becomes louder. I can hear her heart echoing with mine.

"Johnny Dobsals," I mutter, like my voice might drown her out. "Who the fuck are you?"

The floor creaks outside my door, and there's no ignoring Mercy now. She's lurking around in the hallway.

"You can come in here!" I call out before I can stop myself, smiling when I feel the jolt of her surprise and embarrassment. She really thought she could sneak up on me.

"Told you—" I push out of my chair and fling the bedroom door open to find her standing sheepishly in the hallway. "You can't hide from me."

"I wasn't trying to." She sounds defensive, though.

"You were trying to do something." I cross my arms and lean in the doorway. She looks rumpled and pretty right now, her hair mussed from sleep. She almost looks the way she does after I've fucked her.

"I just wanted to see if you were awake," she says darkly.

"So you can sneak out?"

Her cheeks turn red. "I don't even have shoes."

"You could stolen some of mine."

Mercy toys with her hair, wrapping it around her finger. "What are you doing?" she asks, not quite meeting my eye.

I hesitate, putting out my senses. As much as I like the idea of her sniffing around for sex, I don't think that's why she's here. I know what her lust tastes like, what it smells like, and I don't sense it now.

Could it be she's just... lonely?

"Trying to find out more about Charlotte's parents." I step away from the doorframe and hold out my arm, inviting her in. "I could use some company."

Mercy peers up at me, the light from my bedroom lamp turning her eyes to stars. "So could I," she says softly.

She steps cautiously into my room, taking it in. Max trots in behind her. Big surprise.

"So Charlotte is real?" she says dully, her gaze settling on the files and laptop, still open to my people search. "You really were trying to get the names of her birth parents?"

"Yeah, I told you. All of that was true." I drag my office chair over and gesture for Mercy to sit down. She stares at it for a moment, then looks up at me—

And then she sits.

"Is she like you?" Mercy studies me. "Is that how you know her?"

God, I really shouldn't be talking about this with a human. But there are a lot of things I've done with Mercy that I shouldn't have.

"She's a Hunter, yes." I kneel beside my chair so I'm not towering over Mercy, and I like how her eyes follow me, dark and cautious. "She was adopted and didn't know what she was until about a year and a half ago, when she met my friend Jaxon."

"Another Hunter," Mercy says. "How many of there are you?"

"Not sure." I look at the laptop screen, *no results for John Dobsals* emblazoned across the top. "I'd guess around seventy-five in North America. Maybe a bit more."

"Why?" she asks. "Why would God create something like that?"

"You think God created us?" I grin at her, and her cheeks turn bright red. "I believe you called me a demon this morning."

"You said you weren't," she shoots back.

It's sweet, watching Mercy try to figure out how my people can fit into her worldview. "Well, I appreciate you believing me, then."

Mercy doesn't say anything, and I just sit back on my heels, waiting for her to respond. She fiddles with the hem of her shirt, twisting it around her fingers.

"You said Charlotte would be my friend," she says suddenly.

I have to admit, this was not where I expected her to go with this conversation. "I meant that, too," I say. "She grew up in the Church of the Well—well, some part of it in California, anyway. That's what kept her from knowing what she was. Those little charms you people make."

Mercy looks sideways at me. "Those are meant to protect from demons."

"Then maybe I'm wrong. Maybe Satan did make us." I grin wickedly at her, but she just scowls.

"Stop making fun of me."

"I'm not." I shift forward, moving a little closer to her. "Look, it doesn't matter if we're demons or not. I do think Charlotte would like you. She grew up around humans, and she has a human best friend, Edie—they're a little older than you, but I think you'd all get along."

"A little older?" Mercy looks at me. "Like two hundred years older?"

"Like ten."

"Oh." Mercy looks down at the birth files and smiles sheepishly. "Right. The files were from the '90s." She studies them, her smile turning to a frown. "Why do you want to find Charlotte's parents?"

"She needs to know more Hunters." I nod at the files. "I thought her father would be a good place to start."

"Just her father?"

I nod. Then I do what I know I shouldn't, which is explain my thinking, about how Hunters don't give their kids up for adoption—way too risky—and that I'm pretty sure this Johnny Dobsals is a fake name for a Hunter. It ought to feel wrong, spilling Hunter secrets like this, but I like how Mercy listens to me, rapt and attentive, nodding along. Once again, she's got me torn in two.

"The name," she says when I'm done. "You think it could be an anagram?"

"Huh." I drag the file over to and look down at *Johnny Dobsals*, typed out nearly on the thirty-year-old paper. "What makes you say that?"

Mercy chews on her bottom lip, long lashes fluttering. "I used to come up with anagrams of my name," she says. "Right after I married Reverend Gunner." She looks down at her hands, her hair falling in her face, and I can't stop myself from reaching over to brush it away, smoothing it over her shoulder. She glances at me, and smiles, and it makes my heart get all warm and tight. "Mercy's not the name my parents gave me," she says. "I was named Kayley until the Gunners took me in and renamed me. But I kept my last name, Hendricks. Mercy Gunner isn't my *legal* name."

"Your legal name is Kayley Hendricks?"

Mercy nods. "But that was—so long ago. I barely even remember my parents. Kayley doesn't feel like my name anymore." She takes a deep breath, and I can feel her bravery surging up inside her, like she's a victim about to make her final stand. "When I was little, I thought that the Gunners changing my name, that was how they claimed me, you know? So after I —" She bites her lips again, and she speaks, it's barely in a whisper. "After I was married, I had this fantasy that I could change my name and I'd be free."

I feel something I haven't felt in a long, long time. Empathy. Pity. I can see Mercy scratching out fake names on a sheet of paper, tears on her cheeks, and it doesn't do anything but make me want to pull her into my arms and kiss her, slow and sweet.

"Stupid, I know," she whispers.

"It's not stupid." I take her hand, braiding her fingers through mine. She looks down at it with mild surprise. "You don't have to change your name," I tell her. "I'm not letting him have you again."

With *those* words, my pity for Mercy disappears, and I just feel the hot flush of need to slaughter Sterling Gunner and the other one who fucked her—Sullivan. It's a much more familiar feeling. A much more *comfortable* feeling.

Mercy smiles a little. "Thank you." She hardly says it out loud.

This time, I do kiss her, rising up just enough that our lips meet. I half-expect her to pull away, but she doesn't. She parts her lips. She lets me in.

"Come on," I whisper against her mouth, pulling her up to stand. She comes with me, eyes shining and bright, the way they were when she still thought I was just a preacher. I guide her to the bed and lay her down, kissing her the whole time. I'm not going to fuck her.

I just want her to not be sad anymore.

CHAPTER TWENTY-NINE

AMBROSE

When the sun rises the next morning, flooding my bedroom with lemony light, Mercy's asleep in my bed, and I know the name of Charlotte's Hunter father.

I slept a little too, after I kissed Mercy's sorrow away and she drifted off to her human dreams. Just for an hour or so. When I woke up, Max was curled up next to Mercy and Roxi was curled at my feet and it was nice, all four of us in one bed. So nice I just stayed there with her, petting her soft golden hair, my thoughts working through anagrams of Johnny Dobsals. And I don't know if it was the sleep or it was the sound of Mercy's soft, heavy breathing, but I figured it out.

Johnny Dobsals *is* an anagram—for a Hunter named Johnson Baldys.

I don't know him well. I only met him once, years and years ago. Sometime in the late 40s, after the war was over. It'd been up north somewhere, Maine or Vermont, one of those leafy New England states.

And I don't think I would have figured it out if Mercy

hadn't told me about inventing anagrams like it might be a way for her to escape Reverend Gunner.

"Muy bien, humanita," I murmur into her ear. She stirs a little but doesn't wake up. I'll let her sleep. The dogs are scrabbling around in the hallway by this point anyway, ready for breakfast.

I slide out of bed, careful not to disturb Mercy, and grab my phone before padding out into the hallway, where Max and Roxi jump around me, tails wagging, tongues lolling. "You're getting kibble," I tell them. "But then we'll do some training."

They both know the word *training*, and they take off like shots toward the back door. It's been about a week since we did it last, since I couldn't very well do it at the Church of the Well. Still, I want to feed them first.

I dump some of the grocery store kibble in their bowls. Max immediately abandons the back door for breakfast, although Roxi takes her time, eyeing me as she strolls into the kitchen. I shrug. "Gotta finish up that kibble first," I tell her. "Then you get your reward."

She relents—begrudgingly.

I brew some coffee and send a text to Charlotte, letting her know the names of her parents. Not even a minute later, my phone rings.

"Are you serious?" she asks when I answer. "This is them?"

"Yeah, I'm pretty sure. I'll let you track them down. You need the practice anyway."

Charlotte scoffs, and I hear Jaxon shout something in the background.

"What's he upset about?" I pour my coffee, watching the dogs. They're almost done eating.

"He's agreeing with you." Charlotte takes a deep breath. It sounds like the phone filling with air. "So, uh, we saw your work at the Church of the Well, by the way."

I freeze, fingers tightening around the phone.

"Yeah, thought you said you were keeping this one clean," Jaxon shouts.

"Take me off speaker phone," I snap. Jaxon cackles.

"I'm not judging," Charlotte says. "I mean, that place fucked me up, so don't get me wrong. I almost kind of admire it. Should have gone after Sterling Gunner, though, not some poor woman."

The dogs have finished eating and are staring up at me, waiting to continue their training. And I debate what to tell Charlotte and her eavesdropping boyfriend.

"The woman's not dead," I finally say.

Charlotte goes quiet. Part of me hopes the line disconnected so I don't have to keep having this conversation.

But then she asks, "Did you pull a Sawyer?"

"Absolutely not. I need to go."

"He pulled a Sawyer!" Charlotte calls out, away from the phone.

"I fucking knew it!" Jaxon's voice is tinny and distant. I hate both of them.

"I'll scan the adoption files and email them to you," I say. "But you need to be looking for Johnson Baldys, okay?"

"Is she at your house?"

"Goodbye." I end the call before she can say anything else. Then, after a moment of consideration, I turn the phone off entirely.

Max and Roxi stare up at me expectantly.

"I don't want to hear it from you two, either." I take a deep breath. "Now, are you ready for training?"

Roxi barks in excitement, and they both tear off for the back door, their nails skittering against the tile. I pick up my coffee and follow behind them. When I push it open they burst out into the back pasture like two sleek bullets. I step into my yard shoes and amble after them, siping at my cooling coffee, heading toward the barn. It's locked up tight—protection for while I was away. After all, it's the place where the truly wicked things are kept.

Things I want to hide from Mercy.

Did you pull a Sawyer? Charlotte's question ricochets around in my head while I spin the dial on the padlock. No, I did not. Sawyer fell in love with a human and got himself shot in the head for his trouble; it took fifteen years for him to revive and the first thing he did was seek her out again.

I just—brought Mercy back to my house because she knows what I am. I'm just keeping her here until I decide what to do.

At least, it feels good to tell myself that, anyway.

I crack open the barn door. The dogs know the sound, and Roxi bays as they come racing out of the pasture and over to where I stand waiting for them.

"Good job," I tell them, giving them both a vigorous head rub for their trouble. This is good, actually. I need some normalcy back in my routine. I can focus on the dogs and not Mercy.

So I follow the dogs into the barn and drag the door shut. It's stifling in here, but I kick on the big metal fan, and that stirs the air around. At least it's still relatively early in the morning, and thus marginally cooler than it will be five hours from now.

I let out a sharp whistle and the dogs come trotting over and sit at my feet. Then I consider my options. I have an array of weapons in here: a wall full of knives and assorted saws and power tools, plus a locked cabinet with some of my more esoteric options—thumb screws, a medieval-style knee splitter, that kind of thing. I keep my rifles inside, out of the heat.

The freezer's out here, too. That's where I keep most of the meat, each victim in their specially labeled bags. I bring them into the house freezer piece by piece.

Raul's out here.

I put the thought aside. I didn't even know Mercy when I

killed him, and killing is what I *do*. It's my entire reason for existing. And I didn't even torture him.

The dogs are waiting for me, tails thumping against the concrete. I force myself to focus.

"Roxi."

Her ears perk up.

"Meat cleaver."

She leaps to her feet and runs over to the wall of knives, grabs the cleaver by its handle from the bottom row, and runs back to me. I take the knife out of her mouth.

"Good girl." I hate that I think of Mercy when I say it.

Roxi barks.

"Yes, yes, you'll get your treat." I go over to the freezer, unlock it, peel back the lid. The cold billows up, a relief in the barn's balmy heat.

Fucking Raul is right on top. I didn't know his name when I killed him, so I wrote CHURCH OF THE WELL DRIVER in big black letters across the bag instead. I don't pull him out, though. I go for George Lakowski, a poacher I had some fun with a few months back. Followed him all over the western half of the state, stalking him the way he was stalking the bobcats and mountain lions he prized so much.

I take out his arm and toss it down on the metal table. The dogs' tails wag even faster.

"Roxi," I say, slamming the cleaver down on Lakowski's thumb. She rises up to her hind legs and when I toss the thumb she catches it and gulps it down.

"Yeah, it's nice having it be frozen, huh?" I hack off Lakowski's ring finger and hold it up to Max. "Your turn, buddy." Then I whistle a sharp, prickly melody.

The transformation is immediate—from sweet, cuddly Max to a vicious, growling monster. I wonder what Mercy would say if she saw this.

Nothing good, probably. Especially with the finger-cicles.

I point to the stack of old boxing dummies I keep in the corner and whistle again. This time, with the code for *attack*.

Max does as ordered, launching himself on the dummy and grabbing the biggest one, just like I trained him. He snarls and bites and drags the thing over to me. Roxi can't help herself and joins in on the attack. But when I whistle sharply, they both stop on command.

"Very good." I toss Max his finger and cut off another piece for Roxi. They both gulp them down in one bite and then sit at attention, waiting for my next command.

"You two want to run in the pasture, don't you?" I grin down at them, and both of them start wagging their tails ferociously at the word *pasture*. I don't blame them; they were cooped up at the cabin at the Church of the Well.

"All right, corpse training it is, then." I whistle sharply in four short blasts, and the dogs rise up to standing. I grab what remains of Lakowksi's arm and a shovel from the hook on the wall and push the barn door open. They tear off again, running in wild circles out in the pasture.

I duck behind the barn, out of the view of the house's windows—I don't know when Mercy's going to wake up, and I don't feel like explaining why I'm carrying around an arm.

Then I hike to the opposite end of the pasture, near the big mesquite tree that marks the edge of my property. The dogs are still closer to the house, running in circles, not paying me any mind.

I start digging, just a shallow little grave for old Lakowski. Or at least his arm. Then I drop the arm in, cover it back up with dirt, and head toward the barn. Once I'm there, I whistle again.

The dogs immediately circle around to me, excited. We've been through this exercise dozens of times—a dog that can clear a crime scene is a useful friend to have, even if Hunters have other advantages that keep us from being found out.

I whistle again, low and fluttery—the order for *scavenge*. The dogs immediately start sniffing around the ground. I check the time on my watch. The last time we did this, it took them nearly twenty minutes to sniff out the meat, but I suspect it might not take as long today, given the heat will start to thaw out that arm a lot faster, even buried.

I follow the dogs as they get to work, snuffling through the dying grass. They haven't caught the scent yet. Or they're lallygagging, hoping to get more time outside.

The sun beats down on me, and I wipe the sweat away from my forehead. The dogs are slowly but surely making their way to the far end of the pasture, but it's a hike in this heat, even for a creature like me. I should have brought out a glass of water instead of my coffee, which I left abandoned back in the barn.

We're about halfway to the mesquite tree when I feel it—a disturbance shimmering through the air like a heat slick. Mercy's fearful about something.

I glance over at the house, frowning. I don't see her, but I can smell the sweet, rich scent of her fear. I wonder if she opened up my laptop and went searching for more information about how Gunner's handling her disappearance. This is what her fear smelled like yesterday when she saw that news report.

Max lets out a volley of excited barks, pulling my attention away from the human in my house. He's caught Lakowski's scent.

"Good boy," I shout, glancing down at my watch. Fifteen minutes. They're probably going to beat last time.

Both of them gallop toward the mesquite tree, but I take my time, weaving through the grass. The wind shifts and Mercy's scent isn't as strong, but it is there, faintly, in the background.

The dogs attack the ground at the mesquite tree, growling and digging. I check my watch Sixteen minutes and forty-five seconds.

"Good job," I tell them. "Enjoy that arm."

And that's when Mercy's fear erupts.

I don't just smell it now; I feel it, like the air's charging up for an electrical storm. And I know, with a sinking feeling in my chest, that she's not reading the fucking news.

Because this is what her fear felt like when she saw me kill Price back at the church.

"Stay!" I shout at the dogs. They look up at me for a second, their muzzles bloody, and then turn back to the arm. I whirl around, racing back toward the house. At least I know that there aren't any other humans here. I would know if someone pulled up to the house—

And like that, I realize why Mercy's fear spiked. She's not in the house at all.

And when she starts screaming, it's coming from the barn.

CHAPTER THIRTY

MERCY

Church of the Well Driver. 8/9. FM 3208.

The freezer's cold air turns to steam around me, billowing in the sweltering heat of this—it's not a barn. It's a torture chamber.

I read once that a poet, Dante, said that hell was a series of layers, and the deepest layer was the coldest, and I think that's what I'm looking at right now. The deepest part of hell.

I drop the freezer lid and stumble backward, jostling up against a nearby workbench hard enough that there's a sharp metallic clatter as a butcher cleaver falls to the ground. It's streaked with red.

I scream again, the sound tearing my throat to shreds, and I try to run away. Except there's nowhere to run, not in here. Weapons are everywhere. Dozens of knives. Gleaming saws. Coils of chains. I really am in hell.

And at the center of it—

I can't look at the freezer, glossy white in the middle of all this grime. All I can think about is getting *out*, but my brain is panicky and stupid, and I'm barefoot. Why did I even come out here? I know what Ambrose is. But I let myself be lulled into a sense of safety because of his tenderness last night. The way he tucked my hair behind my ear and brushed my cheek with his knuckles.

I came out here because I didn't want to be alone and because I thought he might give me more of that tenderness.

Instead, I found Raul. Who else could that be? I know he died on August 9th.

I dart toward the barn doors, still cracked open, the stream of hot bright sunlight my beacon to safety. It's all I focus on, even though it hardly feels as if I'm moving. I keep seeing that neatly labeled bag in the freezer.

The angle of sunlight widens, and then a shadow blocks it again. Ambrose.

I scream at the sight of him and whip around, furiously scanning the barn. There's nothing but weapons and horror. No other exits. No *windows*.

The freezer sits like a toad.

"Mercy!" Ambrose shouts. I ignore him, skittering back and forth, as panicky as a rabbit. "Mercy, be care—"

Pain sears up through the bottom of my foot, as sudden as a lightning bolt. I howl in agony and tip forward, landing hard on my hands and knees on the concrete floor. Screaming, I drag myself forward, my foot throbbing. All I can think about is getting away from him.

"Mercy, you're fucking hurt."

Ambrose's shadow falls over me, and I flip around onto my back, sobbing with terror and pain. His eyes blaze. His swirling tattoos are sheened with sweat.

"You stepped on a nail," he says softly.

"Get away from me!" I scream.

He crouches down and grabs my ankle, lifting my foot up from the ground. I fall backward against the damp cement, grinding my teeth in pain.

"You shouldn't have come out here barefoot."

"You won't let me have shoes!" I try to pull myself out of his grip, but it's no use. He's too strong. "That's how you're keeping me here. *This* is how you're keeping me here—" I gesture down to my foot, blood already puddling on the ground.

"I can't have you going to the police," he says stiffly.

"You have Raul!" I scream, my tears veiling the world with salt. "You have Raul, you monster!"

His grip tightens around my ankle.

"Yes," he says. "Yes, I do."

"You're the devil!" I scream. "I hate you! I *hate you*!"

I try to jerk myself away from him, but Ambrose reacts too quickly, dropping my leg and grabbing me by the waist and then throwing me over his shoulder like I'm not even a person. My anger is swallowed up by terror.

He's going to cut me into pieces like he did Raul.

"No!" I shriek, fighting against him, trying to kick through the pain in my foot. "No! You promised you wouldn't kill me!"

"And you think I'd break that promise?" He stalks toward the barn's entrance, leaving behind the worktable and the weapons and the freezer. It's all I can see, though, as he carries me away. The white glare of the freezer that hides the horror inside it.

I sob and hiccup and try to fight against Ambrose, but it's no use. His arm is wrapped tight around my waist and I'm bleeding from a wound in my foot and I'm trapped here, in hell, with Satan himself.

Ambrose drags the barn door open and carries me outside. "Sit," he barks, and I think he's talking to me until Max runs up behind him, tail wagging, his muzzle covered in blood.

I scream again, panic surging through me like nausea.

"It's not what it looks like," Ambrose says, stepping onto the porch. Max follows behind him, wagging his tail. "I was training him."

"Did you kill someone?" I gasp out.

"Not today, no." Ambrose flings the back door open and carries me inside and then lowers me, with more care than I'd expect, onto the couch.

It's still covered in his blood. It's still marked by his depravity.

The depravity that you enjoyed.

I take deep, ragged breaths. Ambrose runs his rough hands over my bare leg, his touch gentle as he lifts my foot. I try to squirm away from him, but he glares at me and I go limp, afraid of what he'll do. "Hold still," he orders.

"Why did you keep Raul?" I choke out.

He looks away as he slowly lowers my leg to the ground. "Stay here," he says. "I've got some bandages and antiseptic."

"Why did you keep Raul?!" I scream at him, my face hot with rage and fear.

Ambrose fixes me with a look so unfathomably dark that it steals my breath. And I know, in this moment, that he isn't human. What we did yesterday on this couch was supposed to be the proof. But his expression right now, his black and glittering eyes—this is when I *know*.

"I was going to eat him," he says flatly.

And then he walks out of the living room.

I'm too frozen with shock to do anything but stare at the place where he was standing. My foot throbs. Blood drips onto the floor. And I think back to the two meals I've eaten in this house.

No meat.

Neither of them had meat.

I scramble off the couch, knowing I have to get away. I have to get out of here. But I'm not thinking clearly, and I step down on my injured foot and the pain explodes again because the nail is still implanted into my sole.

I scream and slam forward, hitting my head against the

floorboards. The world blinks. Distantly, I hear someone curse behind me.

"I told you to stay." Ambrose's hands are on my waist again, pulling me up. "I didn't want to take the nail out until I had bandages."

"You're going to eat him," I whisper, tears streaming down my cheeks.

Ambrose situates me on the couch and puts his attention on my foot. "This is going to hurt," he says, right before he pulls the nail out.

I scream. The pain is so much more blinding, so much more sudden, than I was expecting, even with the warning and even with my frenzied grief. But it only lasts a second. Ambrose presses a pad of gauze against my sole, stopping the blood.

"I need to clean this and hope for the best." He peers up at me. "I'm guessing you've never had a tetanus shot."

"What do you care?" I try to kick my leg into his face, but his arms flex, pinning me in place.

"I don't want to kill you," he snaps, "and I don't want you to die some other way, either. Hold still."

"Did Raul *hold still?*" I snarl at him. The question surprises me. Mostly because I don't actually want him to answer.

Ambrose dabs the blood away from my foot, then rubs a smear of antiseptic across the wound, the cream cool and burning all at once. I gasp a little, sliding back into the couch.

"Stings, doesn't it?" he says amicably.

"You're a *cannibal.*"

"I know." He wraps clean gauze around my foot, securing it with tape. Then he gently lowers my foot to the ground, his hands still wrapped loosely around my ankle. I'm terrified and sickened and I hate him, but the way he's touching me reminds me of our time together at the Church of the Well, how he pried my legs open and kissed the pleasure into me.

"I told you, though," he says. "I didn't let him suffer."

"What?"

"Raul." Ambrose stands up, towering over me. "I severed his spine before I killed him. He didn't feel anything."

The low-simmering nausea in my stomach surges upward; I couldn't stop it even if I wanted to. The cup of coffee I drank before coming to the barn explodes out of me, splattering across Ambrose's black cowboy boots.

I freeze, expecting him to attack me. To kill me like he did Raul. But instead, he pushes my hair away from my face and sidesteps the mess. "Let me get you some water," he murmurs.

"I hate you." Tears tremble through my lashes.

He doesn't respond, just gets the water like he said. I know I shouldn't, but I drink it, telling myself I want to wash the taste out of my mouth. Ambrose disappears again and comes back with an old towel that he drapes across my mess. "I'll clean it up later," he says, sinking down on the couch beside me.

I instinctually recoil from him.

"I didn't mean for you to find that," he says, after a few moments of agonizing silence. "I should have locked the barn door."

"You shouldn't *kill people*," I hiss.

Ambrose laughs darkly. "Well, humanita, I'm afraid that's non-negotiable. I never claimed to be anything but a monster." He turns toward me. "But I could have done more to protect you from my, ah, darker urges."

I glare at him. "Why do you care?"

Something flickers across his face—a kind of discomfort. "Because I care for you," he says stiffly. "Against my better judgment."

My heart flutters at that, as if it still doesn't understand what Ambrose is.

"If you care for me so much, then let me go."

As soon as I say it, I'm not sure that's even what I want. But how can that not be what I want? He's a killer and a cannibal.

He has a barn clearly designed to torture people. He covered me in his blood and then licked it away.

And you liked it.

"Let me go," I repeat, trying to suppress the thought.

"And where would you go, if I did that?" Ambrose tilts his head. It's not mocking, the way he asks it. "Back to the Church of the Well? To the police?"

"I won't tell anyone about you," I say. "Just let me go back —" The word *home* curdles on my tongue. "Just let me go back."

"Is that really want you want?" He shifts on the couch, eyes burning into me.

No, it's not. I don't want to go back to the church. I don't want to go back to Reverend Gunner, back to being a helpmeet but not really a wife, back to being an object that isn't even treasured. Ambrose is a monster, a demon, but he looks at me like I matter. He's doing it right now. And that's more than I can say for Reverend Gunner or Pastor Sullivan or Madelyn or any of them.

"I hate you," I say, because I do. I hate him for showing me what my life could have looked like but then taking it away from me because he's a psychopath.

"You already said that," Ambrose says softly. "And it hurts just as much the second time."

Then he stands up, his dark eyes fixed on me. I feel faintly stunned—how can he care if I hate him? How can he care about me at all?

And why do I want to believe he's telling the truth?

CHAPTER THIRTY-ONE

AMBROSE

I t's too fucking hot to be out in the barn, but I'm out here anyway, slumped in an ancient lawn chair and smoking a cigarette, a vice I haven't indulged in for a few years. But smoking helps calm me down, and I never have to worry about cancer anyway.

Right now, though, the smoke just tastes like ash.

Roxi and Max sit at my feet, the heat making them lazy. I haven't bothered to wipe down their bloody muzzles after they tore apart Lakowski's arm, and there's a small, petty part of me that wants to send Max into the house to check on Mercy, bloody muzzle and all. A small, petty part of me that wants to hear her screams and smell her fear and jerk off to it.

Pathetic.

The cigarette is almost to its filter, and it's doing fuck-all for me, so I stub it out on the metal cabinet where I keep my various torture devices and add it to the rest of the barn's mess. Like the nail Mercy stepped on.

She doesn't know it, but I licked my fingers clean of her blood after I left her alone in the living room, eyes closed as I ran my tongue around my fingers. She hurt the fuck out of me, saying she hated me the way she did, but tasting her blood was a small consolation. Reminded me, in that moment, of what I am, and what she is, and what creatures like me are supposed to do to humans like her.

It'd be easy, wouldn't it? To grab one of my blades off the wall—the ax, maybe, the ax is always a classic—and stalk inside and swing it down to split her head open. I'd kill her fast, same as I did her precious *Raul*, and unlike Raul I'd eat her right away, cut big steaks off her gorgeous thighs and fry them in butter and garlic and rosemary.

The idea makes my cock swell, and I shift in the chair, angry at myself for wanting her so badly even when I'm fantasizing about destroying her. I shouldn't be thinking about her at all. I shouldn't have felt a stab of panic when I realized she'd stepped on that fucking nail and she might have tetanus and I can't do a damn thing about it without the risk of exposure. I shouldn't have wrapped her foot up so tenderly while she raged at me about what a monster I am, and I sure as shit shouldn't have felt bad about it.

I shouldn't feel pangs of jealousy every time she says Raul's name.

I sigh, exasperated, and pull out another crumpled cigarette. The pack is almost five years old, an artifact I keep stashed next to a box of big metal hooks.

I light the cigarette with my old Zippo and draw the smoke in, leaning back in the chair. Even with the fan blowing on me, it feels like I'm simmering in an oven. Ironic, that.

Max whines and nudges at my foot.

"I'm not letting you go in there," I mutter to him. "She hates us, remember?"

Max licks the sweat off my leg. I pet him and take another drag of my cigarette. Even though I shouldn't, I put my senses out until I find Mercy. She hasn't fled like I expected her to, which is kind of a relief, because I know I would chase her if she tried. Not just because I don't want her going to the cops. But because—

Because you want her, you fucking fool.

I suck down more acrid smoke like it'll save me from myself. That's the truth of it. I do want her. I also want her to be happy, which is the other reason I don't want her to flee. I can hide from the cops easily enough. Go south to one of my houses down in the Rio Grande Valley, take on a new persona for a few years. It's not like I haven't done it before.

But what would happen to Mercy, then? She'd have to go back to that piece of shit Sterling Gunner. He doesn't even have the decency to let her be a wife to some sad sack in the church. He had to claim her for himself.

You're doing the same thing.

The thought hits me hard, and it burns as bad as the cigarette. Something like guilt pulses through me, and that's an unfamiliar fucking emotion, let me tell you.

I seek out Mercy again. Seek out her terror and her sorrow. It's the same intoxicating blend that I felt when I first glimpsed her by the Concho River, her hair almost silver in the early morning moonlight.

I've been chasing that beautiful fear since I heard her elegant scream. Chasing it all the way to this miserable moment, me smoking a crumbling cigarette with an insistent hard-on and the only woman I've wanted in years sobbing and cursing my name.

"I don't know how to deal with this shit," I say to the dogs. Max whines and cocks his head. Roxi ignores me.

I stand up, letting the cigarette burn between my fingers instead of smoking it. I mean to pace around, to try to work off some of this energy, but I find myself drifting over to the damn freezer, the lock still on the floor from where it must have dropped when Mercy opened up the lid.

I open up the lid now and sigh into the cold billowing air. Because there he is, right on top:

Raul.

I wish I hadn't killed him, which is an unusual feeling for me. Wish I'd just talked myself into the Church of the Well without the chaos. Mercy knows I'm a killer, but Raul's the only one she's really angry about. All her rage and suffering and she's never once thrown the others in my face—not that pissant guard and certainly not the asshole who assaulted her, Pierce or Price or whatever his name was.

I hoist out the sack containing Raul and drop it on the workbench. Close up the freezer. Lock it. I tell myself I'm going to cook him, that I'm going throw all his meat in the smoker and get a month's worth of jerky for my trouble.

I tell myself that, but it's a lie. What I want, what I really want, is to undo his death so Mercy will hate me just a little bit less. But Hunters can only revive ourselves, not our victims.

But I can *not* eat him. That's something. I can wrap him up, give him a proper burial someplace. I'm not sure where they buried the remains of his they did find—not sure if they even buried him at all. I dragged Mercy away from the compound before the funeral service.

Christ. No wonder she hates me.

I take my phone out and turn it back on, ignoring the onslaught of messages from Charlotte. Instead, I do a quick search of Raul's name. I'm surprised by what I find.

An obituary page—but not one put up by the Church of the Well. It was put up by his family, and it seems they're the ones who buried him, not Reverend Gunner. Whether that's because I was terrorizing the church this past week or because Reverend Gunner's a hypocritical shithead, I don't know.

But I do know that they laid Raul to rest in Cocana. Not the church compound.

And yeah, I'm jealous of him, even if he is a bag of meat.

Mercy cared for him in a way she'll never care for me. But maybe I can do this thing for her, put his body back together, so the last thing she remembers about me is that I tried. I tried to be good. Tried to act human.

And then I'll let her go.

CHAPTER THIRTY-TWO

MERCY

The back door slams, loud enough I hear it in the bedroom where I've been curled up and weeping for the last few hours. I immediately tense up, trying to draw into myself.

Especially as heavy footsteps thud down the hallway and stop outside my door.

I freeze in the bed as if Ambrose really is the boogeyman, and I'm a little girl who thinks the monster won't see her if she doesn't move.

The door creaks open.

"Mercy."

He says my name the way he did before, when I thought he was a preacher and I liked how his rough hands explored my skin.

And God help me, but my body still reacts as if I haven't learned the truth of him.

"Go away." I face the wall, refusing to look at him.

"I will." Which is a lie, because he steps into the room. "But I need to tell you something first."

I keep staring at the wall, curling my hands into my chest.

"Your clothes got here," he says. "I didn't tell you, but I bought you some shoes."

I don't know why, but that makes me roll over. Ambrose fills up the doorway, half hidden in the hallway's shadows.

"Why?" I mutter. "So you can chase me down and kill me like you did Raul?"

He blanches at that—or at least, it looks like he does. I don't know why he would care. He certainly recovers quickly enough, his features settling into a neutral expression.

"I'm taking you somewhere tonight."

My fear spikes again, and even though I don't move, I can tell Ambrose knows. He smiles as if my fear pleases him, and he shifts his weight, never taking his eyes off me.

I wait for him to explain, but he doesn't.

"Where?" I whisper. "What are you doing to do to me?"

"I'm not going to kill you," he says calmly. "Trust me, if I was going to do that, you wouldn't see me coming."

I bite back another surge of fear, and Ambrose smiles again, teasing and cruel.

"You're safe with me," he says. "I can't promise much, but I can promise that."

I watch him warily. "But you're not going to tell me where we're going?"

"No. I'm just letting you know. We'll leave as soon as it gets dark."

Then he steps back into the hallway, closing the door behind him.

I roll onto my back, not sure what to think. I'm afraid of him, but, perhaps stupidly, I don't think he's a liar. He's been honest about his atrocities.

But I still can't imagine where a monster like him would want to take me after nightfall.

☼

I don't see Ambrose until the sun sets. He strides back into my room, a stack of clothes in one arm and a pair of shoes in the other—flimsy ballet flats. He's not exactly making it easy for me to escape across the scrubby west Texas landscape.

"Get dressed," he says roughly, tossing everything on the rickety old desk in the corner.

"You're still not going to tell me where we're going?" I don't move from the bed.

Ambrose frowns. "You know I'm capable of taking you wherever I want. Now get dressed and make this easy on yourself."

I hate that he's right. I hate even more that he uses that dark, commanding tone that makes my body throb with heat.

"Get out of here," I snap, as if he hasn't seen me at my most vulnerable, legs spread and moaning in ecstasy.

Ambrose smirks, clearly thinking the same thing. To his credit, he does step out into the hallway—although he leaves the door open. Fine.

I dig through the clothes he got me, a knot tightening in my throat. They're nothing like the clothes I'm used to wearing. They're... secular. Skimpy shorts, sleeveless tops. A strappy black dress that might as well be a nightgown, although it's made out of cool, breathable cotton, the hems edged in lace.

I hate that I think it's pretty. Hate that I finger the fabric between my thumb and forefinger and consider how much prettier this dress is than anything I wore at the Church of the Well. And probably more comfortable.

He bought me underwear, too, and a couple of plain bras. Somehow, he knew my size, which makes me feel odd because it makes me feel—*cared for*, somehow, even though it's impossible. That demon doesn't care about anything.

I peel out of the T-shirt and boxers and slide on my new clothes, going with the black dress because it feels the most familiar. Although it's tight around the bodice and shows off my too-big chest, the skirt is loose around my thick hips and falls just past my knees. A semblance of modesty.

I tell myself I still care about modesty.

I put on the ballet flats and slink out of the bedroom. Ambrose waits for me, leaning up against the far wall, his arms crossed over his chest. When he sees me, he seems to go still, his eyes sweeping across my body, lingering briefly on my chest. I ought to feel exposed. I don't.

"Looks good on you," he says roughly.

I ignore him. I also ignore the fact that he's dressed up, too, in dark slacks and a dark button-up shirt. He looks like the preacher I thought he was.

"Come on," he says. "We've got to drive into town."

"Town?" My throat goes dry, and I'm not sure what I'm scared of. Ambrose? Is he lying and this is really an excuse to take me deeper into the desert to kill me? Or is he taking me back to the church like I claimed I wanted?

The idea makes me queasy.

"Yeah," he says. "Cocana. Should take about half an hour."

I want to protest, want to fight him, but I'm completely powerless. I don't have his strength or his ruthlessness or his violence. I don't have whatever demonic magic keeps him from dying.

So I go along with him. I climb into the passenger side of his Oldsmobile and buckle myself in, my fingers squeezing up my skirt the way I always do when I'm nervous. The car's engine rumbles to life, the radio kicking on to the same staticky country music station that was playing when he dragged me out of the church.

The landscape is dark as pitch, with only the headlights illu-minating the two-lane highway. Ambrose sings along softly to the radio, his voice low and dulcet. I hate that he can sing. I hate that he's an evil inversion of what I used to dream about in a husband—a Godly man with a good singing voice, strong enough to protect me from harm.

We don't talk on the trip into Cocana. Ambrose keeps singing, though, and drums his hands against the steering wheel. I stare at my foggy reflection in the glass as we wind through the empty streets, everything already closed up for the night.

Ambrose drives all the way to the other side of town and pulls up to the cemetery there, rolling out away from the highway.

"A cemetery?" My throat is dry again. Of all the things I expected, this was the last one.

"Yes." Ambrose stares out the front windshield, his hands on the steering wheel. "This is where Raul's family buried him."

As soon as he says Raul's name, despair floods through me—all that sorrow I've carried with me since the morning at the river. Because of the despair, it takes me a moment to register what he said.

"Wait." I look over at Ambrose. "His family? Not the Church of the Well?"

"No." Ambrose cuts the car's engine. "I found his obituary online. He's buried here."

"So why'd you bring me here?" Tension squeezes my muscles tight and makes it hard for me to breathe. Tears form in my eyes. "To throw in my face what you did?"

Ambrose clenches the wheel, not looking at me. I suddenly wish I'd kept my mouth shut.

But then he says, "To bury him. The rest of him."

He climbs out of the car before I can respond—not that I even know what I would say. I'm not even sure I heard him correctly. Not sure what to think if I did.

Ambrose opens the trunk and rummages around inside, but all I can do is stare at the cemetery gates. It's locked for the night, a big metal padlock holding the chain in place. But something tells me that's not going to stop Ambrose.

He raps lightly on my window and stares at me, waiting with a shovel tossed over one shoulder.

"I'm doing this for you," he says, voice muffled by the glass. "I was hoping you'd be there."

I shove the door open, hoping, at least in part, that I can slam it into him. He jumps away at the last second, though, too nimble for me, even though he's holding the shovel and—

Raul.

He's holding the bag I found in the freezer, letting it drop at his side.

He really is going to bury him.

"I—You—" I swallow, my throat dry. I don't know how to react to any of this, and so I spit out the first thing I can think of. "Aren't you afraid you'll get caught?"

"No." He tilts his head and his eyes catch some nearby light and gleam like a cat's.

I jerk back in fear. "Your eyes!"

"I told you I'm the boogeyman," he says, his eyes still flat from the light. "I can see in the dark. And I can smell humans. You're the only living one here."

Then he steps back, giving me space to step out of the car. I take a deep breath, trying to decide what to do.

I'm doing this for you, he said, and that makes me feel warm and strange and sad all at once.

"Come on, Mercy," Ambrose says softly. "I can't bring him back, but I can do this."

I jerk my gaze up to him. His eyes aren't shining anymore. He looks like a man.

When I blink, my tears fall. "Okay," I whisper, and I push myself out of the car and slam the door behind me. Ambrose nods and walks up to the gate, sets the bag carefully down on the ground, and then swings the shovel hard against the lock.

The clang is immensely loud and echoes through the night, but Ambrose's blow is powerful enough that the lock scatters across the ground. He yanks the chain away.

His power terrifies me. But that terror does something else to me, too, something I don't let myself dwell on.

He holds the gate open for me. "To the left," he says as I step through.

I walk along the path even though it means Ambrose follows behind me. At least I can hear his footsteps, heavy and ominous.

The night is warm and dry, a wind blowing the cemetery trees around and making it sound as if we're surrounded by ghosts. I don't understand why Raul is buried here and not at the Church of the Well.

Except I do understand, don't I? He wasn't important enough to Reverend Gunner to have a place at the church's cemetery. He wasn't even important enough for a memorial service.

I swallow the lump in my throat, my vision webbing with tears. When Ambrose puts his hand on my shoulder, I jump beneath his touch, my heart leaping to my throat.

"This way," he murmurs into my ear, making my skin prickle.

"How do you even know where he's buried?"

"I looked it up. It's not far."

He's right; it's not far. Even in the dark I can tell which grave is Raul's because the ground is darker than the surrounding grass. Upturned soil.

"When did they bury him?"

"Three days ago," Ambrose says quietly.

I squeeze my eyes shut against my tears. Because three days ago I was still at the Church of the Well. And I didn't know. No one told me. I assumed Reverend Gunner was going to bury him in the church cemetery because I was a fool.

"This won't take me long," Ambrose says. "You can do—whatever you need. Speak to him. Speak to God."

I flutter my eyes open. Ambrose watches me through the dark. "You don't believe in God," I say darkly. "Do you?"

"I do believe in God," he says. "I just know he hates me for the same reasons you do."

And then he starts digging.

CHAPTER THIRTY-THREE

MERCY

While Ambrose digs, I pray.

I haven't prayed since he killed Deacon Price. I haven't prayed since I gave myself to Ambrose in the bunker, which had, at the time, felt like a prayer in and of itself—but a prayer to Ambrose, which made it a prayer to the devil even if I didn't know it at the time. But tonight, in the warm air of the graveyard, I pray to God the Father, and to Jesus the Son, and to the Holy Ghost.

I kneel in the grass and bow my head as Ambrose redigs Raul's grave, my fingers clasped so tight my knuckles whiten. I don't pray out loud; I don't want Ambrose to hear. But I send my thoughts up to Heaven, as jumbled and wild as they are.

I pray that God welcomes Raul into the heavenly hosts, even though I know He already has.

I pray for forgiveness and for deliverance from my sins, as numerous as they are, listing them out by rote. Impurity. Fornication. Blasphemy.

I listen for God's answer, but all I hear is the wind and the quiet powdery thump as Ambrose digs out the dirt of Raul's grave. When I lift my gaze, it falls immediately on Ambrose, a strong dark shadow in the moonlight.

Heat flushes through me. Except it's not lust. It feels like the Spirit, which I would feel during services at the Church of the Well, all those Christian voices joining together in worship. But how can it be the Spirit, when I also felt it that day Ambrose prayed over me? I was so sure it had been the Holy Ghost moving through him.

But it wasn't the Holy Ghost, I realize now. It was Ambrose.

The monster. The murderer. The devil.

He stops, leaning on his shovel, and wipes at his brow. Then he looks at me, still kneeling in the grass.

I feel it again, a spirit arcing between us.

No. He killed Raul.

He did kill Raul. But look at what he's doing now.

"Almost done," he says softly. "Do you need more time?"

To pray, he means. But my prayers haven't done anything for me. Not these prayers. Not prayers to God.

The prayers to *him*, though—

No. That's sacrilege. What we did wasn't praying. It was sin and abomination.

So why didn't it ever *feel* like sin and abomination? Even yesterday, when Ambrose slid inside me, our bodies slippery with his blood—I had begged him for it. I had wanted it more than I'd ever wanted anything.

"No," I finally say. "No, I don't."

Ambrose nods and scoops out another shovelful of dirt. I can't tell how deep the hole is, not in the dark, but I can see that it's smaller than it should be.

"We won't be able to get into the coffin," Ambrose says, as easily if he was talking about the weather. "But we can get him as close as possible."

I go over to the grave and run my fingers over the metal

marker set into the dirt. No headstone. I suppose Raul's family couldn't afford one, and I twist with anger again, that Reverend Gunner didn't cover this expense. Lord knows the church has the money. Lord knows *he* has the money.

There's a thump behind me. Ambrose has hit the coffin.

I look back at him just as he tosses the shovel aside. He picks up the bag—*Raul*, I tell myself. That's Raul. Or at least it's Raul's earthly shell.

"I haven't done a funeral in decades," Ambrose says, a little sheepishly. "But I more or less remember what to do. What to say."

"The devil can quote Scripture for his purpose," I tell him, rising up to standing.

"I sure can." Ambrose watches me in the dark. "And right now," he says softly, "my purpose is whatever will make this right. Or as close to right as I can get."

Something twists in my chest. Nothing can make this right, because nothing can bring back Raul, and nothing can change the fact that I found his decapitated head in the Concho River and stared into his dead eyes and recognized him.

But at least Ambrose is trying. When did Reverend Gunner, when did any of them, ever try to do right by me?

The realization leaves me numb.

"Are you saying you'll do a funeral for Raul?" I ask hoarsely.

"As best I can."

"Is it—is it safe?"

"It's safe." Ambrose tilts his head back and makes a show of sniffing the air. "No one's here but us and the dead."

"Can you smell them, too?" The question's out of my mouth before I can stop it.

"Yeah. It doesn't bother me, though." Ambrose steps up to the edge of Raul's freshly dug grave, kneels down, and lowers him home. The wind picks up again, making the trees rustle around us.

"'Blessed be the God and Father of our Lord Jesus Christ,'" Ambrose recites in a rich, rhythmic preacher's voice. "'The Father of mercies and God of all comfort, who comforteth us in all our affliction, that we may be able to comfort them that are in any affliction, through the comfort wherewith we ourselves are comforted of God.'"

He stands up and looks across the grave at me. "The two of us are here today to celebrate the life of Raul Alvarez, who was taken from this world too soon—" Ambrose hesitates. "That's true, by the way. I shouldn't have—"

"Keep going," I tell him, my heart twisting into knots. "Please. Just—be a preacher right now."

Ambrose nods, takes a deep breath—

And transforms.

He becomes the man I saw in Reverend Gunner's office: a fire and brimstone preacher with one eye on Heaven and the other on hell. I realize now that I was glimpsing his own darkness, but as he launches into a recitation of Psalm 23, his darkness seems to melt away.

"'Jehovah is my Shepherd; I shall not want,'" he says, hands clasped in front of his waist, his eyes on mine. "'He maketh me to lie down in green pastures...'"

I let the familiar words flow over me. My tears brim up again, and I wipe them away with the back of my hand. The truth is I didn't even know Raul that well. We exchanged friendly words here and there. I brought him water, same as the rest of the soldiers. He taught me a little Spanish and waved to me at the services. But I didn't know anything about him. I didn't know he had a family in Cocana. Most people at the church come from elsewhere. They come from far away.

Ambrose's voice is a soft rhythm in the background as I stand by Raul's grave and weep. I hardly knew him at all, but he was the closest thing to a friend I ever had. I went from an orphan to a wife and helpmeet.

Until I met Ambrose. Until I met the devil.

I lift my gaze to him, where he's still reciting Psalms from memory. His eyes shine again, jolting me a little. But it occurs to me *he's* the one I know the best. Not Raul. Certainly not Reverend Gunner. And not God, either.

Ambrose Echeverría, the cold-blooded murderer currently praying over one of his many victims.

"Do you want to say anything, Mercy?" he asks, pulling me out of my thoughts. "About—about the deceased?"

I look down at the gravesite, at the churned-up dirt. "No," I whisper. "He's in Heaven now. He doesn't need me."

Ambrose nods, then starts shoveling dirt back into place. I watch him, the wind blowing my skirt around my thighs, and for the first time since I discovered the truth about Ambrose, I feel calm.

"Have you ever done this before?" My voice is more clear than I expected.

Ambrose keeps shoveling. "Buried a body? Yeah."

"No. Performed a funeral for someone you—" I whisper the last word. "Killed."

This, he doesn't answer right away. He just keeps shoveling the dirt. "Yes," he finally says. "I used to do it all the time. But this is different."

The shovel scrapes and the dirt thumps. The wind blows through the trees. I feel hot and strange and free. Not like myself. Not like Mercy Gunner, anyway.

"How is it different?"

Ambrose throws the last of the dirt into place and packs it down with the back of his shovel. To my untrained eye, the grave looks undisturbed.

Ambrose walks around the dirt, like he doesn't want to step on it—a superstition I learned when I was a child before my parents died and I'd ever heard of the Church of the Well. He tosses the shovel in the grass and takes my hand, hesitantly, like he expects me to pull away. Maybe I should. I don't.

"I've never done it with the hope that someone would forgive me," he says softly.

I jerk my gaze up to him, my breath tightening. His eyes burn like hellfire. That strangeness I feel intensifies, like I'm drifting outside of myself.

"Are you saying you want me to forgive you?"

Ambrose nods, his fingers tightening around my hand. "I hope you'll forgive me," he says. "Although I understand if you don't. Either way, after this—I'll let you go."

I'm stunned at his words. Stunned at the sadness I see crawling across his face, even in the dark.

"Let me go?" I shake my head. "Just like that?"

"Well, on one condition. That you don't go back to that church." Disgust curls in his words. "Don't go back to Sterling Gunner. I'll give you money, a bus ticket, whatever you need. Go to the cops if you want; they won't find me. But don't go back to the piece of shit. Gunner doesn't deserve you."

I can't breathe. I certainly don't know what to say. And still, I keep my hand linked to Ambrose's, my eyes on his face, trying to comprehend what he's saying to me.

This is what I wanted. To escape the church. And then, later, to escape Ambrose. I thought I didn't have the means to do either. It turns out, he'll give them both to me.

So why don't I want to say yes? Why am I standing here in a graveyard, holding his hand and not wanting to let go?

Gunner doesn't deserve you.

Ambrose's words ring in my thoughts. A truth I've always thought, deep down, even though it felt blasphemous. Certainly everyone else in my life told me the opposite—and told me Jesus agreed with them.

But it still always felt like sin.

"Mercy?" Ambrose leans closer, tilting his head a little. I part my lips on instinct, even though he doesn't kiss me. "What do you say? Will you promise not to go back to the church?"

The wind gusts, low and howling, and I think it blows me into him. At least, that's what it feels like, as I fling my arms around his shoulders and press my lips to his.

"Mercy," he murmurs against my mouth, against my cheeks, kissing me and speaking to me at once. "You don't have to do this. I'll help you—"

I kiss him again because I want him to stop talking. I want him to devour me like he did before. I want to spread my legs for him and invite him in.

I want to choose the devil over God.

"Mercy," he growls, nipping at my neck with his teeth. "If you keep going, I'm not going to be able to stop myself from fucking you."

His words shoot straight through me, and I stop, breathing in the dark scent of his skin. My body's on fire, and I can feel his arousal digging into my thigh.

I want you to fuck me, I think, even though he's a monster and a killer. But I can't bring myself to say it. I want him to take me, to absolve myself of this sin.

So I keep going, mashing my lips to his in a hard, fumbling kiss. Ambrose makes a sound like an animal, like the Great Beast itself, and digs his hands into my waist. He hoists me up, and I wrap my legs around his hips, our mouths never breaking. I thread my hands through his hair, pulling on it the way he pulled on mine, and his kiss turns into a bite, hard and sharp.

I jerk back with a gasp, and Ambrose grins at me. "Don't pull my hair if you don't want a little roughness."

My clit throbs at the thought—

And I pull his hair again.

Ambrose growls and drops to his knees, throwing me hard

enough against the ground that my breath shudders. But not so hard that he hurts me.

"I warned you." He shoves my dress up around my waist, shoves my thighs wide. "What do you have to say for yourself?"

A million possibilities flash through my head. But I settle on the one I mean the most.

"I forgive you."

CHAPTER THIRTY-FOUR

AMBROSE

For a moment, all I can do is stare down at Mercy, her body throbbing with heat in the graveyard grass. Her eyes gleam, still damp with tears, but she writhes her hips against me, slow and distracted, like she's not even aware she's doing it.

She forgives me.

"Say it again," I order, because I'm still not sure I believe what I heard.

Mercy looks right at me.

"I forgive you," she whispers again, her voice breathless.

It's all I need to hear. I wrench her arms overhead, pinning her down so I can kiss her like I'm going to consume her. She moans against me, jerking her hips up, and I kiss down to bite at her neck. Her breasts spill out of the top of her dress, and I bury my nose between them, breathing in the confused melange of scents—her fear, her lust, her grief, her doubt, all of it. All those things that make her human.

"Don't fucking move," I growl, pulling myself up to kneeling.

She doesn't, my perfect human. She even keeps her hands overhead.

I slide my hand into my pocket to pull out my switchblade and snap it open, the blade gleaming in the moonlight. Mercy's eyes widen. Her fear spikes. God, I'll never get tired of that.

"I promised I wouldn't hurt you," I tell her, sliding the blade between her panties and her skin. "But I also promised to fuck you."

"You can just take them off!"

"Don't sass me." I jerk the knife up, slicing the fabric in half. Mercy moans, and I slice open the other side of her panties, revealing her wet pussy to the warm night air. Then I flip the knife and slide the cool metal handle up against her folds.

Mercy gasps and jerks beneath me. "Is that—"

"It's the handle." I move it in a slow circle, making her moan and squirm. "And you need to hold still. I don't want you cutting yourself."

Then I slide the handle inside her and draw my hand away to admire the slim silver blade jutting out of her perfect cunt.

"Did you—" She tries to sit up, but I gently press her back down, shaking my head.

"I told you not to move." Then I stand up so I can admire her fully—her gorgeous spread legs, her trembling chest. She watches me, eyes wide with fright and lust, as I slowly unbuckle my fly and pull out my cock. I wish I'd brought some rope with me, something to tie her down. But I hadn't remotely expected her to want to fuck me again.

We'll just have to make do with the threat of punishment.

"You'll stay exactly as you are," I order, lazily stroking my cock as I talk. "If you move in a way I tell you not to, you'll be punished, do you understand?"

"P-punished how?" Her fear and excitement twist around us.

I trail my eyes over her body, lingering on the knife blade

between her legs. God, that's an image I'm going to remember for a long, long time. My dick jumps against my palm.

"I won't let you come, for one," I tell her. "And I'll probably do worse. Now open that pretty mouth of yours."

She does as I ask, showing me her pink tongue.

"I love it when you obey." I straddle her chest, positioning my cockhead in line with her waiting mouth. Her tongue laps at the precum already beading up there, and I wrap her hair in my hands and pull her head up so I can slide my cock over her tongue. "Now, listen carefully, humanita. You're going to be my fucktoy. Do exactly as I say, and you can come. Disobey..."

Her eyes widen above my cock.

"Well, like I said—I'll punish you."

I thrust myself into her mouth, making her moan. She squirms beneath me, but I slap her cheek lightly in warning. "Don't move," I remind her. "You have a knife in your cunt."

Mercy groans and flutters her eyes closed. I start to fuck her mouth, dropping my head back, rolling my hips against her face. I'm sure she expected me to fuck her pussy, the two of us locked in a missionary position and surrounded by the dead. But I want her to never forget what I am. I want her to know I'm not going to hold back with her. That I'm not going to change.

I thrust a little harder, and Mercy, bless her, drags her mouth even further open, like she's desperate to accommodate me. I can feel her body rippling beneath me, hips rocking, and I chuckle as I fuck her sweet mouth. "Don't forget what's inside you, Mercy."

She makes a muffled noise, her eyes rolling back.

"You like how it feels, humanita?" I hold her in place by the hair, still fucking her throat, which is impossibly wet. Impossibly warm. "My dick in your mouth and my knife your pussy?"

The way she shudders against me is all the answer I need.

"That's what I thought." I drop her head and lean forward

so I'm on all fours as I slide my cock in and out of her mouth. Mercy moans around me, and the vibrations are incredible, a seismic rippling that nearly pushes me to the edge.

But then she jerks and makes a kind of yelping sound in the back of her throat. I smell her blood.

With a groan, I pull my cock out of her mouth, her spit trailing after it. "Mercy, Mercy," I chide, crawling forward so my dick trails along her face. "Did you cut yourself?"

"No," she says, somewhat defensively.

"No, *sir*." I miss that, her calling me sir. "And you're lying."

I stand up, dusting the dirt off my knees, and walk over to inspect her legs. Sure enough, a thin dark trickle of blood slides along her thighs. I sniff the air, breathing it in.

"Look what we have here," I purr, swiping my finger through her blood. I keep my gaze fixed on hers as I slide my bloody finger into my mouth to have a taste.

Fuck, she tastes *divine*. She tastes like the roasted oysters I used to eat as a boy, spritzed with lime and dusted with chili powder. I drop down between her legs and lick the cut, drawing more of her decadent blood into my mouth.

Mercy gasps and squirms and the knife blade presses against my cheek. I jerk away from her, hot blood trickling down my face.

Mercy stares at me, trembling. I wonder what I look like to her right now, blood on my face and my lips.

"This is what I am, humanita." I reach up and smear my blood onto my fingers. "I like the taste of blood. Your blood especially."

Then I slide my bloody fingers into her mouth.

"Do you like the taste of my blood? Hmmm?"

Mercy moans, eyes fluttering, and licks the blood away. I draw my fingers out.

"Do you?" I say it more firmly. "Answer me, Mercy."

"Yes," she whispers.

I stare down at her, not quite believing it. She quivers with fear and shame and lust, and I push back her hair and then lean over to kiss her, slow and tender. But I'm not going to stay tender. She's full of surprises, but I also need to know now if this is going to be too much for her.

"Do you want me to fuck you now?" I rasp in her ear. "Next to the grave of your dead friend?"

Mercy whimpers, turning her gaze to meet mine. I can see her considering the options, working through them one by one. It's not that different from what I see in my victims' eyes when I toy with them, when I make them think they have a chance at escape. The difference is, if Mercy says no, I'll let her go.

I think.

"I'm waiting, humanita." I read down and pinch the knife blade so I can pump the handle in and out of her, working it up against her G-spot. Mercy gasps and arches into it. "Answer me, or I'll get you worked up without any release."

Mercy bites her lips and stares at me, her hips rolling against the knife blade, her pupils flooded from lust. I've noticed that she's hesitant to say what she wants.

Well, that's an inclination I'll fuck out of her.

I push the knife up, angling it so I can hit the spot I know she likes. Mercy jolts.

"Answer me," I order, fucking her a little harder with the knife handle. "Right now. Do you want me to fuck you next to the grave of your dead friend?"

There are tears in her eyes. Heat in her cheeks. She nods.

"Say it, Mercy. Out loud." I push the knife handle inside her pussy and wait.

"Y-yes," she whimpers.

It's a start.

"Good girl." I drag the knife out of her. Mercy slumps back, breasts heaving against her low-cut dress, and I slam the blade into the ground next to her head, the handle glistening with her arousal. She tilts her head toward it, eyes glimmering, and I grab her chin and force her to look up at me again. "Eyes on me, humanita."

Mercy softens beneath my touch, yielding to my command. "Yes, sir," she whispers, spreading her legs a little wider in anticipation.

God, she's a fucking treasure.

I press my cock against her pussy, stopping myself from slamming right into her the way I want to. I want to tease her some more, want her dripping wet and dying to be filled. I want her to beg. And I want to make sure she comes.

"How does that feel?" I ask, nudging my cockhead against her fluttering clit.

Mercy gasps and squirms. "G-good, sir."

"Do you want more?" I rub my cock in little circles, gathering up her wetness so I can slick it against her clit.

She moans, digging her fingers down into the grave dirt.

"That's not an answer." I pull away, stroking myself, and Mercy whimpers.

"Please," she says. "Please, Ambrose. I—I need..." Her voice trails off, and she drops her head, looking away. I force her gaze back on me again and hold her there, one hand around her jaw and the other on my dick.

"Need what?"

Mercy gnaws on her lower lip, her cheeks flushed. She doesn't want to say it. Doesn't want to *ask* for it. I think she's been broken down by the church, by Reverend Gunner. Told she exists for his pleasure when he can't even be bothered to make her his wife.

I don't deny I'm a monster. But even I wouldn't do that to a woman.

"What do you need from me, Mercy?" I grin, showing her my teeth, letting us be predator and prey for just a second.

Then I nudge the tip of my cock into her pussy, making her squirm. "Is it this?"

She nods, and I pull my cock out and slap it against her clit, hard enough it hurts me as much as it shocks her. "Say it out loud. What do you want from me?"

"I want you to—" Her eyes blaze through the night, and it takes every goddamn ounce of my willpower not to ravage her the way she wants. But I will hear her say it first. I will know she's willing to fuck me no matter what I am.

"That's it, humanita." I tap her clit again, more lightly this time, a rapid-fire of quick short raps that have her lifting her hips to meet me. The scent of her arousal is so heavy on the night air that it reminds me of jasmine. It's so heavy I think even a human man could smell it.

"You can do it, baby," I say. "Tell me what you want me to do to you or I'll jerk myself off on those gorgeous tits of yours without laying a finger on your needy little clit." To prove it, I rise up on my knees and stroke myself a few times. "Say it, Mercy. Before I come all over—"

"I want you to fuck me!" she screams, then slaps her hand over her mouth, like she's so shocked she could say those words.

I grin and fall back over her, bracing myself on either side of her head, my cock lined up with her pussy. "Good girl," I purr. "And where do you want me to fuck you?"

"Here," she says in small voice.

"And where are we?" I nudge my cockhead into her cunt again. Mercy trembles.

"Next to Raul's grave." Her voice is barely a whisper.

"That's right, pretty thing. But he won't mind. He's not here, is he? He's up in Heaven." I shove myself inside her with a single sharp thrust, and Mercy moans and arches up into me, her hands coming up to grip my biceps.

"Yes," she whispers. "Yes, he's in Heaven."

"You're about to be in Heaven, too, humanita." I roll my

hips against her, angling it so the base of my cock slides up against her clit and my cock massages her G-spot. Mercy groans and rolls her eyes back. "The only Heaven you need."

"That's not—" she chokes out, but I give her a soft, gently slap on the side of her face and grab her chin to make her look at me.

"I'm the only Heaven you need." I thrust into her, wrapping my fingers loosely around her throat. Not to choke her but to hold her down. To let her know I have the power here.

Her pussy spasms with a quake of pleasure. Mercy wraps her fingers around my wrists, her eyes boring into mine.

"Ambrose," she whispers, rocking her hips against me, locking us in an undulating rhythm. "I think— I mean—"

Her pussy contracts around my cock. She's close.

Mercy stares at me, fingers tight around my wrist like she's holding onto a life preserver.

"I think you're the only god I need," she whispers—

Right before she comes.

CHAPTER THIRTY-FIVE

MERCY

I don't know why I said that to him, other than that it's true.

As soon as the words leave my lips, blasphemous as they are, I tip over the edge I've been balancing on since he threw me to the ground and slid his knife inside me. I split open and scream into the night—a scream Ambrose silences when he latches his mouth against mine in a brutal, violent kiss.

And he keeps fucking me, and I keep coming for him, pulse after pulse of pleasure rocking through my body as his tongue grapples with mine, his fingers wrapped around my throat like a necklace binding us together.

Then he wrenches away, rising on his knees. He lifts my legs up so that they're propped on his shoulders. Rests his fingers on my clit, still throbbing and sensitive.

"Say that to me again."

I tremble, gazing up at him, his face carved out by the moonlight. He looks like a god, with me on my back in supplication.

Ambrose pushes into me with long, slow thrusts.

"Say it," he orders, rubbing his thumb against my clit. I cry out, the intensity of his touch lighting me on fire.

"You're the only god I need." My voice rings out, stronger this time, and it feels good to say it. Just like it felt good to cry out that I wanted him to fuck me. It feels *right*.

Ambrose groans and drops his head back as he slams deep inside me, sitting there for a moment before doing it again. He fucks me with such force that I'm shoved back through the dirt, almost like he's pushing me beneath the soil. Down into the darkness, down into the underworld.

This is who I am, that I'd let him do this to me. That I would *like* it, and want it, and crave it.

"You feel so fucking good," Ambrose grunts, wrapping his fingers tight around my ankles as he slams into me and shoves me deeper into the darkness. "Human women aren't supposed to feel this damn good."

"Murderers—" I gasp out. "Murderers aren't supposed to feel this good, either."

Ambrose grins at that and rubs my clit a little faster. My arousal is soaking both of us.

"You sure about that, humanita?"

He punctuates the question with a sharp thrust, then asks,

"You going to come again for me? For your god?"

"Yes," I moan, although I don't know if I can. But I want to. I want to keep falling backward through this pleasure and depravity. I was harmed so badly by the light and the darkness both, but at least the darkness apologized. At least Ambrose saw that he hurt me and tried to fix it.

"Good," he rasps, his thrusts quickening, his fingers furiously working my clit. Tension builds in my belly like a rubber band stretching to its limit. "Because I like it when you come, little human. I like it when you fall apart for me."

I moan and let him fuck me. I let him use me just like Reverend Gunner did, like Pastor Sullivan and Deacon Price.

For three years, I was used.

But it never felt like this. It never felt like the sun was burning inside me.

"Come on, baby," Ambrose rasps. "Come on. I'm close. I'm gonna need you to come again."

"I don't—" I jerk against him, desperate to chase my pleasure. But it's not enough. The tension's there, but it's not ready to break. "I can't—"

Ambrose roars, his hips shuddering against mine, his demon seed spilling inside my womb. I suck down gulps of air, delirious with pleasure, and wait for him to pull away so it can fade.

But he doesn't. He keeps his cock shoved inside me, his thumb on my clit. "Look at me," he says, rubbing my clit in furious circles. "You're gonna look at me when you come."

He's not stopping, I realize. "You don't have to—"

"Shut the fuck up." His eyes blaze. "If I'm your god, I'll give you pleasure if I see fit. Now lie back and come for me, my little human slut."

His harsh words tear a fire through me. All I want in the whole world is to do what he says. To obey him. To worship him. To do the thing I was taught to do but which, until this moment, always felt wrong.

I settle into the graveyard grass, my eyes fluttering shut, and roll my hips against his hand until my pleasure throbs through my core. The rubber band stretches a little further.

"That's it," he breathes, lying at my side, his fingers never once leaving my clit. Warmth leaks out between my legs, and I want it to stay, desperately. It's the same fantasy I had before, of being *his*—his wife and helpmeet, the supportive woman at his side. But this time, I'm not a preacher's wife.

I'm a devil's.

"Ambrose," I choke out, the pleasure building to such a peak that it hurts. "Why are you—"

He rubs my clit harder and slides a finger easily into my cum-soaked pussy. I lose the question into a sea of moans.

"Why am I what, humanita? Why I am still fingerfucking you?"

"No." My hips grind against his hand. "Why are you protecting me?"

"Protecting you?" He puts another finger inside me and curls them both up, making me shudder and shriek and buck against the grass. "Who am I protecting you from?"

"*You*!" I scream. I'm close. I'm so, so close. He knows how to touch me. "Why don't you want to hurt me?"

He grins, his fingers sliding in and out of my body. "You mean kill you?"

My body jerks at that, the first quake of an orgasm. I nod, breathing hard, the promise of release so close. Ambrose leans over me, still working me with his expert touch.

"Because then I wouldn't get to see you do this," he says—

Right before he shifts his thumb ever-so-slightly to the left.

Every nerve in my body erupts. I feel as if I could levitate off the ground, as if I'm flooded with holy light. Not God's light, of course. But my god's light. This murderous, vicious, cruel god, who's still plunging his fingers in and out of my pussy, stroking me to oblivion.

"That's what I'm talking about," he says softly. "That right there. You just completely fall apart for me. Gorgeous. Fucking gorgeous." His lips brush against my forehead, my cheeks, the tip of my nose. "Killing you won't be nearly as much fun. And I'd only get to do it once."

His fingers are still inside me, even though he lifts his thumb off my clit. I stare up at him, wobbly, wet-eyed from pleasure. "Are you going to do it again?"

"I'll keep doing this right here until the fucking sun comes up," he says, fingers working inside me like a promise. "You have no idea how beautiful you look surrounded by death."

I push myself up enough to catch his mouth in a kiss, my fingers twined up in his hair. And he keeps touching me. It's almost too much. It almost makes me feel like my body's going to shred apart.

Almost.

"How many times can I make you come?" he rasps into my ear. "How many times can I make up for what that piece of shit Gunner did to you?"

I can't answer. I can't speak. I'm a web of ecstasy. I just stare at him with my wide eyes and moan—

Suddenly, he stops, yanking his hand out of me. I keen at its loss, but he jerks his head around, his nose wrinkling. "Someone's here," he whispers. "Fuck."

A new terror slams through me. Or maybe it's an old one— the terror I felt before I knew what Ambrose is, when I thought Reverend Gunner might find the two of us together. The terror of getting caught.

"Come on, humanita." Ambrose is already on his feet, and he grabs my hands and pulls me up, even though I wobble a little. "I need to get you out of here."

"Are you sure someone's here?" I don't hear anything. Don't see anything. The cemetery feels as empty as it has the last hour.

"Positive. He's coming from the back. Probably another street entrance there." Ambrose grabs the shovel and then takes me by the hand, his fingers braiding up in mine.

"I don't hear anything—"

"Because you're human." Ambrose jerks me up to him and kisses me with a roughness that makes my legs tremble. "I can smell him."

He tugs me forward, weaving us between the headstones. I glance back over my shoulder for one last glimpse of Raul's grave. I feel like I should be more ashamed of what we did. But the truth is, I just feel free. More free than I have in a long, long time.

A light dances through the trees.

"Ambrose!" I hiss, grabbing at his arm. He glances back and scowls.

"Damn, he got here fast," Ambrose mutters. "Or I was just too distracted to notice him when I should have."

I blush. The light bounces off the top of the gravestones.

"Who's out here?" A man's voice cuts through the night. "Cemetery's closed!"

"Oh, Jesus, I really was distracted." Ambrose laughs and pulls me forward. "Run, baby!"

The man shouts, and the lights flash, and Ambrose and I take off together through the graveyard. The wind pushes my hair back so that it streams off my shoulders, looking like moonlight. I feel like moonlight, actually, something effusive and untouchable and beautiful.

"Hey!" the man shouts. "Stop right there!"

I pump my legs faster, although I'm still not fast enough to catch up to Ambrose, who's already shoving the entrance gate open. I glance over my shoulder at our pursuer, but all I can really see of him is the bobbing flashlight.

"Come on, humanita." Ambrose grabs my hand and pulls me through the gate and kisses me, all in one motion. Then he's dragging me toward his car, and I don't know why, but I can't stop laughing. Because I'm being chased through the night, but it's not by the man who has killed three people that I know of. Because I just went to a funeral and had sex in a graveyard. Because if you had shown me all this a month ago, I would have never believed it.

But I feel better than I have since the day Reverend Gunner took me as his wife.

I fling open the passenger door of Ambrose's car and leap

inside just as the man slams up against the gate. "Stop!" he shouts. "You're trespassing!"

Ambrose ducks behind the wheel, revs the engine to life, and slams backward, grinning wildly. "That was fun as hell," he laughs, peeling out of the parking lot. "I haven't run from a human in a long-ass time."

A human. The word jars at me, a little, that reminder that Ambrose is a demon in a man's skin. But I'm still smiling. Still exhilarated. Maybe I belong with the demon.

The man chases us down the road, our taillights washing him in red light. "He'll get your license plate number," I say.

"Let him. It'll be a dead end." Ambrose turns the car sharply to pull us out onto the highway. I flip back around and sink down in my seat, still giddy with excitement. Giddy with confusion, too.

"What name is the car under?" I look over at him, wondering if he trusts me enough to share it.

"Vincent Fita," he says, his eyes fixed on the road. He's driving too fast, the buildings and street lamps blurring beside us. Chasing death, I think idly. Just like I did when I let him throw me into the graveyard grass.

"You're not afraid I'll take that name to the police?"

Ambrose glances at me. "Will you?"

His question catches me off guard. Because the first answer that pops into my head, the one that feels the most right, is *no.*

Why would I? He just held a funeral for Raul because he thought it would make me feel better. He didn't throw me to the cemetery caretaker so he could get away.

He's shown me pleasure and a strange sort of a kindness and isn't that all I've ever wanted but couldn't get, not in the church?

"That quiet is making me nervous," he says lightly. I know it's a lie. Nothing makes him nervous.

"I want to stay with you."

I hadn't realized that was how I was going to answer until I say it, the words erupting out of me. I go tense, but Ambrose seems to soften. The car slows, too, even though we're reaching the edge of the Cocana city limits and there's nothing but the highway from here on out.

"I really was going to let you go," Ambrose says softly. He doesn't look at me. "I had it all planned out—I was going to give you some money to get you started. Drive you into Dallas and leave you there. Easier to get by in a big city."

I stare at him, at the highway shadows melting across his face. "Why?"

Ambrose frowns. "Why what?"

"Why would you do all that?"

Ambrose doesn't answer right away. There's just the highway and the night, the soft purr of his engine, the frantic thudding of my heart.

"Because I like you, Mercy," he finally says. "And you deserve to be happy."

CHAPTER THIRTY-SIX

AMBROSE

Mercy sleeps with me that night, curled up in the bed at my side, her hair damp from the shower she took to wash the graveyard dirt away. I don't have the heart to tell her I don't need to sleep, but I stay in bed with her anyway, watching news reports on my phone with the sound turned low and one hand trailing through her hair.

I want to stay with you. Mercy's confession keeps marching through my head. I'd been so ready to let her go, and now it almost feels like a trick, her warm body curled up next to me, the steady rhythm of her breath filling up the room.

Because she can't stay with me, not really. I can't have a human woman in my life. My life is too fucking dangerous for something so fragile. Something that can die as easily as her.

Sawyer does it.

Sawyer's a fool. Even if he does seem happy. And, more importantly, so does Edie.

The video I'm watching ends; it was today's news report from Cocana. Nothing of interest. But when the next video starts, Reverend Gunner's face fills up my screen. It was posted two hours earlier by what seems to be an official Church of the Well account. So much for eschewing the secular world.

"My ward, Mercy Gunner, is still missing," Gunner says, and I can tell even through the phone screen that the sadness in his voice is a facade. "We fear the worst, and we're calling on all Christians, regardless of your affiliation, to offer up prayers for her safe return."

I recognize his office behind him, the window open to show the church compound beyond.

"Three of our brothers have joined Christ at the hands of a Satanic madman," he goes on, which makes me snort. Beside me, Mercy stirs, but I stroke her hair and murmur at her to go back to sleep.

"We fear that madman has taken our Mercy," Gunner continues, and my skin bristles at that—*our* Mercy. "That he's doing ungodly things to her as we speak."

Well, that part's true, at least. I bite back a smirk.

"Any information you have about this man—" Reverend Gunner fades away, replaced with that police sketch of the itinerant preacher Ambrose Echeverría, who as far as the state of Texas is concerned, hasn't existed for nearly a century. "Please report it to the Cocana sheriff's department. And if you see any sign of Mercy Hendricks, please, let us know."

Mercy Hendricks, huh? I see he's using her real last name.

Another picture fills the screen: the same one as before, Mercy in her pretty blue dress. She really does look fucking miserable.

I think about her twinkling laughter as we ran away from the cemetery earlier. What sort of Hunter am I, that I like hearing a human's laughter instead of her screams?

Well, in addition to her screams.

The picture of Mercy fades, and three new pictures take its place: my three most recent victims. It's been a while since I've attracted the attention of the media, and seeing my victims lined up like that gives me a delicious little thrill. All the suffering I caused. All the fear I've sowed. It's what I was made for, and the idea that I have a whole church cowering in their beds because of me is—

Well, it's getting my cock hard.

"Three members of our church have gone to Christ," Reverend Gunner is saying. "And we need your help bringing their murderer to justice. Your prayers, any information—whatever you can provide. God bless you. Truly."

He doesn't care about any of them. He didn't even bury Raul on the church compound, and there's no way he officiated Raul's funeral. Contrary to what he made Mercy think when she was still trapped there, she *does* have the power to bring him to his knees. All she has to do is tell the truth about what he did to her, and the good Reverend Gunner will have a good old-fashioned sex scandal on his hands.

I'm not sure my humanita realizes that she could take down the whole damn church if she wanted to.

I stop the video and turn off my phone. Mercy breathes beside me, her scent wafting around through. I can't stop myself from reaching down to idly stroke my cock over my boxers, my thoughts half on the three murders—especially that motherfucker Price—and half on Mercy's soft, warm body.

I lean down to nuzzle her neck and kiss her fluttery pulse. Mercy sighs and turns toward me, muttering something I can't decipher. This is getting me worked up, truth be told.

But I also want to see how much she's willing to tolerate my nature. If she really understands what it means to be stay with me.

"How long will it take you to wake up?" I slide my hand up under her T-shirt and palm her bare breasts, which makes her shiver. She doesn't answer, of course. Still asleep. But her lips part and her nipples sharpen beneath my hand. She moans softly.

"Are you getting wet for me?" I'm already hard as hell for her. Sex and death, there's no better combination. Even she discovered that earlier tonight in the cemetery.

I massage her breasts, slow and lazy, and she moans and shifts around on the mattress. *I want to stay with you.* I still don't really understand why. Not why she wants it. Not why I want it either.

I run my hand over her belly and slip my fingers into her panties, which are as damp as I expect. I tease her clit for a few seconds, keeping my gaze on her face. Her eyes flick beneath her eyelids, and she mutters again.

It almost sounds like she's saying my name.

"What was that, humanita?" I slide the panties off her. "Were you dreaming about me?"

"Ambrose?" Her voice is much more clear now, and her eyes flutter open and look up at me, although they're unfocused, glazed over. She's half asleep.

"I'm going to fuck you, Mercy." Her panties are a tangle around her knees, and I have to resist the urge to shred them into ribbons. "Do you understand?"

"Yes," she slurs, lifting her hips up a little. Then: "Am I dreaming?"

"No, sweetness." I manage to get her loose of the damned panties, and I ball them up in my fist. "Open your mouth for me."

She does, immediately. I press the panties over her tongue, a makeshift gag.

"Keep those in there," I tell her, looking her straight in the eye. "That's where they belong. Do you understand?"

Mercy nods, her eyes wide. She's awake now. And afraid. Aroused. Squirming against the mattress.

"Good girl. You're so obedient." I trace my finger along her cheek, and she moans a little around the panties. "I like that. I like it when you obey me." I wrap my fingers softly around her throat. "But only when you obey *me*, do you understand? Not anyone else."

Mercy nods and then, to my delight, spreads her legs a little wider for me.

"You're a fucking treasure." I push up her T-shirt so her breasts are exposed to the air, and then I pull one into my mouth, flicking my tongue against her nipple. Mercy's moans deepen, and I reach up to press my hand over her mouth, holding the panties in place.

"I want you quiet, humanita." I kiss between her breasts, licking up the taste of her skin. "No matter what I do to you, you're not allowed to scream."

I lift my gaze just as her fear spikes, and I grin wickedly. "I'm not going to hurt you." I kiss her tits again. Suck on her nipples. "But I like how your fear smells. And this frightens you, doesn't it?"

Mercy nods wordlessly. I drop my hand down to massage her cunt. She's soaked.

"But it turns you on, too, doesn't it?"

She doesn't respond right away. I slide two fingers inside her and press upward, making her buck against my hand and cry out, although her cry is muffled. I tsk softly.

"I told you to be quiet, little human. I'm the devil, remember?" I pull my hand away so I can crawl on top of her, settling myself between her spread legs. I press my mouth to her ear. "The truth is," I murmur. "You have no idea the evil I'm capable of."

Her body stiffens beneath mine, and she draws her hands up. I expect her to shove me away, to yank the panties out of her mouth and scream at me to stop touching her.

Instead, she runs them up my arms, like she can't get enough of my skin. Then she pulls me closer to her. I have to bite back a groan of pleasure—I don't want her to see me lose control. Not right now. Not like this.

I need to show her the real me. Let her know what's getting into. So I take a deep breath and press my mouth to her ear.

"If you're going to stay with me," I whisper to her, my cock pressing into her thigh, "then you need to understand what I am. *Fully* understand."

She looks at me, eyes blazing, and says something around the panties.

"Silence," I order, and then I move like a Hunter to flip her onto her belly. She bounces on the mattress, crying out again, and I slap her on the ass, hard enough to leave a red imprint of my hand.

She groans, arching her back in pleasure or pain or both. I yank my cock out of my boxers and stroke it just to try and quiet my lust. "I told you not to make any noise," I tell her, and then I slap her other ass cheek, her flesh rippling beneath my hand.

Mercy drops her head into the pillow and says nothing.

"Good girl. That's what I want to see." I position myself behind her, dragging back her hips so I can shove my cock into her waiting cunt. I know I'm trying to act in control, but I can't bite back my groans as I slide home. She just feels too damn good.

Let's see how much of the boogeyman she can take before I spill inside her.

I start slowly, keeping my thrusts measured and even. Her body trembles beneath me, and I run my hand down the indentation of her spine, which just makes her shiver harder. "You're doing so well," I tell her. "Staying quiet for me. You know why I want you quiet?"

Mercy shakes her head against the pillow and rolls her hips against me. I know she's trying to get some sensations on her clit, but I smack her lightly on her ass in warning. "Not yet, humanita. I'll let you come if you're good, but you need to wait. Do you understand?"

She nods, tilting her head to look at me over her shoulders. Her eyes are wild with lust, and she bites down hard on her panties as she stares at me through the tangle of her hair.

"Good." I quicken my pace a little, keeping my gaze fixed on hers. "Here's what's going to happen. If you want to stay with me, you need to understand what I am—*really* understand. You need to hear the depths I can plunge to." I bottom out inside her, making her grunt around the panties. "And I'm going to tell you with my cock buried in your pussy. Nod if that makes sense."

She hesitates, just for a second, before nodding once.

"If you change your mind about me, and I don't blame you one goddamn bit if you do, take those panties out of your mouth and tell me. I'll stop." I thrust my full length into her again, grinning as she bites back another cry of pain. "But as long as those panties stay, I'll keep going. Do you understand?"

There's no hesitation this time. She nods vigorously, a simple motion that sends heat flooding into my belly. I dig my fingers into the flesh of her hips. Take a deep breath.

"Good," I say. "Now let's get started."

CHAPTER THIRTY-SEVEN

MERCY

I know I should be terrified. And part of me is, the fear twisting around in my belly at whatever it is Ambrose wants to reveal to me.

But he also feels so, so *good*.

I press my cheek into the pillow, tasting myself in the fabric of the panties, as Ambrose thrusts viciously into my pussy. He squeezes my hips, his fingers digging into me enough to cause some pain, but I don't care. I—

I *like* it, the sting of his nails and the steady metronome of his thrusts. My thighs are already slick with my arousal, and I have to swallow every moan and whimper. I know if I could wriggle my hips just right, I'd get the pressure on my clit I'm desperately craving, but I don't.

I trust him to finish me—even if I'm not sure what else he's going to do.

"You know the one thing that would make your cunt feel better?" Ambrose grunts, our flesh slapping together. "If my cock was covered in Reverend Gunner's blood."

The last thing I expect is for Ambrose to say *his* name, and the shock reverberates through me. But I don't take out the panties. Because he didn't *just* say his name, did he?

"Oh, that got your attention." Ambrose chuckles and stops his thrusting, his cock buried fully inside me. "You're wetter than you were a second ago."

That can't be true. I squeeze my eyes shut.

I don't take out the panties.

Ambrose groans and starts up again, faster and harder than before. "Yes, Mercy, I want to kill Reverend Gunner. I want to kill every man who ever laid a finger on you. That's why I killed Deacon Price, you know."

I keen into the panties, and I'm not surprised when Ambrose slaps my ass again, the pain sharpening the pleasure of his cock. The images flash through my head—the blood, Deacon Price screaming—

And I feel something ripple inside me. A jolt of pleasure.

Ambrose laughs. "Oh, fuck, humanita. I felt that." He collapses on top of me, still grinding me down into the mattress, and kisses the back of my neck. "Would you want to watch me kill Gunner, sweet thing? Would you want to sit in the corner and touch your pretty little clit while I cut him limb from limb?"

I bite back a moan—out of shame, not fear of Ambrose's punishment.

"You would," he whispers.

"No!" I scream against the panties, but I don't take them out because I don't want this to stop.

I don't want *any* of it to stop.

Ambrose growls like a hell beast, jerks himself back up, and changes his position in a particular way. Now, when he thrusts inside me, it hurts.

"You know what to do if you want me to stop," he says, and his thrusts slow and feel good again, like hot melting sugar, and I don't do it. I bite down on the panties so hard my jaw aches.

Ambrose makes a kind of startled noise and squeezes his hands into my thighs and says. "On your hands and knees, baby."

He yanks me up, never taking his cock out of me, and then he begins to thrust into me in earnest, lightning-fast. Faster than should be possible. I squeeze my eyes shut and give myself over to it, gasping and panting around the panties.

"I wouldn't just kill him," Ambrose pants. "You need to know that. I'd take my time. Torture him. Cut off chunks of his thigh meat, fry it in some butter, eat it in front of him."

This is terrible. Nightmarish. My thighs are drenched.

"I'd let you have a few bites, if you wanted."

I collapse down on my elbows, squeezing the bedsheet up into my fists. Ambrose never slows, his thrusts so sharp and deep that my whole body shakes with them.

"But that's not all I'd do," he continues. "I'd peel the skin of his face away and expose all the nerves there. He'd be in absolute agony. And you, my pretty little human, you'd be getting off to it. I'd make sure he knows."

I buck back against Ambrose, matching his thrusts with my own. Fire burns up through my core. I know I should stop this. I tell myself it's not even true, what he's saying—about me getting off to it. But I still don't want to stop.

Maybe Ambrose isn't the only devil here.

"I might break a few fingers," he says. "Hold him underwater until he starts breathing it in. I don't know. It would depend on my mood."

The heat flushes even hotter. I know that if I were to snake my hand down between my legs and touch myself, I would unravel instantly for him.

Ambrose falls on top of me again, still rolling his hips up against me as he pushes away damp strands of my hair to kiss and lick at the back of my neck. "I told you I didn't let Raul suffer," he murmurs, "and I didn't lie. His death was easy. Almost instantaneous."

I whimper, tears brimming along my lashes. I don't want to think about Raul dying, but these tears aren't sorrow. They're pleasure.

"Gunner's won't be."

I groan around the panties, my body jolting. One touch to my clit. One touch and I would die in this all-consuming hellfire.

"None of them will have an easy death," Ambrose says, slowing his strokes until they're almost torturous. "Any man who touched you when you didn't want it will beg for the release of death. Do you understand that, Mercy? Do you understand that's what it means to stay with me?"

"Yes!" I scream around the panties, tears streaming down my cheeks. The pressure in my belly is unbearable, and I thrust my hips back against Ambrose, desperate for my own release. For my own death. Not death of body but death of spirit and soul.

Because I know that's what I'm doing here. I'm selling my soul to the devil.

"You're so fucking wet," Ambrose whispers, kissing the top of my shoulders. "You're so fucking wet from this. Do you know that, humanita?"

I sob around the panties and try to reach down between my belly and the bed. Ambrose grabs my wrist.

"Not yet," he snarls into my ear. "You don't get to come until I've tasted you." He presses his mouth against my shoulder again. It's not exactly a kiss. And instinctively, I know what he's going to do. I know what he wants to taste. Because I know what kind of meat he keeps in his freezer.

"Last chance, baby," he breathes, shoving my wrist away. His voice is ragged. "I'm going to take a big bite of your sweet flesh while I pump your womb full of my seed. This is your last chance to stop me."

My heart feels like it's going to explode out of my chest. Every nerve in my body is screaming for release. And all I do is tuck my hands underneath me, as far from the panties in my mouth as I can get them.

Ambrose lets out a dark, shuddery breath. Braces his hands on my waist. I squeeze my teary eyes shut.

My shoulder blooms with agony. I scream and buck up against him, but he's too strong, and he pins me down against the bed, his teeth sinking deeper and deeper into my flesh. The pain is exquisite, as exquisite as the fire coursing between my legs,

Suddenly, all that tension tilts and spills. I didn't need him to touch my clit. All I needed was for him to devour me.

I scream around the panties, bucking and jerking against the mattress, the orgasm searing through my body. I'm distantly aware that he's still biting me, that he's tearing and chewing and dragging my flesh away. Distantly aware that blood runs hot down my arm. But I don't feel it anymore.

All I feel is pleasure. It feels like the end of the world. It feels like God.

I collapse face down on the pillow, pulses of heat still racing through my core. Ambrose licks my shoulder, his tongue warm and soft against the pain of the wound. "You're delicious," he pants between licks. "You're sublime. I want to eat every fucking inch of you."

Then he jerks me up so we're both kneeling on the bed, my back pressed against his chest. I can't move. I'm boneless, still quivering with aftershocks. Ambrose reaches around and gently pries the panties out of my mouth, and I suck down a lungful of air and slump back against him, staring first at the wall and then down at the bed, where my blood stains the sheets.

My shoulder howls with pain.

"It hurts," I say softly. "Where you—"

I turn toward him, and I'm not terribly surprised by what I see: Ambrose smiling gently down at me, his mouth smeared with my blood.

"I know, baby." He pushes my hair out of my eyes, then runs his thumb over my cheek, following the tracks of my tears. "I can't believe you didn't stop me."

I sway, woozy from what we did. From all his violent words, from the pain in my shoulder, from the lingering bursts of pleasure between my thighs.

"Do you really want to eat me?" I ask, my words slurred.

Ambrose smiles, my blood gleaming on his teeth. "Fuck, yes, I do. But I'd rather have you around, so I won't." He presses his forehead against mine. "But I had to show you all of me. I needed you to *see* it. If you don't want to stay—"

I kiss him.

I do it without thinking—it just feels like the right thing to do. Even if tasting my own blood startles me. Even if he pulls me roughly up against him, and it makes pain bloom in my shoulder. When I cry out, he deepens the kiss to silence me. For a moment, I wonder if he really will try to eat me someday.

But the thought doesn't disgust me. It floods me with warmth, actually, that Ambrose would want me enough to pull me into him like that.

I break the kiss with a gasp, still tasting my blood. Ambrose smiles at me, looking as much like the devil as he ever has. "You really aren't what I expected when I first met you in Gunner's office."

I blush and wipe the back of my hand across my mouth. It comes away bloody. My shoulder's still burning, too.

"I need to dress that," Ambrose says.

It takes a moment to realize he means the bite. I hadn't looked at it yet, but I do now. It's messy and violent, a jagged hunk of my flesh missing from the familiar curve of my shoulder. I can see the muscle tissue, impossibly red and shiny.

I feel dizzy. That part of me is inside him. Forever.

"I don't want it to get infected." Ambrose guides me down so I'm sitting on the bed, then kisses my temple. "Wait here."

He ducks into the attached bathroom, and all I can do is sit and stare dazedly at the doorway, listening to him dig around in the cabinets. His vicious words circle through my head. All that talk about killing Reverend Gunner. *Every man who touched you against your will.*

There have only been three of them. Deacon Price, Reverend Gunner, Pastor Sullivan. And one of them is already dead.

Heat coils in me, strange and unfamiliar. Ambrose steps out of the bathroom holding the first aid supplies and comes and sits down next to me. His closeness is a comfort.

"This is going to scar," he says, wiping the blood away with a soft towel. I suck air through my teeth. "Nothing I can do about that."

"I don't mind."

Ambrose fixes me with his dark eyes. "You don't really mean that."

I look right back at him. "I do, actually. I could have stopped it but I didn't."

Ambrose is the first to break eye contact, dropping the towel on the bed and reaching for the antiseptic. "You're full of surprises, humanita."

"So are you."

He grins. Squeezes a dollop of the antiseptic directly on the bite, which makes me cry out. "Yes, but I don't imagine any of my surprises have been particularly pleasant."

I don't say anything, just bite down on my lip as he gently works the antiseptic into the wound. It hurts, but I can tell he's trying to make it hurt less. And I imagine that's not easy for him.

"I have a friend," Ambrose says softly. "Sawyer. He's like me. And he's got a girl like you."

I lift my gaze to his face. He's not looking at me, though. "What do you mean?"

"She's human. I mentioned her to you once. Told you she's Charlotte's friend. And she is." He picks up a pad of gauze and presses it against the wound. "But she's also Sawyer's girl. And he bit her in the shoulder, left a scar a bit like this. Yours will be a lot worse, though."

I frown, watching Ambrose work. I still can't get over how gentle he is, especially compared with just a few moments ago. "Does that happen a lot?" I say. "For, um, people like you—" I almost said *demons*, "—to marry humans?"

"They're not married." Ambrose looks at me. "Don't know if they ever will. But they're *together*, and yeah, it happens. Not frequently, but it happens."

He smooths the gauze tape over my skin, and I'm not sure what I'm feeling. Hope or disappointment or confusion or disgust or affection. Or all of them, all at once. Maybe that's why I say what I say next.

"I always wanted to get married." I pull away from him and run my hands over the wound dressing, the tape rough beneath my fingers. I keep my gaze fixed on it as I speak. "I thought—I thought it would make life a little more bearable, having a husband who loves me. But Reverend Gunner—" My voice catches. "He took that away from me."

The mattress shifts and creaks. I moved away from Ambrose, but now he's moving closer. Chasing me.

He grabs my chin, pulls my gaze toward him. And what I see there, in his expression—

It terrifies me.

His eyes are flat. Empty. Undeniably cruel. But he still cups my cheek like a lover.

Like a husband.

"Everything I said about him," Ambrose says in a dark, rough voice. "Earlier? While I was inside you?"

My body flares at that, like it wants to invite him inside again.

"I meant it." His fingers tighten against my cheek, and I gasp in a soft breath. "I'll do every goddamn thing I promised. Just say the word."

Those promises flash through my head.

"You'd make him beg for death," I whisper.

"I'd make all of them beg for death." His eyes are as black and empty as Hell. "Give me their names, and I'll slaughter every single one of them."

Ambrose pulls me up to him, presses a bloody kiss against my forehead.

"And I'd do it all for you."

CHAPTER THIRTY-EIGHT

MERCY

I lie in my own bed that night, in the clean sheets, and I consider what Ambrose told me.

He assumes I'm sleeping, I'm sure—he helped me wash off the blood, then tucked me into bed, his goodnight kiss deep and treacherous, as if he might start devouring me again. But he didn't. Only whispered, "Try to sleep," before he slipped out of the room.

I can't sleep, though. I listen to the creaks of the house, the moans of the wind across the flatlands. I replay what we did, and I run my hands over my body, shuddering at my own touch. I imagine it belongs to Ambrose.

Just say the word.

For the first time in my life, I feel something like power. It feels strange, like a hand-me-down dress, but I could get used to it.

I think about the day I swore myself to Reverend Gunner, that I'd be his wife and helpmeet. And I think about that night, when I was terrified and asked him to stop because it hurt, and he didn't. I think about how he slapped my face for crying and told me I needed to behave because my disobedience was displeasing to God.

He said the same thing when I told him I didn't want to sleep with Pastor Sullivan. And how I did it anyway, trying to numb myself as Pastor Sullivan panted above me. I think about the shame I felt as I stretched out on the bed, my eyes fixed on the ceiling.

For weeks afterward, anytime Reverend Gunner touched me, it was like he was dragging a knife over my skin.

Ambrose actually *did* draw a knife over my skin, but when he touches me, it feels like coming home. I want to beg him to do things that would turn my stomach if Reverend Gunner did them. I want to beg him to do far worse things, too.

The difference, I think, is the power. In the end, Ambrose gifts it to me.

Footsteps echo outside my door, followed by a soft knock. "Mercy?"

"Ambrose?" I sit up, and he steps into the room, warm soft light spilling in from the hallway. "What's wrong?"

"I was going to ask the same of you." I can just barely make out his silhouette in the darkness. "You're not sleeping." He moves closer to me, and his eyes shine in the darkness, turning to illuminated glass. "You feel—upset. Confused."

Something shudders through me. "How'd you know that?"

"Same reason I can hunt humans so easily." He takes another step closer and his eyes are normal again. "I hear your heartbeat, your breath. I can smell your emotions."

He kneels down in front of me, and I feel it again, that strange surge of power. For a reason I don't fully understand, I touch the top of his head, the way he touched mine back on the church campus. It feels like a lifetime ago.

Ambrose gazes up at me. "You can leave anytime you want."

"I don't want to leave." My vehemence surprises me. "I want—"

I cut my words off. What I want to say is too dangerous. The worst kind of sin.

But Ambrose knows anyway. His eyes glitter, and he smiles that cruel killer's grin, and he licks his lips like he's starving. "Just say the word, Mercy."

I push my fingers through his hair, staring down at him. "I'm afraid. But you knew that already."

He rises up enough to kiss me, and this time, there's no taste of blood. "Yeah," he murmurs into my ear. "Yeah, I did."

Then he stands, and our positions are flipped, me gazing up at him. But I still feel that power. He may as well be kneeling. He looks down at me as if he is.

I lean forward and press my cheek against his belly, my arms wrapped around his thighs. He strokes my hair.

"I want you to do it," I whisper, squeezing my eyes shut. I practically have to spit the words out, but now that I've said them I feel lighter. I let out a long brush of air and bury my nose in Ambrose's shirt, breathing in his scent. "I want you to kill them."

Ambrose goes still, his hand resting on the top of my head. But I can feel the hard ridge of his cock where I couldn't before.

And my own sex pulses.

"Names," he says.

I take a deep, shivering breath. This will make it real, won't it? As real as his hand combing over my hair. As real as the power he cracked open inside me.

But I still can't quite bring myself to say their names. So I kiss him. I kiss his belly, and then I kiss a little lower, worshipping him through the fabric of his pants, trying to conjure up the strength to wield my power.

"I want you to kill them," I whisper, my rage surging up in me, as hot and terrifying as my lust. I think I'm trying to convince myself.

"Tell me their fucking names, Mercy." Ambrose tightens his grip on my hair. "Tell me who you want me to kill."

I nuzzle against his erection. I don't know why, but it soothes me, that reassuring hardness. "There are only two," I whisper, lifting one shaking hand to undo Ambrose's zipper. He grunts softly, presses his hand more firmly against my head.

"I want to hear you say their names."

My heart feels like a hummingbird. "Reverend Gunner."

"Who else?" This time, he tugs hard on my hair so I have to look up at him, at the twisted desire on his face as I pull out his cock. He bats it gently against my cheek.

"Pastor Sullivan."

And like that, I've condemned them to death, and I'm free. My heart feels like it's going to erupt out of my chest. Ambrose's cock is a rod of fire against my face.

He smiles. "Consider it done, humanita."

My only response is to take him into my mouth.

It's an act of worship, not debasement. I draw him over my tongue, pulling him as deep into my mouth as I possibly can. For a moment, I just hold him there, my eyes watering as he strokes my hair. Then I pull my head back, dragging my tongue along the underside of his cock until I reach his cockhead, which I swirl and suck, lapping up the salt of his precum. Ambrose sighs, his fingers braiding through my hair. But he holds still and lets me worship him.

I bob up and down his length, fucking him with my mouth. At the same time, I grind my pussy down onto the mattress, desperate to find pressure on my clit.

"How do you want me to do it?" Ambrose asks, his voice ragged.

I release him with a *pop* and look up at him, numb to the horror of what I've done. He keeps stroking my hair, his touch shockingly gentle.

"However you want," I whisper.

He smiles, and I kiss his cockhead like a lollipop, swirling my tongue around his hot flesh. "Tell me what you'd do," I whisper. "Like you did before."

I swallow him again, and Ambrose groans, dark and throaty. His fingers tighten slightly against my head.

"I'd have to get them alone first," he rasps. "Out of the compound. Down by the Concho, maybe."

I moan at that, rocking my hips against the mattress.

"You like that idea, do you, humanita?"

Ambrose pushes my hair away from my face as I suck him more fervently. *Worship* him more fervently. Just for a few seconds. Then I release him and stroke his wet shaft as I say, "It's where I was baptized."

"Mmm. I think you need a new baptism." Ambrose pushes my hair away from my face, and I lick down his length and then pull one of his testicles into my mouth, still stroking him. He groans. "I think *I* need to baptize you."

I can't even imagine what depravity his idea of a baptism would be. But still, I look up at him again. "I want that."

"Finish me with your mouth," Ambrose orders. "And I'll baptize you into a new church."

"Tell me what you'd do to them," I counter.

Ambrose's eyes flash, and he grabs his cock from me and bats it against my lips with firm hard slaps until I open up for him.

"You'll get them to the river for me," he says, rolling his hips against my face—gently, but still with enough force to remind me that he is the god and I am the worshipper. I swallow him as best I can, wrapping my arms around his legs to brace myself. "I'll be waiting for them with my long-range rifle." He groans. "Then I'll hunt them, one after the other. I'll wound them. Let them suffer in the heat."

His thrusts grow sharper, but I match their speed and he stills, letting me take over. Salt blooms on my tongue.

Ambrose grabs onto my hair, his words punctuated by sharp breaths. "Once I've got them where I want them, we'll track their blood trails together, you and I."

I moan, knowing I'm condemning myself to hell but not caring because hell is better than Heaven ever could be. My clit burns—the pressure of the mattress isn't enough, but I'm afraid to let go of Ambrose's legs to touch myself.

"I'll gut them," he rasps, thrusting his cock over my tongue. "Field dress them. Then I'll cook you a god damn wedding fea—"

The word *wedding* sears through me, but only for a second, because Ambrose shoves his full length into my mouth and releases his seed with a roar. It shoots down my throat, making it easy to swallow, and I keep sucking on him until he wrenches himself away. He stares down at me as he tucks himself back into his pants, his face flushed and his chest heaving.

"Strip for me," he says.

I want to ask him what he was going to say, about a wedding —but, in this moment, he seems more demon than man. I would also rather die than disobey him.

I fumble with my sleeping clothes, dragging the shirt over my head, yanking down the boxers. Ambrose just watches me, his eyes shining in the dark.

"Lay back," he says when I'm naked. "Show me your cunt."

I do, pushing my legs wide, my breath shallow. Ambrose falls to his knees and attacks me with his mouth, plunging his tongue up inside my body. I shriek and lift my hips to greet him. He pushes me down and kisses my sex as if he were kissing my mouth. And he keeps doing it, unleashing an unrelenting onslaught of pleasure.

I moan, jerking up toward him, thighs trembling, orgasm surging—

But then, just as I'm about to come, Ambrose pulls away.

"Get on the floor," he orders.

"Why?" I can barely get the word out. It's like the pleasure is shredding me to ribbons.

Ambrose tilts his head, and his eyes turn black again. "So I can baptize you, Mercy Hendricks." He reaches behind him, into his back pocket, and pulls out the same slim switchblade he used on me in the cemetery.

"With what?" I whisper. Even though I know.

The blade flashes out, as bright as starlight.

"With my blood, Mercy. I'm not letting you leave this house until I've bathed you in my fucking blood."

CHAPTER THIRTY-NINE

MERCY

I knew what he was going to say, but hearing it still sends frissons of fear snaking through my body. I look past the knife to Ambrose's face, half-expecting to see a demon there, but of course I don't.

It's Ambrose. My protector, in his way. My savior.

My pussy throbs with a sudden, violent pulse.

"If you want me to kill those pieces of shit," Ambrose says softly, still holding the knife. "Then I'm gonna have to use you as bait to lure them away from the compound. And I'm not doing that—"

He steps closer to me, pushes the hair away from my face.

"—Unless I've claimed you as mine."

I look Ambrose straight in the eye."'For my flesh is meat indeed, and my blood is drink indeed,'" I whisper. "'He that eateth my flesh and drinketh my blood abideth in me, and I in him.'"

Ambrose runs his thumb along my lips. "Exactly." Then he steps back and orders, "On the floor. I'm going to drench that gorgeous body with my blood."

Hearing him say it out loud makes me dizzy. Not with

disgust, which is the only thing I think I should be feeling. But with desire. With—affection. Warmth.

I look at him again.

"I'm not letting you anywhere near Gunner or Sullivan otherwise," he says.

I take a deep breath. My clit throbs again, and I drop my hand down to touch it with slow circles. Ambrose notices, because he smiles a little.

"When you do this," I whisper, working through my thoughts, which feel thick and strange. "When you do this, it'll bring me into a new church. A new faith."

Ambrose's eyes bore into me as he touches himself over his clothes. He's getting hard again, which seems like it should be impossible, but then—

He's not human.

"And what faith is that, humanita?"

"You," I whisper, still touching my clit as I slide off the bed, my movements shaky and uncertain. My behind hits the cool hardwood floor, and I scoot forward so that I'm angled toward him.

Ambrose kneels between my spread thighs. Takes my hand away from my clit. Looks me dead in the eye.

"When I do this," he murmurs. "You'll belong to me. Is that what you want?"

My body pulses with desire. "Why did you say you wanted to turn Reverend Gunner and Pastor Sullivan into a wedding feast?"

Ambrose tilts his head and leans closer. "Because I'll belong to you, too."

Then he kisses me, soft and sweet, and I melt into it, my body screaming for him. Screaming for *this*, this blasphemy. This darkness.

"Do it," I whisper against his rough lips. "Baptize me."

Ambrose lets out a sharp, shuddering sigh. "Touch yourself," he breathes.

Then he stands. I lift my gaze to meet his and slide my hand down to rub my clit, stoking my fire even further. Ambrose's expression is deadly serious, and his eyes never leave mine.

"No other man will ever touch you again," he says darkly. "Do you understand?"

Heat courses through me. "Yes, sir."

"I'm about to mark you as mine. Do you acknowledge that? What it means?"

I swallow, my fingers rubbing even more furiously against my clit. I'm so close to coming. So close to giving myself to this monster completely. "Yes, sir." The words come out hitched, my orgasm surging closer.

"Keep touching yourself. Do not stop. Do you understand?"

"Yes, sir."

Ambrose nods once, satisfied, and holds one arm over me. He holds the knife in the other. I stare up at him, panting and trembling, burning up from anticipation.

Then he shoves the blade into his arm, so quickly I hardly see it. But I feel it. I feel the hot, thick blood splatter across my bare breasts and streak down over my belly. And I keep touching myself, the way Ambrose asked, because I want to obey him. Obeying him makes me feel like a treasure.

Ambrose tosses the knife aside with a clatter as his blood flows out of the long, jagged cut on his arm. It splatters over me, streaking my face and my body and pooling around my hand as I touch myself.

"Drink me." Ambrose drops to his knees and presses his bleeding arm to my lips. I part them and lap up his blood like a cat, my eyes fluttering closed, my fingers still thrumming my clit. His blood is salty and thick and I have one quivering thought—

I can't come like this.

But then I do, moaning and bucking against the floor as all my pleasure surges through me, pulled forward by the baptism of Ambrose's blood. Ambrose pulls his arm away but keeps bleeding over me, never breaking eye contact. I gaze at him, gasping and quaking, forcing myself to hold still so he can baptize me as he sees fit.

"You're mine," he says raggedly, pulling his arm away. "No man will ever touch you again."

I can't stop trembling with aftershocks. I can't stop staring at him in adoration, his blood hot on my skin.

"Yes," I whisper. "Yes, I'm yours."

Ambrose grabs my shirt from where I discarded it on the floor, wraps it around his arm, and knots it off. All I can do is watch him, breathing heavily. He doesn't seem as composed as he usually does—there's a kind of dazed expression in his eyes, like he feels as overwhelmed by this as I do.

Then he launches himself at me, dragging my blood-soaked body up to him in a messy, frantic kiss.

"Mercy," he breathes. "How are you fucking real?"

"How are you?" I whisper back, drawing back to look him in the eye. "Are you really going to kill them for me?"

Ambrose pushes my hair back and kisses me again, although it's more gentle this time.

"Yes," he whispers into my ear. "I'm going to hunt both of them through the desert until they're nothing but blood and bone."

I sag against him, listening to the slow, steady rhythm of his heart. My own heart is still racing, and being close to him, wrapped in his arms, doesn't help.

"But before we talk more about that—" Ambrose nuzzles the top of my head, breathing in deep. Then, he sweeps me up in one smooth motion, pulling me into a bridal carry despite his injured arm. I cry out and loop my arms around his shoulder for balance, but he doesn't seem bothered. He smiles softly down at me as he carries me out of the bedroom, into the dark hallway, and into the main bathroom, with its big tiled shower.

"I guess I do need to rinse off," I say, heat flooding into my cheeks.

Ambrose doesn't answer except to set me down and turn the water on. Then he strips out of his own clothes, tossing them out into the hallway along with the blood-soaked T-shirt, and helps me under the hot, steaming spray. The water streams over my body in warm rivulets, and it reminds me of his blood.

"Let me wash you," he says softly, cupping my face with his hands, giving me a soft kiss on my lips.

"What about your arm?"

"You know I don't need to worry about that."

I nod, breath tight in my chest.

When Ambrose starts to wash me, it's slow and methodical, as if he's afraid he might hurt me. He lathers up the bar of soap between his hands and then rubs it over my shoulders, my arms, my breasts, his touch gentle and lingering. The red water turns pink, and Ambrose kisses me as he moves down my body—first on my mouth, but then on the places he cleans, like he's anointing my skin.

Eventually, the water runs clear. That's when Ambrose kneels down in front of me and washes my sex with his hands, rubbing the soap between my legs with careful determination. "Balance yourself," he mutters. "Against the wall." When I do, he hoists my left leg over his shoulder and continues to clean me, the shower pounding over us.

It feels good, of course, because of where he's touching me, but it also feels chaste somehow. Holy. I drop my head back as the shower beats across my chest, but all I can think of is Jesus washing the feet of his disciples. That is what this feels like, as Ambrose bows in front of me, worshipping me with his careful touch.

He sets my foot down on the tile and tugs me forward at

the hips to wash the soap away. I lay my hand on the top of his head as he's done to me so many times, and he tilts his gaze upward.

My monster, my demon. Kneeling before me after claiming me as his own.

No man will ever touch you again.

That's all I want. To belong to one person who loves me—

The thought jars me. He can't love me, can he? Not a killer like him.

Except this feels like love.

"I'm not done, humanita," he says, right before he kisses the damp triangle of my pubic hair, his lips too far away from my clit to do anything but make me sigh.

Then he keeps going, washing my thighs, my calves.

My feet.

He guides me backward to do that, until my back is pressed against the cool tile, and lifts up one foot to lather with soap. I stare at him through the steam, my breath shuddery.

He's the devil.

He's Jesus Christ.

He's *mine*.

And when he finishes, he sets my foot down and rocks back on his heels. The shower pounds around us, almost uncomfortably warm. Or maybe I'm just warmed by his touch.

"There you are," he says. "All clean."

"Thank you," I whisper.

Ambrose smiles, and he looks at me in a way no man has ever looked at me before.

And I know this doesn't just feel like love.

It *is* love.

CHAPTER FORTY

AMBROSE

I think I understand Sawyer and Jaxon a lot better now.

Mercy sits across from me at the dining room table, eating the omelet I made for her—by the time we got out of the shower, it was nearly dawn. I tried to get her to go back to sleep, tucking her into my bed before I went to clean up the mess I made in her room. I didn't mind, though, just as I didn't mind washing her. Blood sure as hell doesn't bother a creature like me.

It was worth it anyway, to see her come as my blood poured over her. As I marked her as *mine*.

Mine. That's all I can think, looking at her now. Mine to feed and protect and care for. Mine to fuck. Mine to pleasure. And the fact that Gunner is still searching for her, wanting to drag her back into fucking servitude, enrages me.

But then Mercy gives me a shy, somewhat confused smile, and the rage recedes. Because he might think he still has a claim on her, but I'm the one that baptized her in *my* name.

And she let me. She came while I was doing it.

"This omelet is delicious," she says, taking a sip of her coffee.

"Good to know." I made one for myself, although unlike hers, mine has meat layered in with the cheese and vegetables. Dane Weeks, a man I hunted a few months back.

Just like I'm going to hunt Sterling Gunner.

We eat in silence for a few minutes, forks scraping against the plates. And then Mercy asks,

"Were you serious?"

I look up at her, but she's got her eyes on her plate as she pushes a bit of omelet around. I know what she's referring to, but I still wait for her to say it.

"About—" She swallows. "About Reverend Gunner?"

"Of course I was serious." Excitement works through my veins. "But I will need your help, like I said." I take a big bite of my omelet, biting down on a hunk of Dane Weeks. Gunner will taste even sweeter, I'm sure.

Mercy finally lifts her gaze. She looks so damn pretty, the morning sunlight turning her loose hair to spun gold. I want to see her at my table every morning, her big brown eyes and soft, lovely lips. It's a startling thought. An unfamiliar thought. But it makes me feel good anyway.

"You said I would be bait," she says softly.

Hearing it like that, I have to resist the urge to cringe. It does sound callous. "I need to get Gunner and Sullivan out in the desert. But I'm not gonna let anything happen to you."

"I know." She looks right at me as she speaks, and I feel it in my chest, her trust in me. Another weird, unfamiliar sensation. "What would I need to do?"

I'd be lying if I said I haven't been thinking about this since last night. "I'll tell them I kidnapped you, and I'll return you if they bring some money out to a meeting spot."

"In the flatlands," Mercy says.

I nod. "Someplace isolated. I'll attack before they can take you anywhere."

Mercy takes a deep breath. I can tell she's thinking things

over. And I let her, even though I've got my own fantasies about how this will play out.

"How much money would you ask for?"

I blink, surprised by the question. "What? Why does that matter?"

She looks up at me, a coy smile on her lips, and I realize she's teasing me. "I was just curious how much you think I'm worth."

I grin. "You're priceless, humanita. That's why I'm not gonna let them take you back."

It's the right thing to say: her eyes light up and she ducks her gaze down, her hair falling into her eyes. And suddenly I wish she wasn't on the other side of the table. I wish she was sitting right beside me so I could grab her chair and pull her over and kiss her.

"No one's ever called me priceless before," she mutters.

Rage flares in my chest again. "Well, you are. As for how much money I'll ask for, you tell me. It needs to be something reasonable that Gunner can get together in a few days. We want to make sure he and Sullivan actually make it out there."

"Oh. Yeah, that makes sense." Mercy frowns. "Money's not an issue, really. It's just a matter of what he thinks would be worth it. For me, I mean. I—" Her voice catches a little, and she looks toward the window. "I know I'm not worth *that* much to him."

"You can expose him," I say sharply. "And as far as he's concerned, that's why I *kidnapped* you." I say the word dripping with sarcasm. Mercy smiles devilishly, a look I like on her.

"You did kidnap me."

"Has it been so bad?" I know I'm treading on thin ice, asking this, and I brace myself for Mercy to unravel the nice little fantasy I have set up here, me and her and sunny breakfasts after a night of depraved fucking, every morning until she does what humans inevitably do. But that's a long, long time off, and I don't dwell on it.

But she doesn't shatter the fantasy at all.

"No," she says. "No, it hasn't been bad at all." A smile dances across her lips. "I don't know what that says about me—"

"It doesn't say anything about *you*." I push my plate aside and lean forward, never taking my eyes off her. Pinning her down with my gaze. I like the way she squirms against it. The way her lips part and her eyes gleam. "But it does mean you've found a place you can call home, for as long as you want it."

It's a risk, saying shit like this to her, but I mean it. Especially when her eyes get all wide and disbelieving and shimmer like she's about to start crying. And I know they aren't tears of fear or pain or sadness, but I still don't want her crying anymore. So I fly around the table, moving faster than I should until she's in my arms.

"You've got to stop doing that," she says with a nervous chuckle. "Moving so fast. It's unnatural."

I just nuzzle against her hair, breathing her in. "That's just one way I'm gonna keep you safe," I whisper. "Now. Say the word, and I'll get things started."

Mercy lays her cheeks against my shoulder, and I pull her up to me, holding her close. It feels good, holding a woman like this. Promising to protect her. I never gave a shit about being human or doing things humans do. But this one thing? Caring for a woman? Making sure she's happy?

It's the one thing I'm willing to make an exception for.

Even though I'm still gonna do it in the way only a Hunter can.

CHAPTER FORTY-ONE

AMBROSE

The next day, I make the arrangements. It starts with a few snapshots of Mercy's pretty face in low light, her hair mussed and hanging in her eyes.

"Shouldn't I look more—messed up?" she says, looking over the pictures with me.

"Nah. I just need to show you're still alive." I kiss her temple. "These'll work just fine."

I make contact out in the barn, using one of the gas station cell phones I keep on hand. Mercy's in the house, Max keeping her company. I've got Roxi, though, my hand pressing into her fur while I send the pictures via text, along with a single message:

> I hear you're looking for someone. Want to make a trade?

I toss the phone on my workbench and wait, stroking Roxi's bristled fur. I don't have to wait long.

> Who is this?

I grin, excitement sparking in my blood. It's been a few weeks since I've had a proper hunt. I've missed it.

Who do you think?

Then I send a picture of Charlotte's files, although I obscure the name and dates. Let him wonder which ones I stole.

I heard some interesting things about what you do with your adoptees.

I settle back in my lawn chair, feeling pleased with myself. This time, the phone rings.

"Reverend Gunner," I say when I answer.

"Who is this?" His voice is sharp. "What are you doing to Mercy?"

"Keeping her safe and sound." I lean forward, my heart racing with excitement. "And you know who this. So, what do you say? Want to make a trade?"

"What do you want?"

"Two hundred fifty thousand dollars," I say. "You give me that, and I'll give you back Mercy. You don't, I'll make sure the FBI knows about the human trafficking the Church of the Well has been involved in."

"You can't prove that," Gunner snarls. The terror and panic are clear in his voice, though.

"I can," I say. "And unless you give me that two hundred and fifty thousand dollars tomorrow morning at 7 AM, I'll prove it to the goddamn FBI. Texting you the coordinates. No fucking cops."

"You think I'm stupid enough to go out there without police support?" he says.

"You want the girl or not?" I grin, relishing the tremble of fear in his voice. "Because I've already got everything I need to bring you down. If I see a cop out there, I'm shooting the girl in the head and you'll still be fucked."

"Who the hell are you?" Gunner demands. He sounds terrified. "Really?"

"Exactly who I told you." I settle back in my chair, feeling pleased with myself. "Just an itinerant preacher doing the Lord's work. I'll see you tomorrow morning, Reverend."

I hang up before he can say anything. Then I send the coordinates over, as promised. It's an area I know well, an area I've hunted in before: about forty minutes off-road from the Concho River. Middle of nowhere, hard to access. I've got a blind set up out there that can be our base of operations.

Time to free Mercy once and for all.

SIXTEEN HOURS LATER, I go hunting with my girl.

I didn't let her see me loading up the car with weapons, but rest assured I packed the goddamn works: my favorite long-range rifle plus a bandolier of ammo, my whole set of hunting knives, my switchblade—which I keep in the holster at my ankle for sentimental reasons more than anything else —and an axe just in case I want a bigger blade. Plus ropes, some meat hooks, and a five-gallon bucket. Best to be prepared.

And Max and Roxi, of course. They sit in the backseat, tails thwapping the seats, as I drive us into the open desert. They know what we're doing. Their sense of smell is almost as good as mine, and they can smell the bloodlust on me.

Good thing Mercy can't. She's nervous. I can sense that, too, radiating off her from the front seat.

"Hey." I rub her bare knee—she's in a pair of jean shorts that show off her long, muscular legs, with a loose, oversized white blouse that'll keep the sun off her shoulders while she waits for Gunner to show up. "Don't be nervous, all right? I'll have sights on you the whole time."

"I know." She smiles weakly at me. "It's not that. It's just—" She sighs and looks out the windshield at the highway. The sun's just starting to come up behind us, a thin pink line in the rearview mirror. We're driving west, into the darkness. "What if it doesn't work?" Her voice is quiet. "What if he doesn't come, or he sends someone else?" She works the hem of her shirt, her anxiety spiking. "What if he sends the cops and I have to go back—"

"I'll shoot them." I glance sideways at her. "You're mine, remember? And I don't let people take what's mine."

Mercy's eyes glimmer. God, I want to kiss her. Tell her it's going to be all right.

But I've got to focus on the upcoming hunt.

"Thank you," she whispers. "For doing this for me."

I fix my eyes on the road and squeeze the steering wheel. "I'd do anything for you, Mercy."

I realize what I just said, then add, "Well. Most anything." I can't *not* kill; that would lead to a darkness not even I want to think about. I don't want to frighten her, though, so I just say, "But you can bet your pretty ass I'll kill for you."

Mercy laughs, kind of disbelieving. "You really are the boogeyman."

"*Your* boogeyman, baby. Now, take some deep breaths for me. We're gonna be there before you know it."

It's not long before we reach the turn-off—a narrow, dusty road barely visible from the highway. My Oldsmobile groans as we crunch over the gravel, kicking up a plume of dirt that, thankfully, isn't visible in the dim light of early dawn. Once we're out of view of the highway, I pull off the road, parking the car between some scrub brush. The sky is streaked with pink and red, a bloody sunrise that bodes well for the hunt today.

"You should eat something before we hike out there," I tell

her, shutting off the engine. I made breakfast tacos this morning and wrapped them up in foil—egg and potato and cheese for her, egg and meat for me. "Get your energy up."

"I'm too nervous to eat," she says, still worrying her shirt hem.

"You don't need to be nervous." This car's old enough that there's no console between us, and I scoot closer and wrap my arm around her shoulders. "I told you I'm not gonna let anything happen to you."

"I know." Mercy smiles at me, but she's terrified. I've been smelling it the whole way here, a scent that's got my blood up for the hunt. "I still don't think I can eat."

"Have some water, then. It's gonna get hot once the sun comes up."

That, at least, she agrees to, nodding a little. We get out of the car, and while I pull out the tacos and a bottle of water, she sits on the hood, facing the sunrise.

"It's pretty, isn't it?" she says when I hand her the bottle. "I always liked watching the sun rise over the Concho."

"It is pretty." I want to tell her about all the sunrises I've seen in this desert, waiting for my prey to come across my path. Hundreds. Thousands, probably. But she's already scared enough of me as it is, trembling with anxiety, and I don't want to add to it.

She makes me soft, my little human. But maybe that's not as bad as I thought it could be.

I eat my tacos quickly, wash them down with the last of the coffee I brought out in a Thermos. Mercy sips at her water, stewing in her thoughts, and I put my hand on her thigh and lean over to her, mostly so I can breathe in more of her scent. "You really need to drink that whole thing, darling. I don't want you getting dehydrated."

Mercy looks at me sideways, a smile dancing on her lips. "I like the way you worry over me."

I grin. "And why's that?"

She shrugs and takes a big long swig of her water before answering. "Because no one ever has before."

That stabs me like a knife. I almost want to call this whole damn thing off, toss her back in the car, and start driving south until we pass into Mexico. Just start over. Let her disappear and not have to put her through what I'm about to put her through.

But then she says, "All my life, the Gunners said they were protecting me." She looks over at me, hair falling into her eyes and her lips wet from the water bottle. "That's why they brought me into the church. But he was just shaping me into whatever he wanted. You're—I know you're a killer, but I feel like you actually *want* to protect me."

Bloodlust surges through my veins. Not just at the thought of killing—but at the knowledge of who I'm killing. That I'm doing it for her.

"I do want to protect you." I nuzzle against her neck, breathing her in. "And I'm going to."

"What are you doing?" She laughs a little, and I just keep nuzzling at her.

"Getting your scent." I kiss her pulse, then move up along her jawline. "I'm not gonna lose you out there, Mercy. I swear to you."

"I know." She winds her hands through my hair, holding me in place, and I bite down gently on her tender neck flesh, making her moan and shudder. It's not enough for her to bleed, but it is enough for me to taste her.

"It's almost time," I whisper against her skin. Against her heartbeat. "Finish your water. And then we can set our trap."

CHAPTER FORTY-TWO

MERCY

We hike to the coordinates, walking side by side across the scrubby landscape, the dogs trotting beside us. Ambrose brings a big duffle bag with him, long enough I know a rifle's in there, although I don't know what else. It's clearly full, and it lets out a metallic clatter every time he takes a step.

By the time we arrive, the sun is just above the edge of the horizon, and the light is clear and bright across the desert. I wipe sweat away from my brow with the back of my hand, grateful that Ambrose made me drink the entire bottle of water.

"Here we are," he says suddenly, stopping in the middle of a dried-out stretch of scrub brush. Even though it's not even seven o'clock yet, insects trill and rattle around us.

"How do you know?"

"Because I've hunted out here before." Ambrose tosses the duffle bag to the ground and points off to the left. "Got a blind set up over that way. That's where me and the dogs will be. Watching you."

Max barks once as if he's agreeing.

I follow the direction Ambrose is pointing, but I don't see anything, just the glare of sunlight.

"You," he says. "Are gonna go right there." He points to his right, and this time when I look over, I do see something: a metal post jutting out of the ground.

"Did you put that there?" I ask, vaguely dizzy. *This is real. We are really doing this.*

I'm *really doing this.*

"Nope. Used to be a fence out here. But it'll work just fine for our purposes."

But before I can step toward the post, Ambrose grabs my wrist and pulls me around to face him. His expression is firm. Serious. He reaches up and brushes my hair out of my eyes, his gaze deep and searching.

"This is your last chance to back out," he says in a low voice. "If you don't want to do this, we'll leave right fucking now."

My breath shudders. I understand the gift that Ambrose is offering me. The thing is, the thing that scares me—

I don't want it.

"I want him dead," I say, my voice harder than I've ever heard it. Ambrose's eyes widen and flash with something like delight. Something like madness. Something like lust.

He leans close and brushes my lips with a kiss. "Your wish is my command, humanita."

Then he presses his hand against the small of my back and guides me over to the post. It's one of those little possessive gestures that would make my skin crawl anytime Reverend Gunner did it. But with Ambrose—

I know I'm in good hands.

He helps me sit down in the dirt beside the post. I know what he's going to do because we talked about it earlier, when we worked out the details of our plan, but it still feels bizarre and frightening to *actually* go through with it, to fold my hands behind me so he can tie me to the post.

"Are you comfortable?" Ambrose squats down and weaves a smooth, silky rope around my wrists. Max sniffs around us and licks the sweat off my knee. Roxi, as usual, keeps her distance, pacing back and forth like she's holding watch.

I nod, swallowing a lump of fear. He keeps the rope loose, though, and doesn't tie it off.

"All right." He stands up and takes a step back. "Practice run."

I strain against the rope. It catches for a moment—but only a moment. Then it unravels and I hold my hands up triumphantly.

"Good girl." Ambrose winks and kneels back down to redo the rope. "You remember what we talked about." He looks at me, expression serious again.

"Yes."

"Tell me."

His eyes are as black as night as I repeat the plan back to him, all the details of our little ruse. And even though I'm sitting in the dirt, my hands behind my back, gazing up at a murder, I feel an immense surge of power.

"Perfect," he breathes when I'm done, and then he kisses me, slow and hard and deep, his hand curling around the side of my neck. It's the kind of kiss that sends heat flooding between my legs, and when he pulls away, I whimper at the loss of his mouth against mine.

"When you get scared," Ambrose tells me, our foreheads pressed together, "I want you to imagine me kissing you, okay? Can you do that for me?"

"I'm not going to be able to concentrate if I think about that." I try to laugh, but it comes out strained and nervous.

Ambrose doesn't laugh along with me. He just pushes my hair back, kisses my forehead. "Then think about how I'm going to kiss you like that when we're all done."

"Yes, sir."

I know the effect those two words have on him, and I smile, seeing it now: the hot surge of desire in his eyes, the way he darts his tongue out to lick along his lips.

"Be careful," he says. "Or I'm going to do more than kiss you when this is over."

I smile coyly at him. "I was hoping you would, *sir.*"

Ambrose grins, and for a moment, he doesn't look human at all. "I'll hold you to that."

Then he stands up, the desert wind blowing hotly around us. He shoulders his duffle bag, the contents clanking ominously, and gives a short, fluttering whistle. Both of the dogs trot over beside him.

"See you soon, humanita," he says, right before he turns and walks away, his steps quick and self-assured. I watch him and the dogs go, fear pounding in my chest. He says he can sense my fear, and I'm sure he senses it now.

But I wonder if he senses the other things I'm feeling, all this confused blend of emotions. My attraction to him. My worry for him. My—

My *love* of him.

I slump back against the post, lifting my gaze to the pale sky. I can't love him.

Can't I?

When I look back to my left, Ambrose and the dogs are gone. My fear quickens. But he said he would be watching me from his blind, and I believe him. I trust him.

I love him.

I squeeze my hands into fists, careful not to move them too much so I don't disturb the ropes. It needs to look convincing when Reverend Gunner gets here.

The wind blows dust into my eyes.

The sun beat down on the top of my head.

And I wait.

It's miserable, the waiting, although I am prepared for it.

The heat is as bad as Ambrose said it would be, especially since I'm out in the open, without any shade. Even this early in the morning, I can feel it scorching the bare parts of my arms and the tops of my thighs.

Still, there's nothing I can do but wait. I shift in the dirt, trying to keep my legs from falling asleep. The insects scream and chitter. Birds caw out overhead, although I can't see them. I have no sense of what time it is. Reverend Gunner is supposed to come to the coordinates at 7 AM—Ambrose wanted to do this during the day. *So they can see what happens to them*, he said in that cold, gravelly voice.

He told me that we're so far from civilization, so far even from the church, that we don't have to hide under cover of darkness and he can unleash his horror in the sunlight.

The wind picks up, cooling my sweat-damp skin. And eventually, I hear something: the faint rumble of a car engine. It's time to play my part.

So I suck down a deep breath of air and scream as loud as I can.

"Help me!" I shriek, kicking at the dirt to stir it up. "Help me, please! Anyone!"

A dust cloud appears on the horizon. The sound of the engine grows louder. I scream wordlessly.

The front grill of Reverend Gunner's Escalade materializes through the dust, and I gulp down air. I don't have to fake my fear. I just have to fake who I'm afraid of.

"Sterling!" I scream as the SUV slams to a stop. The passenger door swings open, and Reverend Gunner spills out, clutching a battered old briefcase. My heart seizes—is Pastor Sullivan driving? Or did they bring someone else out here with them? I don't want anyone innocent to die.

"Mercy?" Revered Gunner calls out, voice uncertain.

"Help me!" I scream, a beat too late—now that I can see him, some primeval part of me recoils at the thought of calling out to him. *Ambrose has sights on me*, I tell himself. Although I suspect, by now, he has sights on Reverend Gunner.

The driver-side door opens, and Pastor Sullivan steps out. My skin crawls at the sight of him, although I feel some measure of relief, too. They seem to be alone.

"Is that her?" he asks, squinting at me.

"Of course it's her!" Reverend Gunner stalks around to the front of the SUV, swiveling his neck around. "Where is he?" he barks. "Where's Echeverría?"

"He said he'd be right back!" I wriggle my wrists against the rope, my heart pounding furiously. Ambrose said he wanted me to escape as soon as he fired his first shot. But if Reverend Gunner or Pastor Sullivan try to untie me, they'll immediately know that something is wrong.

"Right back?" Pastor Sullivan frowns and reaches for the pistol he always wears on his hip. "Where did he go?"

"I don't know!" I scream, tears in my eyes. Why hasn't Ambrose done anything? "Please! Help me!"

Pastor Sullivan looks over at Reverend Gunner, who gives him a short nod of permission. I glance off to the left, but of course I see nothing but desert grass and dust glinting on the wind.

"I don't like this." Pastor Sullivan walks toward me, his steps slow and cautious. "Why did he tell us to come alone?"

"Dammit, Henry, just help the girl." Reverend Gunner keeps scanning the horizon, too. "Maybe we can get out of her before—"

Sullivan's right leg turns to pink mist a split second before the sound of a rifle report shatters through the sunlight. He topples forward into the dirt, howling in pain.

And this time, when I scream, it's for real.

CHAPTER FORTY-THREE

AMBROSE

God damn this fucking wind. It's blowing in from the east, and I haven't fired a long-range rifle in nearly two years. The last thing I want is to miscalculate and hit Mercy instead.

Fortunately, I get Sullivan in the leg.

I immediately jerk my sight over to Gunner, who snatches up the briefcase and dives into the car. Selfish fucker. I know Sullivan is still alive—even at this distance, I can hear his heartbeat. Hear Gunner's, too. And Mercy's, of course, although I can't risk taking eyes off Gunner to make sure she's gotten her hands free like we talked about. Her heart's been racing since Gunner pulled up in that slick Escalade.

The Escalade that's still sitting in the dirt. Sullivan must have the keys, and Gunner's too much of a coward to dig them out.

I shoot twice: once through the tire and another into the engine. Then I fire a third shot through the driver's side window. Gunner's smart enough to keep his head down, I'll give him that, but hopefully, the shattered glass will do some damage. Can't smell it over Sullivan's blood, though.

I need to get over there. Not just to finish it up for Mercy but because—

Well, I *want* to. Haven't had a proper hunt in ages.

I sling the rifle over my shoulder, grab my hunting knife, and whistle for the dogs to stay. They both whine in protest, especially Max—he can tell Mercy's in trouble.

"Let me handle it now," I tell them. "If I need backup, I'll call."

Then I duck out of the blind and run as fast I can over the open desert. Black spots swirl overhead; the buzzards are already here, waiting for death. Even after me and the dogs take our fill, they'll have plenty to eat.

I put out my senses, taking stock of the situation. Sullivan's suffering. Gunner feels like he might be running. And Mercy—

Mercy's getting closer. I can smell her fear, rich and sweet and sharper than I expected. She knows I'm not gonna hurt her. But I realize death is a hard thing for a human to witness.

Sun glints off the Escalade's metal, a flash on the horizon. But two dark figures are surging toward me. One's Mercy.

And the other's Gunner, in pursuit. Motherfucker. No wonder she's scared.

"Ambrose!" she screams, her voice lifted by that damnable wind. "He's after me!"

"I'm coming, baby," I mutter, pumping my legs harder, gun bouncing against my hip. I clutch the knife and surge forward, moving faster than a human can, the landscape blurring around me. All my focus is on Mercy: her blonde hair streaming out behind her red, panicked face. The sound of her racing heart. The scent of fear. Her tears.

"Ambrose!" she screams, and then I'm on her, grabbing her by the waist and throwing her behind me.

Gunner shouts when he sees me and stumbles to a stop, sweat pouring off his brow.

"Hello, Reverend," I say with a smile.

He yelps in fear and stumbles backward, kicking up dirt. He's got his eyes on my knife, and I don't blame him. "I've got your money," he says, lifting his hands in surrender. "Back at the car. You didn't need to shoot Henry."

"You're right." I stalk toward him, twisting my blade back and forth so the light dances in the sunlight. "I was actually aiming at you, Reverend."

Gunner's eyes widen in fear, and then he turns and takes off the way he came. His breaths are thunderously loud, louder even than Sullivan's whimpers of pain.

I flip my knife around and catch it by the blade. Close my eyes to feel the wind. It's slowing down. Fucking finally.

"Not yet, asshole," I mutter, throwing the blade with a precision I learned decades ago. It flashes like a camera and embeds in Gunner's back with a satisfyingly wet thud.

I breathe out, pleased with myself. Hard part's done. Now the fun can really begin.

"A-ambrose?"

Mercy's voice is small and terrified and I cringe with a little burst of guilt—I'd been so caught up in the hunt I nearly forgot she was there, watching me. I turn around to find her standing with her arms wrapped around her chest, her whole body shaking, tears turning the desert dust to mud on her face.

"Oh, fuck, Mercy. He didn't hurt you, did he?" She's not bleeding, I can smell that much, but he might have done something else. To my relief, though, she shakes her head.

"There was so much blood," she whispers. "When you shot—"

"I know." I draw her close to me, half-expecting her to pull away. She doesn't, though. In fact, she buries her face in my neck.

"I was afraid they were going to come untie me," she sobs. "I thought you had left me. They were just standing there and nothing happened. And then when Pastor Sullivan—" She chokes, takes a deep breath. "I got out of the ropes but Reverend Gunner came out when you shot up the car and he started screaming that he was going to kill me—"

"No one's going to kill you." I rock her back and forth and smooth my hand over her hair. "Because the only one doing any killing here is me."

Mercy shudders at that, and I pull away and look down at her, searching her tear-streaked face. I want to torture both of these men for hours. I want to set them free so I watch while the dogs hunt them down. I want to languish in their screams. But I also don't want to see Mercy cry.

"I need to finish them," I say softly, wiping her tears away with my thumb. "I'll do it quick if you want. Then it'll be over, okay?"

I can't believe I'm fucking saying this. Can't believe I'm saying it to a human woman, of all people. But it's not just any human. It's *Mercy*. My Mercy.

"Th-thank you," she stammers. "I'm sorry, it's just—it's too much. It's—"

"Shh." I pull her into me one last time. "I know. But it'll all be over soon. I promise."

She nods against me and then steps back, wiping her tears with her hands.

"You don't have to watch if you don't want to," I tell her. "If you keep going that way—" I tilt my head to the left. "You'll see the blind I've got set up. Looks like an old shed. The dogs are there. You can wait with them." I don't mention my full arsenal of weapons will be in there with her. Don't want her thinking about what I planned to do with them all.

But she shakes her head. "I don't want to be alone. Even with the dogs."

"Well, then." I smile at her, trying to be reassuring, but the wind shifts and I get a hot whiff of blood, and it makes my eyes water and my cock ache. "Then you're gonna need to be brave for me."

Mercy stares at me with a hot fire in her eyes. And that makes my cock ache, too. "I know how to be brave."

"Good girl." I grab her hand and braid our fingers together. "Then you can watch me work."

She shudders at that, but when I pull her forward, she comes with me. I'm vaguely aware of her storming emotions, but I set them aside for the time being to focus on my two kills.

We hit a blood trail first, bright red splatters against the dirt. "Looks like Sterling thinks he can escape." I drop Mercy's hand to bring the gunsight up to my eye, and I take a look at the kill site. Sure enough, there's Gunner, stumbling toward the car, my knife sticking out of his back. Sullivan's slumped on the ground, passed out from shock or blood loss or both. Not dead, though.

I whistle for the dogs, the sound tearing across the desert.

"Is he getting away?" Mercy asks quietly.

"No." I drop the gun and stalk forward, the wind pushing my hair back from my face. Mercy follows behind me, and although I thought she might be distracting, I find that I like it, having an audience. I like the musk of her fear, the way it layers over the musk of Gunner's and Sullivan's blood.

I just hope she can handle seeing me at my best.

"Sterling!" My voice rings out into the wind. The shift in his body is palpable, and I grin and run my tongue over my teeth. "Don't even fucking think about running."

His head pops up, wild and frantic, and when his gaze lands on me, his fear becomes overwhelming, drowning out even Mercy's sweet scent. Of course, he doesn't listen and tries to take off running in a sloppy, stumbling lope. My knife is still sticking out of his shoulder blade, and the blood waterfalls down his back, splattering across the dirt. He doesn't know he's leaving a trail for Max and Roxi to track him down.

"I told you not to run!" I shout at him, which just spikes his terror. It also makes him look back at me again—which means he's not looking where he's going, and his foot catches on some loose rocks and he goes sprawling across the dirt.

"Told you!" I taunt him, laughing. Gunner desperately tries to get away, but he's in too much of a panic. Probably in too much pain, as well.

Footsteps patter behind me, along with a pair of panting breaths. The dogs are here, hackles raised and ready to hunt. They fall into step beside me, and by the time the three of us reach the meeting point, Gunner's still scrabbling around in the dirt, sobbing in terror.

"Why?" he gasps when I approach, his eyes glazed over. "Why are you doing this? I brought the money like you asked!"

I don't answer him, just tower over him with one hand on my rifle butt. Max and Roxi step out from behind me, growling and baring their teeth. He yelps and tries to drag away.

"Why?" he asks again, gaze flicking from the dogs up to me —and then past me, at Mercy. My good mood is swallowed by a sudden flare of rage. I kick him square in the chest, hard enough that he slams down on his back, howling as the knife jams up to the hilt. Fortunately, it was on the right side, not the left. I'm not sure if it missed his lung, though.

Gunner keeps screaming, arching his back up, smearing blood everywhere. The dogs wait for my orders, both of them slavering for meat. "Hold," I tell them.

Then I leap onto Gunner, pinning him down by the throat and pressing my knee into his belly. He goes rigid beneath me, blood-flecked spit bubbling up between his lips.

Yeah, I definitely nicked his lungs.

"Why?" he whispers.

I look away from him. To Mercy.

She stands a few feet away, her arms in fists by her side.

And she's not afraid anymore.

"Her?" he sputters, and then he laughs a little. "She did what all women should do. Marry a good man. Keep a clean house. All she needed was the bab—"

I squeeze his throat tight enough that the words strangle in his mouth, and he flops beneath me, trying to grab at my wrists. He's got fight in him, I'll give him that.

"Here's what's going to happen," I say, leaning close to him, my hair hanging in damp curls between us. "I need to field dress Sullivan over there—"

Gunner panics, but I grind my whole weight into him.

"Listen," I snarl, tightening my grip on his throat again. I can feel Mercy behind me, watching this, her emotions flat. She's not scared. She's not pleased. But she accepts it. "I'm going to field dress Sullivan. Won't take me long. Once he's draining out at my blind, I'll come for you."

I let go of his throat and grin down at him. Gunner trembles, his eyes wide, his breath shallow.

"Think you can escape, Reverend? I'll even let you have a head start before I send my dogs after you."

On cue, Roxi starts to growl.

"Demon!" he shouts, but I just grin wider.

"I suppose I am," I say. "My question still stands."

I jump off him, landing deftly on my feet, and Gunner immediately scrambles up, his limbs shaking and his torso covered in blood. He's not going to bleed out anytime soon, but there's also no way in hell he's going to get to safety.

Gunner's gaze flicks over to Mercy again.

"Don't look at her!" I roar, and his flinch is immediate and satisfying. Tears shine in his eyes. Good.

"Run, Reverend." I swing my gun around and point it at his chest. He looks at the barrel. A tear falls.

I notch a bullet into place. Gunner cries out and stumbles backward.

"Go!" I shout as he turns and starts his escape in earnest,

loping awkwardly over the desert. Every system in his body is lit up in panic. Tracking him will hardly be a challenge—I doubt I'll even need the dogs. But it'll scratch the itch.

I whistle the stay command to Max and Roxi. They both sit back on their haunches, even though I can tell they want to start the chase.

There's a sharp intake of breath behind me. A hot flash of anger.

"Why you'd let him go?"

I turn. Mercy stares at me, her expression imploring. Furious. I want to fuck the rage out of her, but we don't have time.

"I didn't." I stroll up to her and cup her face, leaving smears of Gunner's blood on her cheeks. "He thinks I did, but I didn't."

Mercy stares up at me. Her eyes are dry. "If he gets back to the church—"

"He won't." I kiss her, sweetly, to scratch *that* itch. "Trust me, darling. I've been doing this for two hundred years."

Then I pull out my gutting knife and get to work on Sullivan.

CHAPTER FORTY-FOUR

MERCY

I can't watch. I know Ambrose kills Pastor Sullivan quickly because I hear the metallic *shink* of the blade and a wet gurgle and then a kind of puddling noise. When I glance over, my breath shaky, all I see is Ambrose, my savior and my demon, hunched over Sullivan's supine body. I see Sullivan's feet. I see a widening pool of blood.

My stomach turns, but there's nothing to throw up, not really, and I swallow back the nausea. Then the wind blows the smell away, and I totter sideways, trying to clear my head.

Something wet nudges against my hand—it's Max, looking up at me with big brown eyes, his tail wagging furiously. He looks like a completely different dog from just a few moments ago.

"Hey, boy." I scratch between his ears and walk over to Reverend Gunner's SUV, Max trailing behind me. Glass from the broken windshield glitters everywhere, looking like stars in the sunlight.

The briefcase that holds my hostage money is lying in the dirt. While Ambrose works a few yards away, filling the air with the most horrible noises, I pick it up.

It's light. Too light to hold $250,000 worth of bills.

My stomach turns again, but this time it's with rage. The same blinding, iridescent rage I felt earlier, when Ambrose was taunting Reverend Gunner, telling him to run and letting him escape. I squint out at the horizon, bright in the morning sun, and I can see Gunner moving in the distance, limping and slow.

No wonder Ambrose wasn't worried.

I throw the briefcase on the car and snap it open. It's empty.

"What were you going to do?" I whisper softly, watching Gunner retreat. Pastor Sullivan had a gun. Did they think they could just shoot Ambrose?

After he shot me?

The thought turns my blood cold. Colder than it's been.

I snap the briefcase shut and hurl it out in the desert with a scream, all my tension erupting out of me. Max nudges at my thigh. The terrible wet noises behind me stop.

"Mercy." Ambrose's voice is calm, soft, reassuring. "He's not going to go far."

"He was going to let me die." I whirl around without thinking and then gag when I see Ambrose crouching in the dirt surrounded by glistening viscera. He frowns as he stands, wiping his knife on his pants. Roxi looks up at me, her snout covered in blood.

"What do you mean?"

"There was no money." Blood pounds in my head. "He thought you had kidnapped me for real. You told him you were going to kill me if he didn't pay, right? But he wasn't interested in saving me."

"Humanita," Ambrose says. "This whole thing was a ruse to murder these two pieces of shit."

"But he didn't know that!" I squeeze my arms around my chest. "I thought—I thought *some* part of him would think I was worth saving."

Ambrose frowns and walks over to me. "You are worth saving," he says softly, brushing my hair back, smearing me with more blood. "Why do you think I'm here?"

His black eyes search my face. He doesn't look human right now. Doesn't *feel* human. But for the first time since my parents died—

Someone actually cares about me.

"I love you," I spit out.

It slams between us, cold and electric. I know I shouldn't have said that.

"I—I don't expect you to say it back," I add. "I don't expect you to feel it about me. I mean—" I gesture over at Pastor Sullivan. "Look at you. You're the devil."

"The devil can love," Ambrose says quietly. So quietly I almost think I imagine it. "But that love doesn't look like God's love."

I stare up at him, taking deep breaths even though it means I can smell the coppery stench of Pastor Sullivan's insides. Reverend Gunner's right-hand man. They shared everything, even me.

Now they'll share the same sort of death.

"I feel sick," I whisper.

"Because you're human," Ambrose says. "I'd be worried if you didn't."

A beat passes between us. The sun bakes down.

"Come on," he says. "I need to get the meat to the blind to drain."

The meat. That was how Sullivan treated me, wasn't it? Like meat.

"And then we're going to hunt down Sterling Gunner, and I'm going to show you just how much I fucking love you."

I whip my head over to him, shock rippling through my body. But Ambrose has already turned around, stalking back to his prey. He hoists Pastor Sullivan's body over his shoulder and glances back at me. "Come on," he says. "We don't want Gunner getting too much of a head start."

"I thought you said we don't need to worry about that."

"We don't need to worry about him getting to safety." Ambrose whistles and starts walking off to the west, and I jog up so I can be at his side, rather than behind him. "But the dogs are getting antsy."

I glance down at them, trotting alongside us.

"I still don't understand why you let him go."

"I told you, baby. I didn't." Ambrose glances at me, and his eyes flash dangerously. "It's all part of the hunt. And I haven't hunted properly in a long time."

A million thoughts flash through my head. Like how often he does this. And whether or not he'll ever hunt me.

"Stop worrying," he says softly. "You don't need to worry ever again, do you understand?"

"Not even about you?"

Ambrose stops. He doesn't look at me, but straight ahead, and my heart palpitates.

"Mercy," he says. "You're *mine*, remember?"

A different kind of heat flushes through my body and pools between my thighs. I should not be feeling that out here, in this moment. "Yes," I mutter.

"Well, I don't kill what's mine. I protect it."

I suck in my breath.

"Now let's get Sullivan situated so we can focus on the real prize." Ambrose moves forward again, his cowboy boots scraping against the dirt. "You don't have to come with us if you don't want to." He smiles, and he really does look like the devil. "But I hope you do."

CHAPTER FORTY-FIVE

MERCY

Ten minutes later, Ambrose leads me through the desert, his blood-streaked hand in mine. I'm as culpable as he is, and I know it.

But I don't mind.

You're mine. His voice keeps rumbling through my head. *You're mine.*

When Reverend Gunner said things like that to me, it made me feel small and dirty. When Ambrose says them—

I feel safe.

Ambrose stops and sniffs the air. The dogs are up ahead, snuffling in the dirt, guiding us along the scent trail Reverend Gunner left behind. For a while, even I could see the blood splatter from where he had stumbled away. But that's disappeared.

"He's heading toward the Concho," Ambrose says.

The Concho River. The first place Ambrose ever saw me, even if it wasn't the first time I saw him.

"He's going to make it to the church," I whisper.

"Not on foot." Ambrose whistles to the dogs, who take off

in a cantor. Ambrose strides ahead, pulling me along with him. "He's slow. We'll catch up."

I'm doubtful, but I just squeeze his hand a little tighter. Part of me wishes I had stayed behind at the shed, but that would mean being with Pastor Sullivan's empty body, his blood dripping slow and steady into an ancient metal bucket. And even in death, I don't want his eyes staring at me.

We walk quickly, cutting across the empty field. Despite the rain we've had, the grass is dry and crackling. Sweat drips down my spine and beads along my forehead. Everything looks the same, flat and scrubby, and the pale sky is so enormous it feels as if it might crush us.

But then the dogs go still. Roxi leans forward, pointing at the horizon with her nose.

Ambrose stops and pulls me behind him. "Stay close," he breathes. "I can smell him."

I can't smell anything but sweat and dirt—and the faint, steely scent of river water. The banks are just up ahead, covered in short, spiny shrubs.

Ambrose lets go of my hand and pulls an ax out of the sling he has around his waist, tightening his fingers around its wooden handle.

"There you are, you ugly motherfucker," he murmurs.

I don't see anything but the land. But then there's a flicker of movement up ahead, like a bird taking off. Except it's not a bird.

It's Reverend Gunner.

He's threading through the brush, trying to stay low. Trying to stay hidden, I think, but he's not doing a very good job, if even I can see him.

"Do you want to watch?" Ambrose doesn't take his eyes off Gunner, but I know he's talking to me.

I suck in my breath, my heart hammering. My lips want to say no, but that's just muscle memory. The truth is—

I do want to watch.

I want to know my nightmare is over.

"Yes." I exhale it out, like a sigh.

When Ambrose glances back at me, he's smiling a little. "Stay close."

Then he glides forward, lazy and unhurried, swinging the ax back and forth so the blade catches in the sunlight. I scurry up so I'm walking beside him, opposite the ax, and I take deep breaths, trying to calm myself. The dogs swarm around our feet, and they're breathing heavily like they're excited.

"He sees us," Ambrose breathes.

I don't know how he knows, but a split second later, there's a sudden explosion of rustling shrubbery, and then a splash.

"Fuck," Ambrose spits. "Come on, darling. We're going swimming."

He jogs toward the river, clutching the ax up to his chest. Something like panic seizes at me—panic that Reverend Gunner is going to get away, swept up on the current of the Concho. Although I had told Ambrose that I wanted to see, to know Reverend Gunner is gone for good, I hadn't realized just how *much* I did until this moment, when there's the threat of him escaping.

We skitter to the edge of the bank, the river glittering in the sun. Gunner splashes around—not trying to swim downstream, I realize, but trying to make it to the other side.

Ambrose chuckles softly.

Then he leaps.

I cry out—the river isn't deep enough for diving. But Ambrose doesn't move like a human, and he lands with a small, elegant splash on his feet. The dogs wait on the bank.

Gunner screams, his voice carrying on the wind. Then he stumbles sideways and splashes into the water, limbs flailing

I slide down the bank, stepping out onto the smooth flat stones to watch. Max and Roxi both follow me, sticking close.

Gunner shoots up, sputtering water, and sees me—for the first time, I think.

"Mercy!" he screams. "Help me! For the love of God!"

I don't say anything, just stand on the stones with the river splashing around my ankles, my hand and face sticky with Pastor Sullivan's blood, the wind blowing loose strands of hair into my eyes.

"Mercy!" Reverend Gunner wails, trying to splash toward me, his arms outreached. But Ambrose grabs the scruff of his shirt and drags him under the water. Reverend Gunner kicks up a froth as Ambrose pulls him toward me, yanking his head up only when they're a foot away from where I stand on the bank with the dogs.

"You know why I'm doing this?" Ambrose asks, curling his arm around Reverend Gunner's throat to pin him in place. He wails, water streaming over his face. Ambrose jerks his arm and Gunner's head slams back so he's looking right at me.

I've never felt so powerful in my entire life.

"To protect her," Ambrose says in a dark, thorny voice.

"I t-took her in," Reverend Gunner stammers. "I g-gave her a h-home. She would have been a wh-whore on the streets—"

"And what was I in the church?" I shout, so loud I surprise myself.

Ambrose watches me, his eyes burning, his ax swinging at his side. Reverend Gunner opens and closes his mouth like a fish.

"You didn't give me a choice, *Sterling*." I hiss his name. "I never had a choice, because you shaped me into the perfect helpmeet for you." I'm trembling with rage, flames shooting through my body.

"He's a killer," Gunner whimpers. "He'll kill you when he's done with me."

Ambrose meets my gaze and electricity arcs between us. *You're mine, and I don't kill what's mine.*

"He's not even denying it!" Gunner shrieks hysterically. "Please, Mercy! Get his gun! Shoot him in the head! You can end this!"

"I know I can." I take deep, slow breaths. Ambrose watches me, his fingers gripped tight around his ax. He's barely concerned about Gunner. All his attention is on me.

"He will kill you!" Gunner screams.

"No, he won't," I say evenly. "Because he's mine."

Ambrose breaks into a terrifying, feral grin. Then, in one lightning-fast moment, he slams Gunner's head against the rock I'm standing on, the dogs flanking me on either side.

"Bow to her," Ambrose snarls.

I do feel like a queen.

Gunner sobs and lifts up his head, blood pulsing out of his mouth. He tries to say something, but the words are slurred and distorted, like his tongue doesn't work. He bit it.

"Bow to her," Ambrose repeats, slamming Gunner against the rock again. Blood splatters across my shoes, but when Ambrose lets go, Gunner doesn't move, just slumps there, his back rising and falling with his panicked breaths.

Ambrose lifts his face and looks me in the eye. "'And she, being put forward by her mother, saith, Give me here on a platter the head of John the Baptist.'"

Then he swings the ax down. There's a clean, wet ripping sound and the clank of metal hitting stone.

A breath of silence. Of stillness.

And then Reverend Gunner's head rolls sideways. Ambrose catches it by the hair and hoists it up, and for a moment I think of Raul, of the last time I was in this river. The pain I felt. The terror.

And I think of all the pain I've felt in my life. All the times I bent to meet Gunner's needs. The tears I sobbed in my bed, a pillow pressed over my mouth to muffle the sound even though I was alone. The prayers I whispered in the shower after

Sullivan took me for the first time, how I turned the water on so hot it scorched my skin. The loss of Madelyn, the closest thing to a mother I had, because her husband decided he wanted to fuck me.

I think of all that pain—

And I know that it's gone.

Ambrose tosses Reverend Gunner's head to the riverbank, where it lands in the scrub brush, his eyes turned up toward God. He slides his ax back into his belt and holds out his hand to me.

"Come here, humanita."

I slide my palm against his and step delicately around Gunner's headless body. The rock is already slick with his blood, and I have to take care not to slip and fall face forward in the water. But Ambrose is there to keep me steady as I take one step down into the current, then another. After being out in the heat for so long, the water's chill makes me yelp as it swirls around my bare legs.

Ambrose whistles a lilting little melody, and the dogs descend on Reverend Gunner's head. But he cups my face in his hands and presses me toward him so I can't watch.

"We can't stay here," I murmur.

"No one's here but us," he answers, right before he kisses me like he wants to prove it, his tongue sensual and probing. When he eventually breaks the kiss, he nuzzles against my neck, his breath warm on my skin.

"I need to dress the body," he whispers. "But I have something to ask you first."

I pull away to look at him, his hair wet with river water. He's always hard to read, with his flat dark eyes and predator's expression. But right now, illuminated by the blazing sun, I think he almost looks—nervous.

"What's wrong?" My chest gets tight, and suddenly I'm

afraid that I've been so, so stupid, and he is going to kill me after all.

But then he takes my left hand, rubbing it between his palms.

"Marry me," he says.

I blink, certain I misheard him over the rush of the river. "What?"

Ambrose never breaks his eye contact. "I'm asking you to marry me."

I stare at him. The wind pushes down across the river, lifting up sprays of cold water that, just for a brief second, shimmer into rainbows.

"Can you do that?" I blurt out.

Ambrose laughs and rubs his hand along the side of my neck. "I can do whatever the fuck I want," he says. "And I want you to marry me." He drops his forehead against mine. "Only if you want to, of course."

I laugh, feeling delirious. "I daydreamed about this," I whisper. "When I thought you—when I thought you were a preacher—"

"So what do you say?" He grabs my chin and lifts my head, his eyes burning into mine. "You're already mine. Nothing's going to change that. But you can be Mrs. Echeverría if you want."

This time, when I laugh, the laughter turns to tears, hot and wet and impossibly happy. I can't think about the logistics of this—that he's immortal and I'm not. That he's a killer, not a preacher.

But here is, giving me the two things I've always wanted. The two things I never thought I could have.

Freedom—

And love.

EPILOGUE

THREE MONTHS LATER

MERCY

"Don't you dare come in here!"

I turn away from the mirror just in time to see Charlotte slam the bedroom door shut. "You can't see her yet!"

"I will break this door down," Ambrose says from the other side.

"No, you won't." I stand up, the long skirt of my wedding dress swishing as I walk. Charlotte's pressed against the door, squeezing the handle in place as Ambrose tries to rattle the doorknob to get in. She grins at me and winks.

I only met her a week ago, but she already feels like my friend.

"Let me see her!" Ambrose shouts.

"Calm down." I slide up against the door and press my ear to the wood. "What's wrong? I thought you said everything was ready to go."

"It is. I just wanted to make sure *you're* okay."

324

Charlotte makes a show of rolling her eyes. "He's so dramatic," she whispers to me, which makes me grin.

"I heard that!"

"Baby, I'm fine." I know what he's worried about: that I'm going to change my mind. About him. About the wedding. About this life we're starting together. For the last two months, he's asked me over and over if this is what I want, being with him. And every time, I told him the same thing.

"I haven't changed my mind," I say to the door. "Now go down to the beach like you're supposed to."

"Say it again," Ambrose orders in that way he does, which makes me blush since Charlotte's here. She notices, too, since she's a Hunter, and gives me a rather lascivious look that just makes my blush deepen.

"Stop teasing her, Charlotte," Ambrose snaps. "Humanita, say it again. One more time before we start."

"I haven't changed my mind." I turn toward the door and press my hands up against the wood, imagining that Ambrose is doing the same. "This is what I want. To be with you."

When I glance sideways at Charlotte, she has her hands squeezed up to her chest, her eyes as big as saucers. "You two are so *cute*," she whispers. "I have to tell Edie."

Edie, the other human woman in love with a Hunter, also wasn't what I expected when I met her.

Ambrose makes a kind of grumbling sighing noise and raps against the door. "That's all I wanted to hear," he says. "I'll see you soon."

"You will," I tell him.

"He is such a softie," Charlotte says, tapping on her phone. "I hope he fucking heard me say that, by the way"

I roll my eyes, but if Ambrose does hear it, he doesn't respond—although the front door of the beachside hotel clicks shut.

I always dreamed of getting married in a church, but that was just from growing up in the Church of the Well. I didn't know there was any other way to get married, not really. When Ambrose asked me if I wanted a beach wedding, a little over a month ago, the idea shimmered like a diamond. I hadn't been to a beach since before my parents died, but I remember going when I was a child: the salty wind and rhythmic rush of the waves and the cries of seabirds.

He asked me after he had been gone for a few days to help Charlotte take care of something with her half-brother Rowan, leaving me alone not in the ranch house near Cocana but in a pretty Victorian house along the border, where he took me after the hunt in the desert. We've been living there since, and I thought we'd get married in the big backyard, beneath a cathedral of orange trees. But when he came back from his trip, he had another idea.

So that's how we ended up here, in a little seaside town in South Texas called Rosado. It's not much, but when I saw the waves cresting against the pale sand, I knew this was where I wanted to get married: holding Ambrose's hand by the sea.

"Okay." Charlotte slips her phone in her pocket. "Edie says everything's good to go down on the beach. Let's just finish getting you ready."

Charlotte pulls me back over to the vanity, settling me down on the seat. She's been helping me for the last two hours—doing my makeup so my eyes look big and bright, pulling my hair back in a complicated bun that looks nothing like the braids I had to wear at the Church of the Well. We bonded over those braids because her mom used to wear them.

"Here you go." Charlotte pins the veil into my hair. She made it herself, out of fresh roses and a long trail of organza silk. When it's situated, she steps back, and all I can see in the mirror is myself, looking like the bride I never thought I'd be.

"If Ambrose ever fucks up," Charlotte says. "You come find me. Jaxon and I will get it sorted. He doesn't scare us."

I glance over my shoulder at her, flush with warmth. I know I don't know her *well*, but she's more protective of me than anyone I've ever met other than Ambrose. Edie, too. They're like a family, the five of them, and they welcomed me so easily that I realized I never really understood what a family was before now.

"He's not going to fuck up," I say. "But thanks for the offer."

Charlotte grins and pulls me back up to my feet. "You ready?"

I nod.

She leaves the bedroom first, making a show of checking for Ambrose as if he might be lurking around to get an early peek at me. He's not, though. When it's clear, she gestures for me to join her, and we go out into the open walkway, the breeze warm and balmy. It's early September, still warm enough for a beach wedding in Texas, but out of season so that Rosado and its beach are mostly abandoned. Plus, Charlotte's half-brother Rowan runs the hotel, and he apparently made sure everything is empty just for us.

Charlotte taps out something on her cell phone, then nods when it dings. "All right," she says. "Ambrose is where he needs to be. Edie says you're good to make your entrance."

I smooth down my skirt. I'm not nervous about marrying Ambrose—nothing feels more right to me—but I am nervous about the wedding itself, even though hardly anyone is here. I'm not used to being the center of attention.

"Come on." Charlotte loops her arm in mine, and we take the stairs to the hotel's courtyard, walking together past the glittering swimming pool and out to the rickety boardwalk that leads to the beach. I can't see anything, just mounds of vine-covered dunes and the glassy water glimmering in the distance.

"You ready?" Charlotte asks.

"Ready," I say.

Together, she and I walk down the boardwalk. I never

dreamed about being given away at my wedding—I don't have a father to do it. But Charlotte volunteered and said it made sense since we had both escaped the Church of the Well. I agreed.

There's no music, just the rhythmic swell of the ocean. Charlotte and I crest over the dunes, and I see what Edie and Charlotte's boyfriend Jaxon have been working on for the first time:

An altar made out of driftwood and flowers and antlers and animal bones. Jaxon stands in front of it, Ambrose at his side. The altar is beautiful and strange, but when I see Ambrose, he's all I can see—especially as his eyes drink me in, making me feel like I'm the only human in the world.

Charlotte laughs. "Oh, he's down bad."

I blush and focus on walking down the aisle that Edie and Jaxon created out of stones and seashells. She's sitting in a folding chair next to Sawyer, her Hunter boyfriend. Rowan is there, too, big and hulking as he watches silently from the back row. Another Hunter, like Charlotte. He has a date with him, a dark-haired woman named Abi who curls her fingers protectively around his hand.

But all I care about is Ambrose.

Charlotte guides me across the beach, the wind whipping my dress and veil out behind me. When we reach the altar, she looks Ambrose dead in the eyes and says, "Don't fuck this up."

"Get out of here, Charlotte." But he's looking at me as he says it, his lips curled up in a smile.

She does, scurrying over to join the others. Ambrose takes my hands, pulling me around so that I'm facing him. His eyes pin me in place.

Jaxon clears his throat.

"Welcome, everybody," he says. "We're gathered on this beach beneath the eyes of the gods to bind these two people together in blood."

I take a deep, shaky breath. I definitely never fantasized about a *pagan* wedding, but I don't need the Christian god anymore. I only need Ambrose.

He squeezes my hands. I squeeze them back, and he smiles.

"Mercy Hendricks," Jaxon says, offering me a small, sleek dagger. "You may begin."

I take it from him, the weight smooth and cool in my palm. A wedding dagger, Ambrose told me when he gave it to me, nestled in velvet like a ring. To seal our commitment.

I step up to Ambrose, who offers me his left hand, palm up. I press the dagger's blade into his flesh. Breaking his skin is harder than I expect, and he pushes up, doing the work for me. Red blood blooms.

"Mercy," Ambrose murmurs. "I mark you as mine until the universe ends."

And then he smears his blood gently across my forehead. I shiver at his touch, at the warmth of his blood, at the way this ceremony mirrors the night he claimed me as his.

Then I hand him the knife and offer him my left hand. He cuts it so quickly I hardly feel the sting.

"Ambrose," I say, my voice shaky. "I mark you as mine until the universe ends."

And then I bless him, dragging my bloody palm across his forehead. He catches my wrist and presses his cut palm against mine.

"Our blood will mingle until we are one," he says softly.

"Our blood will mingle until the death of all things," I respond.

And then he drags me up to him, more roughly than you would expect for a wedding, and kisses me in a way you *definitely* wouldn't expect. But this is Hunter's wedding, after all.

"Okay, cool it," Jaxon says. "We're still in public."

Ambrose pulls away from me, grinning, and brushes his knuckles against my cheek. "More of that later," he whispers.

I grin back at him.

Jaxon rolls his eyes. But he's grinning, too. "I present you Ambrose and Mercy Echeverría, joined by blood until the end of time."

I'm distantly aware of the others applauding and cheering, but it just blends into the sounds of the ocean. All that matters right now, to me, is Ambrose.

All that matters is that I finally found my way home.

THE END

Thank you for reading *Turn That River Red!* I hope you enjoyed it.

The series continues with Rowan and Abi's story in Half the Summer's Night.

If you'd like to read an extended (and very spicy) epilogue about Mercy and Ambrose's honeymoon, you can access it by signing up for my newsletter here: rosebitterly.com/newsletter.

HALF THE SUMMER'S NIGHT

COMING 10.17.25

ABI

People say my hometown of Rosado is cursed. There are too many disappearances. Too many accidental deaths.

And they aren't wrong. As the town's coroner, I see those deaths firsthand. But I don't think a curse is responsible.

I think a killer is.

No one believes me. But I'm determined to get to the truth—

No matter what it takes.

ROWAN

For as long as Rosado has been my hunting ground, I've been in love with Abi Snow. Every time I kill, I show my devotion to her in the mayhem I leave behind.

But when she starts to actually investigate the clues I leave behind, it leads her down a dangerous path. One that I didn't intend for her to follow.

Now, *she's* at risk of dying. And I can't have that.

So I'm going to do something I've never done before.

I'm going to save a life instead of take it.

Get It Here

ABOUT THE AUTHOR

Rose Bitterly is a hopeless romantic who has been reading and writing scary stories since elementary school—imagine her excitement when she learned you could blend the two! Today, she writes dark, immersive horror romances featuring slashers and other monsters, all shot through with a hint of the occult. Visit her online at rosebitterly.com.

Never miss a new book! Sign up for Rose's mailing list and receive free bonus stories: https://www.rosebitterly.com/news letter.

www.ingramcontent.com/pod-product-compliance
Lightning Source LLC
Chambersburg PA
CBHW020243010826
48973CB00006B/1640